VOW OF VENGEANCE

DANNY T. FERGUSON

Alliance Books
an imprint of Harlan Publishing Company
Greensboro, North Carolina USA

Published by Alliance Books
an imprint of Harlan Publishing Company
5710-K High Point Road #280
Greensboro, NC 27407 USA

Visit our web site at: http://www.alliancebooks.com

Book design by Jeff Pate

Area maps drawn by Janice Stevens

FIRST EDITION

Library of Congress Control Number: 2002114519

ISBN: 0-9676528-9-8

01 02 03 04 05 06 07 08 09 10

ACKNOWLEDGMENTS

Many thanks to the wonderful people who helped me along the way to publication. Thanks to my friend Bobby Quinn, who introduced me to the waters of coastal North Carolina. Also, my deepest gratitude to my stepson Fletcher Thompson, my nieces Dill O'Hagan and Kay Hagan, and my nephews Stuart Jackson and Andrew Hagan, as well as to my friends Toni Radler, Sally Taff, and Ken Harris for their assistance and advice. Also, thanks to my sister Mary Jane Hagan, for providing me with the never-quit motivation that brought this story to fruition.

Particular thanks goes to my friend and secretary Janice Stevens, who not only used her artistic abilities to draw the maps in the book, but also also retyped this manuscript perhaps a thousands times. Her advice, dedication, and hard work has been invaluable.

Also, much thanks to Jeff Pate of Alliance Books for his suggestions and expertise. Without his assistance, I would have been clueless about the intricacies of publication.

My wife Betty Ferguson deserves the lioness' share of the credit. Her many readings, her sharp pencil, and her literary talents made this writing possible. Also, her patience with a sometimes-wild man is what really made it happen.

CONTENTS

Of all the things of a man's soul, which he has within him, justice is the greatest good and injustice is the greatest evil.

—Plato

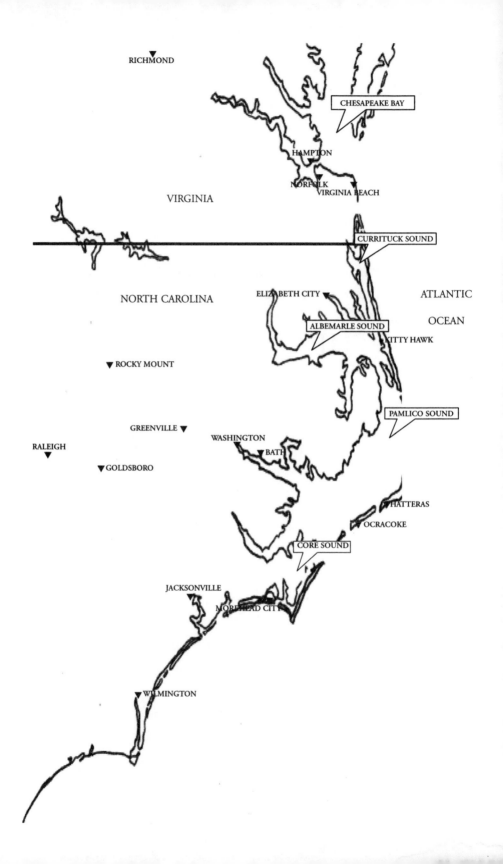

I

THE PRECURSOR

CHAPTER

1

THE AXE blade reached its apex, stopping momentarily in midair, then fell downward on a lethal trajectory.

His eyes sprang open, but his vision was obscured by blood oozing from cranial contusions. In the glare of the morning sunlight, he could only vaguely discern the wedge of death racing toward him. The doomed pirate felt no fear, only resignation. His final moment was upon him.

Royal blades had slashed away chunks of flesh, leaving bleeding chasms in his side. Sword-jab punctures and musketball holes had peppered his now dying, prostrate body. With only a blink of time remaining, his own pain was of no consequence. Rather, he was focused on a myriad of scenes that fleeted across his mind's eye.

His happiest moment had been at the helm of the *Queen Ann's Revenge* as it cut through the sea with its unfurled sails billowing. Mounted with forty guns and crewed by more than three hundred men, this magnificent vessel had enabled the pirate to capture many fine prizes of battle.

In the split second of life that remained, still another image flashed, an image so awful he beckoned the axe blade to hurry. Never to have another woman was worse than death!

But truly, with fifteen wives to his credit, now the only

woman who mattered was his beautiful Mary. He had married young Mary Ormond only four months earlier, and her lovely image overshadowed all else. Mary, carrying his child, was in nearby Bathtowne awaiting his return. He now knew he would never again lie beside her, nor would he ever see their child.

If only he had taken advantage of the governor's pardon, he could have grown old with Mary and their child while enjoying the incredible wealth he had amassed. If he had just listened to her pleas, he could have become a respectable member of his community. But no! Instead, an insatiable emptiness in his very soul craved the taste of blood, the smell of battle.

His eyes wide open, only a desperate micro-second remaining, it was as though he were not within his own body. Rather he was high in the rigging of this royal sloop looking down upon his own demise. He could see the ship's commander, a young lieutenant dressed in the uniform of the Royal Navy, standing there as the ship's crew eagerly watched.

Then, he saw it. The axe blade was cutting into his very own beard-shrouded neck. With that, his last emotion was anger as his mouth opened to issue his final order. Air hissed through his teeth, his lips struggling to mold words of revenge, but only a faint sound, a barely decipherable articulation, was audible. "Deth to uh..." he gasped. But the splat of the axe abruptly transformed his words into a gurgle of air bubbles, the wedge slicing clean through his neck, then, with a hollow thud, chomping down hard into the wooden deck.

As though the earth's rotation took pause, the moment froze in the minds of the royal crew who were gawking down at the remains of this infamous villain. The good and noble emissary of the crown had just done battle with the surrogate of Satan. Rarely in the annals of history had good versus evil been so clearly characterized as it was on the morning of November 22, 1718.

An aura enveloped the ship, the crew standing motionless in total disbelief, skeptically trying to comprehend the spectacle they had just witnessed. Had they really killed Blackbeard, the scourge of the sea? Well, . . . it had to be true because the hideous head lay three feet away from the body, the eyes rolled back, the skin a pallid white.

The old pirate had to be quite dead, decapitated, five gunshot holes, and twenty-seven sword punctures. But the sight was uncanny. The beard-shrouded mouth remained open, as if he were trying to complete his last command, a command that would not be addressed for nearly three hundred years.

*

In an effort to calm the harrowed crew, Lieutenant Maynard ordered the corpse dumped over the side. Four reluctant crewmen, each as tense as if he were handling a live bombshell, dragged the headless body to the starboard gunwale and dropped it overboard into the briny deep. But the headless body did not sink. Rather, it floated like a log, bobbing up and down at the will of the sea near the ship's water line.

With fear gagging in their throats, and their eyes bugging out frog-like, the crew looked down, each staring incredulously at the unbelievable as their greatest dread became reality. "Oh, uh, oh my God!" a voice stammered. "It's . . . it's alive! It's . . . it's swimming!"

And it was, it appeared. Its arms were moving as the headless body drifted across the bow, then aft and back down the port side. At the stern, it washed back to starboard and was heading toward the bow. The royal crew was dumbfounded, some men even running along the perimeter of the deck, following the body in morbid fascination as it circled the ship.

Although there were doubters, most of the crew would later confirm the headless body rounded the ship a second time, then a third, before finally disappearing into the depths of what later would become known as Teach's Hole.

A young seaman leaning far out over the ship's railing stared wild-eyed down at the spectacle. "Oh, Lord, we have killed the devil himself!" he declared.

THE SLOOPS of war neared the mainland, the *Jayne* in the lead, the *Ranger* following close behind. In single file, the small ships sailed into the channel of the Pamlico River, the bow sprint of the *Jayne* adorned with the remains of Blackbeard's severed head. In her hold were ten captured pirates, all bound and chained.

As he lay in his berth on the *Jayne,* his first mate tending his wounds, Lieutenant Maynard proudly examined his exalted prize of battle, Blackbeard's personal ensign. The bizarre souvenir had been commandeered from the pirate ship just before it was set ablaze. The pennant, designed by Blackbeard himself, depicted the devil stabbing an innocent heart.

Maynard reflected on his good fortune. Not only had he survived, but he had been victorious in the bloody battle of Ocracoke. This was truly the most glorious day of his naval career. Only two weeks earlier he had been dispatched by the royal governor of Virginia to seek out and destroy Blackbeard.

And on this very morning, his small two-ship fleet had confronted the pirate head-on.

"No quarter will be given, nor will any be taken!" Blackbeard had proclaimed.

Deadly barrages of cannonade were exchanged, the pirates hitting their mark with every blast. The maruaders soon became over-anxious, lulled into a sense of false superiority. Wildly and recklessly, they threw grappling hooks into the rigging, then swung aboard, eager to finish off these hated royal invaders.

But Maynard played his wild card shrewdly. At just the right moment, a detachment of soldiers that had been secreted in the hold, poured out onto the deck, primed and ready for battle. Caught flatfooted by the unexpected ambush, the astounded pirates were thrown into a quandary of confusion and could not regroup. As the smoke of death cleared, only one pirate was left standing - Blackbeard, himself.

Against overwhelming odds, he fought like a trapped lion. He swung his oversized sword with his right hand while blasting away with one of his never-ending supply of pistols with his left. He had been shot, stabbed and sliced, his body flinching, his blood spattering with each penetration, but he would not fall. He was invincible, it seemed.

The blade of his sword glistened as it sliced back and forth, cutting a curtain of death for any soldier who might dare to come within range. This monster of a man was about to single-handedly defeat the entire royal crew, it appeared.

But then, the course of destiny drastically reversed itself. Suddenly, Lieutenant Maynard bounded into the midst of the affray. In seconds, he was head to head and eye to eye with Blackbeard as the metallic clang of glancing swords signaled death's warning. Eager to destroy his nemesis, Blackbeard slashed violently downward at Maynard's head, his blade only grazing the young lieutenant's hand.

Then, just as Blackbeard pointed his last pistol at Maynard's head, a bayonet jab from behind jostled the pirate's aim. The pistol fired but the lead ball only tore flesh from Maynard's shoulder. With that, Blackbeard, the most fearsome pirate of the New World, collapsed to the deck, apparently ending his unrivaled reign of piracy.

*

As the royal sloops passed a peninsula of land known as Plum Point, a pretty young woman, pregnant with child, stood on the bank. A grimace of concern on her face, she carefully studied the ships headed toward the Bathtowne docks. Squenching her eyes, she strained to get a better look at the people standing on the decks of these two incoming ships. Focusing methodically on each face, praying her husband was not there, she was relieved to see no familiar faces, only faces of English seamen. But her eyes drifted on toward the bow and stopped abruptly at the sight of a round, spheroid-shaped thing that hung from the ship's bowsprit. In an eerie way, it looked familiar to her.

As the boat grew closer, she could tell the thing was actually a human head. Guardedly, she studied its features until the undeniable resemblance caused her to gasp. Her greatest fear was upon her!

"It's Edward's head!" she cried, tears rolling down her cheeks. "My baby!" she shrieked hysterically. "My innocent baby will have no father!"

Mary Ormond was traumatized; her hopes and dreams suddenly, mercilessly shattered.

The two ships sailed into Bathtowne where Maynard rounded up and captured even more of Blackbeard's crew. Now, with fifteen captured pirates chained in the hold of the *Jayne*, the two vessels set sail for home.

*

Three days later, with the grotesque head still hanging from the *Jayne's* bowsprit, the two ships arrived back in Hampton, where crowds lined the river bank to see the ghastly curiosity. At a gala celebration, the governor praised himself, as well as Lieutenant Maynard and crew, for their courageous efforts in helping to rid piracy from the Atlantic shore.

As a warning of the consequences of piracy, the decaying remains of Blackbeard's head was staked on the bank of the Hampton River for all to see.

Its location would become known as Blackbeard's Point.

II

THE PLAYERS

CHAPTER

3

January 2001

"FRY 'EM in five!" decried the prominent legislator from Richmond.

Alexander S. Brotherton was the well-born, aristocratic sponsor of the most creative revision to criminal legislation in the history of the United States. He stood six feet three inches tall, his head of snow white hair finely styled and sprayed perfectly in place. His fifteen hundred dollar, tailor-made, pinstriped suit fit his trim physique perfectly. Although he was 61, he carried himself with the zest and vitality of a much younger man.

As Delegate Brotherton stood behind the center podium, he scrutinized the Virginia House of Delegates. Although he knew every delegate — friend and foe — by name, this time it didn't really matter how many of them didn't like him, because this time, he had pulled out all the stops.

Brotherton's very presence was charismatic. When his bass voice boomed, there was instant silence.

"The use of illegal drugs preponderates and dominates masses of people in our society!" he bellowed. "Our faithful police are overworked, undermanned and frustrated. Taxes are breaking the backs of our middle-income citizens. Nearly forty percent of our tax revenue is being funneled into law enforcement and prisons, yet crime continues to grow more rapidly than ever. Our middle class is growing poorer, and our poorer class is growing larger."

Brotherton paused and took a sip of water from a styrofoam cup as he surveyed the audience. It was un- usual for the entire one- hundred-member body of Virginia's distinguished House of Delegates to be present at the same time, but today was unique. The Senate had already tacitly approved the proposal, which meant to- day the fate of the controversial Fast Track Death Pen- alty Law would be decided.

If it passed, it would become law.

In his smug, all-knowing way, he carefully explained the upsurge in crime—drug smuggling had tripled, murders had doubled, and house breakings were up sixty per cent.

The legislators were receptive. Hype about this Fast Track Death Penalty Law had been around for more than a year, its relentless supporters spending over twenty million dollars on a massive media blitz. The public had been bom- barded with television clips of convicted murderers enjoy- ing sex and drugs in prison, causing many citizens to be- lieve this was the norm for prison life.

The voters had devoured Brotherton's propaganda, hook, line and sinker. The once silent majority became vo- cal, and now declared loudly and clearly they were fed up with the justice system. The public outcry had continued to escalate until the general consensus overwhelmingly de- manded passage of the law.

Opponents of this bill, including most of the civil liber- ties groups, had vigorously argued that valuable Constitu- tional rights were being overlooked for the sake of political expediency. Nevertheless, today, as the delegates sat there listening to Brotherton's oration, most of them already knew how they must vote if they coveted a political future.

"In the United States of America," Brotherton pro- claimed, his blue eyes sparkling, "we have a record number of criminals behind bars."

Enthralled with his own words, Brotherton paused momentarily to clear his throat. Scanning the distinguished group, it gave him great pleasure to see them spellbound, anxiously awaiting his next words.

"In Virginia alone," he lectured, his voice deepening, "we are supporting a vast population in our jails and prisons at a monumental expense to the taxpayer. We are building new prisons as fast as possible, yet no sooner are they opened, than they are filled to twice their capacity."

Although the vast majority of the delegates seemed mesmerized by his every word, a few glum-faced members were totally bewildered, unable to fathom how such a right wing retrogressive law, totally devoid of genuine due process protections, could have ever gotten this far, but Brotherton could have cared less.

Suddenly Brotherton's right index finger jabbed skyward, and his voice rose an octave. A brash scowl on his face, he began to preach. "Thousands upon thousands of convicted murderers have been sentenced to death! But, because of antiquated technicalities, only about sixty a year are executed in the entire country."

There was a silent pause as he stared out at his colleagues. Then, like the sound of a fast-approaching freight train, his voice began to tone deeper and deeper, louder and louder. "My proposal will change that mockery!" he roared, his words now echoing off the forty-foot ceilings.

Clapping began slowly, quickly increasing into thunderous applause as almost every member of the House of Delegates responded with a standing ovation. For three minutes, the enthusiastic applause resonated through the chamber and waned only after Brotherton raised his hand to silence the group.

A tone of excitement had enveloped the great hall. Like leading a herd of blind mules to the glue factory, Brotherton was ushering the awe-struck delegates down his own self-serving path to power.

"It is taking an average of twelve years from conviction to execution." Brotherton's words quickened as his high passion for the fast track law generated increased energy from the excited audience. "Under our present system, the death penalty is protracted, cumbersome, and practically meaningless. My proposal will fix this malfeasance of justice!" The governor spoke so loudly his magnified voice was beginning to squelch.

After adjusting the microphone, he lowered his volume slightly. In his still vibrant voice, he began to explain the fast track law.

"Under the new law, they'll have one month from the time of arrest until the trial starts. Then, they'll have four months from their sentencing until they're executed. That computes to five months, excluding trial time, from arrest to execution."

A five second pause elapsed allowing Brotherton's most ardent supporters to begin a preplanned chant. **"Fry `em in five! Fry `em in five! Fry `em in five!"** they cried out in unison. At first, it was a mere handful of chanters, but the catch phrase became contagious. More and more of otherwise conservative delegates broke from the House's tradition of quiet dignity and joined in the chant until the sacrosanct chamber echoed so loudly it was reminiscent of a roll tide cheer in Tuscaloosa at the Alabama-Auburn football game.

"Fry `em in five! Fry `em in five! Fry `em in five!"

The sound reverberated off the walls and soon was ear shattering. Brotherton, gloating vainly at his mastery over his peers, looked down on his flock. Then, upon the wave of his hand like a magic wand, the delegates immediately quietened.

With an expression of uncompromising determination on his face, and in his most fervent voice, Brotherton concluded with these words: "Let today be remembered in our nation's history as the day when criminals were put on notice they must, from now forward, answer for their sins!"

The august body applauded like teenagers at a rock concert. Brotherton smiled graciously, but inwardly, he was basking in the exhilaration of the moment. As the applause continued to abound, his humble smile transformed into a glowing, near-regal expression.

The speaker called the bill for a vote, and it passed — not just by the majority, but by a clear two-thirds. This was a great moment for Brotherton. Passage of this law would provide him with a springboard to the fulfillment of his life-long dream.

CHAPTER

4

ALEXANDER S. BROTHERTON, a native of Richmond, had been a member of the House of Delegates for the past ten years. He had long yearned for the power that could come with the governor's office, but it was the momentum from his Fast Track Death Penalty Law that gave him the boost he needed.

The bulk of his campaign funding was provided by one of the world's most powerful evangelical empires. This Virginia-based group had been founded by the outspoken Reverend Rufus K. Jones some twenty years earlier and had rapidly grown from a small church in Portsmouth, Virginia, into a world-wide television evangelical-political organization whose supporters crossed all racial and socio-economic boundaries. The influential Reverend Jones had his own television channel, where he could be seen preaching and praying at all hours. His shows were broadcast worldwide and translated into nine different languages.

Jones preached as much law and order as he did religion. "An eye for an eye, and a tooth for a tooth," were some of his favorite quotes. And it was Jones who created the "fry `em in five" slogan. He was quite proud.

After the passage of the Fast Track Death Penalty Law, Brotherton instantly became a celebrity. Morning, noon and night, he began appearing on national television talk shows. Surveys quickly indicated overwhelming popular support for his Fast Track Death Penalty Law which, for the moment, made Brotherton one of the most up - and - coming personalities in America.

The opportunity of a lifetime now fell at his feet. He seized the moment and allowed himself to be drafted as his party's unopposed choice for Governor of the Commonwealth of Virginia.

He had no scruples. Cheating, fuzzy math and dirty tricks didn't matter. The general election had been a no-holds-barred battle, the type of battle that fitted him to a T. In an unprecedented landslide, Brotherton won the gubernatorial race hands down.

*

On January 2nd, 2002, Alexander S. Brotherton was sworn in as the Governor of the Commonwealth of Virginia. Five months later, on June 1st, his glorified Fast Track Death Penalty Law was scheduled to go into effect.

On the evening of his inauguration, Alex Brotherton, sitting in the den of his Richmond mansion, chatted with Roger Keller, who had been his executive assistant for twelve years.

Brotherton took the last sip of his Glenfiddich, and after momentarily savoring the taste, he slammed his tumbler down on the table.

"You know, Roger," he droned philosophically, a slight slur in his words, "if we can actually fry somebody in five months, I think I'll be the most popular man in America."

"You may be already, sir," Keller replied, always eager to feed the ego of his mentor.

Brotherton smiled. "Now, Roger, if that were true, you know what our next step would be, don't you?"

5

February 10, 2002

IT WAS the coldest February in recorded history as Arctic winds brought sub-zero temperatures across the eastern half of the United States. Frozen precipitation fell as far south as North Carolina, causing treacherously slick roads and nearly impassable coastal waterways.

Notwithstanding these extreme conditions, a 51 foot diesel-powered trawler plowed the icy waters of the mid-Atlantic Ocean, traveling on a compass heading of 270 degrees magnetic. Three men, each cloaked in heavy waterproof parkas, huddled in the enclosed cockpit as the trawler plunged through six-foot swells. A tall, heavy-set, bearded man stood at the helm. He tightly gripped the wheel, his piercing black eyes straining to see through the ice-glazed windshield as he guided the boat through the pounding sea.

"Go below and ready your equipment," he snapped, looking over his shoulder at the two other, much smaller men. "Then get some sleep. That's an order! Tomorrow's gonna' be a tough day for all of us."

The skipper quickly directed his attention back to the helm as he skillfully turned the wheel to starboard, causing the trawler to lurch toward the crest of an approaching wave.

As the boat slowly powered its way through the freezing

waters, the radar screen indicated a solid mass, presumably land, five miles to the northwest. The diesel engine sounded a steady drone-like beat while the ever-present smell of diesel fumes left the crew slightly nauseous. The sea was rough, the swells growing more frequent and increasingly higher. Over and over, the trawler rose, then fell, rolled, then slid.

The two-man crew had retired to their respective bunks and were trying to force sleep, both knowing full well that the skipper would roust them hours before daybreak.

Crewman John Williams, a former Navy Seal, was 37 and had years of commercial diving experience all over the world. This job, however, had the makings of a grand slam windfall. Never had he been offered so much money for such a relatively simple job: fifty thousand dollars for just three days work.

The other crewman, Herb Bonner, had been diving for five years. He was 23 and held every conceivable scuba certification. He had pounced on this opportunity of good fortune, a chance for him to make more money on a three-day diving expedition than he could earn in six months of hard work. Although he had not been told exactly what he would have to do, it really didn't matter. For fifty grand, he'd walk on water if he had to. Bonner tossed and turned in his bunk, as he thought about his new found wealth and what he would do with all that money. He was sure of one thing: he would take a month-long vacation in Cozumel, where he would bask in the sun, sip on margaritas and chase thongs. Finally, with that blissful thought, he began snoring.

The trawler changed course to 305 degrees magnetic. When the radar blip indicated their approach to land, the skipper throttled back a few notches, reducing speed to six knots. In five more minutes, the radar configuration changed, the screen now showing the approach of two land masses with a narrow gap between them.

The digital depth finder had indicated over a hundred feet of water under the keel, but abruptly, a drastic decrease in depth was recorded. The ocean bottom was now just nine feet down and getting shallower as the craft neared the narrow gap. Soon the depth had dropped to eight feet, then to seven, and then it was just six feet. The side scan sonar showed depths to port and starboard as unrecordable, meaning the depth was less than three feet.

With its five foot draft, the trawler was in a shallow ditch, barely deep enough to float the vessel. Surrounded by such freezing and turbulent waters, to run aground here on this dark treacherous night would be disastrous.

But then the water depth dropped again. Just as the depth finder indicated a five-foot depth, the crew was rudely awakened, startled by the grinding sound of the hull scratching over the sea bottom. The trawler's forward movement slowed to crawl-speed as it dragged over the gritty shoal. The boat, it appeared, had run aground and was about to become stuck. Even the salt-worn skipper gave pause as the thought of a ruined dream loomed before him. But seconds later, he exhaled a sigh of relief when he realized that the trawler had slid over the shallows and into deeper water.

The boat rumbled forward on the same heading, traveling at a speed of six knots for another ten minutes when it turned ninety degrees to starboard. After several more minutes, the trawler made another starboard turn, then abruptly, the throttles went to neutral and an electrical whine forecasted the splash of the anchor.

A few final moments of peace allowed the crew time to drift back into a sound sleep, but their quietude was soon terminated when a deep voice from above sounded out loudly.

"Okay, men, out of the rack! Breakfast will be ready in five minutes."

The divers had a hearty appetite, devouring eggs, sausage and grits like there was no tomorrow. But at 4:30 A.M., the cordiality evaporated. The skipper's feigned smile formed into a rigid snarl as he began barking out orders.

"All right! Get your butts in your dry suits! Be on deck

by 0500 ready for work. Now, move out!"

"I think the party's over," Bonner whispered as he and Williams descended the stairway to their cabin. After pulling and tugging themselves into their bulky dry suits, the men now looked like fat astronauts. With no time to spare, they grabbed their gear and lumbered back onto the cold slippery rear deck.

The black-suited skipper, an obsessive gleam in his penetrating eyes, was waiting impatiently. Taking small, deliberate baby steps over the icy deck, he walked cautiously over to a large crate lashed to the rear deck. The divers followed.

"The thing in this wooden box," he instructed, placing his right hand on the corner of the crate, "is gonna be dropped into the water and it'll sink to the bottom."

"What is it, skipper?" Bonner asked.

"I can only tell you that it has to do with an artificial reef," the skipper replied, lying unconvincingly.

The divers were directed to pry the wooden crate open and rip away the plywood. That done, a hard plastic box, eight feet long and four feet high, was revealed. Located at one end of the strange object was a round, hatch-like door with a hard plastic wheel lock.

"Get behind it and push!" the skipper directed.

The three men pushed and strained, but the huge crate would not budge.

"Damn it! Put your back into it!" the skipper growled, his hairy face squenching as he pushed with the determination of a pyramid builder.

They rocked it back and forth, pushing it forward, then pulling it backward, over and over, until finally, there was a barely audible pop, then a crack, followed by ever so slight movement. Struggling, inch by inch, they slowly pushed the strange box aft, until at last, it tumbled over the edge, splashing down into the icy water, its location marked by an orange marker buoy which quickly popped back to the surface.

Next, the skipper directed three other crates to be ripped

open, soon exposing three large round drain pipes, each six feet in length.

"Now, you, Williams," the skipper blasted, his finger jabbing out towards Williams' nose, "Get the hell up there and start the compressor! Bonner, you attach the airlift hose and drop the end into the water!" The skipper's words were sharp, his glare fierce.

With their equipment readied, the dry-suited divers, face masks and mouth pieces in place, stepped off the aft deck and dropped into the 30 degree water. The frigid terror of this cold, dark environment would have been paralyzing to most people, but these divers were focused on their mission, seemingly unconcerned about the perils they might soon be confronting.

As they descended, the skipper kept a gloved hand on the marker buoy line, allowing the line to slide between his fingers. Other than the sucking and gurgling sounds of compressed air bubbling from scuba exhausts, the submarinal surroundings echoed with an eerie silence, a silence that screamed out a warning, a warning that would never be heard.

With visibility less than one body length's distance, the divers sank twenty-six feet down into the murky water, their fin covered feet finally crunching onto the sandy bottom. Impatiently, the skipper immediately snatched the dangling airlift hose and began to vacuum away sand from underneath the plastic box.

An airlift device such as this one had originally been developed for underwater treasure hunting and was used much like a vacuum cleaner to suction away the sand and mud that covered shipwreck debris. Here, however, the airlift was being used to suction away the sand from under the plastic box.

Bubbles sputtered up from the intake as the exhaust end of the hose ten yards away spewed out vacuumed sand. With the divers taking turns operating the airlift, the box was displacing the underneath sand and slowly sinking down into the sea floor. The work moved rapidly, and in less than thirty minutes, only the upper eighteen inches of the box was still exposed.

The job half done, the skipper and his divers surfaced, refueled the compressor, and attached fresh air tanks. One at a time, the three plastic drain pipes were rolled off the stern and into the water. As the third marker buoy popped to the surface, the skipper again began to spew out orders.

"Williams, start the compressor! Bonner, grab the airlift!"

No one noticed the fanatical glint in his dark, sinister eyes, reflecting the skipper's intense commitment to the success of this bizarre endeavor.

In minutes, they were back in the water, this time with Williams operating the airlift and Bonner holding the hose. As the airlift continued to suction away the sand beneath the box, the first circular pipe was attached. With more suction, the box, together with the attached pipe, gradually bored deeper and deeper. As it sank, the second pipe was attached, then the third pipe, until finally, the box was buried eighteen feet below the surface, the upper rim of the third connecting pipe even with the ocean floor. The skipper fitted a plastic cover over the exposed rim of the pipe, capping it off.

On March 1st, the unidentifiable, bloated bodies of two divers in dry suits washed ashore on Assateague Beach near Chincoteague, Virginia.

GRAYSON QUENTIN FORREST, JR. was the treasure at the end of his mother's rainbow. The sun rose and set on him. His father had called him Grayboy and said he was a gift from God. Grayboy had been the unexpected but welcome only child of a 49-year-old father and a 38-year-old mother.

He grew up in Hampton, Virginia and graduated from Hampton High School, an unremarkable student. He played football there, but only third string. He held the record for strikeouts on the baseball team, but in batting, not pitching. Nevertheless, his favorite sport was carousing with his buddies, which he did very, very well.

As a teenager, Grayboy spent much of his spare time exploring the local waters of Hampton Roads and the Chesapeake Bay in his father's unsinkable Boston Whaler. He cruised westward as far as the James River falls near Richmond and southward down the Dismal Swamp Canal into North Carolina.

In spite of his frivolity, Grayboy excelled on the college entrance exam, allowing him admission to his first choice, East Carolina University in Greenville, North Carolina. ECU had an excellent academic name and was also renowned for fantastic football, wild parties and beautiful coeds.

Standing five foot ten, Grayboy was big boned, his muscles rock hard, and he had the stamina of a workhorse. From his father, he inherited a full head of fine, light-brown hair that refused placement, prompting him to frequently use his hand to flick the overhang off his brow.

His face was handsome, his features soft and gentle. His brilliant blue eyes danced with never-ending enthusiasm for whatever might interest him at the particular moment.

At college, academics took a back seat to guzzling suds and partying. So, it came as no surprise, when at the close of his freshman year, the university issued a proviso to his continued enrollment—academic probation and summer school.

The most significant event of his life occurred during that summer school session. It began with a phone call, a call from his minister. His father had died of a massive stroke.

Coping with the reality that he would never see his father again was agonizing, but even worse was his deep sadness that his father had not lived to see his only son become a responsible citizen—just an immature teenager in summer school on academic probation.

After the funeral, when Grayson returned to college, he had a new attitude. He attended classes regularly, he developed good study habits, he even did his homework. And like magic, his grades drastically improved. Soon he was off academic probation and before long on the dean's list. As time passed, a novel aspiration began to occupy his thinking—law school.

At William and Mary School of Law, inspired by his father's memory, he totally devoted himself to his studies. He did well, made law review, and after three years was awarded his JD degree with honors.

The post-graduation family dinner at Hampton's Fisherman's Wharf almost did him in. After Grayson's small family had over-indulged in the bountiful buffet, his Uncle Sterling stood and dramatically raised his glass of wine.

"I propose a toast to Grayson Quentin Forrest, Jr.," he

said. In unison, Grayson's mother and his Aunt Mary Jane raised their glasses of iced tea.

"Here's to my dear nephew who has made our family proud today," Uncle Sterling announced as he looked down at Grayson.

Then, he raised his glass a bit higher as he beamed from ear to ear. "And I speak for his dad, my brother, and tell you Grayson Sr. would be the proudest father in the world."

With those words, Grayson had to choke back the tears. *Maybe his father really did know.*

Soon after graduation, Grayson joined Navy JAG where he saw the world, sailed the seas and gained invaluable experience as a trial lawyer. But, shortly after his 29th birthday, his naval tour came to a close. It was time to return to civilian life, time to become the senior partner in his own one-man law firm back home in Old Hampton.

GRAYSON Q. FORREST
ATTORNEY AT LAW

Grayson rented a second floor walkup office in the old Kresge 5 and 10 Cent Store building on the corner of Queen's Way and Vine Street. He bought a used desk, had a phone installed, resurrected a dusty couch from his mother's basement, and then, on a cold bleak day near the end of February 2002, his long-awaited moment finally arrived. His dream was about to come true.

It had been a proud moment when he nailed the sign to the front of the Kresge Building beside the walkup stairs. But it only took a few weeks for him to realize there was one major ingredient missing in his law practice: Clients.

Desperate for business, Grayson allowed his name to be added to the list of lawyers who would accept court-appointed cases. Although the fees were much less than standard attorney rates, something was better than nothing.

Business proceeded slowly. After four weeks, he had

grossed just $578, but his expenses were $688.

"Is there something wrong with this picture?" a somewhat discouraged Grayson Forrest, Attorney at Law, asked his uncle Sterling. "Maybe I've made a mistake. Maybe I really can't make it in a solo practice."

Uncle Sterling, the family confidant, was a double dipper, first having retired as a sergeant major from the U. S. Army's military police, and then retiring again from the York County Sheriff's Department.

"Look, Gray," Sterling responded sympathetically, his voice warm and consoling, "I've been in the law business fifty years. Trust me, things are gonna' pick up! You just need to hang in there! You hear?"

CHAPTER

7

May 25, 2002

"HELP ME, Daddy! I've been kidnapped!"

"Where are you, baby?" stammered Gunnery Sergeant Lincoln Vernon, but the phone abruptly clicked, replaced by the hum of the dial tone. Gunny's adrenaline shot skyward as a quandary of unanswered questions begged for answers.

Where was his little girl? Who was she with? And worst of all—would he ever see her again?

For the past two days, Gunny had been worried sick after his adopted daughter had failed to return home from an outing with a young man named Rusty Blalock, a 19-year-old high school dropout. Frantically, Gunny looked up the name, Blalock, in the phone directory and found no listing.

Unnerved by her disappearance and desperate for answers, Gunny dried his eyes with a paper towel and comforted himself with the thought that Mandy was still alive, at least for the moment.

Gunnery Sergeant Abraham Lincoln Vernon, USMC retired, loved his adopted daughter, Mandy, more than anyone else alive. He had married her mother Donna back when Mandy was just four.

Donna, a petite blond beauty, had been divorced for

three months when she walked into the Black Cat Lounge, the local hangout for black noncommissioned officers in Jacksonville, North Carolina, the home of Camp Lejeune.

Although the Black Cat Lounge was usually humdrum, Gunny had frequented the place almost every night because it was better than staying home and counting the cracks in the ceiling. There, at the Black Cat, he would drink vodka and ginger, and if he got lucky, he might score a roll in the hay. That was as good as it ever got. That is, until Donna Brown strutted in, wearing her charcoal, ultra mini skirt and her white, skin tight, cashmere sweater.

Donna had taken a seat at the bar, two stools down from him, but close enough for Gunny to look at her from the corner of his eye. Even before a word was spoken, he was captivated. He bought her a beer. They made small talk. He smiled and she smiled back. The chemistry was there as they slow danced, staring at each other as though there was no one else in the room.

Donna's daughter was a miniature, mirror image of her mother. When Donna and Gunny began seeing each other, little Mandy would frequently gaze into Gunny's big brown eyes and tell him he was the handsomest man in the whole world.

When she said, "Gunny, I want you to be my daddy," he would melt like a marshmallow over a campfire.

Gunny's adoration for Mandy partially stemmed from a 1990 pre-Gulf War guilt trip. Gunny had been going out with Kenya Lawford, a good-looking lady from nearby New Bern. They had grown quite serious in their six-month courtship, but when she disclosed her pregnant condition, the moment became bitter, the ending ugly.

In the days that followed, Gunny wrestled with his feelings about the responsibilities of fatherhood and his insensitivity toward Kenya, but before he could reconcile his thoughts, his Marine unit was put on alert. Communications were restricted as Gunny's advanced team of force recon Marines was whisked away to Iraq, where they were airdropped into the desert.

As the days passed, the war going on all around him, Gunny repeatedly pondered his shameful reaction to Kenya's apprehensive disclosure. Days turned into weeks, but his mind continued to vacillate.

The answer to his moral dilemma became vividly clear early one morning in the desert, when his recon team advanced on an Iraqi outpost. The Marines attacked with automatic gunfire and grenades, destroying every living creature in the outpost.

But when Gunny inspected the carnage, he found not only dead Iraqi soldiers, but also dead civilians, probably Bedouins. An elderly woman, two middle-aged men, three younger women, and even their camels were all dead unnecessarily. It got worse. A baby, an infant less than one-month-old, was lying there charred and lifeless. That innocent baby was Gunny's catalyst, a catalyst that molded his future resolve.

The same night, he wrote Kenya and asked for her forgiveness. He told her he wanted to marry her. He wanted to be the father of their child. A month later when the war was over he tried to call her, but her line had been disconnected. Upon his return stateside, he tried to locate her, but she had moved and left no forwarding address.

For more than a year, Gunny was tormented by guilt for his stupid insensitivity and by heartache for the tremendous loss of the lady he loved and the child he would probably never see. So, when he met Donna and Mandy, it was like a gift of renewed hope and a second chance at happiness.

8

IN JUST two months, Donna and Linc, as she called him, were married by the base chaplain. Donna's mother refused to attend the wedding, ostensibly because it was too far over to Jacksonville from the small rural town of Rocky Springs, located in western North Carolina. But, the real problem was the ultimate taboo—Loretta Brown's daughter was marrying a "colored man".

The wedding ceremony had been first-rate Marine style. Initially, the focus had been on the tall, handsome Marine ushers in their dress blues.

Gunny himself was quite striking. Standing six foot one, he had the broad shoulders and slender waist of an NFL running back. In those days, he worked out daily, yielding him washboard abs, a carved chest and a lean torso.

The bride was beautiful in her off-white, full-length wedding gown. However, when the processional began, she was not the center of attention. All eyes were drawn to her darling little daughter, Mandy, who preceded her mother down the aisle, dropping rose petals with each step.

Mandy stole the show. The bride and groom faced each other to exchange their vows, and little Mandy stood between them. Gunny took his vows and said, "I do," then the chaplain turned toward the bride. "Do you, Donna, take

Lincoln to be your lawful wedded husband, to have and to hold, to love and to cherish, through sickness and in health, so long as you both shall live?"

"Yes, we do!" came a high pitched, exuberant voice from below as Mandy slapped her hands up to cover her face as if to hide her embarrassment. The chaplain could not contain himself. His stone face cracked into a smile, then he exploded into gut-busting laughter as tears engulfed his eyes. The entire congregation followed suit.

After the service while the guests stood outside by the front steps, the rhythmic beat of military cadence began to fill the air. "Left—left—left—right—left." Two rows of Marines marched forward, and on command, clicked their heels together, coming to a precise stop. After a precision turn inward to face one another, they stood motionless, their eyes staring straight ahead.

Soon, Gunny and Donna with Mandy still between them, appeared in the chapel doorway. A deep, magnified voice announced, "Ladies and gentlemen, I am pleased to introduce for their very first time in public, Staff Sergeant and Mrs. Abraham Lincoln Vernon and their daughter, Mandy!"

The handsome threesome stepped briskly down the staircase as the Marine columns arched their swords in perfect synchronization to form a sabred archway. The newlywed trio walked forward, passing under the first set of arched swords unfettered, then under the second and third set of swords. There was just one more sabred archway left.

When they thought they were about to successfully run the gauntlet, the sabres of the final arch descended, blocking the new family's passage. The threesome stopped, leaving Gunny grinning apprehensively at his friend, the major.

"Kiss to pass!" the major demanded, his demeanor stern and rigid.

Gunny and Donna beamed like the morning sun, as they embraced, their lips touching. Then, with Mandy giggling and jumping up and down, the new couple knelt down beside her and held the bubbling child, all three kissing and hugging ecstatically.

The sabres raised and just as the new family passed under the arch, the major lowered his sabre, turned the blade to its flat side and very gently tapped the bride on the fanny. "Welcome to the Marine Corps!" he exclaimed.

The honeymoon endured long past the one week trip to the Bahamas, and for a while, it appeared it was going to be a storybook marriage. Gunny and Mandy bonded. She was the child he had lost; he was the father she'd never had.

When Gunny was not on assignment, he was home with his family enjoying this opportunity to make up for the mistakes of his past. His most gratifying moment came when he received the court papers which certified him as Mandy's adoptive father, and Mandy was so proud she took the papers to school to show to her teacher.

Five near-blissful years passed and all appeared well. But when Gunny returned from a three month stint in the Mideast, his world fell apart. The first thing he noticed was the knee-high grass in the front yard and when he went inside, he was flabbergasted. The furniture, the lamps, the stereo and the television were gone. On top of a clump of clothes piled up on the bedroom floor was a note:

> *Linc,*
> *I can't live like this any more. Mandy and I are leaving you. You will hear from my attorney.*
>
> *Donna*

Gunny was mortified. This loss was deeply personal. Mandy and he were bound by mutual love and admiration; nothing could tear them apart. She was not just his daughter but also his best friend. Now, however, he stood to lose her, just like he had lost the others. This had been his last opportunity to prove his worthiness as a human being, his final chance to make amends. Instead, his adopted daughter was going to grow up in Rocky Springs, North Carolina with a self-centered mother who was so focused on herself she didn't have time to attend to the needs of her 12 year old daughter.

Gunny wanted custody, but his lawyer offered him little hope. The likelihood of him getting custody of a white teenage girl who wasn't biologically related to him, particularly in Rocky Springs, would be next to impossible. The best he could hope for was supervised visitation every other week.

CHAPTER

9

GUNNY'S FIRST and only visit with Mandy was a disaster. They met at the social services office in Rocky Springs and were supervised by a social worker. Mandy, stoic and detached, spent most of the visit looking at her watch.

The next two visits were cancelled, presumably by Mandy, and Gunny's phone calls were always refused. Over and over his efforts to see his daughter were met with uncompromising resistance. It began to seem hopeless.

Then, out of the blue, Donna called. After strained introductory cordialities, Gunny asked her what she wanted.

"Gunny, I can't handle Mandy," she said whining. "She's slipping out of the house at night. She's drinking beer and smoking marijuana. I'm not sure, but I think she's having sex."

"Damn it, Donna! She's just fourteen years old. How could she be having sex? Who's looking after her?"

"Well, Gunny, you know my mother is getting pretty feeble, and uh, the guy I'm seeing, well, he and Mandy don't see eye to eye."

"So, nobody's looking after her, right, Donna?"

Gunny was sizzling.

"There's another little problem," Donna added. "Mandy got kicked out of school yesterday for smoking marijuana."

"Well, what the hell do you want me to do?" Gunny was now boiling.

"Let Mandy come live with you. You know how much she loves you. She needs a strong male influence. Besides, we just can't look after her anymore. She's just too much for us to handle."

Gunny's eyes lit up. Finally there was a bright spot in his life. "You'll sign the court papers?"

"I will."

"When?"

"Tomorrow."

"I'll be there tomorrow at six. Have her stuff packed!" Gunny's level of excitement was about to shoot through the roof.

Things had changed considerably in the two years since Donna and he had split. He was older—51, but hopefully, much wiser. Last year, he had reluctantly retired from his beloved Marine Corps and moved to Morehead City, where he had bought a bungalow a block away from Bogue Sound. He had planned to renovate the house, and spend his spare time fishing and clamming. But, unfortunately, his plans had not jelled. He soon learned he was a lousy carpenter, and it was easier to buy his fish at the market. And without his daughter and the Marine Corps, there had not been much left in life for him, so instead, he drank.

But now, with this wonderful news, he was certain things would be different. He brought Mandy to her new home in Morehead City, helped her decorate her room, and bought her a stereo system with a DVD player. He even gave her his credit card and sent her to the mall for new clothes.

Mandy, elated with her new life, was a changed girl. Her attitude was wonderful, and she even obeyed her father since she did, in fact, adore him. She didn't even recall the terrible visit in Rocky Springs. Her grades improved, and for a time, she was a model young lady.

Nevertheless, Camelot did not last forever, and as she neared her 15th birthday, she met Rusty Blalock, a 19 year old hooligan. She became unruly and smart-mouthed. Rusty would keep her out until the early hours of the morning, and she wouldn't tell where they had been.

Now, because he had not taken a firmer hand, it appeared he stood to lose the only person in the world he loved unconditionally. But, he could not just stand by and let that happen!

CHAPTER
10

GUNNY WAS determined to find Mandy. He called the local police who told him matter-of-factly that teenagers run away all the time. "Don't worry," they said. Another call, this one to the local high school principal, yielded Rusty Blalock's address. Ten minutes later, Gunny stepped onto the front porch of the two-story frame house. He knocked on the door.

"Is anybody home?" he yelled.

A longhaired, teenaged greaser opened the door.

"Is Rusty Blalock here?" Gunny asked, his voice firm.

The greaser, a puzzled, marijuana muse on his face, finally grunted a response. "Uh, yeah man...uh, I'll get him."

Gunny entered the living room, which was dark, dingy and reeked of marijuana. Momentarily, Rusty, attired in faded jeans and a Jack Daniels T-shirt, came to the doorway. "Hi, Sarge. What's up?" he said.

"I'm looking for Mandy. Do you know where she is?"

"I haven't seen her since the other night, you know, the night I took her out. You mean she ain't come home?"

"That's right, Rusty, she ain't! Not since she went out with you." Gunny, his eyes narrowing to slits, leered accusingly at Rusty. "Where'd you take her, Rusty?"

Rusty scratched his head sheepishly and looked at Gunny

with a cat-ate-the-canary expression on his face. "Well, you see, I got sorta' bombed, and Mandy got pissed. She took up with some other guy, so I got mad and left."

"Who the hell did you leave her with, Rusty?" Gunny demanded.

"I don't know. Some big old guy with a beard. He was giving her reefer and hitting on her."

"Damn it, Rusty! Where had you taken her?" Gunny's voice was strained and his blood pressure was rising.

"We were at a little bar up there off Highway 70, Dixie Belle's Lounge, you know, up past Otway.

Gunny went ballistic.

"Rusty, I ought'a whip your ass! You took my daughter out and left her with some redneck in the middle of no-where?"

Rusty's middle finger suddenly jutted upward as words he would soon regret spat out of his smart mouth.

"Don't threaten me you washed-up relic just `cause your daughter's a trampy little bitch!"

The boy's injudicious choice of words pushed Gunny past his control point. Rusty's nose was instantly smashed level with his face. Gunny hit him once more for good mea-sure, leaving the boy moaning on the floor.

Storming out the door, Gunny jumped into his ma-roon Dodge Ram and headed for Dixie Belle's Lounge. He sped across the bridge toward the historic town of Beaufort, whizzing down Highway 70 at twice the speed limit. Panic-driven, he was focused on just one thing: find-ing his daughter. He hoped, just maybe, she was still up at Dixie Belle's Lounge.

Dixie Belle's Lounge was known as a hangout for rednecks and cluckers. Recalling many years earlier, when he was full of piss and vinegar, he and some of his leatherneck home boys had gone up to Dixie Belle's as a joke, just to see if any of the local crackers wanted to give them grief. *Damn, we must've been crazy!* Gunny reflected, somewhat astonished at his old antics.

He couldn't remember exactly where Dixie Belle's was located, but he was pretty sure it was on a side road off Highway 70. Passing a Citgo station, then a caution light, he spotted an intersection that looked familiar. He stomped down hard on the brakes and turned to the right. The truck skidded, then fishtailed. Gunny accelerated, regaining control, then blasted down the road. Nothing would stop him, he thought.

Sergeant Clyde Pitts of the North Carolina State Highway Patrol was cruising southbound on Highway 70 toward the Harker's Island intersection. As he approached, he spotted the maroon Dodge Ram as it skidded, then fishtailed onto the side road. The dutiful trooper quickly hit his brakes and switched on his blue light before making a three-point turn-around.

Gunny groaned when he saw the flashing blue light in his rear view mirror.

"The hell with it," he muttered. "You'll just have to catch me, Mr. Cop. I've got to find Mandy!"

The land on both sides of the straight flat road was low and marshy with scrubby pine trees sporadically dotting the terrain. The trooper's speedometer was almost buried, his speed well over ninety miles an hour, but the maroon pickup truck was only an elusive blur somewhere up ahead of him. The trooper continued to accelerate, his speed increasing to well over a hundred miles per hour as the gap began to close.

Dixie Belle's Lounge, Gunny recalled, was about a mile off the hard surface road, down some rutty dirt road. Gunny had to figure out just which rutty dirt road. There were dozens of dirt lanes, and they all looked alike. If he made the wrong choice, he couldn't turn back or the cop would nab him for sure.

With the trooper closing fast, Gunny saw the dirt road up ahead. He turned the wheel and sent the Ram into a power slide, quickly recovering before disappearing down the narrow road in a cloud of dust.

Trooper Pitts was not quite so fortunate. Racing along at a hundred plus, he hit the brake and turned, but he was going much too fast. The patrol car broke loose, slid out of control and skidded across the road, then careened down a slope, slamming headlights first into a murky ravine. The car was hopelessly stuck up to its axles in Carteret County swamp mud.

CHAPTER
11

AS THE dust cloud settled, Gunny rolled to a stop in front of a raggedy honky tonk bar, a shanty so dilapidated it looked like it might collapse at any moment. Dixie Belle's was a weather beaten, wood-frame building in dire need of painting and repair. It had broken window panes, holes in the weathered siding, and missing roof shingles. The sagging porch was propped up by makeshift, two-by-four studs. Two rusty pickup trucks were parked in the dirt lot.

After parking on the far side of the lot, Gunny exited his truck, Beretta in hand. He tucked the gun down into his waistband, then walked cautiously toward the front door of the lounge. Taking a quick look over his shoulder, he felt a slight sense of relief that there was no sign of the cop that had been chasing him.

Before entering, he peeked inside the dimly lit lounge and quickly scanned the layout. To the right was a pool table, to the left a small bar. Cautiously, he stepped inside. The place smelled of stale beer and cigar smoke. As he took his next step, his boot soles stuck to the gummy floor. It crossed his mind these rednecks probably hadn't mopped the floor since the last time he was here, maybe twenty years ago.

A scrawny white guy in an unbecoming, black Harley

Davidson tank top, his tattooed arms the width of a garden hose, was tending bar. He was talking to his only customer, a slithery man with a pony tail who was sipping on a long-neck Budweiser. Although there were several beer cans along the edge of the pool table, there was no one else around.

Watchfully, Gunny approached the bar and fished a photograph of Mandy from his shirt pocket. When he showed it to the bartender, the little man, a dumb expression on his face, made a token glance down at the photo. But, too quickly, he looked back at Gunny and shook his head sideways.

Sensing a bad attitude, Gunny blew up.

"You didn't even look!" he thundered. "Look at it again; this is important!"

Stepping closer, extending his hand across the bar, Gunny stuck the photo squarely in the bartender's face, directly under his nose.

Obviously intimidated by the aggressive nature of this tall, black man, the bartender pretended to carefully study the photo, this time looking at it for a full ten seconds.

"Nev . . . never seen her before," he finally stuttered, his eyes staring back past Gunny toward the pool table. But then, the flush of a toilet seemed to change the barkeep's attitude. Suddenly, he sounded more self-assured.

"And who cares anyway!" he blurted out, sending a spray of saliva into Gunny's face.

The previously timid man now seemed to have suddenly acquired the courage of a lion. "This is a private club," he yelled, "so get the hell outta' here, jigaboo!"

"A what?" Gunny retorted incredulously, not believing what he had just been called.

Abruptly, a loud, obnoxious voice sounded from the other side of the room. "What in hell's a nigger doing in here?" it howled.

Gunny turned to see a gigantic white man with a huge beer belly, long hair and no teeth, standing next to the pool

46   DANNY T. FERGUSON

table armed with a cue. The blimp-shaped man was reaching under his belly, trying to zip up his pants, which were several sizes too small.

It was then, when Gunny noticed the full, wall-sized, Confederate flag draped down from the opposite wall, a perfect backdrop for this toothless beer-bellied bigot. And worse, like a rabid warthog, the overwrought slob, his pool cue leading the way, was now plodding menacingly toward Gunny.

Out of the corner of his eye, Gunny saw the bartender reaching for something under the counter, but the foreboding pool cue was already within range and reared back ready for a swat at Gunny's head. Instinctively, as the cue began swinging forward, Gunny spun into a flying side kick, thrusting his right foot hard into the toothless slug's protruding belly. Instantly, a loud burping groan gurgled through the toothless mouth of this grotesquely obese man. His rotund torso bent forward, and a swash of slime green regurgitation spilled from his mouth, splattering onto Gunny's Air Jordans.

At that very moment, the bartender raised the barrel of a blue steel weapon from under the counter and pointed it even with Gunny's head. Gunny, well versed in the art of urban combat, snatched the vomit-sprayed pool cue from the floor and threw it at the bartender. The cue spun through the air like a fan and slammed squarely into the scrawny barkeep's face, the impact dropping the little man and sending his sawed-off shotgun clanging noisily to the sticky floor.

"Put your hands up, you're under arrest!" ordered an authoritative voice from the doorway. Gunny whirled around to see a highway patrolman brandishing a .45 caliber Glock, the barrel pointed directly at him.

"You need to arrest them, not me!" Gunny protested.

"Shut up and put your hands up, now!" the trooper commanded.

The next morning, after making bail, Gunny was determined to get back to his search for Mandy. Day after day, he drove to honky tonk beer joints throughout the county, where he asked questions, showed Mandy's photo, and ostensibly in the line of duty, drank large quantities of beer. Occasionally, he would see a big, bearded man who fit the general description of the kidnapper, but to Gunny's mounting disappointment, so far, every lead was a dead end.

Two weeks of relentless searching passed. Gunny had posted a $20,000 reward; he'd put up reward posters; he'd advertised in the newspaper, and he'd even gotten one of the local AM radio stations to announce the reward on the radio. Although he did receive some leads, unfortunately they all seemed to take him nowhere.

Gunny dwelled on the burning question of whether Mandy was even still alive. He agonized until his frustration gave way to depression, which deepened to desperation and despondency. His only remedy for such times—a half-gallon bottle of Absolut vodka.

III

THE PLIGHT

CHAPTER

12

June 3rd, 2002
10 A.M.

"**THIS IS** Coast Guard Dolphin 5654 ZULU. We have the suspect vessel in sight. Looks like a red Cigarette boat. It's traveling on a due west heading about ten miles east of Cape Henry. It's maybe going sixty miles an hour. Am I cleared for intercept?"

Based in Elizabeth City, North Carolina, the Coast Guard HH-65A Dolphin helicopter had been ordered out early that morning and directed to patrol the waters off Virginia Beach, south to Nags Head. Its mission was to seek out possible drug courier boats en route from the high seas.

An hour earlier, the Coast Guard's aerostat radar had detected suspicious movement off the Virginia shore. A blip on the screen, thought to be a small seacraft, had converged with a much larger, ship-sized blip some 150 miles out in the Atlantic Ocean, due east of Cape Charles.

The aerostat was actually a huge unmanned blimp-like airship which was tethered to a mooring platform. Inflated with helium, the airship rose to altitudes of up to 15,000 feet where its radar could be effective for over two hundred miles.

"Coast Guard Dolphin 5654 ZULU, you are cleared to intercept the incoming vessel for purposes of identification," came the radio dispatch.

"Roger on your last," the pilot of the helo replied, as he

nodded to his co-pilot. "Stand by as we approach for interception. Lock and load, Smitty," he ordered, directing his command to the petty officer seated behind him responsible for armament.

Lieutenant Ben Martin had been a Coast Guard helicopter pilot for almost five years and was an old hand at interdiction operations. Co-pilot Ensign Stephen Brooks, however, was a rookie. This was his second month on assignment and his very first order to intercept.

"Locked and loaded, sir," responded Petty Officer Second Class Ronald J. Smitherman, now seated in the starboard hatchway with his safety harness attached. The palm of his left hand rested on the bolt and his right hand gripped the trigger guard of the Browning M-2HB .50 caliber machine gun already prepared for action.

Maintaining his visual on the Cigarette boat, Martin began pushing the stick forward.

"Its destination seems to be the mouth of the Chesapeake Bay. Okay men, here we go!" Martin said, his voice ringing with the exhilaration of the moment.

In sixty seconds, the helicopter was a hundred feet above, slightly aft of the rapidly moving boat. The slender red craft continued to speed on its westward course, its helmsman, the lone person visible on the boat, showing no overt concern about the pursuing helicopter.

As Ensign Brooks looked down at the airspeed indicator, he noted they were flying nearly eighty miles an hour and the Cigarette boat was going even faster. "Damn!" he exclaimed. "That thing is really hauling ass!"

Skipper Martin kept a wary eye on their interception target. "I see a man driving, but I don't see anybody else. Can you make out anything?" he inquired.

Just as the words were coming out of Martin's mouth, Petty Officer Smitherman spotted a black-skinned man exiting the boat's cabin. He appeared to be carrying something. "Lieutenant, that black man's got a gun, and he's pointing it..." Smitherman's words abruptly ended as automatic gunfire erupted, a string of bullets tearing through the helo's port hatchway.

"I'm getting us the hell out here! Call for backup!" Lieutenant Martin directed as he pulled back on the stick and increased power. The Dolphin responded instantly, rapidly veering up and away from the Cigarette boat. In a heartbeat, the helicopter was out of range.

A faint voice could be heard over his headset. "Lieutenant, sir, I'm hit!" it cried out in feeble desperation. Looking back over his shoulder, Martin saw Smitherman. He was dangling from the hatchway, held only by his safety harness. Bloody faced and panic stricken, he was thrashing about, waving his arms wildly, trying to grab the lower edge of the hatch.

Then, suddenly, an ear-shattering explosion! The craft lurched violently to starboard. The entire fuselage began to vibrate.

"Wha...what the hell was that?" Brooks was stammering, his voice strained.

"We've been hit! We've lost our starboard engine," Martin exclaimed. "Hurry, pull Smitty back in!"

Brooks unharnessed himself and crawled back to the hatchway, where he reached down with his right hand and grabbed the terrified petty officer by the safety strap. Holding onto the bulkhead with his left hand and pulling with his right, he dragged Smitherman back up into the cabin.

A cloud of black smoke billowed out of the starboard engine as the vibration quickly became even more extreme. In a deep, formal tone, Lieutenant Martin spoke into his microphone. "Mayday! Mayday! This is Dolphin 5654 ZULU! Repeat. Mayday! This is Dolphin 5654 ZULU! We've been hit by hostile gun fire. One engine is out and a crewman is injured! Our location is eight miles due east of Cape Henry. We're headed toward Virginia Beach, but we're not maintaining altitude. She's going down. Do you copy?"

"Roger, Dolphin. This is Norfolk Base; we read you loud and clear, standby." The seconds seemed like an eternity, until finally, the voice was back on the air. "We have you on the screen. All available rescue aircraft are being launched. Repeat your location for verification, Lieutenant."

"Norfolk Base, now, we're about four miles from the beach, but our altitude is only eighty feet and falling. A crewman has taken a hit. He's alive but bleeding and going into shock. Get us some medical help ready...over!"

"Dolphin, did the hostile fire come from the vessel you were attempting to intercept?" asked the base radio operator.

"Affirmative, Norfolk Base, some black guy opened up on us with an automatic weapon."

"Could you describe the people on board?" inquired the radio man.

"Stand by, Norfolk! Now our port engine is starting to misfire. There's smoke coming out of it." Martin's words abruptly stopped, and he broke into a cough. Gasping, he managed to stammer, "Uh, we got smoke in the cabin, but we're in sight of the beach, maybe a half mile, but we're falling fast! We're only twenty feet above the water." Martin was yelling, his raspy voice panic-driven and strained. "We can't hold her. We're not going to make it!"

He was screaming in desperation as he pulled all the way back on the stick. The rotors could no longer hold the helicopter airborne; it began to fall. Ten feet above the water, the port engine stopped completely, and the craft dropped like a rock, splashing down hard into the breakers less than fifty yards off the beach.

Jostled, but undeterred, Lieutenant Martin jumped out of the hatch into the churning waist-deep water.

Through black smoke still billowing out of the starboard engine, Brooks hastily lowered Smitty down into the water as Martin grasped the collar of the wounded petty officer's orange life jacket.

As the helicopter was being buffeted about by the breakers, Martin and Brooks dragged their wounded comrade to the safety of the beach.

13

FOUR HELICOPTERS had been launched by the U.S. Navy to support the rescue/interdiction operation. Two helos veered south toward the downed airship, and the other two set a course in pursuit of the bandit Cigarette boat.

The red boat's engines were screaming, pushing the craft to top speed—over 120 miles an hour. Soon, however, the helicopters began to close in, prompting the fleeing boat to whip sharply to port, its new heading, Virginia Beach, dead ahead. It closed on the beach rapidly and in a blink it was there.

The roar of the Cigarette boat's twin 600 horsepower engines blended deceptively into the buzz of the personal water crafts flitting about in the surf. The sunbathers had almost no forewarning.

The huge red blur crashed through the breakers, instantly destroying everyone in its path. Two small children were crushed to death. The body of a young woman in a red bikini was sent cartwheeling through the air.

Carving a deadly path beachward, the Cigarette boat, its bow stem emblazoned in blood, finally came to a grinding halt. Hanging headfirst over the transom was the body of a white man, red ooze dripping from his mouth.

In the next moment, a handsome young man, a harrowed look on his face, came stumbling toward the boat. He was enraged, crying, cursing and screaming out of his mind. He reached up and yanked the corpse's head upward and yelled into its dead eyes.

"You son of a bitch!" he screamed, his voice quaking. "I'll kill you!"

An adrenaline surge sent the berserk man catapulting over the gunwale into the cockpit. In a frenzy, he struggled to his feet and stared down into the cabin's hatchway. A pair of eyes looked back at him.

"Come out of there, you murdering bastard!" he demanded, as a beast he had never known emerged from his inner being. "I'll tear you apart with my bare hands!" he growled, a savage snarl covering his face.

He began to step down through the hatchway when someone grabbed his shoulder.

"Hold on sir, this is a matter for the police," a suntanned lifeguard said, his voice kind but commanding. But the man's emotions were like a roller coaster, irate one moment, distraught the next.

"This bastard murdered my family. Let me loose!" he wailed. "I'll kill that son of a bitch if it's the last thing I ever do!" His screams were vicious and hysterical, then he broke into gutwrenching tears.

More lifeguards arrived and manhandled the man over the side of the boat into the waiting arms of a group of well-meaning beachgoers. Mercifully, just as they gently laid him down onto the beach, the young man fainted, his body unable to cope further with this hellish ordeal.

Uniformed Virginia Beach police officers soon arrived and climbed onto the beached yacht. One officer cautiously stepped down into the cabin. Momentarily, an EMT was called aboard. An injured man had been found inside.

A medical team, just arriving, boarded the beached vessel and lifted a young black man out of the hatchway and onto a stretcher. In seconds, the patient was whisked away in an awaiting ambulance.

Another officer climbed down into the cabin to assist. With flashlights shining, they continued to search the cavernous-like area, finding nothing unusual until a beam of light was shined underneath the bow V-berth.

"Well, look what I found. Bags of a white powdery substance!"

CHAPTER
14

Monday, June 3rd, 2002
10:50 A.M.

VIRGINIA BEACH Police Lieutenant Leon Veneable sat at his desk, perusing over a hodgepodge of bureaucratic paper work and munching on his second honey bun of the morning. His secretary buzzed on the intercom.

"Leon," she said, in her sweet Georgia peach brogue, "they need ya down on th' beach; there's fatalities, some kinda boat crash."

As the Central Investigation Duty Officer that day, it was Veneable's job to oversee all major crime scenes occurring during his shift.

"No rest for the weary," he casually remarked as he pulled on his wrinkled, size 52, herringbone sports coat and adjusted his too-short, paisley tie that lapped down to the middle of his round stomach.

"Where on the beach?" he asked.

"They told me up between 52nd and 53rd Street," the Georgia peach replied.

Veneable tightened his tie and brushed down the few hairs remaining on his thinning scalp.

"I'm goin' on out there. Maybe I can head off some of the usual problems."

A frown of boredom on his face, he sauntered out the door and climbed into his unmarked Chevrolet sedan. Momentarily, he was speeding down the road, northbound, siren screaming and blue light flashing. Approaching an intersection, he slowed for the red light, then blasted through like a 16-year-old out in his daddy's car.

In record time, he arrived at the intersection of Atlantic Avenue and 52nd Street where he saw five parked patrol cars and several police officers guarding the pathway to the beach. Also, surprisingly, he saw a Navy helicopter hovering over the beach and two other helicopters off in the horizon.

He parked curbside next to a fire hydrant, grunted a hello to the officers on guard, then tromped beachward. Up ahead he spotted the boat.

"God almighty!" he exclaimed.

This was more serious than he had originally thought.

The portly detective forced his five-foot nine-inch frame, which bore the burden of his 240 pound body, to break into a jog. Already sweating and now gasping for air, Veneable made it to a yellow strip of plastic, which outlined the perimeter of the police crime scene.

The boat, a red Cigarette boat, was high and dry a hundred feet away from the receding tide. Emergency medical teams were fitting plastic body bags over three victims.

"What in the hell happened here?" Veneable demanded of a nearby police officer.

"Drug dealers were chased onto the beach by the Coast Guard and smashed into these people. They didn't have a chance."

Veneable squenched a frown on his face and shook his head in disgust. After a pause, he asked, "Who are they?"

"It's a woman and her two children."

"Did we get the bastard who was driving the boat?"

"Yes sir! One's dead, shot by the Coast Guard or somebody. His body is over next to the boat. The other one's a black guy. Found him in the cabin of the boat with thirty kilos of cocaine. Looked like he was hurt pretty bad. They've already carted him off to the hospital."

"You got any names on these dead people?" Veneable asked coolly, as though he had been through this a thousand times.

The uniformed officer pointed toward an EMT team located just beyond the boat. "The man they're loading in the ambulance is the husband of the lady killed, and the two kids were his, too."

"What's his name?"

"I don't know, but he claims his uncle's the governor."

"The governor? Oh, sure! And my mother's the Queen of England," Veneable said, rolling his eyes.

"Well, sir," the officer said unflinchingly, "he didn't sound like he was making it up."

"Well, check it out!" Veneable snapped, already irritated with the situation.

Veneable could see it coming—*if this guy really was related to the governor, then they were in for a world of shit. When a bigwig politician gets involved, the investigation has to be letter perfect. No bungling; no screw-ups; and the bottom line was: Somebody's gonna' have to burn!*

"Why me, Lord?" Veneable mumbled, his eyes looking skyward. "I'm just a year away from retirement. Please tell me these dead people aren't related to the governor."

*

Tuesday, June 4th

God did not act favorably on Veneable's plea.

The next morning news media stormed Virginia Beach, swarming like famished mosquitos looking for raw flesh. Newspaper headlines read,

GOVERNOR'S FAMILY MURDERED BY DRUG DEALERS.
Dope Dealers Attack United States Coast Guard

It was major news of profound proportions as the

beached Cigarette boat, surrounded by body bags, greeted early morning television viewers.

Venable grew immediately concerned with all the hoopla. After all, retiring with his generous pension was everything. Although he was totally burned out, he decided it was imperative to give this particular matter his personal attention.

He drove over to Virginia Beach General, where he scouted out the young black man found on the beached boat. The suspect had been treated in the emergency room, then admitted to the hospital later that evening.

As Veneable skulked his way down the hallway near the suspect's hospital room, he learned from a candy striper the man was awake. He peeked at the chart, noting the patient suffered multiple contusions, broken ribs, and a punctured lung, but nothing sounded long-term or life threatening.

The wheels in Veneable's head were already turning, spinning a scheme to insure certain conviction. He pushed the preset caller button on his cell phone.

After a thirty second pause, a male voice came on. "Jamison here, chief, what's up?"

"Get off your butt and meet me in the lobby of Virginia Beach General Hospital. Right now! We've got a hot potato!"

CHAPTER
15

JAMES "JAMIE" JAMISON was much like a Labrador Retriever, obedient and constantly trying to appease his superiors. That's what Veneable liked about him.

Soon Jamison arrived, scurrying into the lobby of the hospital where Veneable was waiting. Jamison had a baby face and big ears. Attired in a double-breasted beige suit and black over brown saddle oxfords, he looked like a nerd from the 1980s.

After directing Jamison to a secluded corner of the lobby, Veneable began to speak in a loud whisper. "Jamie," he said, "we got this Cigarette boat carrying thirty kilos of cocaine, slamming onto our beach and killing a woman and her two little children. Guess who their uncle is?"

"I heard, sir."

"Right, our illustrious, brand new, law and order governor."

"It's terrible. I feel so sorry for him!" Jamie said.

"You're goin' to be feeling sorry for yourself if you don't shut up and listen!" Veneable snapped, already getting annoyed at Jamison's denseness.

"Huh?"

"We got to make sure we get the jerks who did this, and more importantly, we got to do it quick! This is going to get big-time press coverage. This will be the first test of the Fast Track Death Penalty Law."

"So, who do you want to convict for this?" Jamison asked, still oblivious to his new mission.

"Well, it just so happens there was a black guy on the boat. They found him hiding right smack in the middle of the cocaine," Veneable said, as he rubbed his palms together. "The only other person on the boat was a dead white guy, and we can't convict a dead guy."

"So what do you want me to do?" Jamison asked, a clueless expression on his face.

"Jamison, the black guy is here in the hospital all busted up. I want you to get his confession."

"No problem. I can schmooze with anybody."

"Now this is what I want you to do." Veneable's index finger shot skyward. "First, you buddy up to him and gain his confidence. You get him talking, tell him everything is going to be okay. Then, get his confession. Be sure you have a tape recorder going, and we'll cut and splice it later. That way," Veneable said, now smirking, "they can't claim we put words in his mouth." Veneable's eyes narrowed as though he sought to transmit a telepathic message to his gullible associate. "You know," he said as he began to over-enunciate every syllable, "We - wouldn't - want - him - to - be - coerced, - would we?"

"But, Lieutenant, I'll have to tell him, you know...he has a right to a lawyer and all that stuff...won't I?"

Veneable, shaking his head in disbelief, frustrated at Jamison's stupidity, began to speak slowly and patiently, as if explaining something to a child. "You - only - have - to - do - that - if - he - is - in - custody. We're not going to arrest him...not yet that is."

"We're not?" Jamison was scratching his head.

"No! Damn it! Right now, we have this golden opportunity. If he's not in custody, we don't have to give him his rights."

"Well, what if he gets up and walks out of the hospital?

Should I arrest him then?"

"That's the beautiful part, Jamie, my boy. He can't leave 'cause he's all busted up from the boat crash. You see, we don't have to worry about all that technical stuff 'cause he's not in custody, and we don't have to worry about him absconding 'cause he can't even walk."

Jamison, finally beginning to get it, was now listening intensely as his head began to nod approvingly.

"Now listen to me Jamie, I want you to get up there and get a confession any way you can do it, 'cause if we don't have a confession, then we might not be able to convict this turkey, and if we don't convict him, we can't fry him. And if we can't fry him, we all might get fried ourselves. Do you follow me?"

"Ten-four, boss!"

Detective Jamison walked steadfastly up to room 371 to visit the patient. The name listed on the door was Dani Alverez: black male; birth date: January 15, 1980; residence: Grand Cayman Island, British West Indies. He gave a token knock and opened the door. Entering the room, he saw a young black man lying in a hospital bed. The patient's face was bruised and swollen. An I.V. hookup was plugged into his arm.

"How ya feeling, little buddy? I understand you took a pretty nasty spill out there," Jamison said, displaying a candy-coated smile and speaking as though he were chumming up to his long, lost brother. Jamison closed the room door and pulled a chair up bedside.

"Now, let's have a little chat," he said, his eyes twinkling with superficial concern.

*

Wednesday, June 5th

The media was relentless. The horrific slaughter of two innocent children and their mother on the beach would be etched in the memory of the people of America for years to come. The morning talk shows devoted their entire program to the event. One of the more popular shows even televised live from the beach itself, overlooking the crash scene.

The editorial headline in the leading Virginia Beach newspaper asked:

IS THERE ANY PLACE SAFE ANYMORE?
First, it was sharks. We were scared out of the water onto the beach. Now, it's the dope dealers who have scared us off the beach...

*

On the religious network, Evangelist Rufus K. Jones pounded on the Bible as he orated to his worldwide flock.

"The audacity of this alien drug dealer," he preached, using his most effective fire and brimstone technique. "They shot at a United States helicopter in American waters right off the coast of Virginia."

"It's the work of the devil!" he proclaimed, words spewing out so rapidly a lesser person would likely have gotten tongue tied.

Reverend Jones raised his fist in the air, then slammed it down hard on the desk in front of him.

"We must rise up and smite Satan!" he screamed. "We must take the devil by the horns and let Lucifer know the Christians in our great Commonwealth will not stand for this!"

Reverend Jones had gotten himself so worked up he had to reach into his hip pocket for his handkerchief, on which he first blew his nose, then wiped his brow.

CHAPTER

16

Friday, June 7th

THE DAY before the funeral, Governor Brotherton accepted an invitation to appear on a national morning television talk show. Before the nation, he talked about his love for his departed family and vowed to avenge their deaths for the sake of justice in America. Charming and charismatic, he epitomized the image of a warm, caring grandfather. The millions who saw him that morning cried with him as they eagerly awaited this drama to unfold.

Across the nation, the television news programs conducted interviews with people from every walk of life, asking them how they felt about the tragedy and the Fast Track Death Penalty Law. From congressmen to ministers, from police officers to prosecutors, from white collars to blue collars, and from virtually any citizen on the street who would comment, the public was bombarded with questions. It was becoming a media circus.

The comments of an unidentified gentleman interviewed on Wall Street typified many of the responses from across the nation when he said that Governor Brotherton was the hero of his generation. "He's a man that doesn't mollycoddle criminals. He's a man who can make our streets safe again!" the man proclaimed.

Sitting in his office at the governor's mansion on Friday

night, Alex Brotherton sipped on his GlenFiddich while looking at his big screen television. His face glowed in delight when he saw the articulate gentleman on Wall Street praise him.

"Roger," the governor said, an ice-cold grin on his face, "I think it's time to get on with the show."

Saturday, June 8th

Three hearses and eight stretch limousines, all black Cadillacs, were parked in front of the opulent Cathedral of the Abiding God. Designed by the Reverend Rufus K. Jones, the cathedral was a mammoth structure composed of glass, chrome and marble. The blue neon cross mounted at the top of its 300 foot steeple could be seen for miles and was sometimes mistaken by seafarers as a beacon from a lighthouse.

At 2 P.M. the cathedral doors closed, and the capacity crowd rose. The family of Susan Johnston, the young mother who had been killed on the beach with her twin three year olds, entered the enormous sanctuary from the vestibule and walked slowly down the center aisle to the reserved front-row pews as the cathedral's own orchestra played "Rock of Ages".

Leading the processional was her husband, the father of the twins, Dr. Jim Johnston, whose grimaced face and clenched fist revealed his internal torment. He walked between his parents, Beatrice and Arthur, their faces solemn, their eyes red.

Behind them came Dr. Johnston's uncle, Governor Alexander S. Brotherton, his face somber. He walked erect with his shoulders back, and as always, he cast the ambiance of a strong leader dedicated to goodness and morality. Walking close beside her husband, hand on his arm, was the governor's delicate wife, Priscilla. After a recent bout with breast cancer, Priscilla rarely appeared in public. A former runner-up in the Miss Virginia pageant, Priscilla had once been a gorgeous woman, but now she looked frail, her complexion pale, yet she still wore a gentle smile.

Next came the deceased mother's parents, Randolph and Florence Bradford, both outwardly distraught over the loss of their only child and the only grandchildren they would ever have. Hand in hand, they walked slower than the others in the processional. Randolph, a tall man with a protruding stomach, stared at the floor, his eyes squinting, nearly closed. Florence, a short, slightly stout lady, could not contain her grief and sobbed uncontrollably. Randolph tried to console her, pulling her close to him as she turned her teary face against his lapel.

With thousands of floral wreaths as the backdrop, the three unopened caskets, each adorned with sprays of fresh roses and baby's breath, occupied the front of the sanctuary. Television cameras mounted on both sides of the U-shaped balcony zoomed down to telecast the spectacle.

The sanctuary was packed, not a vacant seat anywhere. The bereaved family sat on the front row, and over a thousand guests were squeezed into every available pew. Ten state governors were present as was every member of Virginia's General Assembly. Scores of Tidewater politicians, hundreds of Virginia Beach police officers, the chief and mayor were in attendance. This was unquestionably the place to be.

Behind the altar was the cathedral's one-hundred voice choir, its members attired in bright purple robes. Between the sanctuary and the altar, an orchestra pit held the Cathedral of the Abiding God's eighty-piece orchestra. A six-foot chrome railed bridge crossed over the orchestra pit to the raised pulpit area.

Center stage in a king-like chair sat the renowned Reverend Rufus K. Jones, founder of Grace of God Ministries and chief minister of the Cathedral of the Abiding God. Jones wore a flowing fire engine red robe adorned with hand-woven, gold crosses. His long, styled hair was jet black, which was quite amazing for a man in his mid-fifties who claimed never to have dyed his hair.

The service began as Reverend Jones stepped to the pulpit and orated a long, rambling prayer. When the Amen finally came, Jones introduced Governor Brotherton who rose from his seat and made his way across the chrome-railed bridge to the pulpit. Dramatically, he looked down, his face displaying a melancholy expression. His voice cracking, his eyes tearing, he said a grief-filled thank you to the mourners.

"Some say the good die young," he reverently declared, then added, "We all know Susan, Jimmy and Jenny are safe in the bosom of the Lord Jesus Christ. They shall never want for anything again."

As the zoom-in brought Brotherton's face closer to the viewers, the governor closed his eyes tightly, squeezing the last bit of moisture from his occipital pockets.

"Ladies and gentlemen," he said solemnly, forcing his voice to tremble with sincerity. "Please pray for my family as we strive to endure the future without our loved ones."

Suddenly, as if it were part of the script, Reverend Jones jumped to his feet and hastened to the rescue. Placing his arm around the governor, the Reverend gently guided him back across the chrome-railed bridge, down to his seat on the front pew.

To the sound of "Onward Christian Soldiers," the caskets were rolled down the center aisle into the vestibule. There, Virginia Beach's finest, eight officers per coffin, carried the caskets, marching slowly to the waiting hearses.

With Brotherton leading the way, the family, still grim faced, eyes all cast down, filed out of the cathedral behind the caskets. A Virginia Beach Police motorcade led the funeral procession to the nearby Peacehaven Acres Cemetery. Tens of thousands had gathered within earshot of the graveside service as the three caskets were made ready to be buried together in one grave. Reverend Jones read from the Bible, then said a prayer while distant bagpipes played the Scottish rendition of "Amazing Grace."

The funeral, the procession, and the graveside service had occupied four hours of live television. It was estimated Governor Brotherton had been seen and heard by over 140 million people.

17

Monday, June 10, 2002
10:30 A.M

"**NURSE, HAVE** you seen Mr. Jamison this morning?" Dani asked anxiously. "He should be here by now." Dressed in jeans and a polo shirt courtesy of Jamie Jamison, Dani, sitting on the edge of the bed, was ready to go home.

"No, I haven't but there's some, uh, police officers out here in the hallway who say they want to talk to you," the full-figured nurse replied, a concerned look on her face as she left the room.

Dani was confused. He was supposed to be discharged today. Jamie had assured him that by noon today he would be on a flight to Miami to connect with a Cayman Airlines flight. Why would there be police officers there to see him? Where was his friend, Jamie?

Suddenly, his door exploded open, and Lieutenant Veneable stormed into the room followed by a SWAT team of uniformed officers. Veneable, red faced and sweating, looked like a heart attack waiting to happen.

"Dani Alverez!" he boomed, "I am police Lieutenant Leon Veneable!" He was yelling so loudly his voice was echoing off the bare walls. "I have warrants for your arrest for murder! You have the right to remain silent..."

Dani could only stare blankly into the lieutenant's dart-shooting eyes. Dani's arms were jerked violently behind him and handcuffs pinched down hard against his wrist. He couldn't believe this was happening to him.

"Where's Detective Jamison?" Dani protested, but no one responded. Dani repeated his plea. "Where's Jamie?" His voice was louder and more desperate.

Two officers, one on each side, manhandled him to the elevator, took him down to the ground floor, then dragged him out the door to a waiting unmarked car. A short ride later, a Virginia Beach magistrate summarily denied bail and appointed counsel.

Panic seized him. Nervously, he peered through the bars of solitary confinement at the Virginia Beach Detention Center, as it finally dawned on him the untenable corner in which he had painted himself.

*

The phone call came at 4 P.M. Deputy clerk Lisa Davenport greeted him cordially, then quietly turned cold.

"Mr. Forrest," she said, "you allowed your name to be placed on the court-appointed list of attorneys to handle capital cases. Is that correct?"

"It sure is!"

"The court clerk at Virginia Beach called asking whether we have an attorney here in Hampton who would handle a capital case there. Would you be interested?"

"I sure would!" Grayson's response was much too exuberant.

"Very well, Mr. Forrest, the man's name is Dani Alverez, and he's in the Virginia Beach Detention Center. He is scheduled for arraignment tomorrow at 9 A.M. in the Circuit Court there."

"Well, uh, that's uh, great!" But then, Grayson's voice dropped, revealing a hint of hesitancy as he made a telling inquiry. "Uh, ma'am, what do I do now?"

"Mr. Forrest, you're the lawyer. You'll have to figure that out yourself," she replied sharply. "Now, goodbye."

The thirty-minute trip in his old Jeep Cherokee took him across the Hampton Roads Bridge-Tunnel, through Norfolk and on to Virginia Beach. Arriving at the detention center, he parked and marched staunchly toward the jail, legal pad in hand. At the counter, he told the deputy he wanted to see his client.

"You must be the lawyer for Alverez, the guy who killed those kids and their mother," the tall, heavy-set jailer replied accusingly, a crooked snarl forming on his pitted face.

"Well, I don't know about that, but I do represent him. Can I please see my client?" Grayson asked.

"Lawyer, I don't mean no disrespect, but can I ask you a question?" inquired the jailer who apparently had been salivating for an opportunity to confront Alverez's lawyer.

"Uh, sure."

"How the hell can you represent a foreign dope dealer who runs down two children and their mother? How do you sleep at night?" The officer's sneering eyes and condescending voice caused Grayson to shudder. He was not accustomed to such a direct attack.

Before making a reply, Grayson took a deep breath, gathered his composure, then calmly said, "Sir, in America everyone accused of a crime is entitled to a lawyer to see that his Constitutional rights are protected."

The jailer, a large man with a Neanderthal forehead had swelled up like an indignant toad. "Who the hell protected the rights of those innocent children?" he retorted, his words seething, his tone sarcastic. "If you ask me, this jerk should be taken out and shot!"

Knowing this was not the right battlefield on which to fight the war, and further response would have been a waste, Grayson waited patiently until the tirade faded.

Finally, shaking his head in disgust, the deputy pointed toward a hallway and directed Grayson to follow him. Unlocking a steel door, he motioned Grayson inside where a dark-skinned man sat at a wooden table. The prisoner, wearing an orange jumpsuit, sat with his head lying on his folded arms. He appeared to be asleep, but when the steel door clanged shut, his head lifted.

"Mr. Alverez, I'm Grayson Forrest. I'm your lawyer." Grayson took a seat in the opposite chair.

Dani's eyes widened, a broad smile flashing on his face. With a pause, he looked up at his caller, his starry eyes traveling up the yellow brick wall to the ceiling. Then, he made a startling declaration: "Oh, Lord," he suddenly exclaimed, "You have sent me your angel!"

Grayson was stunned. As a criminal defense lawyer, he had never before been labeled an angel—a devil, maybe, but not an angel. Now, having been sanctified, he was not quite sure how to begin.

18

AS GRAYSON gathered his wits, trying to figure out how to begin the interview, he reflected on the legal responsibility before him. He was all too aware that clients frequently lie to their lawyers. This man before him might be getting ready to dish out an outlandish crock. But it didn't really matter at this point. After all, he was this young man's only lifeline to the American justice system. Like it or not, he had to program himself to listen patiently and objectively to his client's story. At least for now, he would not suggest his client might be lying. He would only gather the facts in an effort to create a theory of defense.

Grayson's new client's full name was Daniel Quiermo Martinez Gomez Alverez, but he went by Dani Alverez. Born in Jamaica, 22 year old Alverez moved to the Grand Caymans with his parents when he was very young. He dropped out of school in the fourth grade and worked mostly on fishing boats but also on two commercial ships.

Having established some measure of rapport, Grayson decided it was time to get down to the nitty gritty. "Dani, you're charged with murder by intentionally driving a high powered boat into three innocent people." Grayson's voice was deep, his tone serious. "So, I just want you to start from the beginning and tell me the truth."

The young Caymanian scooted to the edge of his chair, cleared his throat and began by explaining he had worked on a freighter, the *Jamaican Maiden,* which shipped out of Jamaica supposedly delivering bananas to ports in America.

"But truthfully, sir," Dani said, a confused expression on his face, "I never saw any bananas, and the ship never went into any ports."

According to Dani, the ship would stop offshore at coastal cities like Savannah, Charleston, Myrtle Beach, and Morehead City. A speedboat would come out with teenaged girls who would be taken aboard, bound and gagged. It happened each time the ship stopped.

"Off Morehead City," Dani explained, "a power boat brought more teenaged girls out. But this time a great big hairy, woolly bully man all dressed up in old timey clothes was in charge." Dani contorted his face and drew an imaginary beard under his chin, as if to illustrate the face of the woolly bully man.

Grayson continued to listen intently, but he couldn't help but think— *this kid has been watching way too much television.*

The story got even more bizarre. When they were somewhere off the coast of Virginia, the Cigarette boat, driven by the woolly bully man, appeared from out of nowhere, its cargo: teenaged girls. A while later, Dani said he'd sneaked down to the stateroom where the girls were being held, and actually tried to talk to one of them, but she was too groggy to make much sense.

"Go ahead, continue," Grayson urged.

"I heard someone coming. I tried to run but they caught me and began hitting me. They kicked me, they slapped me, over and over. I just couldn't take it anymore!" Dani's voice cracked and his hands trembled. "I broke free and ran toward the bow, but, uh, but..."

"So what happened next?" Grayson prodded.

"I jumped off the ship and swam over to the red boat."

Dani's story, outlandish maybe, continued. "Then, I

snuck aboard, slipped in the forward hatchway and hid out under the front V berth."

As Grayson listened, a fleeting caricature passed through his wandering mind. He saw himself on stilts, striding through a field of fathom-deep manure, which was getting deeper as Dani talked.

"The boat started up and got going really fast. I heard a helicopter, then gunfire. The next thing I knew, the boat slammed onto the beach." After breathing a long insightful sigh, Dani added the obvious. "It must have been when the people were killed."

A mournful expression formed on Dani's face and his eyes dropped. "That's all I know, honest to God," he mumbled softly.

IV

THE PROCESS

CHAPTER
19

Tuesday, June 11, 2002

AS HE drove back to Hampton, the sting of reality slapped him in the face. His mind was preoccupied with the awesome duties that lay ahead. There was so much to do, but so little time to do it. He had to investigate, obtain expert witnesses, bone up for jury selection, cross-examinations, final argument, jury instructions, sentencing — the list went on and on.

Although it was late when he arrived back home, Grayson decided to try to reach Dani's mother in the Cayman Islands. He dialed the number, and after a short delay, a female voice answered. Introducing himself to Mrs. Alverez, he explained he was an attorney in Virginia appointed to represent her son. Finally, taking a deep breath, he broke the bad news.

"Mrs. Alverez," he said. "Your son is in some very serious trouble. He's been charged with murder, uh, three counts."

The background static roared as Grayson waited uneasily for a response, which soon came in the form of a cry of desperation. "No! No! That's impossible!" she screamed. "My Dani is a good boy. There's been a terrible mistake."

"Ma'am," Grayson said, searching for a way to make this woman deal with reality, "Dani's trial will be held in about four weeks. It would be good if you could be present."

There was no reply, just more long-distance static. Rosa Alverez's heart dropped like a rock. She was totally bewildered and absolutely unable to contain herself. This could not be happening. It was inconceivable that her only son could be capable of hurting anyone.

As Grayson hung on, he heard commotion, voices, crying, then a clump, as though the phone had fallen to the floor. After a short pause, a different voice spoke. "Hello, this is Martina Alverez, Dani's sister. What's going on here?"

Grayson again explained the situation to the sister, who like her mother, went into immediate denial.

"Sir," she said emphatically, "there has obviously been some kind of mistake! Where's Dani?"

"The Virginia Beach Jail, ma'am."

"Oh my goodness! Dani's in jail?" she cried hysterically. "That can't be!"

Grayson decided he would have to be firm, otherwise, these people just wouldn't listen.

"Ma'am," he said, his tone cold and objective, "Your brother may well be innocent, but he's charged with murder. Only a jury can decide his future. I'm sorry, but that's just the way it is."

"That's absurd!" Martina Alverez snapped.

Grayson could hear voices in the background. Apparently the sister and mother were talking, then Martina spoke once again. "Mr. Forrest, is that correct?"

"Yes, Grayson Forrest."

"I'll be in Virginia tomorrow. Could you meet me at the Norfolk airport?"

"Sure."

"I'll call and tell you my arrival time as soon as I make reservations."

It was after midnight when Grayson finally climbed into bed determined to get some sleep, but his eyes refused to close. He tried to force himself to lie still, but a vision of Dani strapped into the electric chair kept haunting him.

He tossed and turned, trying to clear his head of the night-marish thought, but all he could see were huge flashing letters that spelled out—*Death penalty for innocent man— Grayson Forrest incompetent—You can't screw up any worse than that!"*

With sleep hopelessly eluding him, Grayson climbed out of bed and headed downstairs to the kitchen. He poured a glass of Gatorade and took a seat at the breakfast table, where his mind continued to roam. He just couldn't rid himself of the same haunting image, except now, it was more vivid than ever. He saw young Dani Alverez, cuffed and shack-led, being led into the execution chamber as a host of gawk-ing spectators watched. He could see the governor, itching to tell the world he had accomplished his objective in his war on crime.

Grayson tried to force himself back into the real world, but instead, it got worse. Dani's face wrinkled, his mouth and nose contorted in agony. The smell of burning hair dominated the air as electricity sizzled into his dying body. His head was smoking, his eyes were bulging and his skin was blistering.

He was crying out, "Mr. Forrest, Mr. Forrest, this is America! How can you let them do this to me? I'm innocent!"

CHAPTER

20

AT 5:00 A.M. the insufferable wail of the clock radio sent Grayson springing out of bed like a Pop Tart. Instantly, he was wide-awake, wired and ready to tackle the case of his career.

In a surge of adrenaline, he showered, dressed and sat down to plan his day. At 6:30, Martina called, saying she would arrive at Norfolk International Airport that evening at eight. After arranging to meet her there, he drove to Virginia Beach for the 9:30 arraignment.

It was short and not so sweet. Amidst a gallery of reporters, Dani, handcuffed and shackled, was brought into the courtroom. An assistant commonwealth attorney sat at one table, Grayson and Dani sat at the other. With the enthusiasm of a geriatric jellyfish, the prosecutor read the indictment accusing Dani Alverez of three counts of murder and one count of drug trafficking. Grayson entered a plea of not guilty, and the judge set the trial date for July 5th; no bail allowed.

That was it. Fifteen minutes later, as Dani was being taken back to lockup, Grayson walked over to the prosecutor's table, his hand extended. "Hi, I'm Grayson Forrest," he said cordially.

Ignoring the offer of a handshake, the assistant, his eyes

uncaring and callous, looked up at Grayson. "Yeah, so?" was his cold reply.

"I just want to know if you will be prosecuting the case?" Grayson inquired, his demeanor still controlled and pleasant.

"You need to talk to the head commonwealth attorney, Arnold Bledsoe. I've been instructed not to discuss the case with you!"

Down the hall, Grayson recognized the great seal of Virginia on the door of the Commonwealth Attorney's office. Upon entering, he was greeted by a slender young receptionist, who informed him the Commonwealth Attorney had been expecting him.

"That's his office," she said, pointing to an open doorway. "Go right on in."

Grayson walked into a palatial office dominated by heavy mahogany furnishings. Numerous awards, certificates and framed photographs adorned the walls. One photograph in particular caught his eye. In glossy color framed in gold leaf, the photo depicted the illustrious Governor Alexander Brotherton and this tall lanky man in his early fifties, the same man who was at this very moment rising from behind his desk and holding out his hand.

"Mr. Forrest, I'm Arnold Bledsoe," the man said. "I understand they had to go all the way to Hampton to find a lawyer qualified to handle this case."

Grayson forced a courteous smile. "Not really, sir, nice to meet you."

Bledsoe offered no further pleasantries, nor did he invite Grayson to sit down. Rather, hands on his hips, he waited defensively, silently itching for an opportunity to make a verbal jab at his new found foe.

"Mr. Bledsoe, I just wanted to meet you and obtain any discovery and exculpatory evidence as soon as possible."

"Hold on, young man. You're going much too fast." The semblance of a smile crooked onto Bledsoe's long, narrow face as the volume of his voice began to rise.

"Mr. Forrest, trust me! We'll give you everything you're entitled to. But I'll tell you right now, there's not going to be any exculpatory evidence!"

The initial hospitality was history, now replaced with an air of hostility so thick you could cut it with a butter knife.

"And I'll tell you one more thing," Bledsoe said, his face squenching into a sinister sneer. "I'm - gonna - put - that - murdering - bastard - in - the - electric - chair! Do you understand?"

Bledsoe was thoroughly enjoying the put down.

"In fact," he growled angrily, "five months from this day, your client will be toast!"

Grayson cleared his throat, then looked upward, directly into Bledsoe's eyes.

"Sir," Grayson replied, his voice trembling with conviction, does it matter to you that Dani Alverez might be innocent?"

"Innocent, my ass!" Bledsoe retorted as he gasped deeply, displaying his exasperation at the naivety of the question. "Did you just fall off the watermelon truck, boy?"

What an arrogant prick!

Aristocratically, Bledsoe began waving his finger at Grayson's nose. "And one more thing!" he added, his voice steaming with insolence. "This case is set for trial in exactly twenty-nine days. Be ready! I don't want to hear any sniveling motions to continue. You hear me, boy?"

Instantly startled, Grayson paused but quickly collected himself. Unfettered by the self-righteous pomposity, Grayson stared point-blank into the prick prosecutor's cold eyes and began to advance aggressively toward him. "You need to re-read your oath of office. You're trying to execute an innocent man!"

Momentarily speechless, surprised this upstart would speak to him in such an impertinent tone, Bledsoe stepped back, shaking his head.

"Boy!" he finally screamed. "If you want to practice

law in my court, you'd better learn to play the game. You understand me?"

Grayson's exit was less than cordial. "Go to hell!" he yelled, as he violently slammed the door so hard the coveted photograph of Governor Brotherton was jarred catawampus on the wall.

CHAPTER
21

U.S. AIRWAYS flight 379 was on time, landing precisely at 8 P.M. Dressed in a blue blazer and khaki pants, Grayson watched through the concourse window as the airliner taxied to the deplaning area.

With passengers exiting and walking past him, Grayson waited patiently, looking for a woman who matched the description of Martina as given by Dani. Then, he saw her. Walking briskly toward him, a rolling suitcase in tow, five feet six maybe, her hair black and flowing, her skin dark and flawless. Under her chic beige suit, accented by an orange scarf, there appeared to be a slender, but enticing silhouette.

It had to be Martina Alverez.

Grayson observed her intensely. Clearly, she was special. Maybe it was the glow on her face, or perhaps the brash look in her eyes, or maybe even the spring in her stride.

Grayson fought an urge to become blindly smitten, keenly aware of the ethics opinion prohibiting a romantic relationship with a client. And worse, trying to explain to his cavalier mother he might be interested in an African-American would be imponderable. He was determined his relationship with this beautiful woman would remain strictly professional.

He walked toward her, head held high, trying to put forth his most dignified look.

"Are you Martina?" he asked, the tone of his voice friendly, but formal and business-like.

The woman stopped and looked up at him. "Yes, and you must be Attorney Forrest," she said, a polite smile on her face as she held out her hand.

Their eyes met, Grayson's fanciful and blue; Martina's, beautiful and brown. Grayson gave her soft, smooth hand a gentle shake.

"Nice to meet you," he said, still formal and business-like. "Sorry it's under such difficult circumstances."

With a gravely serious expression on her alluring face, her eyes coolly detached, Martina wanted to get down to business.

"Now, Mr. Forrest, please tell me what's going on!" There was a no-nonsense tone to her voice.

As they walked toward the baggage area, Grayson explained the situation. When he told her Dani would be facing the death penalty, Martina lost it.

"Oh God, no!" she exclaimed as she wiped away tears that had begun to trickle down her cheeks.

A sense of bitterness overtook her. Angrily, she began to lash out.

"I thought this was the great United States of America! What's happened to the human rights this great country tries to impose on the rest of the world? I thought you had a Constitution here."

Martina was spewing fire and on the attack.

"Excuse me, ma'am, but, uh, I'm on your side, remember?"

Pausing, she looked up at him and apologized.

"I'm sorry. It's just that I can't believe this is happening. Forgive me for sounding angry at you, but I'm just very upset."

Grayson gazed into her hypnotic eyes.

"Oh, that's okay. By the way, would you call me Gray, please?"

Soon they were headed for the Virginia Beach Detention Center in Grayson's Cherokee. Not only did they talk about Dani's dire plight, but Grayson learned a bit about Martina who he found to be as bright and personable as she was beautiful. Nevertheless, true to his vow, he reaffirmed not to let hormones interfere with his responsibility to his client. However, a fleeting ping of curiosity entered his mind. *Why do I keep thinking about this?* he queried.

At the detention center, they were directed to the visiting area - thick jail windows and telephone receivers. Momentarily, Dani's face appeared in one of the windows.

It was a tearful reunion. Martina held her hand against the glass separating them, while Dani's hand lay flat opposite hers. She expressed her love for her little brother. He reciprocated, then expressed his concern for their mother. Dani vowed his innocence, and Martina pledged her support. But, finally, after more words of concern, their time for commiseration came to an end. Now, according to Martina, it was time to get to work and prove her brother innocent!

CHAPTER

22

AS THEY headed for Richmond, they were a dismal duo. For Commonwealth Attorney Arnold Bledsoe and Detective Lieutenant Leon Veneable, the visit to Virginia's capital city was at the personal invitation of Governor Alexander S. Brotherton.

Veneable, the driver of the unmarked green Chevrolet, quietly listened to Bledsoe's know-it-all bullshit about his glorified achievements as the Commonwealth Attorney and his grave concerns about this case.

Finally, Veneable decided to speak up.

"Don't worry, sir. I think we've got locks on this case. I can't imagine a jury letting that little murderer go."

Bledsoe's eyebrows jutted upward as he twisted toward Veneable.

"Don't take anything for granted," he cautioned. "I want no stone left unturned. Pull out all stops! Do you hear me, Leon?"

Leon Veneable, just over eleven months from retirement, knew how to play the game, and if need be, would have agreed the moon was made out of blue cheese!

"Yes, sir, I totally agree," he declared.

Arriving in Richmond, the Chevrolet Impala pulled up

to the gate of the governor's mansion. After flashing IDs to the guard, the twosome were waved through and directed to a small parking area. They entered the mansion and were ushered into the parlor.

A well-dressed woman appeared. "Gentlemen, the governor will see you now," she announced.

The two men, both clad in dark suits, marched single file down the hallway and into a large oval office. Until recently, the office had been rectangular, but the governor, controlled by his visions of grandeur, decided to have it reshaped.

Brotherton was waiting. He stepped from behind his antique satinwood desk and held out his hand.

"Arnold," he said warmly, "it is indeed a pleasure to see you again. How are you?"

After introducing Veneable, along with standard cordialities, smiles and handshakes, Brotherton announced it was nice to have them aboard. Then, like going from Dr. Jekyll to Mr. Hyde, his expression abruptly transformed from a smile to a frown, his voice deepening, becoming ominously serious.

"Now, gentlemen, please take a seat so we can get down to business. I have something of the utmost importance to discuss with you."

The governor sat down in his overstuffed leather chair located behind the ornate desk and leaned forward.

"Gentlemen," he said, a flair of drama in his voice, "you are embarking on a crucial test of the new crime bill. If you prevail in the prosecution of this Alverez man - if Alverez is executed - we will all be victorious!"

His eyes opened wide, his brow furrowed and his vocal cords tightened.

"Gentlemen," the governor gleefully declared. "If we are successful, we will go down in history as patriots!"

But then, a lull of silence filled the air, the governor's eyes focusing sharply on his guests with a gaze that cut to the quick.

"But let me tell you the downside of this." A foreboding tone began to dominate the governor's voice.

"If this murderer beats this case, the consequences would be politically devastating. If he slips through the cracks, I will look like a failure. It would be the end of my political career."

Brotherton's eye slits narrowed and his voice deepened.

"Should that occur, then quite frankly, it would also be the end of your political futures as well."

Suddenly, the governor sprang to his feet as his manic side regained control.

"Gentlemen!" he screamed, "Working together we can win! Working together we can save America!"

Then, in a blink, he shifted from warrior to pacifist. Relaxing, he leaned back in his chair.

"Would anyone like a cup of coffee?" he asked, a wide smile re-appearing on his face.

When his guests nodded, he pushed a buzzer. Shortly, a young woman entered and took coffee orders. A minute later, she returned with four cups of coffee and an inverted pear-shaped silver pot on a matching silver tray.

After taking a sip of coffee, the governor's tone changed again. He began firing questions about trial strategy. First, he asked about Alverez's lawyer.

"Who is he? Is he any good?"

Bledsoe was ready for this one.

"Sir, his name is Grayson Quentin Forrest. He's thirty years old, right out of Navy JAG. He's a Hampton boy, went to William and Mary Law School. Must be fairly smart because he was on law review, an editor, I think."

"Why didn't you get a Virginia Beach lawyer appointed for the case?" Brotherton asked.

"Well, sir, this was such a controversial case, we suggested to the judge it might be unfair to appoint a local lawyer since the adverse publicity could be devastating to a law practice." Bledsoe grinned and gave a sly wink.

The truth was, however, Bledsoe had cajoled the local judge into appointing Attorney Forrest in order to give the prosecution a distinct advantage from the get-go. The fewer the resources, the more ineffective the lawyer. Also, the farther away the lawyer was from Virginia Beach, the more inconvenient it would be for him.

According to Bledsoe's calculations, Grayson Forrest would be wasting at least two hours a day in travel time alone.

Grayson Forrest was a perfect choice. On paper, he had four years experience defending and prosecuting in the Navy. Also, in JAG, he had prior experience trying a first-degree murder case. Therefore, he met the basic qualifications, yet he had zero experience in Virginia's civilian court system.

Next, the governor inquired as to who the judge would be.

Bledsoe smiled, proud of his conniving ways. "Our local resident judge, the Honorable Buford H. Bullins," he replied.

The governor returned the smile.

"The old Bull!" Brotherton exclaimed. "He's known far and wide as the toughest judge in the Commonwealth. That sounds great!"

Brotherton asked about the confession which prompted Veneable to chime in.

"Governor," he said, "I've been a police officer for twenty-seven years and have personally reviewed the confession. It's as solid as I've ever seen. No young whipper-snapper lawyer is going to break this confession. I can personally guarantee you that!"

Brotherton nodded courteously, then rolled his chair back from his desk and stood up.

"Well, gentlemen, I like what I'm hearing. Please know you have the total support of this office."

After the pair confirmed their dedication to the governor's hallowed cause, there were firm handshakes and eye-to-eye commitments. Brotherton, now satisfied his team would do its job, resurrected his former congenial personality and congratulated his henchman, wishing them well.

Shortly, the unmarked Chevy headed back to Virginia Beach, its occupants now totally committed to their renewed calling to make sure Dani Alverez fried.

23

GRAYSON STOOD up from the makeshift counsel seat on the closed-lid commode. An expression of confidence on his face and purple flip flops on his feet, he swaggered over to the lavatory where a yellow legal pad lay open.

Making eye contact with his mirror image, he began his practice session. "May it please the Court, my first motion is for the Fast Track Death Penalty Law to be declared unconstitutional."

Reversing roles, he began to mimic the judge.

"You may proceed, Mr. Forrest," Grayson growled in his best judge-like voice.

Switching back, he began his presentation. "The defense contends the new death penalty law is unconstitutional because it denies due process of law and is blatantly unfair."

He concentrated on trying to look squarely into the eye of his judicial reflection as he consciously slowed his tempo and carefully articulated his words.

He pounded his fist on the make-believe podium. "Your honor, this law allows the prosecutor to select who will live or die. What's worse, it denies equal protection under the 14th Amendment!"

Grayson's soiled white tank top and purple and gold

boxer shorts detracted significantly from the already questionable decorum of the imagined moment. Nevertheless, he thought he sounded pretty good, particularly the way his voice resonated so aptly off the ceramic tile walls of the bathroom.

*

Ready or not, morning came quickly. Grayson in his charcoal suit, so new the coat pockets were still stitched together, and Martina, an eyecatcher in her gray business outfit with crimson trim, walked briskly toward the courthouse, each lugging a heavy briefcase.

They made their way past a news van, its antenna raised high. As the couple neared the courthouse, a mob of reporters began to swarm around them, hungry for a story, but Martina and Grayson ignored them and rushed up the steps to the courthouse.

Grayson, expressionless as he entered the courtroom, placed the briefcases on the defense table and turned around to give Martina a reassuring smile. She reciprocated with an intriguing wink.

In short order, the rear door swung open and two seemingly paranoid bailiffs marched into the courtroom, both scrutinizing everybody and everything. Moments later, Dani Alverez entered, another bailiff trailing close behind him. Dani walked slowly toward the counsel table where he took his seat beside Grayson.

Grayson, his stomach churning, forced himself to display an air of calmness, a rather difficult task when it seemed as if all the alligators in the swamp were about to be unleashed against him.

Actually, Grayson was not a total neophyte when it came to trying controversial cases. Back in JAG, he had been involved in a number of serious trials, but it was different then. In JAG, there had always been plenty of backup, law clerks, investigators, social workers, secretaries and practically anyone and anything he needed. But now, here, he felt virtually alone in a life-or-death struggle.

Court opened with Judge Bullins making his grand entrance. He took his exalted chair and looked down from his pedestal, peering over his reading glasses.

"Okay," he snapped unemotionally, "Commonwealth, call your case!"

Bullins, sixtyish, baldheaded and bespectacled, did not strike Grayson as being particularly intimidating. Certainly not as bad as his reputation.

"We call the case of Commonwealth of Virginia versus Dani Alverez," the prosecutor announced.

"Counsel," the judge said, as he stared coolly at Grayson, "I understand you have some motions?"

"Yes, sir!" Grayson replied assertively, quickly rising.

"Let me tell you this before you waste your time and mine," Judge Bullins barked. "I've read your motion where you claim the Fast Track Death Penalty Law is unconstitutional. Well, your motion is poppycock! This new fast track law was prepared by legal scholars with great deliberation and the deepest consideration for the Constitution. It has built-in safeguards specifically designed to protect and preserve due process. Mr. Forrest, your motion has no merit whatsoever. Therefore, it is denied!"

On the outside, Grayson maintained his composure, but internally he was stewing. It was clear this *pompous, black-robed jackass was putting on a show for the press.*

"Any other motions, Mr. Forrest?" Judge Bullins chided.

"Yes, your honor," Grayson answered, feigning respect and hoping the tremble in his voice would not reveal the fury welling inside of him.

"Your honor," Grayson protested, "To be pushed to trial in just one month is absolutely outrageous! I move to continue this case!"

"That will be denied," Judge Bullins snapped. "Now, is that all, Mr. Forrest?"

"No, sir, it is not!" Bloodied but not beaten, Grayson

reloaded and fired again, this time with his motion for individual *voir dire.*

"Denied!"

"There's a motion to dismiss on grounds of selective prosecution."

"Denied! Anything else?"

One by one, Grayson announced his motions, each of which were summarily denied.

Damn, Grayson mumbled under his breath, *This is going to be a long trial.*

*

The final week passed quickly. Martina, aided by an investigator, scoured the beach area for witnesses while Grayson prepared his trial presentation. But, before they knew it, the trial was upon them, the time for reckoning was here.

CHAPTER
24

THE SENSATION of heartbeat triggered a faint aware-
ness of mortality. She resisted the invasion of consciousness
as she struggled to maintain herself in this sanctuary of drug-
induced hibernation. Nevertheless, unwelcomed reality
seeped through the ramparts of her mind, worming its ugly
self in to confront her cognitive processes as she lay on her
back on a lumpy mattress.

Panic shot through her mind, which provoked the hysterical imponderables of why, where, and what. She tried
to shout a plea for help, but no sound was forthcoming, not
even a feeble whisper. Stubbornly seeking to shake off this
muddled stupor, she forced herself to silently mouth words,
then sentences.

"Where - am - I? What - is - happening - to - me?" Her
lips moved, but her apathied vocal cords continued to
fail her.

Now, except for an occasional rustling sound, there was
silence. Pangs of fear shot through her mind, rational
thoughts scattered about like dust in the wind.

With her breathing short and shallow, she desperately
tried to move, but was too weak. Forced, without option, to
remain and endure the horror of the unknown, she prayed

this ordeal would soon be over, one way or another.

She moved her fingers across the thin gown that covered her body. As her hands moved medially, her finger tips touched, then both hands slid upward over her flat stomach, passing across the small mounds of her chest. Moving up her neck and over her chin, a finger slid across her parted lips and touched her teeth, then it moved to her nose.

Am I dead? she wondered. *Is this hell?*

Minutes turned to hours as her desire for refuge from this unrighteous place overrode her trepidation. Moving her mouth, moans were gradually molded into whispers.

"Someone, anyone, please help me!" she begged. At first, her cries were soft and low, but quickly, they grew louder and more shrill. Soon, her trembling voice began to shriek out in a bloodcurdling plea, a plea that would have been bone chilling to all but the coldest of heart, that is, had there been anyone to hear it.

A span of time passed, how long, she did not know. Her thoughts became clearer and more vivid than at any time since she had found herself in this hellish dungeon. But, still she could not remember her name, nor from where she had come.

As she peered up through the darkness, a faraway glow shone dimly down upon her. The faint glint from a distant light allowed her to distinguish the old brick walls that surrounded her. Pushing herself into a sitting position on the cot, she felt aches and pains all through her midsection, and when she swallowed, there was a raw soreness in her throat. She could not fathom what had happened to her.

Hoping to spur her memory by increasing the oxygen to her brain, she inhaled deeply, filling her lungs to capacity, then she slowly exhaled. The air had a musty smell with a slight hint of fishiness.

When she wiggled her big toe, her leg twitched, then her foot moved, then both feet. She bent her knees upward, causing the blanket to slide away, exposing her naked thighs to the cool dampness of the brick-encased pit.

Could she climb off the cot and explore these dark surroundings? Not yet, she decided. The pit was too dark; she was barefooted; she was not ready to leave the relative sanctuary of her cot; thoughts of rats or, heaven forbid, snakes held her there.

Vague memories seeped into her mind as she remembered a tall, hulking man with a long, black beard. He had been dressed strangely, like a pirate. She had some memory of being tied up, maybe drugged. And she vaguely recalled being in a locked cabin aboard a ship with some other girls her age.

Having no concept of how long she had been in this dark place, or what was happening to her, frustration generated by utter futility brought tears to her eyes until the image of a familiar face brought her consolation. It was a reassuring face, obscure at first, but ever so gradually, the image began to focus. It was strong and masculine. She recognized the comforting smile. "Oh, Daddy!" she cried softly. "Where are you? I need you so badly! Please find me!"

*

As though doused with ice water, Gunny sprang instantly wide awake from a sound sleep. He had just dreamed Mandy had called for him. Sitting on the side of his bed, he played back the vision that had burst into his restless mind. *Oh, Daddy! Where are you? I need you so badly! Please find me!* It had sounded so real, almost as though she were right there beside him.

The pathway through his cobwebbed brain let him visualize Mandy's image, but when he reached out to touch her, it was like trying to grasp a cloud. Abruptly, the cloud dissipated, his obsession replaced with harsh reality.

He was desperate, more desperate than he had ever been in his life. Through his Marine career, he had been in many dire straits: fire fights, parachute drops, rock climbs, and shark dives. But now, despite the many obstacles he had overcome in his life, he was at his wits end.

Then, for reasons unknown, he sat down, cupped his chin in his palm, and closed his eyes. His mouth opened as unfamiliar words came out:

"Dear Lord, please help me find Mandy. She hasn't had much of a chance in life, and I've made so many mistakes with her. Oh Lord, give me another chance, and let me find her. Thank you for hearing me out. Amen."

When Gunny was a child, growing up in Smithfield, Virginia, his mother had been very spiritual, insisting he attend church each and every Sunday. He had never known his father, and his wonderful, God-fearing mother died when he was just seventeen. Three months later, he enlisted in the Marines, where he moved into a lifestyle that didn't include much church-going. To Gunny, church had seemed hypocritical, particularly since he spent most of his time learning how to kill.

After praying about Mandy, he felt better. He sensed he was not alone. That out of the way, he headed for the kitchen to prepare his favorite breakfast: a bloody Mary and toast.

25

Monday, July 7th
THE TRIAL BEGINS

EXCEPT FOR the first two rows of reserved seating, the Virginia Beach Circuit Court was packed with an anxious press corps and two hundred prospective jurors.

Judge Bullins, for the first time in twenty-five years on the bench, was allowing television cameras in the courtroom. Several news commentators, relying on anonymous sources, suggested the governor's office had encouraged Judge Bullins to reverse his longstanding ban of courtroom video.

The bailiff opened court: "All rise...Oh yez, oh yez, the Circuit Court of the Commonwealth of Virginia in and for the City of Virginia Beach is now in session..."

The oration was appropriately ceremonial to announce the entry of high royalty. Instead, however, the not-so-regal Judge Buford Bullins, his bald head shining, entered the courtroom and took his throne on high.

The clerk called twelve prospective jurors to the jury box, and the judge rotely instructed them on their duties, then turned the questioning over to the Commonwealth.

Bledsoe stood up and gave his introductory speech, then scanned the jury, looking each juror directly in the eye. He explained this was a capital murder case and after the defendant is found guilty, the Commonwealth will be seeking the death penalty.

Next came his most important question, a question designed to weed out the squeamish. He didn't want any finicky jurors on the panel when nut-cutting time came. "Could you vote for the death penalty if the law required it?" he asked demandingly.

Most of the jurors nodded yes, but Bledsoe noticed juror number twelve, a black housekeeper and mother of six was stoic and non-responsive. Moving in for the kill, Bledsoe asked point blank.

"Could you, Ms. Goins, vote for the death penalty?"

She shook her head. "No sir," she replied calmly.

Bledsoe paused, his face projecting a conceited smirk.

"Now, ma'am," he said, his words short, his manner condescending. "Are you saying if the law mandated the death sentence, you would not follow the law?"

Mrs. Goins was unfettered. She stared directly into Bledsoe's eyes and spoke emphatically. "The Bible says, 'Thou shalt not kill' and I will not violate God's word!"

God's word or not — Mrs. Goins was gone, challenged for cause by the Commonwealth.

The Commonwealth's jury selection continued until mid-afternoon recess when Bledsoe finally announced the prosecution was satisfied with the jury.

Grayson already knew the types of jurors he needed: younger people rather than older; single people rather than married; educated people rather than uneducated; people who really believed a person was innocent until proven guilty.

He questioned each prospective juror, trying to determine the juror's ability to be fair and impartial. He explained the presumption of innocence and reasonable doubt; he cautioned that the death penalty could be rendered only if there were aggravating circumstances.

Finally, by 11 A.M. the next day, eleven jurors had been selected. At this point, Grayson used his last challenge, excusing juror number seven, an angry-faced man who carried himself like a storm trooper. From here on out, the defense would be stuck with the very next juror called.

Braxton Hornsby was the name called out by the clerk. A white man, perhaps late thirties, red hair, six feet tall, medium build, took seat number seven. He was a low-level engineer; he had served as an MP in the Army; he was all law and order and a devout Christian, he volunteered. Could he impose the death penalty?

"I sure could!" he responded, too enthusiastically.

Could he be fair and impartial?

"Oh, sure, no problem."

Now, with the second day of trial behind him, Grayson and Martina returned to his office in Hampton.

As they turned onto Queen's Way, Grayson expressed his concern about time for preparation.

"Gosh, I thought we'd never get here," Grayson said. "I've got to work on my opening statement. I hope I can stay awake long enough to put the finishing touches on it."

"You work; I'll get dinner-to-go," Martina volunteered.

Grayson had worked for an hour when Martina returned with Chinese food. As they sat at the conference room table eating, Grayson took a long, in-depth look at Martina. She really was beautiful with her dark, chocolate-brown skin, big brown eyes and high cheekbones. She could easily have been a fashion model.

"This sweet and sour shrimp is really good," he said as he munched away.

"Do you think so?" she responded.

"Yeah," Grayson mumbled, still chomping on the shrimp.

"Actually, it's not as good as mine."

Grayson's mind floated into forbidden territory. *And she can cook, too.*

26

WITH THE jury seated, the trial began with opening statements.

Bledsoe rose, buttoned his coat and straightened his tie. With a buddy-buddy smile toward the judge and a token sneer at Grayson, he swaggered to the podium which was centered in front of the jury box. He said a patronizing thank you, then told them irrefutable evidence would show the defendant was an alien drug trafficker who brought drugs and disaster to the shore of Virginia Beach, which resulted in murderous death of the Johnston children and their mother.

Next came Grayson's turn. He looked the jury in the eye. "May it please the Court, Ladies and Gentlemen," he began, the boldness of his words disguising the internal fear that threatened to overcome him.

"I represent an innocent man!" he loudly proclaimed. "A man who was in the wrong place at the wrong time."

As he proceeded with his presentation, trying to explain that Dani Alverez was a hardworking, Christian seaman from the Grand Caymans, he noticed the jury was distracted, their attention focused somewhere beyond the prosecution table. He glanced right and spotted the problem. It was the governor, right there in open court, reaching over the railing and handing Bledsoe a note.

Grayson's mouth was suddenly dry, and he felt a lump in his throat. Nevertheless, he struggled to carry on. He told the jury about Dani discovering the kidnapped children, about him stowing away on the red Cigarette boat, and about the terrible crash onto the beach.

Finally, after taking a deep breath, a somber grimace formed on his face. "Ladies and gentlemen, the evidence will show Dani Alverez is innocent! Thank you."

Judge Bullins recessed court for lunch until 2 P.M. As the crowd was filing out, Bledsoe read the note the governor had passed to him. As he read, a grin appeared on his face. The note read:

> *Great opening, Arnold! Will you join me*
> *in the library for lunch? I'm having it catered.*
>
> *Alex*

Bledsoe's grin widened noting he was Arnold and the governor was Alex. He liked the sound of that. Note in hand, he walked anxiously down the rear hall annex to the back door of the Commonwealth Attorney's office, where he punched in the secret combination.

In the library, sitting at the conference table was Governor Brotherton and his, nephew, Dr. Jim Johnston. Both of them stood to greet Bledsoe.

"Arnold," the governor said enthusiastically, "I just want to tell you how great your opening statement was. Everything I've heard about your ability is true." For the next several minutes, the governor continued to gush lauds of praise, until finally, a knock came on the door.

Two men dressed in white, caterers from the prestigious "Ole Virginia Men's Club entered carrying large silver trays with plates of savory prime rib, twice-baked potatoes, salads, vegetables and the trimmings. It was a gourmet feast.

Bledsoe wasted no time delving into his prime rib while Brotherton, always conscious of his slender physique, nibbled on his vegetables. As they ate, another knock came on the door. Without invitation, the Honorable Buford Bullins stepped into the room.

"Governor, I just wanted to stop by to say hello," Bullins said, a cat-ate-the-canary grin on his face.

"Oh, come in, Buford," the governor said cordially. "Sit down, and let's have a little chat."

CHAPTER
27

THE FIRST witness was Jim Johnston. He was tall and slender, almost too slender. He had dark, neatly-cut hair with a visible tint of emerging gray along his temples. The ordeal of the past month had added an aura of sadness to a once youthful face, as well as the hint of newly-formed crows' feet at the corners of his eyes. He stepped up to the clerk, placed his left hand on the Bible, raised his right, and was sworn. His testimony would be emotional and devastating.

He talked about his beautiful wife and wonderful children. The kids were laughing and giggling, "just having a wonderful time on the beach." He explained that he'd left his family to go back to the car to get the cooler.

"As I was returning, I...I heard a terribly loud roar." His voice began to quiver. He lowered his head, searching for the strength to repeat the recurring horror one more painful time.

"What happened, Dr. Johnston?" Bledsoe asked.

The young doctor sat up straight in his chair and began to speak haltingly.

"The roaring engine got louder and louder. Then, I saw it! This red racing yacht was traveling at an incredible speed, headed right...right for my family. Before...before I could react, it shot through the breakers and crashed into my...my beautiful wife and children."

Dr. Johnston lowered his head as more tears slid down his cheeks. Sobbing, he told the jury about that terrible moment when little Jimmy and Jenny were struck by the Cigarette boat.

"I began running toward them, then I saw Susan's red bathing suit. Her body was lying on its side not ten feet in front of me." Dr. Johnston's voice began to break and tears reappeared as he labored to continue.

"I...I rushed to her and immediately knew she was dead. Then, I went to my daughter, lying there motionless. Her limp, little body was on its back with her arms resting on her chest."

Bledsoe paused and handed Dr. Johnston a cup of water. As the young doctor sipped slowly from the paper cup, the only sound in the otherwise hushed courtroom was the hum of the air conditioning. Finally, abruptly, Dr. Johnston's raspy voice broke the silence.

"I went totally berserk! I had just lost my entire family, my wife, my wonderful children were gone forever."

His face grimacing, he struggled to explain the rage he had felt when he found the black man hiding on the boat.

"I cursed him and started in after him. I would've killed him with my bare hands, but someone grabbed me and forced me off the boat."

There was a long pause of silence, a silence that brought out tears—until finally Bledsoe, in his smug tone, said, "Your witness."

Early on, Grayson had decided to play it safe by asking just one question. "Dr. Johnston, sir," he said, his tone much softer than usual, "You didn't see who was driving that boat as it came ashore did you?"

"No, sir, I did not!" Jim Johnston retorted, his words distinctly over-enunciated. "I was focused on my children rather than on who was driving the boat." Hesitating, his face turned pink, then quickly red, red as a ham. With vengeance eking from his voice, his long pent up anguish exploded.

"But I'll tell you this!"

At the moment of this dreaded interlude, Grayson knew whatever Johnston was about to say was not going to be good. "Objection, non-responsive," Grayson shouted.

"Denied! You may answer, Dr. Johnston," the judge instructed.

Damn, I should never have opened this can of worms, Grayson thought.

Jim Johnston exploded.

"There were only two people on that boat," he screamed hysterically, "and one was dead! So, who the hell do you think was driving the boat?"

BY THURSDAY, the fourth day of the trial, Grayson was beginning to feel the draining effects of minimal sleep, nonstop planning and continuous stress. The witnesses he expected to cross-examine on this day were extremely important, and with a little luck, he might score a few points by capitalizing on their vulnerabilities.

The first witness was the pilot of the helicopter that intercepted the red Cigarette boat. Lieutenant Benjamin Martin, wearing his dress white service uniform, testified about the helicopter patrol and the drug interdiction attempt. He explained that the helo had hovered over the red Cigarette boat, preparing to make a loudspeaker request for the vessel to heave to. Suddenly, a black man appeared on deck and began shooting. The doomed helicopter, smoke pouring out of its starboard engine, limped back toward the mainland, only to crash in the Virginia Beach surf.

When Grayson's turn came for cross-examination, he was ready.

"Now, Lieutenant Martin," he said, "you only had a matter of seconds to observe the man who shot at your helicopter. Is that correct?"

"Yes, sir."

"So, all you're really saying is the man looked black or was dressed in black, correct?"

"Well, uh, I guess that's true," the lieutenant responded, his eyes dropping.

"In fact, sir, this person shooting at your helicopter could have been a white man wearing a black dive suit. Isn't that true?"

Martin raised his head, his eyes averting Grayson's stare. "I don't know, uh...maybe. I really can't say for sure."

Grayson knew he should stop on a high note. And this was as high as it was going to get.

"No further questions."

The testimony of Ensign Stephen Brooks, the co-pilot, and Petty Officer Ronald Smitherman, the gunner, was almost identical to Lieutenant Martin's. Both said the man on the Cigarette boat shooting at them was black or appeared so, but both conceded it could've been a white man in a black wetsuit.

By the end of the first week of trial, the prosecution had called a total of twelve police witnesses, each of whom provided cumulative testimony about the horrible carnage they had witnessed on the beach.

An officer who had seen Dani Alverez being taken away by stretcher from the beached Cigarette boat was called to testify.

"How was the defendant dressed?" Bledsoe inquired as he set up the play for the snap.

"Black shorts and nothing else," was the reply.

"So, he appeared black all over. Is that true, sir?"

"Yes, sir. Black from head to toe," the officer replied, the dialogue seeming to ring suspiciously of rehearsal.

As the weekend approached, the news media remained in a feeding frenzy, reporting every available morsel of trial information. The case was continuing to receive national coverage by all the major networks, including *Live Trial Television,* which was covering the trial in its entirety.

CHAPTER
29

"**THE COMMONWEALTH** calls Detective James J. Jamison," the prosecutor announced.

Jamison entered the courtroom and walked quickly through the swinging gate without so much as a glance toward Dani.

Dani lowered his head, his eyes focused on the table top as an aura of sadness came over him. He recollected how lonely he had been after the accident, and how warm he had felt when he finally accepted Jamison as his friend. Now Dani felt a bitterness he had never experienced. His personal trust had been betrayed by a man who manipulated him into signing a false confession —a confession that might cost him his life.

Standing and buttoning his coat, Bledsoe began his direct examination with standard introductory questions: name, employer, experience, involvement in this case, and the like. Jamison answered in a rote, rehearsed fashion, completely indifferent to the role his chicanery had played in bringing Dani to trial.

"Tell us about your first visit with Alverez, detective," Bledsoe asked.

"I went to see him at Virginia Beach Memorial Hospital

on the evening of June 3rd," Jamison responded, as he twisted to the left so he could look eye-to-eye with the jury. "I didn't go to arrest him, I went just to see how he was doing and to talk about what had happened."

Rat shit! Grayson scratched on his note pad.

"Tell us what happened," Bledsoe directed.

Jamison, still looking at the jury, began to explain the conversations during the visits.

"Without hesitation, Mr. Alverez informed me he stole the boat and took it offshore where they picked up a load of cocaine."

Cat shit! Grayson scribbled.

Jamison paused, his eyes now staring out into space rather than at the jury. Finally he managed to push the words out.

"It...it was then," he asserted, a slight stutter to his voice as his eyes glanced fleetingly at the jury, "that, uh, that the suspect fully admitted his guilt and signed a full confession."

"And what did he say, Mr. Jamison?"

"He, uh, confessed he, and he alone, drove the red Cigarette boat onto the beach, and it was he, and he alone, who killed the people on the beach."

Dani was aghast, his face wrinkling in bewilderment as he shook his head in denial.

"Did you give him his Miranda Rights?" inquired the prosecutor.

"I certainly did." Jamison asserted.

Finally, Bledsoe, still a goofy smirk on his face, asked, "Mr. Jamison, did you in any way coerce this defendant into signing this confession?"

Jamison cocked his head back. "I most certainly did not! In fact, Alverez seemed glad to be getting it off his chest."

Bull shit! Grayson whispered a bit too loudly, causing a nearby bailiff to look up and take pause. And for a moment, even Judge Bullins hesitated as he adjusted his hearing aid, his eyes staring down menacingly toward the defense table.

At last, it was Grayson's turn. He stood up and walked

toward Jamison until they were eye-to-eye.

"Detective Jamison," he demanded. "Isn't it true that hospital records indicate you visited with the defendant a total of twelve times while he was in the hospital. That's at least twice a day. Is that correct?"

"Sure, what's wrong with that?" Jamison responded defensively, fidgeting slightly.

"You told him, didn't you, if he would confess, he would get to go back home to the Cayman Islands?"

"I said nothing of the sort!" Jamison's tone was self-righteous and indignant.

"You told him, didn't you, if he didn't cooperate by giving a confession, he would most certainly be convicted of murder?"

"Absolutely not!" Jamison sang out, now with a dramatic flair to his denial.

"Isn't it true sir, you told him if he didn't confess, he would never see his mother and sister again? Isn't that a fact, Mr. Jamison?" Grayson demanded.

Over and over, Grayson hammered Jamison with leading questions for more than an hour, but despite his most arduous efforts, he couldn't break through the chain of lies. Rather, Jamison continued to adamantly deny he had lied to, browbeat, or in any way coerced Dani into signing the confession.

Finally, deciding he had dribbled this ball as far as it would go, Grayson reluctantly announced, "No further questions."

At last, the Commonwealth's case began to wind down. After hearing from more police witnesses, then the corporate president of the conglomerate that owned the *Jamaican Maiden,* that was it. The Commonwealth rested.

"Now, Mr. Forrest, does the defense desire to offer evidence?" the judge asked condescendingly, seeming to imply that Dani Alverez's goose was already cooked.

30

THANKS TO Martina's hard work, a possible fantastic defense witness had been uncovered, a witness who just might save the day.

"The defense calls Marvin Elwood Simmons!"

Simmons, clean shaven, his thinning gray hair combed into place, took the witness chair. Wearing his green work pants and a white short-sleeved shirt, he was quite a distinguished elderly man.

Mr. Simmons identified himself and told the jury he was a commercial fisherman. On June 3rd he had been a half mile off Virginia Beach in his skiff, fishing for Spanish mackerel.

"Been out there 'bout an hour when I heard them helicopters," he said. "Out in front of 'em was this red Cigarette boat headin' right at me. It looked like it was gonna' run me right over, so I speeded up to get out of its way. It couldn't have missed me by more'n ten or so feet."

Grayson paused and took a deep breath. *Now, the biggie for the whole ball of wax,* he murmured to himself. "Mr. Simmons, did you see anybody on the boat?"

"I sure did!" Simmons replied. "When it passed me, I saw a man dressed in all black at the helm. He had dive tanks on his back. And, there was another guy on the boat too, a white guy."

Standing up and stepping behind Dani, Grayson placed his hand on his client's shoulder. "Mr. Simmons, I ask you whether you saw the defendant here on that boat?"

For a full ten seconds, Simmons looked point blank at Dani. Finally, emphatically he replied, "No sir! Uh, the guy with the scuba tanks was a real big white man. In fact, both of `em were white. I didn't see this feller."

Simmons testified he had told the police about this, but they called him a liar and didn't seem interested in what he had to say.

"Are you telling the truth here today, Mr. Simmons?"

"Yes sir, as God is my witness," he replied solemnly, "that black man there was not in the cockpit of that red boat. I swear!"

With those words, a contrived expression of shock on his face, Bledsoe looked dramatically up at the ceiling—but only for a sharp second. Quickly, his prosecutor mode returned as he began his cross-examination attack.

"Mr. Simmons, or can I call you Sippy?" he asked slyly, a gremlin-like grin on his face.

"Sure, you can call me Sippy. Everyone else does."

"Are you the same Sippy Simmons who was convicted of drunk and disorderly conduct thirty-four times in the last ten years?"

"Well, I s'pose so."

"How many times have you been convicted of driving while impaired?"

"A few times, sir."

"Five times to be exact! Isn't that true, sir?" Bledsoe demanded sharply.

Glaring at Simmons, Bledsoe prepared to go for the jugular.

"Sippy Simmons, your only truth is in a bottle! You didn't see any such man in a scuba outfit. That was just alcohol talking. Isn't that true?"

Before Simmons could respond, Bledsoe theatrically shook his head in feigned disgust, then theatrically slammed his legal pad down on the table.

"No further questions!" he blasted disdainfully.

Grayson's great fear had just been realized — the cross examination of Marvin Elwood Simmons had been devastating.

CHAPTER
31

CLAD IN his Marine issue, desert tan, camouflage boxer shorts and matching T-shirt, Gunny sat in his recliner, glumly eating a bologna sandwich. His own criminal charges were set for trial the next morning, and it didn't look promising. He might even go to jail.

With such pressure facing him, he knew he would yield to the temptation of alcohol today, but he told himself he must wait until at least ten o'clock before pouring his first cocktail. Nibbling on his sandwich, he looked at the clock, anxiously awaiting for his happy hour to arrive.

"What the hell; it's ten o'clock somewhere," he finally proclaimed as he uncapped his Absolut vodka, anxiously poured a triple over ice and splashed in a thimble full of ginger ale. Remote in hand, he plopped back down in the La-Z-Boy and began idly surfing past the same old interview shows, the same old movies and same old fruity religious shows. When the *Live Trial TV* channel came on the screen, he removed his thumb from the flicker and waited to see if there was anything worth watching.

Shortly, a voice announced the continuing *Live Trial* telecast of the Alverez trial. The defendant, Dani Alverez, accused murderer of the Governor of Virginia's family was scheduled to testify.

Normally, Gunny didn't watch court-type stuff, but like most of America, this case had him captivated.

"Let's see what this little jerk has to say," he mumbled as he quickly sucked down the last of his cocktail. "I'd like to personally blow his friggin' brains out."

Gunny mixed a fresh drink and once again nestled down in his recliner, his curious eyes fixated on the television screen. He saw a bespectacled judge staring angrily down at a youthful white lawyer. As the camera focused on the lawyer, Gunny erupted into an angry tirade, blasting ferociously at the television.

"What kind of low life, ambulance-chasing lawyer would represent a foreign scum bag who would shoot down an American helicopter?" he screamed. "That damn lawyer ought'a be found guilty too! Both of 'em ought'a be taken out and hung from the highest tree!"

Meanwhile, in the courtroom, the defendant, dressed in dark trousers and a white shirt, took the witness chair. He identified himself as Dani Alverez of Grand Cayman, British West Indies.

He stated he had been a cook on the *Jamaican Maiden,* which had left Kingston on a Monday and sailed for the southeastern coast of the United States. The freighter would stop offshore near a number of coastal cities. Speedboats would come out to meet them where a group of teenaged girls were brought aboard.

"Something wasn't right," Dani said. "It just didn't make any sense. We weren't going into any ports. I, uh, just didn't know what was going on. But somewhere off the Carolina coast, about dusk, a power boat approached and came up alongside the ship and again, girls were brought aboard.

"Then, later in the evening, the captain and a big, bearded man came into the galley for coffee. I heard one of them say something about, uh, having to keep the children doped up. But, I didn't know what they were talking about."

Bledsoe had been caught daydreaming, but when he

realized what he had just heard, he bounced to his feet. "Objection! Move to strike!" he screamed. "That's rank hearsay, your honor!"

"Sustained!" Judge Bullins snapped. Leering at Grayson like he was the scum of the earth, Bullins' face formed into a mean-spirited scowl and his words took on a hostile bite.

"Mr. Forrest, you know better than to try to sneak in inadmissible hearsay. Don't let it happen again!"

As he was being admonished, Grayson could only stand there and dutifully take his medicine, all the while wondering why law school hadn't offered the course "Ass Kissing 101."

Proceeding with his testimony, Dani explained that his curiosity finally got the best of him. He went to the forward stateroom, peeked in and found it packed with teenage girls. Most were unconscious, although a few were awake but in a doped-up condition.

"One girl was able to talk a little bit. I don't remember her name, but she was from North Carolina, Morehead, I think she said."

At the words *"North Carolina, Morehead,"* Gunny's head shot up from the recliner. Incredulously, he stared at the TV screen, not believing his own ears. "What did she look like?" Gunny asked, his words identical, word for word, in unison with Grayson's direct examination question.

"Oh, she was slender and petite. She had blond hair and was very cute. She was really groggy and I only got to talk to her for a minute before she went back to sleep."

"Oh, my God," Gunny exclaimed, as he jumped up like a jack in the box. "That was Mandy! You're talking about my kid!"

Dani went on to explain that he returned to his cabin, but soon the big bearded man busted in and started beating him. He managed to break away and escape to the main deck. But then, someone started shooting at him.

"I had nowhere else to go except over the side, so I jumped overboard!"

Gunny's alcohol-dulled mind pondered the plausibility of this young man's story. He located the morning newspaper and skimmed the daily synopsis of the trial, quickly determining the date of the beach tragedy to be the 3rd of June. *Mandy turned up missing early June - that matches!*

Gunny was instantly cold sober. He now knew for sure he was no longer panning for fool's gold, this was the real thing! Nervously, he began to pace back and forth in front of the TV as he pondered his next move.

His first conclusion was obvious. He had to talk to Alverez.

*

Back in the courtroom, Dani's testimony continued. He stated he had jumped off the ship and hid himself against the ship's hull for a few minutes, but soon they spotted him and started shooting at him again. Bullets were striking the water all around him, so he swam to the red Cigarette boat, sneaked aboard and hid down in the cabin. Shortly, the boat took off and sped westward. As it raced along, he heard a helicopter and gunfire. It was a few minutes later that the boat crashed onto the beach.

Grayson paused, took a deep breath and prepared himself for the finishing stroke. In his most sincere and somber voice, he asked his final question.

"Mr. Alverez," he said, his eyes making direct contact with Dani's. "Mr. Alverez," he repeated, "Were you driving that boat?"

"No, sir, I was not!" Dani's voice was somber and sincere.

"No further questions."

As Grayson walked to the defense table, he rationalized that Dani had sounded very believable. *Maybe, just maybe, we might win this case after all,* he thought.

What came next, however, was to be a stellar performance by Bledsoe. With the governor and national press watching, Bledsoe knew this could be his ticket to fame and fortune. Rising to his feet, his blood-thirsty eyes affixed on his prey, he clenched his fists like he wanted to start a fight.

"Isn't it true, Mr. Alverez," he roared, "you were caught in this red Cigarette boat with thirty kilograms of cocaine?"

"No, sir. It wasn't mine, sir."

"Isn't it true the red Cigarette boat crashed into little Jimmy and Jenny Johnston and their mother, snuffing out their lives forever?"

"No, uh...well, yes, but..." The questions were coming too fast. Dani didn't have time to think.

Grayson had warned Dani an aggressive cross-examination was likely, and he should remain absolutely calm and take his time answering the questions. But Dani was not emotionally prepared for the rapid fire intimidation. He was already near panic.

Without pause, Bledsoe let go with another volley.

"Alverez!" he screamed viciously. "Do you expect us to believe you were a crewman on a ship for which there is no record of even being in Virginia waters?"

Before Dani could respond, Bledsoe was already firing another salvo.

"You don't give a damn that you killed these innocent children, do you?"

All Dani could say was "But, but, but." When the barrage finally subsided, his credibility was shot. Dani's story had come across as outlandish.

"Call your next witness, Mr. Forrest!"

Grayson wished there were more, but that was it. All he could say was, "The defense rests."

CHAPTER

32

RACING OUT of Morehead City like a Winston Cup contender, he weaved through traffic, breezing through New Bern, zipping past Little Washington, then whizzing across the Pasquotank River at Elizabeth City. In record time, he had crossed the Virginia line, and in thirty minutes more, he was at the Virginia Beach Court Complex. It was nearly five o'clock when he rushed into the courthouse.

After passing through the metal detectors and getting directions to the courtroom, he ran down the hallway and up the staircase to the second floor. At the third courtroom on the right, a black deputy sheriff, a bailiff, stood guard. "Excuse me, deputy," Gunny said.

The bailiff, in his drab brown uniform, turned around, his eyes immediately focusing on Gunny's much-adorned dress blues. "Yes, sir," he snapped in reply, obviously impressed.

As he gawked at Gunny's array of medals and ribbons, the ex-Marine bailiff told Gunny the lawyers were making their final arguments. He could take any vacant seat.

Gunny entered the courtroom, careful not to let the door slam, then squeezed into a seat on the back row.

*

Grayson, his palms damp, his breathing irregular, stood up and walked to the podium. With his right hand, he flicked the overhanging hair from his brow. His moment to proclaim to the world his client's innocence had finally arrived! He gripped the sides of the podium and paused as a solemn expression spread across his face.

Thanking the jury for their attention, he then forged ahead. His words were forceful and heartfelt.

"There is no credible evidence that Dani Alverez was driving the boat, nor that he had anything to do with the Johnston family deaths. Like the twins and their mother, Dani Alverez is also a victim of this tragedy!"

Grayson's delivery flowed smoothly. He stressed the unrefuted testimony of Mr. Simmons. He emphasized the inability of the helicopter crew to say whether the man who shot at them was white or black.

"Each of us," Grayson reminded the jury, "is presumed innocent and remain innocent unless the prosecutor can prove guilt beyond a reasonable doubt."

For the entire thirty minute oration, the eyes of each and every juror—except those of juror number seven, Braxton Hornsby—followed Grayson's every movement. Hornsby, however, stared out into the audience, his eyes unswayed from the governor's entourage in the center section.

Pausing to take a deep breath before throwing his final pitch, Grayson looked imploringly at the jury.

"Ladies and gentlemen," he finally said, his tone deep and sincere, "We ask that you find the only fair and just verdicts, verdicts of not guilty!"

Grayson nodded respectfully and returned to his seat, hoping for the best, but silently conceding *it actually seemed like the sharks were circling closer than ever.*

*

Arnold Bledsoe strutted arrogantly toward the jury box. Using his most persuasive pitch, he spoke to the jury theatrically, his eyes panning to each member.

"This alien," he said, pointing his finger at Dani, "snuffed out the lives of two innocent children and their mother." Bledsoe's voice was soft and low at first, but as he proceeded, it began to crescendo.

He began prancing back and forth like a drum major, then as slithery as a snake, he slid into his preaching mode.

"Ladies and gentlemen, this cockamamie story about pirates and kidnapped children and a non-existent ship is hogwash! This alien claims some bearded pirate drove the boat, shot at the helicopter, and then scuba dived away. Now, come on! This isn't fantasy world! Rather, this is a ludicrous story by a desperate liar. No sensible person on God's green earth would believe this fairy tale!"

As the jurors' eyes followed Bledsoe's every move, Hornsby was nodding and Bullins was beaming as they both silently conveyed their approval. And in the audience, Governor Brotherton was feeling a sense of satisfaction, all but certain there would be a conviction.

Bledsoe shifted gears once more, and the fire and brimstone began to fly.

"We ask that you be Virginia patriots here today. We ask you to return a verdict that will tell the drug smugglers around the world if they commit a crime in our fair Commonwealth they will pay for it in the most extreme way!"

With that, like an overgrown banty rooster, Bledsoe strutted back to his seat, a vainglorious glow of confidence on his face. He was positive he had won!

*

The trial recessed until the next day. As the courtroom emptied, many eyes focused on the rugged Marine who was making his way up the aisle against the flow, dodging the exiting crowd.

"Grayson Forrest?" Gunny asked.

Grayson and Martina were sitting side by side at the coun-

sel table, both physically and emotionally exhausted, neither in the mood to chat with anyone. "Yeah, that's right.
Who are you?" was Grayson's half-hearted reply.

Gunny stuck out his right hand. "I'm Lincoln Vernon.
I need to talk to your client. He may have some information that may be mutually beneficial to both of us." Gunny
was quick to explain that his kidnapped daughter matched
the description of the teenager Dani had spoken with on
the ship.

Grayson's first impulse was to tell Vernon to get lost,
but something made him reconsider. Although the man
was probably a crackpot, if there really were an outside
chance this could be of some benefit to Dani, why not
hear him out?

"Okay, I'll bite," Grayson said. "What the heck are you
talking about?"

Gunny hastily presented a capsule briefing about
Mandy's disappearance and the big, bearded man. Then
he made his desperate plea.

"Mr. Forrest, I heard part of your client's testimony and
I think the same bearded man who was driving the Cigarette boat also kidnapped my daughter. Please, let me talk
to your client. I've got to!"

Together, Gunny, Grayson and Martina walked over to
the nearby Virginia Beach Detention Center where a deputy
escorted them to the visitor's viewing window.

Soon, Dani's face appeared on the other side of the thick,
wire meshed glass window. As Dani put the phone to his
ear, he immediately wondered why this tall, black stranger
was standing there before him.

"Dani, this man is from Morehead City, North Carolina,"
Grayson told him. "He's looking for his daughter and thinks
you may have some information that could help him find
her. Indirectly, it might even help our case. Do you mind
talking to him?"

"Uh, sure. Anything I can do to help...uh, but sir, I don't
think I talked to his daughter."

"Why do you say that?" Gunny responded, having just taken the phone from Grayson.

"Well, you see, sir, the girl I talked to was, uh, was caucasian with blond hair."

A sudden grin flashed across Gunny's face.

"Let me explain," he said. "I'm looking for my adopted daughter. She's white with blond hair."

When Gunny asked Dani to describe the girl he had talked with, Dani replied, "Sir, she was maybe five foot two, blond, a bit on the skinny side."

Gunny reached into his shirt pocket and pulled out a photograph.

"Mr. Alverez, would you look at this photo and tell me if this is the girl you talked to?"

"I'll try."

With Gunny holding the photo against the glass, Dani studied it carefully. Soon, a smile slid across his face.

"That's her, that's her!" he exclaimed excitedly.

As Gunny gazed into Dani's eyes, he couldn't help but feel a sense of shame about how judgmental he had been. He had been calling this man a lying scumbag, but now, here he was, face to face with him, hoping against hope this same man could help him save Mandy's life.

CHAPTER
33

PROMPTLY AT 9 A.M. the next morning, Judge Bullins instructed the jury on the law, then jury deliberations began. With Dani locked in the holding cell, Grayson and Martina remained in the courtroom with nothing to do but wait and worry.

"What do you think is going to happen?" Martina asked, hoping for a sign of optimism from Grayson.

A serious expression on his face, Grayson looked into Martina's brown eyes.

"I really don't know," he replied, wishing he could be more optimistic, "but it's best to prepare for the worst and hope for the best."

He put his arm around her shoulder as his voice softened. "Oh yes," he said, as he sought a temporary respite from the tension of the moment. "Did I tell you what my mother said about you?"

"What?"

A rascalian grin slid onto Grayson's face. "She said she really likes you and wishes I'd find a girl as nice as you."

"Really?"

"Yeah, and you know that's pretty significant when you consider her feelings on interracial romances." Grayson's eyebrows arched, nearly touching his hairline.

They looked at each other as the words, "*interracial romance*," reverberated in their respective minds. Grayson could feel himself being drawn toward her - she made him feel warm and comfortable. After all, she was caring, thoughtful and highly principled, not to mention exceedingly beautiful.

Minutes turned into an hour as they waited, both wondering what the future held. Two hours slipped by, then three hours without a word.

"How much longer, Gray?" Martina asked wearily.

"I don't know, but usually, the longer the jury stays out, the better it is for the defense."

Another hour passed; then another thirty minutes, still without a word. But at 8:30, a bailiff rushed into the courtroom through the side door. He had a note in his hand and was walking directly toward the judge's chambers.

"This could be it," Grayson whispered to Martina as he felt his heartbeat quicken.

Several minutes later, Bledsoe entered the courtroom and took his seat. A bailiff led Dani back to his seat, court personnel took their places and the legion of reporters and spectators filed back into the courtroom. The tension was palpable, the parties waiting with grave anticipation for the historical verdict.

The judge appeared and the jurors filed back into the courtroom, each eye looking straight ahead, every expression poker faced, no one divulging their collective secret.

The butterflies in Grayson's stomach were fluttering. All he could do was close his eyes and pray.

"Has the jury reached a verdict?" inquired the judge.

Juror number seven, Mr. Hornsby, stood up. "Yes, we have your honor."

Oh crap! Not Hornsby, anybody but him.

"Mr. Hornsby, you're the foreman of the jury?" the judge inquired.

"I am, your honor."

"Please hand your verdict form to the bailiff, sir," the judge instructed.

The bailiff passed the verdict form to Judge Bullins who reviewed it, then handed it to the clerk. "Take the verdict, Madam Clerk!"

Grayson knew he had to be strong. No matter what the verdict, he had to respond in a dignified manner. *But, maybe, just maybe, the system will work. Maybe they will see through this mockery of justice.*

The clerk, jaded from thirty years in the criminal courts, took the verdict form from the judge. She began to speak.

To Grayson, the moment seemed almost surreal, like he was watching a movie, like looking down on the courtroom from the ceiling above. He could visualize himself sitting at the counsel table as he waited for the verdict while everything around him seemed to be moving in slow motion.

"We, the jury," the clerk read loudly, "find the defendant, Dani Alverez, on the charge of murder in the first degree of Susan Johnston, guilty!"

"The word *"guilty"* reverberated inside Grayson's head like a jack hammer. As his spirit sank, his heart pleaded - *No, no, it can't be! Our system is supposed to work!* Grayson's mind was in shock. He heard the words, but the reality was an illusion. *It wasn't real. It couldn't be!*

Her awful words continued.

"We, the jury, find the defendant, Dani Alverez, on the charge of murder in the first degree of James Johnston, Jr., *guilty!* We, the jury, find the defendant, Dani Alverez, on the charge of murder in the first degree of Jennifer Johnston, *guilty!*"

Judge Bullins, his eyes magnified by the coke-bottle lens of his glasses, was gloating. "Any motions now, counselor?" he asked, his voice near song-like as a twitch of a smile flicked onto his face.

Grayson reached down into his very soul as he struggled to stand up and respond. Clearing his throat, he was barely able to find enough saliva to swallow. "No, your honor," he finally replied as he felt a dark wave of despair looming, ready to crash upon him.

"Mr. Alverez, stand up!" the judge ordered.

Piously eyeing Dani Alverez, Judge Bullins seemed anxious to utter the words he had been waiting to say for the past two weeks. With a subdued grin on his face, reminiscent of a man about to experience an erotic moment, the judge proclaimed, "Dani Alverez, this Court hereby adjudges you guilty of three counts of murder in the first degree! The sentencing hearing will begin Monday at 9 A.M. Adjourn court, Mr. Bailiff."

Just like that, it was over. It seemed there should have been a drum roll or some extraordinary decree from on high, but there was no such pomp. Grayson's heart sank into his stomach. How could he look his client in the eye?

BEFORE GRAYSON could react, Dani was dragged toward the exit door by the bailiffs, a fleeting expression of horror on his face.

Grayson and Martina, both dumbfounded and still in shock, left the courtroom and walked down the corridor, sidestepping reporters and dodging cameras along the way. They made it to the parking lot and into the relative solitude of the Cherokee. Suppressing the temptation to slam the accelerator to the floor, instead Grayson calmly started the engine and slowly drove away, headed for the Virginia Beach Detention Center.

Upon arrival, they were escorted into the prisoner visiting area where Dani waited, red-eyed and solemn faced.

"Are they going to kill me, Mr. Forrest?" Dani's voice quaked, reflecting an anxiety too frightening to disguise.

Grayson was determined to be upbeat.

"Dani, I know you're innocent. I know you're just as much a victim as was the Johnston family."

Compassionately, Grayson explained the process.

"On Monday, we will try to convince the jury you don't deserve to die. Regardless of what happens, your case will be appealed to the highest court, even to the United States

Supreme Court if necessary."

Dani was having a difficult time comprehending what was happening to him. Until the verdict just minutes earlier, he had believed truth would prevail and acquittal was the only possible outcome.

"What does all this mean?" he asked, a puzzled expression on his face.

Grayson realized he needed to simplify the explanation. "It means, I will never give up on you. I will fight in every way I can!"

Sunday, the work was intense and unrelenting. For three solid hours, Grayson pored through law books, brainstormed for ideas, and looked for any helpful hints for the sentencing hearing. Then, shortly before noon he and Martina headed to the Virginia Beach Detention Center.

"Dani, the way you tell your side of this is very important. You must speak clearly and slowly."

"I will tell the truth, Mr. Forrest. That's all I know to do."

"Dani, the prosecutor is going to try to make you sound like a liar. First, when he asks questions you don't understand, say you don't understand."

"Also, no matter what he says to you, don't! - I repeat - don't get angry. If the jury even suspects you have a temper, they may equate that with you being an evil person. Do you understand?"

Dani nodded.

For two hours, Grayson worked with Dani until it seemed he could absorb no more. As the sun was setting, Grayson and Martina bid Dani goodnight and headed home to get ready for the next day, when literally, "life or death" would be decided.

CHAPTER
35

THE PENALTY phase was underway with Bledsoe belaboring everyone's patience, even Judge Bullins'. He recalled the same cumulative blood and gore evidence, the same police officers and the same pathologist. His plan was calculated to elevate the jury to its maximum level of passion. He wanted them to be so enraged that death could be their only possible verdict.

The final bombshell was a repeat of Dr. Jim Johnston's earlier testimony. Just as before, when the bereaved widower left the witness chair, there was not a dry eye in the courtroom.

Grayson's first witness was a psychologist, Dr. Antonio Vansetti, a heavy set man over six feet tall, wearing a bright green blazer and matching green polka-dot tie. Dr. Vansetti, speaking with a European accent, testified that although Dani had an overall I.Q. of 91, which was in the low average range, no anti-social tendencies had been detected. Dani seemed to be quite well adjusted.

Because of Dani's adjustment to the local jail, Dr. Vansetti opined Dani would also adapt well to a life in prison. But on cross, Bledsoe shot a big hole in the doctor's testimony.

"Now, Dr. Vansetti." Bledsoe said, his forehead wrinkling into tight ridges. "Alverez has been in jail only six weeks. Correct?"

"Yes, I think so." Dr. Vansetti acknowledged.

"That's hardly enough time to evaluate his long term adjustment to confinement, is it?"

Dr. Vansetti squirmed in his seat. "It gives some indication."

"So, sir," Bledsoe impugned. "You really don't know whether Alverez would be a dangerous trouble maker in prison or not, do you?"

"I guess not," Vansetti said, backpedaling, "but, but, that would be very unlikely."

Martina was called as a witness. She spoke softly, but her quivering voice and trembling hands betrayed her emotions. She talked about Dani's childhood, about their parents and the tragic loss of their father. She explained Dani's devotion to the Roman Catholic faith.

"Everyone likes Dani. He's honest, peaceful, and loving. He's a good brother and a good son. He doesn't use drugs of any kind, including alcohol." With her voice cracking and tears coursing down, emotionally, she begged for her brother's life to be spared.

Bledsoe was unmerciful on cross-examination. Like a hound dog on a hot trail, he could tell Martina could easily be pushed over the brink. He stood up and buttoned his coat. Then, with the intensity of a bear chasing honey, he attacked.

"Ms. Alverez, you ask for mercy for your brother, but he has shown none for his victims." Bledsoe's voice was angry and demanding. His eyebrows rose dramatically toward his receding hairline as he waited like a vulture for Martina's response.

"Sir, uh, he's sorry these people died, but...but he didn't kill them!" Martina, her words strained, shook her head in frustration.

Bledsoe's cruel eyes were boring into her. He increased the intensity of his attack. "Your brother brutally murdered three fine people! He's lied to you! He's lied to his lawyer! And he's lied to this jury! Isn't that true?"

"Objection!" Grayson yelled but his attempt to buffer the verbal assault was too late. Martina exploded into a new round of tears. Bledsoe had done it again!

Almost too quickly, it was time for the final arguments. Bledsoe went first, claiming the law required "an eye for an eye, a tooth for a tooth, and a life for a life. He's killed three times. Three strikes and you're out in baseball and with three murders, a criminal should also be out — out forever!"

When Grayson's turn came, he reiterated the reasons for sparing Dani's life: he has lived a good Christian life; he has a mother and sister who love him; he would be a model prisoner and would cause no trouble while incarcerated. Grayson, in contrast to Bledsoe, quoted from the New Testament, "Vengeance is mine saith the Lord."

The jury deliberated until nearly 5 P.M. when the judge called them in and asked if they were close to a decision. Hornsby, still the foreman, sprang to his feet. "Almost judge," he chirped out gleefully.

Deliberations continued, but not thirty minutes later a long series of intrusive knocks came on the jury room door. Shortly, the court personnel re-assembled and the jurors, their eyes looking downward, filed back into the courtroom. *Not a good sign,* Grayson reflected.

The all-too-eager judge asked if they had reached a verdict. Hornsby stood up. "Yes, we have, your honor," he replied, his face sparkling like a well-paid whore.

Hornsby passed the verdict sheet up to the judge who silently reviewed it, then handed it to the clerk. "Take the verdict, Madam Clerk," he ordered.

Grayson could hear the beat of his own heart as he nervously watched the clerk begin to speak. He closed his eyes as if in prayer.

"In the case of the murder of Susan Johnston, we, the jury, find aggravating circumstances exist beyond a reasonable doubt."

That's no surprise, Grayson thought.

The clerk continued. "We, the jury, find no mitigating circumstances."

What! Grayson murmured, astonished the jury had not considered Dani's good reputation nor the fact he had no prior record.

"We, the jury, find the aggravating circumstances outweigh any mitigating circumstances."

Oh, no! I can't believe this is happening! Grayson thought, his mind racing.

"We, the jury, find the aggravating circumstances are sufficiently substantial to call for the death penalty."

Oh, my God, no! Grayson began to feel the sharp stab of defeat.

And then they did it. "We, the jury, recommend the defendant be sentenced to death."

Before his brain could process the unfathomable verdict, a second death verdict was proclaimed — this one for Jenny, then, a third for Jimmy. Grayson felt flush, his mind threatening to shut down. He dared not look at Martina who he knew must be going into shock. But when he looked over at his client, Dani appeared amazingly composed, much more so than his lawyer.

Judge Bullins nonchalantly thanked the jury for their service, then stood up, his right hand raised. "The defendant will rise!" he commanded in a God-like tone.

Dani and Grayson stood up, both staring up at the judge, both feeling naked and vulnerable.

Stern faced, without so much as a blink, the judge piously boomed out his hallowed sentence as though he were on a sacred mission. "Dani Alverez," he exhorted, his words biting and cold, "I hereby order, adjudge and decree you be, and hereby are sentenced to death! That on the 22nd day of November you shall be executed by sufficient amount of electricity passing through your body as to render you dead, according to law."

Then, as if it were an afterthought, Judge Bullins paused,

his vacant eyes looking over the rims of his glasses. "And May God have mercy on your soul!" he declared as though he had a close tie with the Lord God, himself.

Martina began to cry, her wails of sorrow overriding all other sounds in the courtroom. Grayson, standing motionless and at a total loss at what to do, stared blankly at the floor and could only wince when Dani was jerked violently to his feet by the bailiffs and dragged like a rabid animal toward the exit.

Grayson gathered his papers from the table in front of him and stuffed them into his brief case. Martina, still sobbing, moved up beside him at the counsel table, her hands covering her teary face.

Trying his best to be strong, Grayson dared a look at her. "Marty, uh, don't, don't worry," he said, a slight stutter in his voice, "there, there will be an appeal. We'll not let this terrible injustice win out!"

V

THE PROBE

CHAPTER
36

ATTIRED IN faded jeans, a denim shirt and Air Jordans, Gunny gazed out the window of his U.S. Airways flight to Miami. The plane lifted off from Norfolk Airport, gained altitude, then gradually turned onto a southerly heading. Through wispy clouds that partially obscured his view, he could soon see the solid strip of coastal land below known as Currituck Banks, an elongated barrier island which separated Currituck Sound from the Atlantic Ocean.

What a quandary of events! Just yesterday, the only person who had given him any viable hope in his search for Mandy had been sentenced to death. Gunny's mind returned to the terrible final moment of the trial when the death sentence was pronounced. It was like being slam-dunked. It had been devastating. An hour later, Attorney Forrest had taken him to see Dani for a second time. He had taped the interview with Dani, which he now planned to listen to en route to Jamaica.

As the flight attendant rattled down the aisle with the refreshment cart, Gunny, earphones in place, pushed the play button on his Walkman. He heard his own voice ask Dani to tell him about this ship. "Where did you board it? Who is the owner?"

Dani's recorded voice was soft but audible. He stated he

had left home from the Grand Caymans and ferried over to Kingston, Jamaica where he signed on with the *Jamaican Maiden*. Dani told about the *Jamaican Maiden,* the teenagers brought aboard and his brief encounter with Mandy.

When asked whether there was anyone else aboard the ship who might be able to help, Dani suggested a friend, Oliver Weaver, a messman. Oliver lived in Kingston with his very pregnant wife.

In Miami, Gunny changed planes, boarding Air Jamaica's nonstop flight to Kingston, and an hour later landed at Kingston International Airport. After clearing customs, he hailed a cab. Climbing into the front seat, Gunny asked the cabby to stop at a phone booth so he could find Oliver Weaver's address.

With a grin on his face, the driver identifying himself as Cash, reached under the seat and handed Gunny a Kingston phone directory. In the dim light, Gunny paged through the directory, straining his eyes until he found the name Weaver, Oliver, 268 Gem Road. "Do you know where that is?" he asked Cash.

"Over near Trench Town, not too far away," Cash replied. After a wild thirty minute ride through a maze of dark Kingston streets, Cash steered his taxi into a driveway. "This is it," he announced.

After handing Cash a twenty dollar bill and asking him to wait, Gunny walked up the sandy walkway to a small stucco cottage. His knock was answered by a young Jamaican lady. She opened the door a few inches and peeked through the crack.

"What do you want?" she asked cautiously.

"Is Oliver home?"

The lady, apparently Oliver's wife, gave Gunny a leery look, a slight grimace on her brow. "Uh, please wait," she replied. Then, she closed the door.

A full minute had passed when a man in a tank top and shorts reopened the door. "Hey, mon, I'm Oliver. Who are you, and what do you want?" he demanded sharply, his Jamaican accent pronounced.

"Well, Oliver, it's a long story. It's about Dani Alverez. He said I should come see you. May I come in?"

Oliver forced a smile, then invited Gunny inside to a small, dimly lit living room. Sitting on the sofa, Gunny told Oliver about his kidnapped daughter and his suspicion that she had been a prisoner on the *Jamaican Maiden*.

"I don't know nothing about that," Oliver said, folding his arms defensively out in front of him.

Gunny slapped a one hundred dollar bill on the coffee table. "No one will ever know who told me, Oliver, and if it leads to my daughter, I'll pay you five thousand dollars; that's a promise!"

Oliver looked up at his wife who had entered the room just in time to hear the words, *five thousand dollars.* For a second, their hungry eyes met in silent conversation. Then, as though there had been an invisible consensus, Oliver sighed. "Okay," he conceded, "I suppose I may remember. Uh, by the way, how's Dani?"

"Not so well, Mr. Weaver," Gunny replied. "Dani was convicted of murder and sentenced to death."

"Death!" Oliver's eyes sprang widely open, as he shook his head in amazement. He was stunned.

"Tell me now, Oliver. You were on the *Jamaican Maiden* with Dani, weren't you?"

Oliver stared down at the floor. "Uh, I'm afraid I was," he replied sadly.

Gunny passed Mandy's photo to him. "Was this girl on the ship?" he asked.

Oliver looked down at the photo, studied it momentarily, looked up and nodded. "Yeah, mon! She was on the ship, but she was taken off."

Gunny's head popped upward. He couldn't quite believe what Oliver had just said.

"Did you say taken off?"

"Yeah, mon, she was on the ship, but she was taken off."

"When? Where?" Gunny exclaimed as he held his breath,

anxiously awaiting the answer.

"It was a few days after Dani jumped over the side," Oliver explained. "The pirate came back and got the little blond girl. He took her back to his boat, then headed back to the mainland."

"Whe, where? Wha, what mainland?" Gunny stammered, so excited his brain was outrunning his words.

"Um, I'm not really sure," Oliver replied thoughtfully as he rubbed his chin. "But I'd say it was off the North Carolina coast."

Gunny laid two more one hundred dollar bills on the table, then looked into Oliver's eyes. "Thanks, man. If this checks out, I'll send you forty-eight hundred more.

Gunny rushed back to the cab with one thing in mind. "Cash, get me back to the airport pronto!"

The Air Jamaica flight ascended over the Caribbean, heading north. Time being of the essence, Gunny was now fairly sure Mandy was most likely somewhere on the North Carolina coast with this weird pirate.

The sky was cloudless and the water, twenty thousand feet below, appeared calm. Gunny had been unable to sleep the night before as he waited at the Kingston Airport for the departure of the early bird flight to Miami. Even now, he was so excited he couldn't keep his eyes closed.

The flight attendants served refreshments as Gunny contemplated making an exception to his vow of temperance, rationalizing a double vodka Bloody Mary would sure taste good, and he deserved to celebrate this breakthrough. But turning toward the flight attendant, he heard himself say, "Coffee, black, please."

For the next hour, he peered out of his window, looking down at the sea, totally mesmerized by the vibrant cerulean blue of the water below. His mind began to drift to those horrid days in Viet Nam, when he had seen so many people die needlessly. It had caused him to grow detached, impassionate and thick-skinned. His heart had hardened, and his personal life had become a disaster. But years later,

Mandy had crept into his inner soul and taught him what love was all about. When she would look up at him and call him "Daddy," it would touch his heart. Now, she was gone, and so was his heart.

Methodically, Gunny began to assess the information he had gathered. He knew before the crash of the Cigarette boat, this pirate guy had been near Beaufort at Dixie Belle's Lounge from where he had kidnapped Mandy. He also knew the pirate drove an old pickup truck.

But there seemed to be more questions than answers. Still, one hypothesis stood out and rang true: *This psycho dresses like a pirate and acts like a pirate.* "Hmm," Gunny mused. *Maybe, he really thinks he's a pirate, somebody like Blackbeard for instance.*

Two hours after changing flights in Miami, Gunny landed in Norfolk, deplaned, and headed for his truck. His destination, the Hampton Public Library, located across the James River. It was time to do some research.

As he rambled through the stacks, he must have looked like a fish out of water, because a middle-aged lady with a tag on her blouse identifying her as an assistant librarian soon came to his rescue. He was looking for books on pirates and particularly Blackbeard, he told her. The lady scurried into the stacks, returning with a mountain of books almost as tall as she was.

Gunny read intensely for the next two hours until eventually his long day caught up with him. Surrendering to total exhaustion, he called a temporary halt to his research and checked in at the nearby Radisson. For the next three days, he continued his research, studying every available resource on pirates, particularly on Blackbeard. *Maybe, just maybe, he could put together a composite which might somehow lead him to Mandy.*

CHAPTER

37

SHE DRIFTED from the coldness of reality to the warmth of fantasy. Even in her lucid moments, she could make no sense of what was happening to her.

She looked around through the blackness but was only able to distinguish the shadowy outline of her doorless, rectangular prison, the brick walls of which extended as high as she could see. Her living area was small, less than eight feet across, and damp and musty. There was a chill that caused goose pimples on her naked arm, which protruded out from under the single blanket covering her frail body.

Soon, she fainted back into oblivion, where she remained for a time. Eventually, however, she was forced to open her eyes to the continuing horror of her hellish dungeon. This time when she awoke, she sensed something was different. She felt warmer, much warmer than before. Exploring her bedding with her hands, she felt the weight of a second blanket and wondered how it got there.

As more time passed, it began to seem as though she were being watched, but when she looked up, only brick walls stared down at her from as high up as she could see.

After a time, she began to perceive the light from above was gradually getting brighter. She discerned movement as the light moved closer and closer to her. Futilely, she tried to stare through the increasing brightness, but the blinding glare forced her to look away.

Fear induced panic, her heart racing and her breaths quickening. She pulled the covers over her head as if she could hide from the impending answer she desperately wanted but was afraid to face.

Something clattered on the floor nearby. *Was it a small animal, maybe? Oh, God, not rats!* Then, there was a rough, sliding noise. Holding her breath, she felt the throbbing of her heart which beat like a bass drum.

Now, desperate to end this horrid existence, she gathered the courage to peek out from under the blankets. It was then she saw it! Peering through the glare, she glimpsed the hulking mass edging down a rope ladder, a mass so large, it now eclipsed the beam of light. In seconds, it would be on top of her.

Desperately, with all her heart and soul, she wanted to escape this thing that was descending upon her. Nevertheless, despite her efforts, when she tried to push herself out of its way, she was too weak and too terrified to move.

She struggled to roll off the cot and onto the floor. She had to get out of its path, but it was too late - she was trapped. The mass was now over her, straddling her frail body. She tried to scream, but an immense hand covered her mouth while thick fingers grappled with her gown, pulling it up. The last thing she remembered was her panties being snatched down. As the nauseating reality of what was about to happen entered her panic-stricken mind, mercifully, she lapsed into semi-consciousness.

Hours had passed, how many, she could not say. She opened her eyes once again. She had no concept of how long it had been since the horrible man had left, but she was grateful he was gone.

She felt more alert now, like she had awakened from a long night's sleep. As she sat up, her legs hanging off the cot, she felt an aching sensation in her breasts. When she moved her legs, there was a painful rawness between them.

She pushed herself off the cot and stood up. A little shaky on her feet at first, she had to hold her arms out for balance. Like a toddler, she hesitantly put her left foot in front of her right and took small steps until she reached the wall. Then, cautiously, she walked the perimeter of her rectangular prison, her fingers dragging along a mortar joint of this slimy brick-encased pit.

Walking blindly through the darkness, her leg bumped into something that blocked her pathway. Bending over, she touched the obstacle; it was round, bowl-like, and there was a hole in the top. She put her hand down into the hole; it felt wet. She bent down toward it and sniffed. "Yuck!" she shrieked, instantly repulsed by the smell of urine. "Oh, God. Is this my toilet?"

As she returned to her cot, she suddenly burst into tears. The repressed reality of the awful personal invasion into her body would not remain buried. No matter what she did, the memory of that loathsome man forcing her legs open kept re-surfacing in her mind. She gagged when she recalled the bad breath she had been compelled to endure when he panted lustfully against her cheeks. Even more sickening was the thought of the slobbering kisses on her mouth and the course bristles of his beard scratching her face raw. He had squeezed her small breasts until they hurt. And worse, she vaguely remembered him being inside her and the pain she'd felt as he pushed himself deeper and deeper to the end of her vagina. Desperate for his incessant pumping to stop, she faked an orgasm, which prompted him to become more gentle. Apparently he had thought she also enjoyed it. It made her nauseous to think about it.

Suddenly, interrupting the silence of the pit, a bass voice boomed down from above. "All is well," it announced.

When she looked up, all she could see was a shadow, but soon she realized something was being lowered into the pit. Momentarily, a basket landed gently on the floor beside her.

"Eat!" roared the voice.

She gazed upward. "Please, let me out of here!" she begged.

"Eat, I say!" the voice bellowed unresponsively.

Stumbling over to the basket, a picnic basket covered by a red and white checkered cloth, she removed the cloth, which set free an aroma of freshly broiled seafood. Excitedly, she removed the styrofoam cover, revealing fresh flounder, scallops, fried oysters and her favorite, fried shrimp. It was a virtual feast from the sea, freshly cooked and piping hot. There were even french fries and hushpuppies.

Feeling thin and weak, she had nearly forgotten what food looked like. Famished, she began with a hushpuppy, which tasted delicious and felt nourishing, then, voraciously, she attacked the shrimp.

As she ate, her mind wondered about this hypocrisy in which she found herself. She questioned why this man would imprison her in this pit, rape her repeatedly and treat her like an animal, yet after all that, prepare for her this fantastic meal. Mandy suddenly paused as an appalling thought entered her mind - *Could he be fattening me up for the kill?*

38

GRAYSON AWAKENED to the hellish thoughts of yesterday. The jury's death verdict seemed like a shadowy fig-
ment of his imagination, but the ever-present ache in his
heart made him acutely aware it was indeed real.

As his feet hit the floor, he reflected on Martina, who
had left the night before to fly back to the Caymans. She
wanted to be with her mother when she broke the bad news
about Dani's death sentence.

The night before at the airport, they had hugged affec-
tionately and said warm goodbyes. Watching her walk away
to board the plane was terribly upsetting.

Now, having mustered the fortitude to face the day, he
stripped off his boxer shorts and stepped into the shower
where the hot water in his face felt soothing. "Maybe I'll
live after all," he mumbled feebly.

After a Krispy Kreme donut and hot coffee from the
drive-thru, Grayson arrived at his office, sat down at his
desk and opened a paperback manual labeled, *Guide to Fast
Track Capital Appeals.* He had to determine what course
lay ahead for Dani Alverez.

According to the guide, Grayson himself would be pro-
hibited from handling the appeal since there was the po-

tential for a conflict of interest. Rather, new lawyers would have to be appointed.

The appeal would be on an extremely tight schedule—thirty days for the briefs, thirty days more for oral arguments before a joint panel of judges from the Virginia Supreme Court as well as the U.S. Court of Appeals. If error or violation of Constitutional rights were found, the execution would be stayed. Otherwise, the death sentence would remain on the fast track, and Dani would be executed on schedule—November 22nd.

For the next two days, Grayson pored through the ten volume, 1597 page trial transcript, taking notes and making memos of potential error. He specifically sought out instances where Judge Bullins had been blatantly one-sided and unfair. To his great dismay, however, the written words of the transcript reflected neither the judge's scouring expressions nor the prejudicial inflections in his voice. Also, it failed to disclose the judge's condescending attitude, an attitude, which had conveyed to the jury that Dani was guilty as sin.

As Grayson began his second reading of the transcript, he couldn't help but think how dangerous judges like the Honorable Buford Bullins were to the freedom of our great country.

*

In another part of the Commonwealth, a very jubilant, highly restricted private celebration was being held. Governor Brotherton's retreat, nestled in the mountains near Galax, Virginia, was the site of this elite event. Prominent party loyals had been invited for a lavish, aristocratic affair resembling a private caucus but with caviar and champagne.

Governor Brotherton entered the great ballroom of his Victorian mansion, crossed the foyer and climbed half-way up the spiral staircase. Smiling, he greeted his guests below, all of whom were wealthy conservatives devoutly loyal to his cause.

He raised his cordless microphone. "May I have your attention please!" he said, his resonant voice electrifying to his guests. The chatter immediately quieted, one hundred faces instantly looking up as he stood on the staircase like a king.

The great hall was totally quiet until Brotherton broke the silence as his microphone generated a static squeak.

"Ladies and gentlemen," he began, his voice deep and controlled. "I'm here to say thank you for your faith and trust in me. With your support, our new criminal legislation is proving that we can take America back from the criminals who have threatened our entire system of justice. Ladies and gentlemen, justice will be avenged when the murderer is put to death on national television!"

Intermittently, the crowd applauded enthusiastically, but when the governor raised his hands, the room always fell quiet.

Brotherton, abounding with energy, continued to steam ahead. "Ladies and gentlemen, this murderer will be put to death on the 22nd day of November, exactly 116 days from now. With your support, I propose on that day, we announce our new outline for America."

He smiled graciously as his guests interrupted with more applause, which quickly faded when their exalted leader's expression turned solemn. After a moment of silence, so silent you could hear the crickets chirping outside, Brotherton, a twinkle in his eye, made his long-planned declaration.

"Ladies and gentlemen," he boldly proclaimed, "I hereby humbly accept your challenge. On November 22nd I will announce our candidacy for the President of the United States!"

The ballroom became instantly silent as the elite group stared at the governor, everyone totally mesmerized. This was breaking news!

For a moment, the faithful patrons seemed locked in a

time warp, everyone astounded such a profound announcement had just been made before their very eyes. This was history in the making! The silence was soon interrupted when someone began to clap, others quickly joining in, until finally, thundering applause enveloped the entire ballroom.

Savoring the moment, Alexander S. Brotherton smiled approvingly at his ability to bring a crowd to such a frenzy. He now felt certain his plan was going to work because these dedicated supporters would literally walk off a cliff for him. They were his, just like the rest of America was going to be.

CHAPTER
39

THE DAY after the death verdict, Dani had been transported to maximum security at the Commonwealth's most secure prison, located in Mecklenburg County. Not coincidentally, this also was the site of Virginia's newly reinstated electric chair. There, in a block containing 125 other condemned men, Dani was locked away in a six foot by eight foot cell. Because of the new fast track law, Dani's execution date was given top billing, even though he was the row's newest resident.

*

Bleak and dismal, death row was a constant wide-awake nightmare. Dani could neither understand nor accept this terrible thing that had befallen him. Even as a child, he had felt a strong faith in God's plan, but now, he began to doubt faith was going to be enough.

Good fortune did finally smile on him, however. He met the prison chaplain, Father O'Reilly, a short, rotund man who had joined the priesthood and dedicated himself to prison ministry. In his twenty-seven years as a prison chaplain, he had met thousands of prisoners, most of whom were guilty, but many had stubbornly maintained their innocence until the bitter end.

To Father O'Reilly, Dani Alverez seemed different. His whole persona was that of a kind-spirited, truly good man. During their daily visits, they would read the Bible and discuss its divine message and how it related to Dani's life on death row. Dani continued to struggle with the destiny that had befallen him.

*

Although Grayson was no longer officially Dani's lawyer, he could not focus on anything except Dani and Martina. Tormented by his role in the ill-fated defense, he allowed himself to be haunted by his performance as he harangued himself about what he might have done differently.

Much to his delight, bright and early on the tenth day after her departure, Martina showed up in his office. They embraced warmly, and she confessed how much she had missed him. She was chirpy and full of herself, and before Grayson could say a word, she was spouting encouragement. Martina was so stunning and full of hope Grayson couldn't help but become energized. Still he didn't have a clue about what else he might do. Except, of course, there was that crazy Marine out there chasing Blackbeard's ghost.

"Rots of ruck on that," Grayson quipped.

*

For much of the next four weeks, Martina and Grayson were together constantly. They brainstormed for ideas, researched the Constitutional issues, and twice a week, Martina would travel to Mecklenburg prison to visit Dani. But the problem was—time was racing by and they were gettng nowhere fast!

CHAPTER
40

MARTINA AND Grayson's relationship grew closer than ever. They spent nearly every waking hour together. Nevertheless, it never failed, Martina would always insist on going home promptly at midnight.

It was quarter 'til twelve, the first Friday in October. They sat on Grayson's sofa watching the late night news on television. Grayson, in his favorite blue jean cutoffs and a Washington Redskins T-shirt, couldn't take his eyes off Martina who had changed from her formal business suit into her white shorts and Dive Cayman tank top. She was braless with just the tip of her nipples outlined through the thin top.

Grayson could not shake his crush on her. He had never known anyone so beautiful, nor so perfect in every way. Trying to snap out of his smitten state, he stepped into the kitchen, hoping to exchange his love sickness for a chocolate chip cookie. "Want a cookie, Marty?" he asked.

She shook her head, then paused, her brown eyes looking up at him alluringly. "Just come over here," she murmured softly.

His need for a chocolate chip cookie instantly evaporated. He hastened back to the sofa and eagerly, optimistically, placed his hand on the back of Martina's neck. Scrunching down beside her, he nudged closer, his hopes high that tonight might be the night he'd been long awaiting.

As he gazed into her eyes, his right hand slyly slid around her neck and accidently - on purpose - dropped gently down onto her shoulder. They seemed magnetically drawn together.

Their lips connected, and Grayson's hand meandered across her chest, coming to rest near the v-neck of her tank top. Tightly, they embraced. She did not resist.

Again, their lips touched. As Grayson allowed his hand to slide down between Martina's luscious breasts, her hand dropped and gently came to rest on his inner thigh. Their passions rose, their breaths quickening. The time had finally arrived! Grayson was sure of it. But then, tactlessness overruled his good judgment.

"You know, Marty," he whispered, "I'd never kissed a black girl before you."

Martina pulled back. "Is that right? So what do you think?" she said, miffed by the distinction he seemed to be making.

"It's no different than kissing a white girl," Grayson replied dumbly.

Martina pushed him back, then sprang upright.

"Well, thanks a lot!" she snapped. "Maybe you should go find yourself a white girl!"

"No, no! I didn't mean it like that."

"Grayson, I know what you meant, and you know, you're not bad yourself." Martina hesitated as an agonizing expression scrolled onto her face.

"But, Gray," she finally said, her voice strained, "I don't know about this relationship."

"But...but Marty." Grayson was stammering.

"Gray, listen," she said grimly. "We come from very different ethnic backgrounds. Maybe this whole thing is wrong."

Grayson sat there feeling stupid he had even broached the subject of kissing a black woman.

41

TIME WAS slipping away—only six weeks left before Dani was to die. After his Hampton library research, Gunny had scouted through most of coastal North Carolina, looking for any clues as to his daughter's whereabouts. He had even toured the Blackbeard exhibit at ECU where artifacts from the recently discovered *Queen Ann's Revenge*, Blackbeard's heralded flag-ship, were on display.

Gunny extended the range of his nightly bar hopping, now traveling to the outlying counties of Beaufort, Hyde, Pamlico, and Dare. Regrettably, however, despite his valiant efforts, he was still nowhere in his quest to find Mandy. But, he did have an idea!

Gunny let his mind slide off into the world of far-fetched fantasy. He realized he was toying with the incredulous, but at long last, he could stand it no longer; he had to tell Grayson about his crazy idea. He phoned and Grayson answered on the second ring. Exhilaration was apparent in Gunny's voice.

"By day, I'm a nerdy book worm, and by night, I'm an O'Doul's drinking barfly."

Grayson, only mildly humored, shook his head in frustration. "That's just great, Gunny, but do you have any leads, anything at all that might help us?"

Gunny was a motor mouth. "I've been to every library around, and I've checked all the courthouse records in most of the counties of eastern North Carolina. I've got some leads, but so far they don't seem to be getting me anywhere."

"Gunny, we're open to any ideas, far out or not. As you know, we're desperate."

Gunny paused, then let go with his strange theory. "All right, now listen!" he said, his voice half giddy. History tells us that Edward Teach, Blackbeard, temporarily gave up pirating and settled in Bath, North Carolina, Bath Towne as they used to call it. He even got married; married a young girl named Mary Ormond who was pregnant when he was killed at Ocracoke."

"So what happened to the child?"

Gunny's voice dropped. "What I'm trying to tell you," he said, distinctly enunciating each and every syllable, "is - Blackbeard - died - in - 1718 - and - his - child - was - born - in - mid -1719."

Gunny, beginning to sound like a history professor, told Grayson about William Ormond, the first sheriff of Bath Towne and Wyriott Ormond, Bath Towne's representative to the North Carolina General Assembly in 1746.

There was a long period of silence as Grayson tried to assimilate the significance of what he had just heard. Finally, he shook his head. "Just what are you getting at?"

"Well, what if this somehow leads us up the family tree to the kidnapper and then to Mandy?"

"That's sure a long shot," Grayson replied, his eyes squenching, his face furrowing.

"Well, anyway, I'm going down to Bath and look around. Want to come with me?"

"I guess. It's better than sitting here in Hampton counting the cockroaches crawling across the carpet."

"Okay, y'all meet me at the Bath Visitor's Center at noon tomorrow."

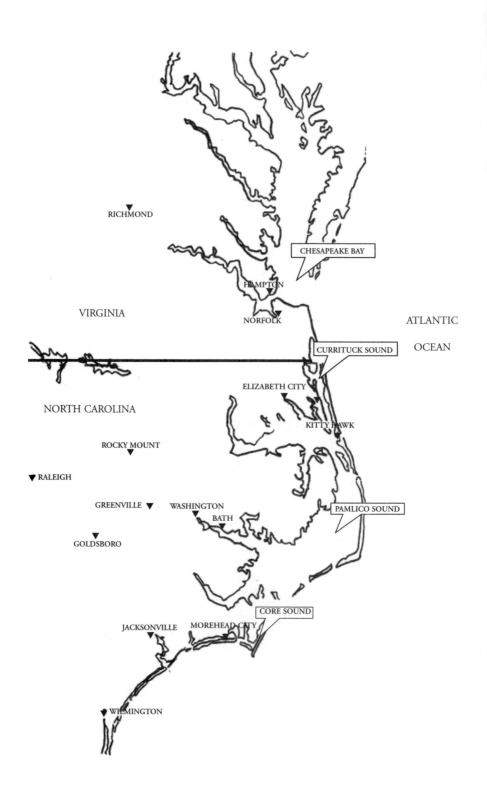

RICHMOND

CHESAPEAKE BAY

VIRGINIA

HAMPTON

NORFOLK

ATLANTIC

OCEAN

CURRITUCK SOUND

NORTH CAROLINA

ELIZABETH CITY

KITTY HAWK

ROCKY MOUNT

RALEIGH

GREENVILLE   WASHINGTON

BATH

PAMLICO SOUND

GOLDSBORO

CORE SOUND

JACKSONVILLE   MOREHEAD CITY

WILMINGTON

CHAPTER
42

THE NEXT morning, Grayson and Martina headed for Bath, North Carolina, an ancient village located on the Pamlico River. The three-hour drive took them through Elizabeth City, Williamston, and little Washington, where they turned east on Highway 264. They found themselves passing through a bucolic countryside lined with furrowed tobacco fields and dotted with houses, mobile homes, and an occasional mom and pop general store.

After crossing the bridge at Bath Creek where scores of sailboats bobbed at their mooring lines, a drastic change in the scenery occurred. It was almost like the hands of time had been turned back two centuries. Surrounded by calm blue water, the quaint village of Bath lay on a peninsula, its streets lined with well-kept homes of yesteryear. One could almost envision Blackbeard himself sauntering along the creek bank.

Parking beside a modern brick structure, the Bath Welcome Center, the only person in sight was Gunny. He was standing beside his truck, a look of impatience on his face.

After a grumpy, it's-about-time greeting from him, the threesome entered the building, where they were welcomed by a tall, white-haired lady standing behind a counter.

"Hello, welcome to Bath. North Carolina's first town. I'm Lora Greene."

"Hello," Grayson said, a smile on his face. "So this is where Blackbeard used to hang out?"

Mrs. Greene, dressed in Colonial attire, smiled broadly. "It sure is. Would you like a tour?"

"We sure would, Ma'am, and we have a few questions for you," Grayson replied.

Mrs. Greene directed them to her blue Honda out in the parking lot.

"If y'all will just jump in, I'll show you around."

With Gunny in the front passenger seat and Martina and Grayson in the back, Mrs. Greene drove a block to the historic village. "Folks," she said, beginning her canned tour speech, "this is the oldest town in North Carolina, established in 1705." She drove three more blocks, passing a number of century-old creek-front homes. Slowing down, she extended her arm and pointed out the car window.

"That's St. Thomas Church. I'm a member there. It's the oldest existing church in North Carolina and one of the earliest built in the state."

A few blocks further, she stopped at the Bonner House. As they stood on the expansive front porch, Mrs. Greene directed the group's attention to the panoramic view to the south. "If you'll look out Bath Creek as far as you can see, you'll see the Pamlico River. They say Blackbeard used to sail right up toward us into the creek." Mrs. Greene nodded toward a peninsula that jutted out from the eastern bank. "He'd hide his ship on this side of that furthermost point."

"Is that where Blackbeard lived?" Gunny inquired.

"It is," Mrs. Greene replied. "The story goes he married a local girl, Mary Ormond, and they lived in a house on Plum Point. Some say Governor Eden and Blackbeard were in cahoots. Supposedly, Blackbeard would bring his booty from his pirating adventures in here and split it with the governor."

"Ma'am," Gunny asked, "Is it true Mary Ormond had Blackbeard's child?"

"So the story goes, but no one ever confirmed it. But, the Ormond name was very prominent in these parts and remains so today."

"Has anyone around here ever claimed to be a descendant of Blackbeard?" Gunny asked, knowing this was a real long shot.

Mrs. Greene paused, a slight grin on her face. Well," she said, "my husband's great, great aunt used to spin a yarn about that. She claimed to have some kind of a Blackbeard connection, but to tell you the truth, folks around here never put much stock in it."

"I guess she's not around any more, huh?" Grayson asked, feeling somebody's great, great aunt must have passed on a long time ago.

"Oh yes, she's alive and well."

"Really?" Grayson's interest was piquing.

"Samantha is the oldest Ormond I know of. Her name is Samantha Broadnax Greene, and she's probably a hundred years old. She's in a nursing home in little Washington."

"Do you know which one?" Grayson asked anxiously.

"Yes, I think it's called the Whispering Pines."

With Gunny's truck in the lead, they retraced their path back to Washington. After a quick stop at a convenience store to check a phone directory, they headed for the Whispering Pines Rest Home, located just off the same road they were on, Highway 264.

They parked their vehicles side by side in the pine tree-speckled parking lot, then rushed inside the nursing home, where they were greeted by a young lady at the front desk. Grayson asked to see Samantha Greene.

The young lady asked them to follow her down a dimly lit hallway past a row of opened-door rooms. Entering the activity room, they saw a number of elderly women in wheelchairs. One lady was moaning and begging for help. Another, mucous on her face, gazed out the window, a faraway look in her eyes.

"That's Mrs. Greene over there," the receptionist said, pointing to a white-haired lady clad in a blue nightgown. She was sitting in a wheelchair, apparently totally engrossed in an Atlanta Braves ball game on the big screen television in front of her.

Grayson approached her. "Mrs. Greene? Excuse me, ma'am, but are you Mrs. Greene?"

The lady looked his way, a surprised expression on her face. "Yes, I am. Who are you?" she asked sharply.

Grayson was not expecting her quick retort.

"Uh, I'm Grayson Forrest. I'm a lawyer from Hampton, Virginia; I need your help."

"What in heaven's name do you want with me?" she replied spritely, her thin, wrinkled face suddenly brightening at the unexpected attention.

Grayson pulled up a chair and sat down beside her, while Gunny and Martina sat on a nearby sofa opposite her.

"Ma'am," Grayson began, "we're working on a case that involves the life or death of two young people. In trying to solve this case, it's very important for us to locate a man who might be a distant relative of yours."

The question mark in Mrs. Greene's eyes instantly vanished. "I'll bet you've been talking to 'em down at the tourist center in Bath, haven't you?"

"Yes, we have," Grayson admitted. "Can you help us?"

Mrs. Greene beamed, her voice rising a full octave. "I'll be glad to tell you everything I know about my family's Blackbeard connection."

"You figured out my question without even being asked," Grayson replied, returning the smile.

Martina and Gunny sat on the edge of their seats, both leaning toward Mrs. Greene. They were all ears.

"It's like this," she began. "I'm one hundred two years old. When I was a little girl, seven or eight years old, my grandma Broadnax used to tell me stories she had learned from her great-grandmother. You see, my grandmother's great-grandmother's mother was Mary Ormond."

"Wow!" Grayson exclaimed exuberantly, as if he had just discovered the Comstock Lode.

Mrs. Greene, her eyes sparkling, making her look thirty years younger, could hardly wait to tell her story. "Anyway," she hastened to say, "when Mary was a young girl, she married Blackbeard, but after only a few months, the old pirate was killed over at Ocracoke."

It was obvious Mrs. Greene enjoyed telling this story, her voice now sounding rhythmic and cheerful. "You understand, Mary was pregnant and only fifteen years old." Mrs. Greene's eyes widened as she shook her head in wonderment. "Can you imagine? At that young age, Mary Ormond was the widow of the most notorious pirate in history?"

Her small audience listened in fascination. "Please tell us more," Grayson implored.

Relishing the attention, Mrs. Greene anxiously continued. "Well, they say Mary and her father, Caleb, who would be my great, great, great, great-grandfather, fled the area because of all the bad gossip against her. Some of `em were calling her a witch and were saying things like she was carrying the devil's child and awful things like that."

"What happened to them?" Gunny inquired.

Mrs. Greene smiled, revealing a perfect set of dentures. "They went way off somewhere and Mary had her baby. It's thought they left the baby with a family who lived up on the Albemarle Sound. After that, Mary came back to Bath and made up a story about the baby dying at childbirth. Later on, she married a fisherman named Broadnax from Bath and lived a quiet life and really wasn't heard of much after that."

"So, would Blackbeard be your great, great, great-grandfather?" Grayson inquired.

"No, I don't think so. You see, Mary Ormond had other children in her new marriage. My great, great, great-grandfather was Thomas Broadnax, the fisherman she married when she returned to Bath after giving birth to Blackbeard's child."

The threesome were spellbound by the story. "What happened to the baby Mary left up near the Albemarle?" Gunny interjected, hopeful for a family tree hookup to the big bearded kidnapper.

"Supposedly," Mrs. Greene said, continuing as if she had told the story many times before, "Mary Ormond died during the birth of her fourth child, never seeing her son by Blackbeard again."

"Did anyone?" Gunny asked.

"Yes, we think so," Mrs. Greene said as she turned to face Gunny. "Mary's daughter, Caroline, who I think would be my great, great, great-aunt, saw a man a few times who claimed to be her half brother and the son of Blackbeard. She wrote in her diary that a young man came to the family farm near Bath Town. He was very tall, quite stout, with a heavy beard." Suddenly, Mrs. Greene paused. "Excuse me, but would you hand me that cup of water?" Mrs. Greene pointed toward a cup on the nearby table.

Grayson handed her the cup and she took a sip of water, then resumed her story.

"Well, anyway, we think he was Blackbeard's son."

There was silence.

"Go ahead, Mrs. Greene," Grayson urged.

"Well, that's where the story stops. That's really all I know."

"That's it?" Grayson replied. "Surely there's more."

"Nope! That's it!"

"Isn't there someone else who could verify this, Mrs. Greene?" Martina inquired politely.

"No, except the family Bible could have." Immediately, however, Mrs. Greene began to shake her head in long-endured despair. Finally, she added a sad addendum to her story. "You see, the Bible along with Caroline's diary and everything else I owned burned in a fire more'n eighty years ago." That said, Samantha went silent, her head bending forward as she focused on the floor.

After a few moments, Grayson interrupted her trance-like mood. "Mrs. Greene, are you sure there's nothing else you can tell us?"

Her eyes traveled slowly up from the floor to meet Grayson's inquiry.

"Well," she said as though she were reluctant to broach the subject. "There was a man, I hear, who was actually a distant relative of sorts, and used to hang around Bath a few years ago claiming to be related to Blackbeard. I never saw him, but they tell me he really did look like a pirate."

"Really, how do you know this?" Gunny inquired.

"My grandson, Archie Greene. He owns the marina down there in Bath. Go talk to him, he'll know about it."

CHAPTER
43

WITH GUNNY'S truck again in the lead, they re-crossed Bath Creek Bridge and passed back through the village. When they arrived at a small marina on the right, both vehicles pulled up and parked next to the boat ramp.

The unlikely trio entered the bait shop where a young lady stood behind the counter. Gunny asked if Archie Greene were there, and the lady, in the midst of a cloud of exhaled cigarette smoke, nodded toward the back door.

"Grandpa's out there fishin'."

They walked out the back door onto the porch, which overlooked the creek where they saw an elderly man in bib coveralls. The scrubby-faced senior citizen was seated in a lawn chair, a fishing rod in his hands and two paper cups on the porch railing in front of him. A purple and gold cap on his head, gray hair frizzing out underneath, he appeared to be seventyish. His eyes were unswervingly fixed on a red float bobbing in the waters of Back Creek.

"Mr. Greene. Are you Mr. Greene?" Grayson asked.

"Yeah, what'd ya want?" the man snapped.

Grayson introduced himself, then explained that Greene's grandmother had suggested they talk to him.

"I'll be damned!" Archie exclaimed. "Has Granny Sam

been tellin' them stories again?" His frown deepened.

"Sir," Grayson quickly responded. "We need to find out about a man you know who claims he's a descendant of Blackbeard."

Archie looked up from his fishing, as a scornful stare on his face homed directly in on Grayson. "Why in the hell would you be lookin' for that son-na-bitch?"

"You mean you know who we're talking about?"

"It sounds like you're talking about that damn fool distant cousin of mine, Toby Greene. He used ta go round callin' hisself Blackbeard. But you know," Archie said, shaking his head disgustingly, "Toby's crazy as a loon."

"What does Toby look like?" Gunny asked, pleased Archie was becoming somewhat more conversant.

Archie suddenly jerked upward with his fishing rod.

"It's the same damn one! He bites at the same damn place, same damn time every damn day."

Archie began to wind his baitcaster reel vigorously. "By Gawd, I got him this time!"

A silver glimmer flapped about beneath the water as it was drawn slowly toward them. Just as the fish got within reach, it thrashed and jerked violently, and in a flash, it was off the hook, disappearing back into the depths of Back Creek.

Archie angrily popped the shaft of his fishing rod against the railing and shook his head in disgust. "Damn! Damn! Damn!" he exclaimed.

Waiting a moment for Archie to calm down, finally, Grayson, his words cautious, asked, "Now sir, about this Toby Greene. What does he look like?"

Archie spit a stream of brown liquid into one of the cups on the rail. "Well, he does look the part. He's probably six-foot four, maybe taller, and he must weigh nigh onto 260 or 70 pounds. He has a thick black beard, but if he's Blackbeard's relative, I'll kiss your butt."

Archie took a swig of clear liquid from one of the cups, then put it back on the rail beside the other cup.

"Have you seen him lately?" Grayson asked as he wondered how Archie could chew tobacco and drink at the same time.

Archie scratched the stubble on his chin. "I reckon I ain't seen nary a hair of him in a month of Sundays."

"How old is Toby?" Grayson asked as he pondered - *How long is a month of Sundays?*

"I reckon he's forty or so. He grew up somewhere up `round the Pungo or maybe the Alligator River."

"Does he have a boat?" Grayson asked.

After spitting a stream of tobacco juice up and over the railing, Archie wiped the brown slime from his mouth with the back of his hand.

"He used-ta have a deadrise fishin boat." Archie's words were slow and mushmouthed. "Uh, but it seems like somebody said they saw him a while back in some kinda' fancy play-purdy boat."

"What kind of a fancy boat was it?" Gunny asked.

"Damn if I know; never seen it, just heard about it," Archie said as he spit out another spurt, which arced out over the rail.

"Do you know if he has family up there where he grew up?" Martina asked.

"Oh yeah, his mama's Minerva Greene. She lives up 'bout Englehard. They're some kin to us, but we ain't never had much to do with 'em. Sort'a felt like they was white trash, ya know?"

After thanking Archie for his help, the trio departed. Walking back to the Cherokee, Grayson told Gunny he had to be in court tomorrow in Hampton, so he would have to be heading home.

Gunny's adrenalin was churning. "Not me, man! I'm going to spend the night around here and check out Minerva up in Englehard tomorrow."

CHAPTER
44

BRIGHT AND early the next morning Gunny was up
and out, heading for Englehard, located on the banks of
the Pamlico Sound. He drove through the quaint village
of Belhaven, known for the River Forest Manor, a popular stopover for yachtsmen traveling the Intracoastal Waterway. Some miles farther down the road, he passed the
shoreline of Lake Mattamuskeet, a fifty thousand acre
water fowl refuge.

Reaching for a cigarette, Gunny found his Camel pack
empty. Longing for a smoke, his heavy foot mashed down
on the gas pedal, pushing the speedometer needle to 80
miles an hour. He whizzed past soybean fields, mobile
homes, scrubby forests and swamps, but still, there was no
sign of a tobacco outlet.

Finally, after crossing into the town limits of Englehard,
the Ram pickup screeched to a halt at a convenience store,
where Gunny bought cigarettes and got directions to
Minerva Greene's trailer.

Five minutes later, he pulled into a dirt driveway, which
led up to a mobile home. No vehicles were visible in the
unkept yard, strewn with old tires, an engine block, an old
outboard motor and miscellaneous debris. In a ditch beside

the driveway lay a small fishing skiff in desperate need of a patch job. The mobile home was rusting and in a state of general disrepair. A cement block was used as a step up to the front door.

Gunny, standing on the cement block, knocked on the door. "Hello, is anybody home?" Momentarily, he felt movement inside. Somebody had to be there.

The door finally opened and the figure of a large woman became visible through the rusty wire mesh of the screen door. "What do you want?" she asked, a suspicious tone in her voice.

"My name is Lincoln Vernon," Gunny answered politely. "I'm looking for your son."

The lady moved closer to the screen door. "Has he done something wrong?"

"Well, ma'am, I'm not sure, but it sounds like he may know the whereabouts of my fifteen year old daughter. Please ma'am, I really need your help!"

"Just a minute. I just put some tea on the stove; let me turn it down." She departed but soon returned and unlatched the screen door and pushed it open. "Come in."

Gunny entered the trailer, which was furnished with a shabby, rose-colored sofa, some hard back chairs and a small formica and chrome dinette table.

The woman, wearing a frayed Carolina blue house coat and dirty white bedroom slippers, appeared uncomfortable and fidgety. Gunny surmised he was not the first person to have visited Minerva Greene seeking information on the whereabouts of her son.

"Have a seat," she said, pointing to a cane back chair by the chrome dinette table.

Gunny sat down across the table from Minerva. She was a large woman, probably six-feet tall and weighing well over two hundred pounds. Her deeply furrowed face caused Gunny to speculate she must be in her late sixties or early seventies.

"Okay, what's this all about?" she said haltingly, an expression of consternation on her face.

Gunny told his story, omitting accusations of Toby's wrongdoing. He told her about a man dressed like a pirate who had been seen with his daughter, but he was exceedingly careful not to use the word, "kidnapped." Rather, he tried to project the image of a concerned father who just wanted to find his wayward daughter.

"Sir, I don't think it was my Toby," Minerva said, her voice firm. "He hasn't been in trouble for a good while." Her sad eyes looked at Gunny pleadingly. "Please mister, leave him alone. Give him a chance to get his life together."

Gunny, not surprised a mother would take up for her son, knew he would have to be tactful if he were to get any information out of Mrs. Greene about her n'er-do-well offspring.

"Ma'am," Gunny said, "This is a photograph of my daughter. She's fifteen years old." Gunny handed the picture to Mrs. Greene.

"This is your daughter?"

"Well, actually, she's my adopted daughter. Her mother and I married when she was just a little girl."

There was a long period of silence. Finally, Minerva responded, her voice beginning to quake nervously. "I hate to admit it, but this does look like the little girl Toby had down here a few months ago."

"You saw her!" Gunny's heart leaped. "Please, tell me! Was she all right?"

"Of course she was! She looked just fine to me. You see, Toby stopped by to check on me, and this little girl was out in his pickup. I walked him to his truck when he left, and that's when I seen her."

"Did you talk to her?" Gunny asked, now so anxious he was about to burst out of his skin.

"Well, no. She didn't have nothin' to say, but she looked all right to me." Minerva rubbed her cheek, then added, "I asked Toby who she was, and he said she was just a little girl he was helpin' out. A few minutes later they just drove off, and I really ain't seen Toby since."

"How come?"

"I reckon, 'cause the law's been lookin' for him. You see, some busy-body social worker saw Toby and this little girl together and reported it to the high sheriff, so they come out a lookin' for him."

"So what happened?"

"Well, Toby don't take too well to no law, so he went into hidin' for a spell."

"He's been in trouble with the law before?"

"I'm afraid he has, but he's done so well since he got out the last time," Minerva said, her eyes dropping as she stared down at the floor.

"Ma'am, I've really got to find my daughter. You must know where he's hiding out! I'll pay you. I'll give you and Toby both a reward just to bring Mandy back to me. I promise there'll be no questions asked."

"I really don't know where he is. I ain't seen him for several months." Minerva paused, her expression becoming very solemn. Finally, with resolve in her voice, she said, "That's all I'm goin' to say." Her head was shaking as if she were internally denying bad thoughts about her own son.

"Well, ma'am, did Toby live with you before he took off this last time?"

"He has a room here, but he hardly ever stays in it. He likes sleepin' on his old fishin' boat."

"Would you mind if I saw his room?" Gunny asked, hopeful some clue might be disclosed.

"I reckon it wouldn't do no harm."

Minerva led Gunny through a doorway to her left into a small bedroom furnished with an extra-long single bed, a dresser and a desk. On the wall beside an empty gun rack, hung the head of a twelve point buck mounted for display.

Suddenly, the teapot whistled and Minerva abruptly rushed back to the kitchen to turn the burner down on the stove. Left temporarily unsupervised, Gunny seized the moment and quietly opened the desk drawer where he found an array of papers haphazardly scattered about. Rapidly rummaging through the contents, he found nothing of consequence until he spotted a yellow invoice from Jackson Marine Performance Engines, Inc. of Cincinnati, Ohio. Holding the invoice up to the light, an inky smudge on the sales price obscured the total amount.

Minerva's footsteps interrupted the moment. Quickly, the instant before she re-entered the room, Gunny stuffed the invoice under his shirt, then turned nonchalantly toward her.

"Mrs. Greene," he said, his voice soft, his words delicate, "May I ask you a somewhat personal question?"

"I suppose."

"Who was Toby's father? Is he still alive?"

"No, he's dead. Been dead for a long time." Minerva lowered her head, looking down longingly.

"What was his name?"

"They called him Sly Willie Greene; he was some kind of man!" she said, a loving smile flashing across her otherwise stoic face.

"Would you tell me a little about him?"

"I don't see why you'd be interested, but if you want to know..." Minerva's voice trailed off as she looked up, seemingly willing to share her memories of Sly Willie.

Gunny sat back down in the chair.

"Thank you, ma'am, I'd really like to know."

"Willie was a rough and tough fisherman from up here in these parts. He loved to fight and was big enough to take on a whole ship load of brawlers."

"How big was he?" Gunny asked.

"He was maybe, six-foot eight and weighed over three hundred pounds." Her smile suddenly widened. "He was a whopper!"

"You loved him a lot, didn't you?"

"I did that," she said softly, as she nodded devotedly, her thoughts still dwelling on her memories.

"What ever happened to him?"

Minerva, her trip back to the better times of yesteryear now interrupted, wiped the tears from her cheeks as her eyes wandered toward the window.

"Well, a few years after Toby was born, Willie went out a drinkin' one night and got to fightin'. Some old man from up 'bout the Albemarle took a shot at him. Well, you just didn't do that to my Willie. Willie beat the man to death."

"What happened?"

Minerva, tears still sliding down her cheeks, shook her head. "They had a trial and found him guilty and gave him life in prison." Minerva hung her head. "My man got killed in prison the next year."

"I'm sorry." After a polite pause, he proceeded with his inquiry. "Ma'am do you know anything about Sly Willie's parents and grandparents?"

"I knew his father; Willie looked just like him."

"What'd you know about him?"

"They called him Elder Greene. He was as mean and hateful a man as you'd ever find," Minerva said, wrinkling her nose. "I was glad when he got shot by the law back when Toby was just a baby."

"Did you ever hear anything about Sly Willie's grandfather?"

"Well, I never knew him, but I do know his name was Elder, also, Elder, Sr. Some of 'em said he drowned when the *Titanic* sank," Minerva said, shrugging her shoulders. "I really don't know if that's true or not; they used to tell me all kinds of stuff like that. Then, they'd laugh at me if I acted like I believed 'em."

Minerva seemed tired and upset, causing Gunny to sense he should be leaving. After thanking her, he gave her his phone number, then exited the trailer, stepping down onto the cement block. But a feeling of concern made him look back up at her. *God, I feel sorry for this decent woman and the curse of life that has befallen her,* he thought.

45

GUNNY'S NEXT stop was the Hyde County Sheriff's Office in Swan Quarter, an old-fashioned little village on the Pamlico Sound. There, he explained to a deputy-sergeant about his missing daughter and the Toby Greene connection.

The deputy listened politely, then shook his head.

"Mr. Vernon, we're looking for him here in Hyde and also in Dare and Beaufort Counties, but he's pretty slippery."

"What can you tell me about him?"

"He's bad news. Toby's been a troublemaker in these parts ever since I can remember. He's mean and he's smart. Not to alarm you, sir, but if your daughter's with him, then, she's in big trouble!"

The deputy-sergeant ushered Gunny into his office where he pulled a folder from a metal file cabinet.

"This is Toby's criminal record." The deputy held a thick multi-folded computer printout above his head, allowing it to flip-flop down until it touched the floor.

Reading from the printout, the sergeant enumerated Toby's convictions. "Indecent liberties with a minor; three convictions for that, and there's a bunch of assault charges." Pausing as he scrolled further down the printout, the deputy soon began shaking his head. "Now I remember this one.

Should've been murder, but it got reduced to manslaughter. Toby beat a kid to death with a baseball bat. I mean he's a bad one!" The deputy, a kindly expression of compassion in his eyes, turned to face Gunny. "Do you really think the little girl they saw him with was your daughter?"

Gunny nodded, his worst fears now justified. "Do you have a photo of him?"

The sergeant handed him a photocopy of a mug shot, a big, bearded man with dark menacing eyes and a cold, merciless expression.

As Gunny climbed into his truck, a rustle of papers in his midsection drew his attention to the yellow invoice he'd swiped from Toby's room. Pulling it out and unfolding it, he studied the ink-splotched figures on the paper. He couldn't make out whether the invoice amount from Jackson Marine was for $650, $6,500, $65,000 or even more. He decided to call the Cincinnati phone number on the invoice.

After three rings, a perky female voice answered, referring him to the company president, Wyatt Jackson. Gunny was candid. He explained the entire situation to Jackson and asked if he recalled Toby Greene.

"Yes I do," Jackson replied. "It was about a year ago. Mr. Greene showed up at our shop here in Cincinnati driving a tractor-trailer rig, towing a forty-two foot custom-made Fountain racing yacht. He hired us to totally upfit it to his specifications. It turned out to be one of the most unusual crafts we've ever worked on."

"What all did you do to it?" Gunny asked.

"Let me think," Mr. Jackson said. "We put in two large 572 cubic-inch Chevrolet bow tie engines, supercharged, of course. Each engine would put out a thousand horsepower."

"Did you do anything else?"

"I should say we did," was the emphatic reply, a ring of pride in Jackson's voice. "We installed twin Dominator carburetors, Stelling stainless steel exhausts, Gill silencers, Hurst transmissions on each engine..."

"Okay, okay," Gunny interrupted. "Uh, how fast will it go?"

"Tuned up right, she'll go over 130 miles an hour. And let me tell you what else. It's even got Aronson surface penetrating drive trains with clever props."

Gunny was clueless about most of what he had just heard; this guy might as well be talking Chinese. But, he did learn the craft was designed for a crew of two who sit side by side, each person in his very own cockpit with duplicate controls, each enclosed by an F-16 canopy.

"Can you describe the boat, sir? I mean, what's it made of; what color is it?"

"The hull is aluminum, solid black in color and shaped like a bat or a stingray." Jackson paused, then added, "Uh, no maybe more like a shark."

"Can you tell me the cost?" Gunny asked.

Mr. Jackson hesitated, then after a long pause, he said, "I don't think I should. That probably should be kept confidential."

"Well, sir," Gunny said as he held the smudged invoice out before him, "Could you just tell me this; would it be closer to $6,500, $65,000, or $650,000?"

"All I can say is that it was six figures," Jackson admitted.

As Gunny drove out of Swan Quarter, he made another cell call, this time to Grayson to tell him about all the new information he had gathered.

"Grayson, we know he's got Mandy; we know he's on the run; and we know he's in a fancy, black racing yacht. I think I'm going to have to take to the water to find this pirate."

Grayson offered the use of his 23-foot Boston Whaler.

"It's a great boat, and it won't take long to show you how to operate it," he said.

"How can you get it down here from Hampton?" Gunny asked.

"I'll bring it down the Dismal Swamp Canal and meet you in Elizabeth City."

CHAPTER
46

THE PLAN was for Grayson to ferry the Whaler down the Intracoastal Waterway and meet Gunny in Elizabeth City. Martina would drive down from Hampton and meet them there.

Grayson phoned Sunset Marina in Hampton and requested his Boston Whaler be forklifted into the water and filled with fuel. The boat, a 1989 model his father had purchased new, had a small cuddy cabin with a V-berth and a portable head. Powered by twin 135 horsepower Evinrude outboard engines, the boat's top speed was 47 miles an hour, but cruised more economically at 30.

Martina dropped Grayson off at the marina. Moments later, the Evinrudes fired alive, initially coughing out clouds of black smoke. As Grayson eased back on the choke, the twin engines began idling like a well-tuned duet. In just minutes, he had cast off, and the Whaler was creeping through the no-wake zone of Sunset Creek, headed for the nearby Hampton River.

After clearing the river shoals, Grayson turned the helm gently to starboard, forcing the bow to crab into the wind-driven current. As the boat headed out toward the blue water of Hampton Roads Harbor, its fanciful skipper glanced toward the tree-lined shore to his right and was immediately struck by a crazy irony.

There, below the treeline, was Blackbeard Point, the exact spot where Blackbeard's decapitated head had once hung after the old pirate had been killed at Ocracoke in 1718.

Now, here we are some 284 years later, once again chasing another Blackbeard of sorts, Grayson thought.

Gradually, he turned the helm to port, the ride quickly becoming rougher as a rapid rippling effect on the hull signaled the crossing of the confluence of the Elizabeth and James Rivers. The Whaler traversed Norfolk's shipping area and passed the national maritime center known as Nauticus.

Nearby, at Norfolk's famous Waterside Festival Marketplace, Grayson noticed there were thousands of people at Waterside, many decked out in pirate costumes, all gleefully dancing, drinking and frolicking around. It was a festival of some sort.

A mile further down river, the commercial atmosphere abruptly disappeared, replaced by a tree-lined, canal-like stream. Soon, a lock appeared on the horizon, which marked the beginning of the Dismal Swamp Canal, the Intracoastal Waterway passage from Virginia into North Carolina. Locking through, the Whaler was soon purring through the narrow canal, cutting its frothy path through the coffee-colored water. The beauty of the canal was striking and occasionally presented momentary interludes of quaint serenity. Gray moss hung from cypress trees that lined the banks, the gray of the moss contrasting starkly with the thick black forest background.

After an hour of snaking through the crooks and curves of the narrow waterway, the South Mills lock came into view. There, after again locking through, Grayson pushed the twin throttles forward, the engines roaring once more as the bow of the Whaler rose up and the craft zoomed down the Pasquotank River south toward Elizabeth City.

Forty minutes later, a bright blue pelican on the mustard yellow sign of the Pelican Marina greeted Grayson's arrival at his destination. There, sitting on the marina porch, Gunny was sipping on an O'Doul's, and Martina, seated next to him, was nursing a diet Pepsi. As the Whaler approached the dock, the welcome committee walked out to meet him.

"It's about time you got here," Gunny said. Martina, however, was more cordial. With a wide smile on her face, she immediately climbed on board and planted a kiss on Grayson's cheek.

Distracted for a moment, Grayson quickly re-focused.

"Okay, climb aboard," he directed, a business-like tone to his voice. "There's only another hour of daylight left, and I want you to know how to operate this boat."

With the threesome huddled behind the windshield, the Whaler headed out toward the center of the Pasquotank River where Grayson began to meticulously explain the boat's operation.

After a few minutes of instructions, Gunny stepped behind the helm. He pushed the throttles forward, and the boat quickly accelerated, soon plowing a ditch through the water. Without so much as a prompt, he expertly adjusted the trim tab controls and edged the throttles further forward, the boat now running at near top speed.

They had cruised south for ten minutes when Martina spotted an immense wooden building on the west bank of the river.

"What's that?" she asked.

"A blimp hangar," Grayson quickly replied. "Back in World War Two, they manufactured blimps over there. One of the hangars burned down in 1995, but it was rebuilt. It was from this very location the Coast Guard sent up the aerostat radar which located the red Cigarette boat that crashed into Virginia Beach."

"So, our nightmare began right here," Martina commented.

It was near dark when Gunny turned the Whaler 180

degrees and headed back toward the Pelican Marina. Running at top speed for ten minutes, their approach to the marina prompted Grayson to offer a challenge.

"Now, for your final test, Gunny. Let's see just how well you can dock her."

With the Whaler streaming along, a glimpse of a grin flashed onto Gunny's face. Abruptly, he turned the helm toward the fuel dock. Rapidly, almost too rapidly, the bow veered to port on a collision course with a piling. Instinctively, Grayson tensed, certain the speed was too fast and the angle was too sharp. But, just as he braced himself for the collision, Gunny threw the starboard engine into reverse and turned the helm slightly to port. Like magic, the boat turned and came to a dead stop perfectly parallel to and only inches from the dock.

"Not bad," Grayson conceded.

Actually, Gunny had not fully disclosed some of his own personal nautical history. He had not bothered to mention his brown water Navy days when he skippered a U.S. Marine Corps—militarized Whaler on the Viet Cong-infested Mekong River in Viet Nam. Today's little cruise was a piece of cake compared to that.

The hungry crew quickly secured the boat and headed next door to the Marina Restaurant. Seated at a table overlooking the river, they were soon enjoying sumptuous broiled red snapper and fresh vegetables.

It had been a lighthearted evening until just after the banana pudding when the mood switched from cheerful to philosophical.

Grayson stood up, his coffee cup held high.

"A toast to my friends and to our joint venture for justice," he proclaimed solemnly.

"And to my Mandy," Gunny declared as he shot to his feet, coffee cup also held upward. "Please, Lord, let me find her safe."

Martina, not to be left out, sprang to her feet also. "And to my innocent brother. Oh, God, please protect him from this horrible miscarriage of justice!"

A moment of silence passed when Gunny, still standing, smiled widely, then blurted out, "We sound nuttier than a bunch of frigging fruitcakes!"

THE SKULL had rested on a silver pedestal at Nauticus the entire day. The hideous display was part of Norfolk's annual Blackbeard Festival at Harbor Park, located between Nauticus and the Waterside Festival Marketplace. The Blackbeard festival had become one of the most popular of Norfolk's annual outdoor events, always drawing tens of thousands of visitors.

The whereabouts of the skull after it was severed from its owner back in the year 1718 had long been considered a great mystery. The putrid head had originally been displayed on the bank of the Hampton River as an ominous warning against piracy. Later, it was put on exhibit at an inn in Williamsburg. From there, it had been stolen, its path thereafter somewhat uncertain. Over the years, it was rumored the skull might have fallen into the hands of pirates back in Ocracoke, or it might have wound up on the mantle of a fraternity house at the University of Virginia, or maybe, it was in the secret cache of Yale University's Secret Bones Society.

Nobody really knew.

Wherever it had been, the most credible information was that Blackbeard's skull was now owned by a wealthy

New England collector who loaned it to Nauticus for display purposes. The skull was accompanied by documenta-
tion of its authenticity, which led the experts to agree it was
the genuine remains of Blackbeard.

All afternoon, thousands of people enjoyed the festival.
In the harbor, sailboats cruised about imitating pirate ships,
flying their Jolly Rogers pennants and booming their miniature, blank-firing cannons. Crowds lined the water's edge
to watch the boats engage in frolicking water fights as black
water balloons flew through the air like cannon balls.

The melodious strains of sea shanties wafted throughout the park while pirate dancers kicked up their heels in
frivolity. The devil-may-care, swashbuckling attitude of the
fun-seeking pirates-for-the-day turned this year's festival into
one of the most uproariously successful events ever held in
Norfolk.

Wandering through the park were children and adults
alike, most of whom were decked out in pirate costumes in
hopes of winning the Blackbeard look-alike contest. There
were even infants wrapped in pirate flags and old codgers
wearing pirate hats and fake beards. Some of the partici-
pants had gone to great pains to be authentic, a few of whom
were dead ringers for Blackbeard.

There had been song, dance, spirits and even sword
fights, but the final event of the evening was the costume
contest. The winner, an enormous man in his forties, six
feet six inches in height with a huge barrel chest, was dressed
in an all black waist coat, tight black leather trousers and
black boots. A gigantic sword and three flintlock pistols were
strapped to his belt. The winning touch, however, was his
long, jet black, braided beard entwined with tiny fuses, which
when lighted, cast an aura of smoky mystique about his head.
He accepted the grand prize trophy with a certain disdain,
then brashly pushed his way through the crowd and walked
rapidly in the direction of Nauticus.

Darkness had fallen with only thirty minutes left until
closing time. Bold, sinister eyes glared at Blackbeard's skull,

which was exhibited in a clear glass case on a raised silver pedestal. Although it was getting late in the day, throngs of people continued to file through Nauticus, all anxious to inspect the macabre curiosity.

The large, bearded man, his eyes cold and emotionless, was stubbornly refusing to move, preoccupied as he stared at the skull. The man seemed oblivious to the people behind him who were having to either wait or detour around him. Stroking his long beard, he was mesmerized by the skull, beholding it as if it were a shrine.

A security guard, noticing the bottleneck in the line, focused his attention on the strange man. Something just wasn't quite right about this guy. Deciding to report the situation to his watch supervisor, but mindful not to cause a scene, Officer Murphy stepped into the vacant hallway where he unholstered his two-way radio.

"Captain Armstrong, this is Murphy. Do you copy?"

"What's up, Murphy?" Security Chief Armstrong responded as he sat in the control room observing the numerous monitors guarding the displays of Nauticus.

"Hey, uh, you know that Blackbeard skull?"

"Yeah, what about it, Murphy?"

"There's some kind of weird guy down here just staring and staring at it. The people in line behind him are getting pissed. Maybe you ought'a come down here and check this guy out."

"Okay, Murph. I'll be right down."

Murphy then walked back into the display room to keep an eye on the bearded man, but the man was gone - he had vanished. Murphy looked over at the silver pedestal, and to his dismay, it was headless - the skull had also vanished!

*

October 11th

At the governor's mansion in Richmond, a small, elite group of individuals, all of whom considering themselves to be FFVs — First Families of Virginia, sat at a large conference table, each FFV eager to hear the words of their exalted leader. Governor Brotherton, standing proudly at the head of the table, began with the big announcement.

"Gentlemen, we will present my candidacy on national television immediately following Alverez's November 22nd execution."

Executive Assistant Roger Keller, his notebook opened in front of him, sat beside the governor. On both sides of the conference table sat these eight waspy, middle-aged men.

Brotherton, a dastardly leer on his face, began his oration. "This glorious announcement, as well as the execution, will take place exactly forty-four days from today. And gentlemen," Brotherton bragged as he winked, making a victory sign with the first two fingers of his right hand, "I have friends in high places who have assured me there is no chance, I repeat, no chance, the high courts will overturn the execution order. That means, gentlemen, nothing can stop us now!"

His eight followers applauded, each smiling like a clam, happy just to be a part of this.

"Now, Roger," the governor said as he turned to his administrative assistant, "tell my friends where this monumental announcement will take place, and please give us the preliminary details."

Keller, a short stocky man in his mid forties who wore a permanent fake smile, was dressed to the nines in his double breasted gray flannel suit and striped tie.

"Gentlemen, the announcement will take place in Hampton at the newly renovated Chamberlin Hotel at Fort Monroe. The lavish new renovation of the Chamberlin puts this hotel on par with the most magnificent hotels in the world and is a tribute to our past, present and future. The extraordinary hotel stands as the guardian of the Chesapeake Bay, and it will reopen just two weeks before our great announcement."

Clinton Myrick, a long-time Brotherton supporter, interrupted. "Roger," he said inquiringly, "Wouldn't Richmond be a better place for such an important event?"

Governor Brotherton stood up.

"Clinton, this was my idea, and I'll tell you why. You need to understand, my good friend, that Fort Monroe has been in existence for nearly two hundred years. This great fort was built to protect our nation's capital after the British sailed up the Chesapeake Bay to attack and burn Washington, D.C. in the War of 1812."

When Myrick had nodded understandingly, another protest was registered, this protest from chicken baron Averill VonCannon.

"But, Governor," he interrupted, "Richmond is closer to the center of population, much more convenient for everyone."

With self-control, Brotherton forged ahead.

"Now, Averill, you don't understand. You see, it's symbolic to my campaign," Brotherton said, knowing the only thing symbolic to VonCannon was the money he received for the millions of chicken parts he sold around the world. "If we succeed, then for the eighth time in history, a Virginian will become the President of the United States. Ol' Virginia and our Virginia fort, Fort Monroe, will again rise to prominence as the great defender of America."

Brotherton should have been on Broadway. His patriotic oratory ensnared even his most dubious supporters.

Keller, his voice soft and deliberate, spoke up. "Now, let me remind you of a few more things about Fort Monroe." Keller's words so polished it sounded as though he were reading from a prepared text. "First, Robert E. Lee worked on the construction of the fort." With the mention of the name Robert E. Lee, all eight FFVs sat up straighter in their chairs, eyes now riveted on Keller. "And today, it is the headquarters of the United States Army Training and Doctrine Command. Do you know what that means?" Keller paused and stared at the eight FFVs, all staring blankly back at him.

"It means," Brotherton interjected, his blue eyes twinkling, "we can put some of the most powerful generals in the Army on our team if we have this at their base and shine a spotlight on a few of them. Believe me, my friends, Fort Monroe and the Chamberlin Hotel will provide us with an ideal platform for our campaign kick-off."

"Who will be invited?" inquired Barth Fedder, a well-known ultra-conservative legislator from Charlottesville.

Keller, the detail man, quickly responded. "Barth, trust us! We're going to be putting on a ten thousand dollar-a-plate dinner." Keller scribbled on a pad, pretending to be multiplying, then announced his total, a number he had much earlier committed to memory. "That would be seven million dollars right from the get-go to jump-start the campaign!"

After more questions and answers, the prestigious FFVs finally adjourned with excessive handshaking and promises of support. As the members of this elite club departed, each felt he had just become an integral part of the committee destined to elect the next President of the United States. This group, it was projected, would be remembered in history as President Brotherton's inner circle.

As the men exited, their minds swirled with high sounding fantasies of what life would be like in the heady society of Washington, D.C.

CHAPTER
48

October 13th

IT WAS a chilly Sunday morning, no wind, the river mirror flat. Gunny had been the first breakfast customer at the Marina Restaurant, where he'd wolfed down three eggs over easy, cheese grits and orange juice.

Just before the sun peeked over the horizon, he headed down river, ready for whatever challenge that lay before him - but little did he realize the huge adversity he was about to confront.

He wasn't really certain how his search should proceed. He figured he would just ask questions of everybody he saw and keep his eyes peeled for any sign of Toby's deadrise fishing boat or maybe that black, shark-shaped racing yacht.

Near the southern end of the Pasquotank, the Whaler entered an extremely wide expanse of water, an expanse so wide no land was visible on the far side. As his eyes scanned the vast Albemarle Sound, the enormity of his mission came into perspective. Cutting the engines, the bow settling in the water, Gunny rummaged in his duffel bag and pulled out a manual.

Turning to the chapter on the Albemarle Sound, he learned the sound was fifty-one miles in length with a width ranging from four miles at its headwaters to over eleven miles as it approaches the coast. Obviously, to search such a large body of water with no further clues would take forever. He had to scale down his search plan.

It seemed more logical Toby would probably stay out of the more congested rivers and sounds, where he might get himself trapped with no escape route. For instance, if Toby went west on the Alblemarle toward Edenton or Plymouth, his only way out was back the way he came in. If he followed the Intracoastal Waterway across the sound, down the Alligator River to the Pungo and on to Belhaven, he would be too near the Hyde County authorities who were already looking for him.

It soon became clear. Toby had to be somewhere near the Outer Banks, after all, it was the only option that made any sense.

At last underway, his search perimeters now more realistic, Gunny pushed the throttles forward and turned the helm southeast - his first destination, the Croatan Sound.

Passing the brilliant forest green of a point of land to port, which blended warmly with the deep blueness of the northeast Albemarle, the Whaler skimmed gracefully across the calm waters. The sky was teeming with wildlife as a gaggle of Canadian geese glided to the west and a formation of pelicans soared to the east. Near the eastward horizon, Gunny could just make out the sand dunes at Kill Devil Hills on the Outer Banks. It was there, Gunny reflected, the Wright Brothers had launched the first airplane for a brief, but momentous, twelve second flight.

Soon, it was decision time again. If he turned to port and headed north, he would be up near the Currituck Sound, which was much too shallow for Toby's boat. Besides, it was a dead-end with no escape route. Gunny elected the other direction and turned starboard, the boat veering to a due south course.

Soon, the Whaler entered the Croaton Sound, a mild breeze now blowing, which caused a chop in the sea. Shortly, Gunny spotted a twin masted ketch at anchor near

Fleetwood Point. Pulling alongside, he asked the skipper of the *Breezin' Around* if he'd seen anyone matching Toby's or Mandy's description. No such luck.

Farther along, as the tip of Roanoke Island came into view, Gunny reduced speed and guided the Whaler around the south end of the island. At a flashing day beacon, he turned the helm and headed into Wanchese Harbor. Briefly docking at the wharf, he walked door to door, asking the same questions and receiving the same answers. Neither his petite blond daughter nor the big-bearded scoundrel had been seen by anyone. Gunny's resolve was being put to the test, but he'd never give up. Somewhere, someone must have seen them.

Back on board, resuming his course, Gunny had just passed under the Roanoke Island Bridge when he saw a marina with an alluring name he just couldn't resist. Heading into the Pirate's Cove Marina, he tied up at the fuel dock, filled up with seventy gallons of gasoline, then decided to poke around.

The Drafty Tavern, located beside the marina, looked like a good place to start. Only a few people were there, so Gunny sat at the bar beside two weather-beaten cronies. Giving them a friendly nod, he smiled. "How you doing?"

The old salts barely glanced toward him, responding only with a sequence of faint grunts.

"Uh, excuse me, but could I ask a question?" Gunny asked hesitantly.

There were more grunts, which Gunny elected to interpret as affirmative replies, so he proceeded. "I'm looking for my daughter. She's been kidnapped by a big man with a black beard. They're probably traveling on a fishing boat."

In a gravely voice, the man seated closest to him quickly responded, "Sorry, haven't seen 'er."

Gunny handed a photo of Mandy over to them. The closer man adjusted his glasses and looked down at it. Almost immediately, however, he looked back at Gunny. "This your daughter, you say?"

"Well, uh, she's my adopted daughter, actually."

"How, how long's she been gone?" the other, slightly younger man asked as he craned his neck, trying to get a better look at the photograph.

"It's been almost five months now. She disappeared in late May. Do you think you might have seen her?"

"I, I don't know for sure, but, but sometime in the . . . uh, summer, I seen a real purdy, little blond-headed girl on a fishin' boat that stopped by here. A great, uh, great big, ugly man with a long beard was drivin'."

Pausing, the man took a sip of beer, then continued. "I, uh, I was workin' the gas dock, and I 'member this little girl just'a sittin' in a chair on the deck of this boat. She didn't get off the boat or even, uh, even move for that matter. Reason I 'member it is 'cause they looked like a real odd couple."

"Does the photo look like it could be her?" Gunny asked.

"It, uh, it sure does."

Gunny pulled out the mug shot of Toby and passed it over. "Does this look like the man she was with, sir?"

For several seconds, the salty fellow studied the photo, then looked back at Gunny. "Pur, purdy good likeness, I'd say."

"Do you remember what the boat looked like?"

"Not really, but, uh, but it seems like it was a regular commercial fishing boat, maybe thirty foot, dir, dirty, white, wooden. I don't recall th, the name on 'er."

"Can you recall which way it went when it left?"

The man paused, scratching the stubble on his unshaven cheek. A long moment passed, when very deliberately, he said, "It, it, uh, seems like I do remember." He started pointing over his head. "I, uh, think it went back under the bridge and headed south."

Gunny was overjoyed, hopeful his patience was beginning to pay off. "Sir, I really appreciate this! It's the best news I've had in a long time. Thank you so much!"

LARGE, BROAD swells were beginning to develop on the Pamlico Sound, but the weather remained fair. Traveling due south, Gunny held the Whaler steady on course, the small craft positioned on the crest of a large wave. Gunny was excited, optimistic at this new glimmer of hope provided by the fishermen at the Drafty Tavern.

Steering with one hand, he opened the cruise manual again. As the print jiggled with the vibration of the boat, he focused his eyes, trying to get some basics about the Pamlico.

"Damn!" he growled, when he read that the Pamlico Sound is the second largest land-locked body of water on the east coast, only the Chesapeake Bay being larger. Glancing ahead, he turned the helm a few degrees west to avoid a crab pot, then refocused on the guide book.

"Good gosh!" he exclaimed, surprised to learn this sound covered more than 1,700 square miles and extended from the western shore of North Carolina's mainland all the way to the Outer Banks. *Damn, that's a lot of water!*

As the Whaler proceeded on its southerly course down the Pamlico, Gunny stopped several fishing boats to make inquiries, and show them Mandy's photo and Toby's mug shot, but no one could help.

Further south, he made stops at some small fishing villages on the Outer Banks, including Rodante and Avon, but still, nothing.

The evening was soon upon him and frustration mounted. Earlier in the day his hopes had been lifted high, but as the hours dragged on with no new leads, the futility of his search was now becoming all too vivid.

The village of Hatteras was the next stop, which Gunny decided would be an ideal place to spend the night. It had been a long day, and a motel room and hot bath would surely be welcome and a hell of a lot better than sleeping in the Whaler's cramped cuddy.

Rollinson Channel led Gunny to the village, where he docked at Hatteras Fishing Center, which had an appealing alias of Teach's Lair Marina. Trying to get his land legs, he wobbled down the road to a small but friendly-looking motel. After a shower and change of clothes, he hit the street, ready to ask around about Toby and Mandy.

It only took an hour to talk with everyone there. But again, zilch.

Strolling back to the dock, Gunny sat down on the edge of a wooden pier, his legs suspended, hanging over the water. Staring off toward the dimming lights on the western horizon, his mind drifted back to those days when Mandy was a little girl. He recalled the time he and Donna sat in the living room of their home and delighted in watching their little girl hamming it up, pretending to be a high soprano as she squealed out a song at the top of her lungs. They had joked about Mandy becoming a famous opera singer, which had prompted her shrieks to become even more shrill. It had been such a happy time, and Gunny had been so very proud of his family.

But now, he had to force himself to return to the cold, hard world.

That night, as he lay in bed trying to sleep, he thought - *Maybe, just maybe, tomorrow will be the day that I find Mandy.* Gunny's eyes closed as he drifted off, wondering what Mandy was doing that very moment. Mercifully, he had no way of knowing.

*

The benevolence of hot meals being lowered to her twice a day didn't make up for the degradation of the incessant sexual attacks.

"I won't let that asshole ever touch me again! I'll kill him if he gets close!" Mandy vowed, having gained considerable strength over the past three weeks. Previously, she had been too weak to resist, but with the passage of time, together with the nourishing meals, her vitality had gradually increased and a thick layer of resolve had begun to develop.

Hours passed as she lay on the cot, staring out into the blackness of her pit. She kept telling herself she had to be tough like Gunny. After all, the worst thing that could happen was this psycho could kill her, and even death would be better than life in this hell hole.

She had last been assaulted by him just yesterday, and no doubt, he would be back any time for more. Trying to force sleep that would not come, she had been lying there for hours, when much to her dread, she heard the now-too-familiar sound of the rope ladder dropping into the pit. She cringed in disgust, knowing the awful man was on his way back down.

Moments later, there he was. His beard was braided, he had on earrings, and his body emitted a nauseous smell of rum and perfume. Toby began removing his shirt, revealing wide, bulging shoulders covered in a jungle of coarse, black hair.

Suddenly, Mandy sprang up from her cot.

"Don't you come near me, you crazy asshole!" she screamed as she contorted her small body into a head-on defensive position, holding her balled fists in front of her like a boxer.

Toby, weaving slightly, bent forward and burst into a belly laugh at the sight of this petite, little girl who, amazingly, was brazen enough to challenge him. "Yoo - re a little wild cat, are ya?" he stammered, still laughing, as he slowly slid closer to her.

"Come on, mi little Mary; it was so good last night; it'll be even better tonight."

"Go to hell, you goofy bastard!" Mandy screamed frantically as she retreated, backing blindly away from him. "I don't know who Mary is, but it's not me. Now get the hell away from me!"

Between the whiskers of Toby's food-splattered beard, a sadistic grin revealed itself. Robot-like, he began to move closer and closer as Mandy backed further away from him. Just as her back touched the damp brick wall, Toby's right arm shot out, grasping at her shoulder.

"Get away from me, you creep!" she shrieked as she jerked her shoulder away and side-stepped to the right.

Toby, still plodding toward her, was only inches away when she jumped out of his reach and darted across the cell. Driven by his drunken lust for sexual gratification, he lunged clumsily forward in pursuit, his arms reaching out toward her neck.

"Come - oon, mi Ma - ry."

Mandy ducked away from his groping hands, causing the tipsy brute to teeter off balance.

Before he could regain stability, he was caught by surprise when warm liquid suddenly splashed across his face. Cursing and wiping the urine dripping from his braided beard, he looked up only to see the blur of fast-moving plastic headed for him, slamming violently into his forehead. Mandy, adrenalin driven, was gripping the lower section of the portable toilet in both hands and had reared back again, preparing to swing the Port-A-John a second time. Holding it like a baseball bat, and swinging like Hank Aaron, she again slammed the potty squarely into Toby's face, the marauder collapsing helplessly to the floor.

Mandy bolted back across the pit, grabbed the dangling rope ladder, and began pulling with all her strength as she slowly inched up the ladder. But it was more difficult than she had anticipated. The rungs of the ladder evaded her feet, and her grip on the ropes burned her hands. She groaned in agony, her arm and leg muscles crying out in pain, as she pulled herself upward, straining for each and every inch of ascension.

Just when she could see the ledge above, the rope ladder was suddenly jerked vigorously downward and immediately sprang up like a bungie cord. As the ladder went taut, Mandy dared a glance downward, and to her great distress, there he was! Toby, his face bloodied, was climbing the ladder just below her.

Mandy reached up for the next rung, struggling for all she was worth to pull her way to the top, but her frail body seemed to have run out of energy. She winced at the touch of his fingers as he grappled for her feet. Unable to bear the thought of him touching her ever again, she tried to climb faster, but couldn't. He got closer, his finger tips again skipping across her bare skin, this time her lower leg. In her final futile effort, knowing he would be upon her at any second, she pulled her legs upward and held them there momentarily. Then, like releasing a tightly coiled spring, her legs snapped downward with all the fury her little body could rally, bashing Toby point blank, squarely in the face.

Looking down as she continued to frantically climb upward, she saw Toby hanging by one hand, his nose reddened, his eyes glazed and the expression on his face one of utter astonishment, which gave Mandy a fleeting moment of satisfaction. *Maybe, just maybe, I've slowed him down enough to get away,* she prayed.

A newly found surge of adrenaline pushed her up the remaining rungs of the ladder and over the top of the ledge. Scrambling to her feet, she dashed to a wooden door, grabbed the knob, twisted it and pushed, but to her horror, it wouldn't open. She pushed again. "Oh God, it's stuck!" she exclaimed as she looked over her shoulder for Toby.

Inspecting the door, she saw a hook, which she quickly unfastened. Then, with all her heart, she shoved with her shoulder and the door swung open to a dark, moonless night.

Now determined more than ever to escape, Mandy bolted through the doorway, down a step and onto a concrete platform with bricks and debris scattered about. It looked like the ruins of an old manufacturing plant, but the roof was gone, as were most of the walls.

She ran, but tripped. Before she could climb back up onto her feet, she looked back toward the doorway and there he was. He was standing there, puffing like a steam engine and gazing out into the darkness. Suddenly, angrily, he bellowed out, "Come here, you little bitch!"

Mandy lay still until she saw a beam of light emanating from Toby's flashlight. The light was moving in her direction. Just as she crawled behind a pile of bricks, the beam passed over her, missing her by a hair.

She heard footsteps, which seemed to be getting closer and closer, but she dared not look. Her heart pounding, her body trembling, she waited for the dreaded ensnarement of Toby's vise-like grip. But the stepping sound got softer and soon began to fade away. She couldn't believe it! He'd walked past her. *Maybe I've evaded this pervert,* she thought hopefully.

After waiting for another minute, she quietly crawled to another brick pile from where she could see trees and bushes just outside the perimeter of the ruins. She had to get out of here. Maybe she could lose him in the nearby woods. Maybe there was a highway nearby. Maybe she could flag down a passing motorist.

Peeking from behind the brick pile, she could see no sign of him. Everything was perfectly still. *It was now or never!*

She sprang to her feet, and sprinted for the tree line, not more than fifty feet away. She tripped, lost her balance, fell, then crawled, but finally made it out into the weedy field, where she dived headfirst into a clump of bushes. She lay there gasping for breath but with an enormous sense of relief. It looked like she might make it. For a brief moment, there was hope.

"Aha!" Toby roared, suddenly stepping out from behind a nearby pine tree. Viciously, he grabbed her by the throat and forcibly dragged her out of her place of refuge. Throwing her down violently onto the cold, hard ground, she landed on her back, totally demoralized as Toby unbuckled his belt. Then, with a diabolical look in his eyes and his pants down, he dropped on top of her exhausted body as she surrendered to hopelessness.

CHAPTER
50

October 14th

THE MORNING air was crisp, the sky was clear with a stiff breeze blowing out of the northeast. As the Whaler skated across Hatteras Inlet, white caps signaled a much rougher sea than the day before. The Evinrudes purred, the Whaler skimming southward through a relentless pounding of waves that slapped rhythmically at the bow. Gripping the helm tightly as he scoured the southern horizon, Gunny spotted the ribbon of sand known as Ocracoke Island.

He had done his homework. This narrow strip of sand just south of Hatteras was only sixteen miles long, its only town, the village of Ocracoke, located at the southern tip. For centuries, maybe even millenniums, this barrier island had served as a buffer against the hurricanes and nor'easters that pelted the mainland of North Carolina twenty miles westward across the Pamlico Sound.

As the Whaler neared the island, scrubby pines, water oaks and marsh grass came into view. Then, pilings, topped with perched pelicans, could be seen at the North Ferry Landing, one pelican per piling.

With the western shore of Ocracoke off to the left, the Whaler plowed onward until, up ahead, a red inlet marker was spotted.

Meticulously, Gunny steered through the weave of markers that led through a ditch-like inlet when, suddenly, he was bedazzled. It was like leafing through the pages of a children's picture book. There he was, spellbound in the midst of the mystical harbor known as Silver Lake. To his left, a ferry boat was being onloaded, and beyond, an American flag waved its welcome from a Coast Guard station.

Gunny was instantly enthralled by the quaintness of the village. Along the rounding cove were classic-hulled fishing vessels docked in front of small, vintage shops. An historic lighthouse stood guard in the eastern background, overlooking the enchanting harbor.

When he passed the ferry landing, he steered toward a long wooden dock that extended out from the shore. As the Whaler came alongside, a pot-bellied man with a Greek fishing cap on his head came out of the shop. "What can oi' do for you?" he asked.

This guy has a funny accent, Gunny thought.

Gunny headed in toward the dock where the man looped the Whaler's bow line over a piling. "Are you from England, sir?" Gunny asked.

"Oh, no. Oi'm from right here. Oi've only been off this oi'land three ti'emes in mi life. Oi'm an O'Coker," he proudly proclaimed, his accent thick and Cockney-like.

He was a talkative man, quick to explain he was a descendant of some of the early English settlers who made Ocracoke their home in the 1700s. He introduced himself as William Crayton and explained that many O'Cokers as recently as his grandparents' generation had never been off the island in their entire lives. Because of this, many of the Ocracoke inhabitants had retained much of their early English brogue, which has come to be known as a "hoi' toider" (high tider) accent.

Standing on the pier, looking eye to eye with Mr. Crayton, Gunny sensed him to be trustworthy. Maybe he could help.

"Could I ask you a question or two, sir?" Gunny asked politely.

"Aye."

"I'm looking for a bearded man who is very big and tall; he sometimes claims to be related to Blackbeard."

"Whoi'y are you looking for 'em?"

"I think he's got my daughter! He kidnapped her. Have you seen anyone who fits his description?"

"Well, you describe Old Toby. He's a big goaty smellin' feller, and he does have a black beard. Used to go around sayin' he was kin to Ol' Blackbeard, but we're all pretty sure he's offshore."

"Offshore! Where offshore?"

"Oh, that just means he's crazy! I forgot I was talking to a dingbatter," Mr. Crayton said, a chuckle to his voice.

Sensing he'd just been insulted, Gunny responded defensively. "Excuse me!"

"Dingbatter. That only means you're a foreigner. People around here are either O'Cokers or dingbatters. If you aren't from here, you're a dingbatter," Crayton explained. Then, he hastened to add, "That is, unless you're a dit dah."

"Oh, okay, I'll bite. What's a dit dah?"

Mr. Crayton grinned with satisfaction. "That's a dingbatter who comes over here to Ocracoke and won't leave. They're worse than dingbatters."

Gunny had to laugh, finally realizing Crayton was putting him on. After a polite chuckle, Gunny asked, "Mr. Crayton, you were talking about Toby Greene weren't you?"

"Aye, Toby Greene's the one, all right. That Toby is a real wampus cat."

"A what?" Gunny asked, his face displaying a frown of frustration.

"He's a rascal. He's crooked, you know, cattywampus."

"When's the last time you saw him?"

"Well, let me think." Crayton looked at his watch. "I, uh, saw him 'bout an hour ago, I guess."

Instantly, Gunny's face went flush, his heart beating like a drum. "An hour ago!" He looked at his watch. "You mean an hour ago, like at 9:30, an hour ago?"

"Aye."

"Where at?"

"Right here. Almost exactly where you're standing."

"Is he still on the island, do you think?" Gunny's blood pressure felt like it was shooting off the chart.

"Must be. His boat's moored over there." Crayton pointed to a white fishing boat moored to a buoy some 200 feet out, near the southwest side of Silver Lake.

Gunny still couldn't believe his ears. "That - is - his - boat?" he asked slowly.

"Aye, that's it, all right."

"Do you have any idea where he is?" Gunny asked, his stomach doing flip-flops.

"Well, seein' how this island's not that big, he's got to be around here somewhere."

"Did you see a blond-headed teenage girl with him, by chance?"

"No, sorry. Weren't nobody with him."

Gunny thanked Mr. Crayton for his help. As he began to run a spring line from the stern of the Whaler to a piling, Mr. Crayton suddenly had an afterthought.

"Oh yeah, old Toby was a bloody mess this morning. Had scratches on his face and a big red, swollen nose."

"Is that right?"

"Said he got hold of a little wild cat last night," Crayton said, a crooked smile on his face and a cackle in his voice.

Gunny, wondering how this new bit of info might factor into the puzzle, decided to go ahead and search the island. Walking briskly down the lane that bordered Silver Lake Harbor, he first stopped at the post office - but no Toby. He then stopped at a duck decoy shop—no Toby. He next stopped at an intriguing-looking bar overlooking the harbor, the Jolly Roger's—but still, no Toby.

As he walked, he couldn't help but admire the variety of quaint structures that lined the streets, everything from modest frame houses with classic cedar siding to antique, mansion-like hotels. With the ancient live oaks that dotted the area, the village had the picturesque charm of yesteryear.

After searching most of the tiny village, Gunny noticed a white picket fence up ahead. As he got closer, he could tell the fence actually enclosed a small cemetery, where a number of granite grave markers were located. On one of the markers, the inscription read, "Lieutenant Robert Cunningham, died May 11, 1941, British Navy." The other grave markers bore names of other British sailors, all of whom had died on the same date in 1941.

The cemetery was orderly and well kept, except Gunny noticed something just didn't seem to fit. Walking closer to the picket fence, he could see a pile of freshly excavated dirt beside an open trench. It looked like a freshly dug grave, the shovel still leaning against the fence. *That's weird*, Gunny thought as he continued down the street.

Returning to the main road, Gunny continued walking until he was in front of a nostalgic relic of the thirties, Albert Styron's Store. He went inside and struck up a conversation with the clerk.

"This is really a neat store, ma'am. How old is it?" he asked.

The attractive, mid-forties lady smiled.

"Aye, it was built in the twenties by Albert Styron. It even won an award for the historical preservation work!"

"Ma'am, I was wondering if you might know Toby Greene?"

"Oh, yes, oi'm afraid so. Toby's offshore, and you know the fool claims to be related to Blackbeard.

"Yeah, that's him. Have you seen him?"

"Not in a while, sorry. But oi' can tell you this. That Toby Greene is the beatenest person I know!"

"I'm sorry, ma'am, but 'beatenest' - what does that mean?"

"Oh, he's unusual, you know, weird. Really, I mean he's the worst behaveness man oi've ever seen."

"What do you mean?" Gunny was perplexed at her seemingly foreign words.

"When old Toby comes around, he makes me daresome, you know?"

"You mean you're afraid of him?"

"Aye, he's dirty and hard down mean. He's always ill and will have a hissy fit if you cross him. Oi' once saw him mommock a man right out on the public street."

"Mommock?"

"Old Toby beat up a dingbatter right there in front of everybody. Nobody dared to do anything to him for it."

Gunny asked about the curious little cemetery down the road. The lady explained that British sailors whose ships had been torpedoed back in World War Two were buried there. Their bodies had washed up on Ocracoke Island."

"Have there been any recent burials there?" Gunny asked, thinking about the trench, the churned up dirt, and the shovel.

"Heavens no. Oi' think there may have been a very old cemetery for castaways and pirates in the same area back before the British sailors were buried there, but oi' don't believe anyone has been laid to rest in that cemetery since 1941."

"Well then, tell me why there would be a recently dug grave and a shovel there?"

"Oi' can't imagine," the lady said, a puzzled look on her face.

Gunny continued to peruse the store until he saw a giant map of Ocracoke on the wall. Taking a closer look, he saw the name, "Teach's Hole," which identified a coastal indention at the southeast corner of the island. He put his finger on the spot. "Ma'am, how do I get here, to Teach's Hole?"

After getting directions, minutes later Gunny was heading for Teach's Hole, excited at the prospect this might well be Toby Greene's hideout. He walked briskly down the road, heading for the narrow beach that ran along the sound. Once at the beach, he began to jog south until the shoreline began to curve inward.

As he continued down this strip of beach checkered with patches of washed-up seaweed, he saw what appeared to be a barricade ahead. Getting closer, he could tell it was actually a large pile of rocks with intermingled brick riprap. It blocked the entire beach passageway. Gunny climbed to the top of the rubble and stood in awe as he momentarily reflected on the historical prominence of this spot. *It was right out there off shore, where Blackbeard's headless body was unceremoniously dumped into the water for all eternity.*

Continuing to probe along the shoreline, Gunny found the beach to be relatively clean, except for seaweed, sand ponds, a few dead sea gulls and an occasional pile of ocean debris. Further down the beach, he spied a large stone protruding from of the sand. Beside it, partially buried, lay a strange web-like object. As he got closer, he realized it was actually a rubber flipper like a diver would wear. Inspecting it, he was astounded at its extraordinarily large size, perhaps a size twenty.

Nearby, Gunny spotted a trail of enormous footprints in the sand, which led up into high grass toward a large patch of thick bayberry bushes, then into an ancient forest of live oak trees. Ignoring a no trespassing sign, Gunny followed the footprints but they soon began to fade, and finally vanished.

For more than an hour, he continued to search the area, but as the sun began to set, there was still no sign of Toby. Suddenly, a dismal thought hit him like a sledge hammer. *What if Toby Greene has already sneaked back to the harbor and taken off on his boat? If that happened, all would be lost.*

Gunny ran back along the beach, climbed back over the riprap, and waded back through the sand ponds. As he ran, he chastised himself for having wandered so far from Toby's boat. Soon, however, he could see the tip of the lighthouse, which seemed to be getting taller as he got closer. By now he was breathing hard, nearly out of breath, but determined not to stop until he saw Toby's boat in Silver Lake.

As he ran, desperately clinging to the hope that the boat would still be there, he cursed his stupidity for having gone on this wild goose chase. He was panting, barely able to catch his breath when Silver Lake finally came into view. Desperately, he squinted into the glare of the setting sun, trying to spot Toby's boat, praying it was still there.

"Thank God!" he exclaimed, as he exhaled a gasp of relief when he finally saw it moored in Silver Lake, just as it was before. Even William Crayton was still on the dock, now sitting with a fishing pole in his hand and a small sack-wrapped can of beer wedged between his legs. Gunny rushed out on the dock and called to Mr. Crayton, "You seen Toby yet?"

Crayton calmly looked up and shook his head. "No sign of the old pirate, sorry."

Gunny needed time to think. He stepped onto the Whaler and ducked into the cuddy cabin where he stretched out on the V-berth. Lying there, he racked his brain, until finally, he realized what he was going to have to do.

51

GUNNY NIBBLED on a chocolate bar as he patiently waited for darkness to arrive. As dusk passed, a quarter moon peaked from behind a cloud. This night reminded him of another dangerous night more than thirty years earlier. He, along with other Marines and a Navy Seal team, had been dropped into Haiphong to mine the North Vietnamese harbor. It was a night much like this one, Gunny recollected: just enough light to see where he was going, but still dark enough to remain hidden from the enemy.

In another hour, the night had grown very dark, dark enough for a swimmer to be nearly invisible. Gunny donned his black wetsuit, stuck his Beretta in a waterproof fanny pack, then quietly slipped into the cold October water. Surface diving, he swam underwater the entire 200 foot distance over to Toby's fishing boat, coming up for air only once. Amazed at his lung capacity, particularly in view of his insatiable nicotine habit, he congratulated himself. *Quite a feat for 51 years old, even if I do say so myself.*

He swam the perimeter, circling the fishing boat, carefully looking for any signs of life. Detecting none, he grabbed the mooring line and pulled himself up onto the foredeck. Relying on his refined senses to warn him of any sign of danger, he slinked along the deck, confident he was all alone on the boat.

Producing a flashlight from his satchel, he directed a beam of light into the darkness of the cabin. Scattered about inside, he saw fishing equipment, gaffs, line, and nets. He stepped down inside and immediately noticed an odd-looking metal box partially covered by an unrolled sleeping bag. Actually, the box looked more like a large cookie tin with a lid. He pried the lid off and shined his light down inside. There was some kind of an oval object inside. Whatever it was, it looked important, so Gunny commandeered it and stuffed it into his waterproof pack.

Continuing his inspection of the cabin, he saw nothing else of particular interest. He had hoped to find some charts that might lead him to Mandy but none were there. Finally deciding he had pressed his luck far enough, he slipped into the water and sidestroked back to the Whaler.

At last, aboard the Whaler, he felt a sense of relief as he toweled off and lit a cigarette. Then, while sitting in the cuddy cabin, he pulled the tin from his pack and pried the lid off. *What in the hell is this thing?* he wondered.

Reaching inside, he touched it. It felt hard and dry, like bone, perhaps. But as he began to lift it out of the tin, his mission was abruptly terminated.

It was like a ground-zero explosion. The booming thud impacted so violently into the boat that Gunny was slammed down, his head crashing hard on the cabin deck. Seconds later, another blow struck, a blow so violent the boat's fiberglass cracked. Gunny's near-panicked eyes shot upward to the disheartening view of a jagged hole that had just been carved in the aft hatchway. Peering through the gaping hole, he was astonished at the horrid sight of a huge sword brandished by gargantuan hands. Before his very eyes, the sword was descending like a silver streak, whizzing down above him, chopping viciously into the cabin.

To avert the next impending slice, Gunny quickly lunged forward and threw himself as far away from the hatchway as he could get. The sword whammed down again, hacking away a three foot chunk from the fiberglass cabin wall. Then, an even more devastating slice came! With a lightning slash of the blade followed by a reverberating crush of plastic and a star burst of splinters, the sword chopped through the cabin and chomped off a corner of the V-berth.

With escape paramount on his mind, Gunny slithered his broad shoulders through the overhead hatchway and gazed aft to a sight he would never forget. The sword-wielding monster was a giant, so tall he obscured the view of the western sky, so heavy the Whaler listed twenty degrees to starboard. He had a full black beard tied in braids, which extended half-way down his chest. Holstered by his side was a 21st Century laser-sighted Glock.

Toby, his evil leer unswervingly affixed on Gunny, swung his sword back and forth in a fanatic frenzy. Desperate for a weapon, Gunny snatched up a nearby boat hook and parried defensively as he tried to ward off his attacker. His feeble attempt, however courageous, was to no avail.

The lethal edge brought on hell eternal, crissing right, crossing left. When the singe of the blade fanned his chin, Gunny retreated toward the foredeck until he felt the bow pulpit pressing against his butt; he could back up no further.

But Gunny was a fighter. He seized the moment and jabbed the boat hook hard into the Toby's nose. Amazingly, like a freeze frame, all movement instantly stopped. The marauder was stunned, but the moment of reprieve was fleeting. With blood spraying down from his snarling nostrils and his mighty sword at the ready, the mountain stood there, blocking Gunny's passageway to the safety of the dock. Gunny was trapped. Like a buzzard eyeing roadkill, Toby's eyes, dark and cold, were focused on its prey. The razor-like blade of his sword began its downward, deadly swoop. All Gunny could do was run, jump and dodge, but even he could not keep up this cat-and-mouse game forever.

Surprisingly agile, Gunny deftly ducked two sword swings, then leaped off the cabin top toward the stern of the boat. At that moment, as Gunny was in mid-air, Toby's huge sword cut an arc upward and found meat, carving a slice out of Gunny's backside. Gunny landed hard and bloody, collapsing on the aft deck, his head smacking violently into the port Evinrude. He lay motionless, crumpled on the deck, eyes closed.

But the pain in his rear was too excruciating to ignore. It wouldn't allow him to just lay there and take the easy way out. Rather, from out of nowhere, an inner wince re-alerted him of the impending doom. He forced himself upright as Toby slipped closer, preparing for the final attack. With only a folding deck chair between them, Gunny desperately grabbed it and held it in front of him like a lion tamer.

Toby charged, his sword plunging downward, but just before it could subdivide Gunny's skull, the cagey old Marine raised the deck chair, closed his eyes and cringed. The speeding blade sliced the aluminum deck chair neatly in half, missing Gunny's head by less than a centimeter.

Gunny had to get away, but the dock was not within jumping range. There was, however, a sawed off piling he might could reach.

Desperate, with no other option available, he leaped toward the piling, throwing himself out like a broad jumper, the odds of a miracle landing approximately equal to a lotto win. Amazingly, though, one foot landed on top of the piling, which gave him a platform to balance himself. Just as he was about to teeter off into the water, he pushed off from the piling with his left leg, and flung himself toward the dock. Momentarily airborne, arms groping wildly at the empty air, he came down hard, landing half on, half off the dock, his chest impacting with a steel dock cleat and his face scraping along the rough wood planking. Though severely injured, he managed to pull up onto his hands and knees and crawl along the dock back to the shore, a widening smear of blood trailing behind him.

Hearing the ruckus, a small crowd gathered at the foot of the dock. Gunny, now bleeding profusely from his face, chest and rear, continued to crawl toward the bewildered onlookers until finally, in front of them, he collapsed.

As he bled from multiple wounds, a puddle of blood began to form around him. His dark skin soon appeared as a shadowy, maroon precursor of death. In his last moment of consciousness, Gunny opened his eyes and raised up on his elbows. "Stop that man!" he begged. "Please, stop that man!" But then, his head fell back, his eyes closed and darkness engulfed him.

52

October 15th

IT WAS 9 A.M. when the phone rang in Grayson's office. It was a Mrs. Ledbetter at the East Carolina University Medical Center in Greenville, North Carolina.

"I'm calling on behalf of Sergeant Lincoln Vernon who was admitted last night with extremely serious injuries," Mrs. Ledbetter said.

Grayson, stunned at the news, slid to the edge of his seat. "Oh, my God! "What happened? Is he going to be okay?"

"Well, he was injured over on Ocracoke and was flown here by helicopter late last night. That's all I really know except Mr. Vernon is in extremely critical condition."

"How bad is he?"

"Pretty bad, sir. He's lost a great deal of blood. We almost lost him several times, but fortunately, his condition has now been upgraded to 'stable but serious.'"

"Is he conscious?"

"Yes, but he's still quite groggy. He wants you to come down here right away."

Three hours later, Grayson's Cherokee pulled into the parking lot of the ECU Medical Center complex. He rushed to the information desk in the main lobby where he was directed to room 367 in the recovery area. Too

impatient to wait for the elevator, Grayson bounded up
the stairs to the third floor, then rushed down the hall to
Gunny's room.

When he opened the door, he was immediately shocked
at what he saw. Gunny look almost subhuman. He was lying in the hospital bed, head crisscrossed with bandages, an
oxygen tube to his nose, an IV and a morphine drip plugged
into his arm. He resembled an Egyptian mummy.

"Uh, Gunny, how're you doing?" Grayson asked as
guardedly, he touched Gunny's right hand.

At first, struggling to speak, Gunny began to mumble,
his words barely decipherable. "I...uh...I think we're on to
something, Grayson." As he strained to speak, he began to
cough, but he desperately wanted to say something. After
another series of phlegmy coughs, he cleared his throat.
"Black, uh...Blackbeard!" he gasped as he sought to push
himself upright.

Grayson wanted to ask a thousand questions, but was
afraid to right now; it might be too much of a strain on the
old Marine.

"I'll be okay; this is just a scratch," Gunny volunteered, his
voice just a whisper. "You, uh, you know, I've been through
worse. I'm a tough old S.O.B., so don't worry about me."

"Where're you hurt, Gunny?"

"Everywhere, but, but, uh, the worst of it's my butt. I
think I've got three cheeks back there now." Gunny made
an attempt to smile, but the bandages on his face held it
rigid. By now, his voice was a mere undertone, growing
more faint with each word. "He, he, uh, broke my ribs and
punctured my lung."

"That's pretty damn serious!" Grayson replied, mildly
irritated at Gunny's lack of concern for himself. "Listen, you
need some rest. I'm going to check into a motel. Maybe we
can talk more afterwhile."

"No! You listen to me! Before you go, I've got to tell you
about Blackbeard."

"Okay, go ahead, if you feel up to it." It was obvious

Gunny would not rest until he spoke his mind.

"You need to go to Ocracoke and check on your boat." Gunny's voice weakened as he broke into another coughing spell. Grayson handed him a cup of water, and after a sip, Gunny continued. "Toby Greene really did a number on the Whaler with his sword."

"His what?"

Gunny held on long enough to tell about getting on Toby's boat and finding the oval-shaped, bony-feeling object. Struggling, he described the attack, the damaged Whaler and the terrible fight that had ensued. Finally, with no further sound emitting from his still-moving lips, Grayson took his hand and gently shook it.

"Don't worry, Gunny. I'll go over to Ocracoke this evening. Just take care of yourself, and I'll call you tomorrow."

Apparently relieved, Gunny closed his eyes and drifted off into unconsciousness.

Grayson sped east on Highway 264 to Swan Quarter, arriving at the public landing just before the ferry was to depart. Paying the ten-dollar toll, he steered his Cherokee on board.

As he sat in his vehicle, the windows down, Grayson was enjoying the salty breeze. Ignoring the brisk temperature, he stared out into the blue water of the Pamlico as he contemplated this new piece to the puzzle - the mysterious oval, bony object? *What would Toby be doing with a skull?*

An hour later, the ferry passed through the inlet into Silver Lake and docked at the Ocracoke Ferry Landing. After rattling across the ramp onto the island, Grayson drove a half block down Main Street and pulled into a dirt lot near the water's edge.

He rushed onto the dock, eager to see his damaged boat. What he saw nearly made him sick. The raised cabin of the craft was almost nonexistent. Both the hatchway and the aft bulkhead were gone, survived only by a raggedy strip of fiberglass that supported the nearly shredded cabin top.

Extensive blood smears streamed throughout the cockpit, leaving the deck of his once beautiful Boston Whaler looking like the floor of a slaughter house. Blood was everywhere, even on the boat hook lying on the deck.

Grayson had worked with forensic chemists in JAG and knew one of the most important principles about a crime scene was the preservation of evidence. He walked around the cockpit gingerly, trying to avoid stepping in the dried blood splotches. As he inspected the four-foot crevice in the cuddy cabin, he was interrupted.

"Who are you?" came a voice from shore.

Grayson looked up to see a man, perhaps in his sixties, wearing a Greek sailor's hat. "This is my boat. Who are you?"

"Oiy'm William Crayton. This is my dock. Are you a friend of the black gentleman who was injured here last night?"

"Yes, I am. Did you see what happened, sir?"

"Toby Greene did it. He's offshore, uh...you know, a madman."

"Have the police looked at the boat?"

"A deputy kinda glanced at it early this morning, but there's no mystery about who did it. We all know it was Toby Greene." Crayton shook his head in disgust.

Scattered around the cabin were numerous pieces of fiberglass in which were intermingled some odd-looking bony splinters. Grayson decided not to mention the curious splinters to Mr. Crayton. There was no reason to give the locals any fodder for gossip.

"Uh, tell me, Mr. Crayton, did you see the fight?"

"Oiy' saw the last of it. That crazy Toby was all dressed up like a damn pirate and swinging that jumbo sword. That fool must be on drugs."

Mr. Crayton explained that Toby was later spotted paddling back to his fishing boat in a rubber raft, and a short time later, the fishing boat headed out into the sound. Also, according to the captain of the late-night Cedar Island Ferry, he'd seen a fishing boat, probably Toby's, heading south, but he wasn't sure.

Using Mr. Crayton's local contacts, Grayson rented a boat trailer, loaded the damaged Whaler onto it, and headed back to Hampton. After crossing Hatteras Inlet on the ferry, he drove past the recently relocated Cape Hatteras Lighthouse, then proceeded north. Three and a half hours later, he was home in Hampton.

Arriving at his mother's house in the wee hours of the morning, he parked the trailered boat in her backyard. Exhausted from the long day, he climbed into his boyhood bed and pulled a blanket over himself as he reflected on the events of this long day. As he drifted off to sleep, there was no question what his first action of the morning would be.

CHAPTER
53

EVEN BEFORE the alarm sounded, Grayson was up and out of bed. He quickly showered, shaved, dressed, and headed for the telephone in the den, having decided it was time to get the Commonwealth of Virginia back into the ball game. Confident he had absolute proof Dani Alverez had not made up the pirate story, Grayson didn't care how early it was. He dialed the number and two rings later, someone said, "Hello, Bledsoe residence."

"Is Mr. Bledsoe in? This is Attorney Grayson Forrest." Surely, even Bledsoe would help him get a forensic examination of the boat. *After all,* Grayson queried, *the Commonwealth Attorney's primary function is to see that justice is done, isn't it?*

Shortly, a deep voice responded. "Hello, Mr. Forrest, what can I do for you at this early hour of the morning?" Bledsoe spoke curtly, as he sat at his kitchen table, curious what this upstart lawyer wanted.

At first, Bledsoe listened quietly as Grayson explained how Gunnery Sergeant Lincoln Vernon uncovered evidence that would corroborate Dani's story.

Then, abruptly, in the middle of Grayson's narration of events, Bledsoe interrupted. "Now, wait just a damn minute!" he exclaimed, the same twang of arrogance in his voice. "You've already tried to tell the jury that crap and they didn't buy it. Now, you want to waste the taxpayers' money by using the Commonwealth's facilities to try to develop that same fantasy."

"I thought it was the duty of the Commonwealth's Attorney to seek the truth!" Grayson snapped, infuriated at the prosecutor's high-and-mighty attitude.

"We've got the truth! Your client's a murderer and he's going to get a ride on big sparky in less than a month. Now, goodbye, Attorney Forrest!"

Suddenly, the phone clunked dead. Bledsoe had hung up on him. Grayson was outraged. In frustration, he vented to the only available ears, his mother's. "We need a DNA expert, but the Commonwealth won't help. What in the heck am I going to do?"

Mrs. Forrest didn't know DNA from AM/FM, NRA or PTA, but as usual, she offered a solution anyway. "You ought to call your Uncle Sterling. You know, he's been in law enforcement fifty years. I'm sure he can help." Mrs. Forrest made her suggestion as though it were quite simple. In fact, she couldn't understand why Grayson was so upset.

Grayson took his mother's advice and called his uncle, who told him to bring the boat up to the York County Sheriff's compound tomorrow. He would see what he could do.

Upon his arrival there the next day, boat in tow, he was warmly greeted by his uncle.

"Grayson," Sterling announced, "I want you to meet Dr. Bryson Broadhurst, a chemistry professor at William & Mary and a retired forensic chemist for the Commonwealth of Virginia."

Grayson shook hands with an elderly, bushy-haired professor, then quickly told his story. Shortly, he and the professor climbed onto the boat for a closer look at the blood smears and other forensic evidence that might be detectable. Not realizing its significance, Grayson pointed out the bloodstains on the boat hook, as well as the splinters found inside on the cabin floor. Dr. Broadhurst took tissue samplings of the blood and picked up the splinters with a tweezer, placing each splinter in a separate bottle.

Holding one of the bottles up to the light, he inspected it. "It looks like bone splinters to me," he announced, but he wasn't sure. He would analyze both the blood and the splinters and get back to Grayson as soon as possible.

"Doctor, I don't mean to push you," Grayson warned, "but this is literally a matter of life or death!"

CHAPTER

54

October 27th

ANOTHER MAJOR setback—Gunny was diagnosed with pneumonia. That, along with two weeks already wasted in the hospital, was disconcerting to everyone. Although Gunny had a burning desire to get back out on Toby's trail, his coughing fits triggered excruciating pain deep in his chest, which tempered his headlong notion to ignore doctor's orders. To have any chance of ever finding Mandy, not only did he have to be smart, but he also had to be both strong and healthy. He couldn't allow himself to act impulsively. He had to use his brain; a lesson he learned the hard way over the years.

During most of his days in the hospital, he lay propped up in bed, studying a map of the Outer Banks and planning his search strategy. While counting the days until the fateful November 22nd execution date, it suddenly dawned on him November 22nd had another significance: It was the 284th Anniversary of Blackbeard's death at Ocracoke.

*

Martina had accumulated enough air miles for a free flight around the world, maybe twice. She tried to divide her time between her ailing mother in the Caymans and her condemned brother at the Mecklenburg Penitentiary. As for Grayson, she was usually able to rendezvous with him at least once a week, either in the town of Jarrett near the prison or in Hampton. Of course, there were numerous phone calls between them, sometimes three a day.

As their relationship grew stronger, they began to feel bonded by a mutuality created only by the terrible adversity they had endured. They had become best friends, but much to Grayson's chagrin, there was still no sex, *not yet, but maybe soon,* he hoped.

*

November 5th
17 Days Until The Execution

"Governor, this is Roger. We've got a slight problem with the announcement plan."

Brotherton listened on his intercom as his front man talked to him from the manager's office at the Chamberlin Hotel.

"Yeah, what's up, Roger?"

"Well, sir, it's like this. If the execution is at eight o'clock, we don't have enough time for the alcohol-free cocktail hour, a full course dinner, and then, your introductory speech before Alverez is fried. We really need to put off the execution until nine o'clock."

"So why is that a problem, Roger? I'm the governor, so I suspect I can just call the judge and have it taken care of."

Five minutes later Brotherton called Judge Bullins on the phone.

"Hello, Buford," the governor began, "I need just a little more assistance."

Buford Bullins had been a trial judge for twenty-five years and was burned out. A plush appointment to the Virginia Supreme Court, the United States Court of Appeals or maybe even the United States Supreme Court would be a wonderful way to cap his judicial career.

"Yes, Governor, what can I do for you?" Bullins responded, his thoughts actually focusing on what the governor might eventually do for him in return.

"Buford, I've got a slight logistical problem with the execution of Alverez. We need to change the execution time until nine o'clock. I know I have the power to delay the execution, but I'd prefer it come from you."

"Certainly, Governor," Bullins gushed. "If you can get the warden to make an official request, I'll be glad to put it off an hour; there'll be no problem."

"You've got it, Buford; I won't forget this."

As the phone went dead, Judge Buford Bullins smiled, as he congratulated himself for his clout with the man who might just be the next President of the United States.

The next day, Warden Alton Pugh, known to his friends as "Porky," sat at the massive mahogany conference table in the library of the governor's mansion. Robert Keller sat across from him with Brotherton at the head of the table. The warden had already agreed to make the official request of Judge Bullins for the one-hour delay of the execution.

"Now, Pugh, there's something else I need to talk with you about," Brotherton said, as he pulled his chair closer to the conference table, his voice taking on a very serious tone. "You know how hard I've had to fight to get this Fast Track Death Penalty Law through the General Assembly, don't you?"

"Oh, yes sir and we're proud of you, sir," Pugh replied, obviously flattered the governor had wanted to talk personally with him.

"And you know, Pugh, don't you, one of the most important criteria for this new death penalty law is for it to truly be a deterrent?"

Warden Pugh, gazing attentively at the governor, nodded his round, red-cheeked face solicitously.

"And you know, Pugh, the execution will be on national television. You understand it is very important for it to look painful, dreadful and absolutely awful."

Warden Pugh continued to nod.

"Well, unfortunately, I've never seen an execution. You've been the warden at the state penitentiary since 1977 and seen a number of them, haven't you?"

Leaning his rotund body forward, Pugh placed his elbows on the conference table. A nauseating grin filled his puffy cheeks. "I sure have, Governor! What would you like to know?"

"Everything! First, how does the electric chair work?"

With his pea green eyes glistening brightly and his whiny voice titillating with excitement, Warden Pugh, all too eagerly, began his explanation. "Well, 'bout an hour before we fry 'em, they're usually so cold and clammy we have to shave the back of their head and left calf so the electrodes will stick to 'em."

A possum grin on his face, Pugh rubbed his palms together. "Then, we bring 'em into the death chamber and hook 'em up. After that, we just turn on the juice. Nothin' to it." Pugh obviously loved to talk about executions, his breathing noticeably heavier than before.

"Now look, I can't afford a screw up," Brotherton said. "You know, Pugh, millions of people will be watching. By the way, has there ever been a screw up that you know of?"

"Never by us," Warden Pugh assured, but then hastened to add there had been some mistakes back in the early days of execution by electrocution.

"In fact, at the very first execution, they gave the murderer too much juice and caught him on fire. I heard it looked like he'd gone to hell before he left earth."

Pugh began to chuckle insensitively.

"Now, wait a minute!" Keller interrupted. "What about that guy down in Florida back in 1997 who caught on fire? Wouldn't you call that a major screw-up?"

"Oh, that," Pugh said, a hint of agitation in his voice. "That was a Cuban. They use masks down in Florida, and the mask caught fire. It stunk up the room with the smell of burning flesh. Other than that, it wasn't no big deal."

"No big deal!" Keller exclaimed. "We don't want anything embarrassing like that to happen."

"Oh, don't worry," Pugh replied. "That could never happen here 'cause we don't use masks. Our scumbags have to go to their graves staring the world in the eye!"

"Okay, what other possible debacles do you know of?" Brotherton asked.

Pugh began to giggle.

"One time the chair broke, the condemned man tumbled out in the floor and was knocked unconscious. They moved him to a bed and gave him chloroform and morphine to keep him unconscious while they fixed the chair. I don't know, but I guess they had to prop it back up somehow. Anyway, it took over an hour to fix it and get this guy strapped back into the chair so they could fry him."

Pugh was now grinning sadistically, seeming to enjoy displaying his callous attitude about the death penalty.

"Anything else?" the governor inquired.

"Well, nothing except the stories you've already heard, you know, like the guy not getting enough juice the first time and having to be zapped once or twice more, but all those screw-ups happened years ago." Pugh, his face grimacing, stared into the governor's eyes. "We had it down-pat during the last twenty years until those pussies voted in death by lethal injection," he said, his voice whiny, high-pitched, and irritated.

"Were you present when the last person died in the electric chair?" Keller interjected.

"I sure was. I wouldn't have missed it for the world."

"Tell us how it went," Brotherton asked eagerly.

"Well, it was back in the early nineties. This guy, uh, I forget his name, was about thirty years old and had killed an old lady over in Martinsville."

Keller and Brotherton were listening intensely, both trying to picture how the Alverez execution might go.

Pugh continued. "Less than twelve hours after the governor turned down the petition for clemency, we fried him like an egg. This is the way it went," Pugh's words were shooting out so fast he was barely understandable. "You see, seven people, a coupla' priests or preachers, along with a bunch of do-good lawyers, walked this murderer down the hallway into the death chamber." Pugh's eyes danced as he relived the moment. "They asked 'em if he had a final statement, and he just grunted. Then, some preacher said, 'God bless you.'" Pugh paused and shook his head in disgust.

Shortly, however, the shake of Pugh's head was exchanged for an affirmative nod as a fiendish grin spread across his face.

"But the one I really liked, and I don't know who said it, was: 'Go with the flow!' You know, like the flow of electricity."

Pugh, apparently impressed with his own clever analysis, again burst into laughter.

Even Brotherton was unsettled with the warden's silliness. He looked at Keller with a long, penetrating stare, then shook his head wondering how such a sick puppy could ever have become a prison warden.

"Okay, okay, Porky, get serious," Keller said. "How many people has Virginia executed using the electric chair?"

"In the eighty-six years we've had the electric chair, two hundred and sixty people have been fried," Pugh responded, trying to behave in a more dignified manner.

"What really happens when the juice is turned on?" Keller asked.

"Well, the condemned man's given a two thousand volt shock of A.C. current for fifty-seven seconds. Then, whether he's dead or not, we hit 'em again with another two thousand volts for another fifty-seven seconds."

"How long does it normally take them to die?" Brotherton asked.

"Well, Governor, I hate to tell you this," Pugh said, his voice lowering as though he didn't want anybody else to hear, "but they die instantly. In fact, the speed of paralysis and destruction of the brain is so fast the signal of pain never even gets to the brain. In other words, they never feel a thing!" After another of Pugh's sick smiles, he gleefully added, "Also, the guy's body temperature goes up to 140 degrees fahrenheit. You can stick a fork in him — he's well done and definitely dead!"

CHAPTER
55

November 10th
12 Days Until The Execution

GUNNY, WHEN in the heck are they going to let you out of there?" Grayson asked, the telephone to his ear, a twang of panic in his voice.

Gunny was sitting up in the hospital bed sipping on a glass of milk. "All they say is soon, but they say if I leave now, the pneumonia will come back. There's still enough time!"

"How do you feel?"

Gunny took a deep breath. "My wounds, you know, in the butt and the chest, seem to have healed...uh, excuse me," he gasped as he went into another hacking, coughing fit. "Excuse me, uh, that's the problem. I still have fluid down in my lungs."

"Gunny, I hate to say this, but I think it's hopeless. I don't see any way that we have time to find Toby.

"No! I'll be out of here in a week. I've been studying the chart. I think I've got a good idea of the general area where Toby's hiding out."

*

November 15th

With just over seven days until the execution, Martina flew out of Miami on Air Cayman to see her mother on this, the final trip before Dani was to be put to death. She hoped her mother would be able to return with her to Virginia to see her son for the last time.

When Martina had been home just a week earlier, she had hardly recognized her mother. A very dark-skinned lady clad in a light green house coat appeared in the hallway, her hair much grayer than Martina had remembered, the furrows in her face deeper than ever. Rosa Alverez appeared to have aged ten years in the past month.

This time Martina found her mother sitting on the sofa, staring almost catatonically at the wall. Her eyes were red and blood shot from continuous crying, and her spirit was broken.

"Don't give up, Mama. We're not going to let it happen," Martina promised, her voice crackling, betraying her own growing feelings of hopelessness.

As the evening grew on, they held each other tightly, sobbing together, both dreading the arrival of the fast-approaching final moment. "How's my baby doing?" Rosa asked meekly.

Martina assured her Dani was doing a lot better than his mother.

"I love him," Rosa said, her voice shaking uncontrollably. "I just can't bear the thought of losing him."

Both Rosa and her late husband, Jose' had been born and raised in Cuba. Later, under the Castro regime, Jose' and his parents fled to the Cayman Islands. Similarly, Rosa's parents moved to Jamaica with their six children.

Rosa met Jose' when he came to Jamaica on a fishing expedition. It was love at first sight — they were married within a month and lived in Jamaica until 1982 when the couple, along with their two young children, moved to Grand Cayman.

In 1992, when Dani was only twelve years old, Jose's fishing boat was caught in a gale. A mayday transmission was heard by the Jamaican Coast Guard, but no rescue was ever attempted since the location of the call could not be ascertained. Jose' had been lost at sea — gone forever.

In 1996, after Rosa had suffered a mild heart attack, she was ordered to lose some weight and take heart medication. She did lose a few pounds, but continued to work as a housekeeper. Martina had long been concerned her mother was not taking proper care of herself, and worse, the stress of this ordeal might be more than she could endure.

Later that evening, after a dinner of conch and rice, Martina and Rosa ate homemade ice cream on the side porch. Although Dani had not been mentioned for almost an hour, Martina suddenly looked her mother in the eye.

"Mama, the lawyers are doing everything they can do, but the result is really in God's hands."

Rosa's solemn eyes drifted up from her ice cream as she focused on her daughter.

"Everything is in God's hands, my dear," she said tearfully.

"But Mama, what I'm trying to say is we are hopeful, but we should be prepared for the worst. I want you to go with me to see Dani. He misses you so much."

VI

THE PURSUIT

CHAPTER
56

November 17th
129 Hours Until The Execution

"GUNNY, HOW'RE you doing?" Grayson asked anxiously.

Gunny sat propped up in his hospital bed, the phone next to his ear. "They say I can check out later this morning, but they claim I'll have to be on bed rest for a little while. I'm not worried about that, though."

"Gunny, do you think you'll be up to continuing the search? "You know, we're running out of time!"

"Oh yeah, don't worry, I can handle it. I've crawled out of rice paddies worse off than this and been back in the fighting the next day. Old Marines can do most anything."

"Sure, Gunny, but you're not Superman."

"Now look! I'm supposed to wait until the doc comes by to release me, which should be anytime." Gunny paused, then added, "Oh, yeah, what about the appeal?"

"Oh," Grayson replied sadly. "Uh, I'm sorry to say the Virginia Supreme Court and the U. S. Court of Appeals have both affirmed the death sentence. The Supreme Court is our only legal hope. The certiorari petition is in Washington, but to this point, they haven't acted on it."

As though he expected the worst all along, the pitch of Gunny's voice got higher and the tone became indignant. "So, Mr. Lawyer, does that mean what I think it does?"

"Well, nobody really knows what it means except the

Supreme Court itself, but it seems to me they would have granted a stay of execution by now."

"So, what's next?"

"Not much, except for the Petition for Clemency that's been filed with the governor. Snowball's chance in hell on that!"

Grayson explained he had patched the Whaler's cabin, installed both a radar system and an extended-range cellular antenna. Then, in great detail, Gunny expounded on his new search plan, which was based on information that Toby was last seen headed south out of Ocracoke.

"If I were Blackbeard, I'd probably head down into Core Sound," he said.

"Gunny, how can you say that? In the time that's passed since Toby left Ocracoke, he could've gotten clear to South America."

"Yeah, but the North Carolina coast is Toby's turf. He knows it like the back of his hand. He doesn't have much history south of the Carolina coast."

Grayson played devil's advocate. "Assuming you're correct, even Core Sound is huge. Where do you think he might be?" Grayson asked.

"Toby's on the run, and he knows we're on to him. Core Sound is bordered on the west by the mainland — which he would avoid like the plague because of the local law looking for him. On the other hand, Core Banks to the east is a series of narrow spits of sand that extend down along the eastern shore of the North Carolina coast. Except for surf fishermen, these spits are practically deserted almost all the way down to Atlantic Beach."

"Gunny, I still don't see how you can be so sure."

"Grayson, you're not paying attention. You see, Core Sound is very shallow with channels that tend to shift. A person needs local knowledge to cruise around there, which would be perfect for this old Blackbeard wannabe. He just needs to find a desolate place where he can pull his boat up and hide out until this blows over."

Grayson remained skeptical, but there was no arguing with Gunny. Deciding to move on to the logistics of the plan, Grayson asked, "Gunny, can you get to Ocracoke from Greenville or do you want me to swing by and pick you up on my way?"

"Not to worry. I've already called an old friend over at the Greenville airport. He's going to fly me there whenever I want to go. I'm planning to meet him about noon today. I'll meet you at the Ocracoke Airport about 2 P.M."

CHAPTER

57

MARTINA AND Rosa were met at the reception center by a stern-faced prison guard who led them into the penitentiary. Mecklenburg was a modern facility encompassing a large acreage surrounded by guard towers and multi-layer fencing. Its buildings were one-story, brick structures, the walls thick and secure, specifically designed for housing high-security prisoners.

Martina's uneasiness mounted. Could her mother endure the horrible reality of seeing Dani wearing handcuffs and leg irons?

Rosa Alverez had tried to prepare herself emotionally, yet there was little she could do. She knew she had to be strong for Dani's sake, but she had inner doubts about her ability to withstand the intense pressure she was about to face.

After signing both a visitor's log and a waiver of liability, she and Martina were searched by a female guard. Then, a tall male guard, a blank expression on his face, led mother and daughter through a steel door and down a covered walkway to the building that housed death-row inmates. They were directed into a room, walls yellow and bare, where a long wooden table with eight hard-backed chairs dominated the center of the room.

"Ladies," the guard said drolly, "this is where you will meet with him. We cannot take his handcuffs or leg shackles off. Those are the rules, so please don't ask. You may see him four hours each day. Then on the day of the execution, you can be with him all day up until two hours before the end."

"Can you leave us alone with him?" Martina asked.

"That's optional. We can leave you alone with him unless there appears to be a problem. You see that mirror there?" He pointed to a three by six-foot mirror at the far end of the room. "That's a two-way mirror. There'll be a guard on the other side at all times watching what's going on."

"That'll be fine," Martina replied calmly, her insides secretly fluttering with anxiety.

"Okay, if there are no other questions, Mr. Alverez will be here shortly."

Martina became more disturbed when she noticed her mother's face had grown very pale.

"Mama, you've got to be strong, okay?" Martina reached for her mother's chilled hand and gave it a reassuring squeeze.

"I will. I'll try." Rosa murmured.

For what seemed like an eternity, the two women sat in silence, their hearts pounding, each of them with thoughts of happier days, both wishing for a miracle. For five minutes they waited, each minute dragging on like an hour, until finally, the door opened and a heavy-set guard walked into the room with Dani close behind him.

Martina wanted to scream. She wanted to grab her brother and her mother and run away with them. Now, the silent agony she had long dreaded was upon her. It was real. Her little brother was on death row, and he was going to die — for nothing. She felt like she was going to explode in anger, but when she looked at her brother's sweet face, she smiled, gratified that at least for the moment, her small family was together again.

Dani was dressed in a dark blue prison jumpsuit. His hands were cuffed in front of him and his ankles were shackled, which prevented him from taking steps greater than twelve inches. When he saw his mother, his eyes opened widely, an ear-to-ear smile extending across his face.

"Dani, my baby!" Rosa cried as she rushed toward her son, embracing him. "Oh, son, I've missed you so! I love you so much!" Rosa's voice crackled, her eyes engulfed in tears. "Are you all right?"

"Mama, I'm fine," Dani said, as he clumsily tried to embrace her with his cuffed hands. "I'm doing fairly well, but I've really been worried about you."

Martina observed the interactions between her mother and brother, savoring this precious moment, committing it to memory.

"Let's all sit down," she suggested, as she motioned toward the table. She forced herself to maintain her composure. Both Dani and their mother deserved that much.

They began to reminisce. Rosa recalled the time at church when Dani and Martina were in the children's choir. Dani had gotten upset and started crying. In front of the entire congregation, eight year old Martina left her choir seat, borrowed a tissue from the pianist, and wiped the tears from her little brother's eyes. Their priest, as well as the congregation, marveled at Martina's impromptu display of tender, brotherly love.

Martina recalled when Dani had been an altar boy. During the Christmas service, he had backed into the Advent candle, singeing his robe. There was no fire, just the smell of something burning, but it had been terribly embarrassing. Now, it brought smiles to their faces.

When Rosa told stories about Jose', their father, and his love for his family, Martina and Dani were absorbed by her every word. Rosa reminded Dani of the first time he went fishing when his father had secretly attached a bonito to Dani's fish line. Later that evening, they had celebrated by broiling Dani's first fish for dinner. Dani hadn't known the truth until many years later.

Dani talked about Father O'Reilly and told about the many hours they spent together reading the Bible and discussing why God allowed this terrible nightmare to occur.

"I owe my faith to you, Mama," Dani said. "It was you who encouraged me to go to church. If I hadn't trusted in God, I could never have made it."

Dani and his family were together all morning. They laughed, cried, reminisced — they discussed the unfairness of it all. When Grayson's name was mentioned, Dani and Martina smiled warmly, causing Rosa to wonder about this man she had never met.

The four hours passed quickly. When the guard came to tell them the visit had come to an end, the lightheartedness ended. Rosa, instantly losing her aplomb, began to cry uncontrollably. "Oh, my son, my baby! How could this happen to you? Why has God let this happen?"

"But, Mama, I've been blessed," Dani insisted.

"Uh, how do you mean, Dani?" she asked, wiping her wet eyes.

"I know God is looking out for me. He has given me you and Martina. And he has given me the best lawyer in the whole world. You are all angels. I know God will not let me down!"

With these words, a niagara of tears began to flow, the three of them sobbing like overwrought infants.

"You really are your father's son," Rosa said. "You have his faith, my child."

For Rosa and Martina, however, it was time to go back to the motel and await the bittersweet time tomorrow would bring.

MEANWHILE, AT the hospital in Greenville, Gunny was waiting impatiently for the doctor. Looking in the closet for his clothes, all he found were remnants of his wet suit, which was bloodstained and bottomless. Otherwise, he had no pants, no shirt, not even shoes nor socks.

"Damn, all I've got is this stupid hospital gown with my bandaged ass hanging out." he muttered, a strain of desperation in his voice.

Just as he was about to go into a temper tantrum, Dr. Smedley arrived. "Hello, Gunny. How's the patient this morning?"

"I feel great, but I need to get out of here, Doc."

After listening to Gunny's lungs with his stethoscope, the doctor told his patient to lie on his stomach. He pulled back Gunny's gown and checked the bandages. "Okay, Gunny, your stitches look good. As far as I'm concerned, if you promise to take it easy and not do anything strenuous, you're free to leave."

"Great! I'm out of here. Thanks, Doc."

"Hold on, Gunny, there's one little problem. There's a highway patrolman out in the lobby waiting for you. Something about an outstanding warrant."

"Oh crap! Not now."

"I'm sorry, but I can't do anything to help you out of your legal problems. You know, I'm not a lawyer, thank the good Lord. Goodbye, Gunny, and good luck."

Gunny, still in his hospital gown, sat on the edge of the bed, contemplating his predicament. He concluded the redneck trooper must have identified him from a crime report regarding the Ocracoke attack.

So, Gunny surmised, *this prick came all the way from Morehead to arrest me for missing court.*

Gunny urgently needed an escape plan. In an effort to assess his predicament, he opened his room door and cautiously peeked out. To his right, at the end of the hallway, he could see the nurse's station and the trooper waiting. To his left, an emergency exit, maybe thirty feet down the hall.

Thinking maybe he could make a run for it, Gunny grabbed his wallet and keys, jerked a sheet off his bed and pulled it over his shoulders, allowing it to drape down over his head and body. Resembling an Arab sheik, he once again peeked out the doorway. To his right, he saw the trooper, still watching, still waiting. It was all too apparent if he tried to run for the emergency exit, he would surely be seen, quickly nabbed and locked up. That would be it; Mandy and Dani would certainly be lost forever. *What was he going to do?*

But he had noticed something red on the wall outside his room. *Could I be that lucky?* Not three feet from his doorway he had seen a fire alarm. *Damn, I hate to scare the hell out of everybody, but I don't have a choice.* After taking a deep breath, he extended his arm out of the doorway and slid his palm along the wall until he felt the lever. He took a deep breath, closed his eyes, and pulled it.

The infernal squeal of the alarm interrupted the relative quiet of the hospital. Room doors began to open as perplexed faces peered out into the hallway. It was a moment of chaotic confusion.

Suddenly, like an eagle taking flight, Gunny bolted through the doorway and down the hall. A blur of white with black churning legs was all that could be seen as he scrambled toward the emergency staircase. After leaping down the first flight of steps in two gliding strides, he hurdled the entire next flight, and then took the last flight in four giant bounding jumps. Exiting into broad daylight, he scampered wildly through the parking lot, drawing attention from all he passed. It was difficult to tell whether he was a ghost or a klansman, but there was no question he was a curiosity.

Running through the parking lot, he frantically looked for any opportunity that might allow him to make a getaway. Spotting an old Camaro parked some fifty feet ahead, he darted in that direction. The sole occupant, a black teenager sporting long dreads, was sitting behind the steering wheel tapping his hand on the console in rhythm with the loud rap music on his car radio. He was so mesmerized he didn't see the white-sheeted black man approaching. Gunny opened the car door and jumped into the passenger seat.

"What chu doin', man?" the startled youngster yelled out. "Get outta' my car!"

"Take me to the airport!" Gunny demanded as he flashed a one hundred-dollar bill in the young man's face. "I'll give you two hundred dollars. Now!"

"For real?" the youngster said, surprised such prosperity had befallen him. "All right!"

At two minutes before noon, Gunny, still attired in his white sheet, exited the Camaro and walked out onto the tarmac of the Greenville airport.

"Sharky, is that you?" Gunny shouted when he saw a familiar face peering into the engine compartment of the red and white Cessna 180.

"Damn, Gunny, where's your clothes?" Sharky Turcotte replied, a look of astonishment on his face.

Sharky and Gunny had been friends since the Gulf War when Sharky, piloting a Huey, dropped Gunny's recon detachment into Kuwait, directly in front of Iraqi's so-called elite Republican Guards. How the recons had lived to tell the story is still a mystery.

"Get me the hell outta' here, Sharky! I'll worry about clothes later."

Sixty seconds later, the Cessna lifted off from the Greenville Airport and turned to a due east heading.

Thirty minutes of air time and they landed at the Ocracoke airport, where Gunny exchanged his white sheet for blue jeans, a white Cedar Island Ferry sweat shirt and canvas deck shoes. He then walked up to the Silver Lake Marina where Grayson was waiting, seated on the hood of his Cherokee. After inspecting the jerry-rigged Boston Whaler, which was still on the trailer, Gunny helped Grayson slide the boat into the water, and tie it off to the nearby dock.

After checking into the Pony Motel, they met for dinner at Howard's Pub, a local watering hole that served great seafood. As Grayson drank an Amstel Light, Gunny, still maintaining his vow of sobriety, sipped on black coffee.

"Gunny, what do you think our chances are?"

"I think we're on the brink of proving Dani's alibi, and also, finding my child." Gunny paused, gulped, and for just a moment, was speechless as he wiped the moisture from his eyes. Finally, he spoke, his voice now low and soft. "I just pray to God I find her safe and unharmed."

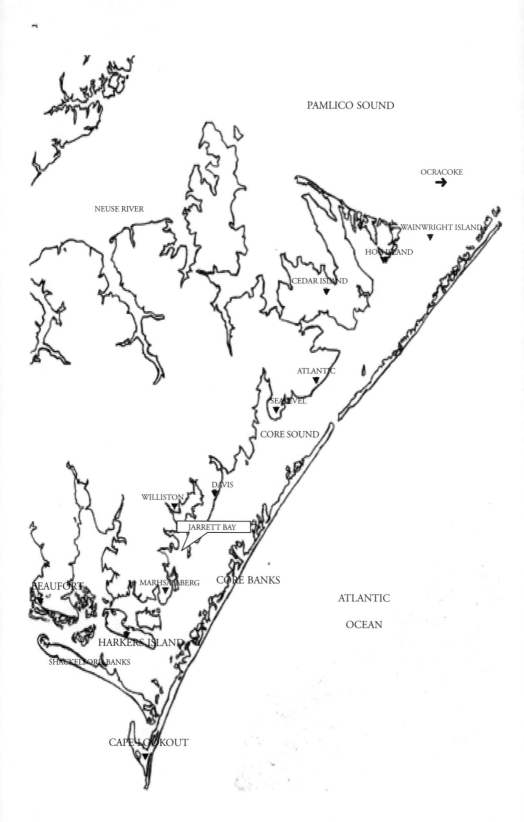

PAMLICO SOUND

OCRACOKE →

NEUSE RIVER

WAINWRIGHT ISLAND ▼

HOG ISLAND ▼

CEDAR ISLAND ▼

ATLANTIC ▼

SEALEVEL ▼

CORE SOUND

WILLISTON ▼

DAVIS ▼

JARRETT BAY

BEAUFORT ▼

MARHSALLBERG ▼

CORE BANKS

ATLANTIC

OCEAN

HARKERS ISLAND ▼

SHACKELFORD BANKS

CAPE LOOKOUT ▼

CHAPTER
59

November 20th
52 Hours Until The Execution

THE NEXT morning the two men said a solemn goodbye.
With only two and a half days before the execution, the extreme urgency of Gunny's mission was all too obvious. Grayson,
deep in thought, stood on the dock watching as Gunny slowly
maneuvered the Whaler across Silver Lake toward the ditch.
When the craft disappeared into the Pamlico Sound, Grayson
walked back to the Cherokee, a growing sense of doom beginning to override his optimism.

The morning was cold and damp, prompting Gunny to
zip up his bright yellow foul weather jacket. Another cup of
coffee would have been nice had there been time.

Gunny tried to keep his spirits pumped and positive,
but a pink overcast sky caused a sailor's weather cliche' to
sound out its foreboding overture: *Red sky at night, sailor's
delight; red sky in the morning, sailor's warning.*

"That's all I need on top of everything else, bad weather,"
Gunny muttered, knowing all too well even with fair
weather, the odds of finding Mandy were not good, but with
a storm, he might as well start planning her funeral.

Heading out of Ocracoke, holding a southwesterly
course, Gunny maintained a constant vigil, careful to steer
between the red nun buoys and the green can buoys and
also careful to avoid any telltale ripples in the water.

Less than fifteen miles out, he spotted a small island. Getting closer, he circled the tiny atoll, looking for any possible signs of life. According to his chart, this was Wainwright Island, once the site of a porpoise fishery. But now, since it appeared deserted, Gunny decided not to waste any precious time there. Instead, he pointed the bow south and continued his quest.

A few miles farther in the distance, he spotted another island. According to the cruise manual, this was Hog Island, which had gained notoriety because of its duck-hunting lodge. Examining the island closer with binoculars, it appeared most of the lodge had been washed away and the island was abandoned. In fact, the entire sound in every direction appeared abandoned.

*

Grayson was back at his office. He had just poured himself a cup of instant coffee when the phone rang. It was Uncle Sterling who told him the report from Dr. Broadhurst was in.

"Great. What does it say?" Grayson asked.

"Well, there's something I just don't understand. Uh, how in the hell could Toby Greene's bone have splintered?"

"Toby Greene's bone wasn't splintered," Grayson replied, feeling his heart skip a beat. "That bone splinter belonged to someone else. I think it came from an old skull Gunny found on Toby's boat."

"Well, according to the doc, DNA from the bone splinters matched the DNA from Toby's blood. Doc said there's a 99.98 per cent chance it was from Toby or someone genetically related."

"Wow!" Grayson said excitedly, the significance of this new clue racing to the forefront of his mind. "You know what that means, don't you, Uncle Sterling?"

"Well, not really."

"Uncle Sterling, it means Toby Greene was carrying

around the skull of his father, grandfather or somebody related to him."

"Well, I'll be a monkey's uncle!"

"Thanks for the compliment, Uncle Sterling, but could you fax me Dr. Broadhurst's report ASAP?"

After hanging up, Grayson pondered this new evidence, soon concluding this could be a major breakthrough. With a little bit of hard proof of Toby's actual existence, and perhaps with a scientifically verifiable connection of his relationship to Blackbeard, it just might be enough to somehow embarrass the governor into staying the execution.

Only five minutes passed when two faxes came in, one right after the other. The first was the worst possible news: The United States Supreme Court had denied certiorari, in other words, it had denied discretionary review of Dani's death sentence. The bottom line now was that the only person who could stop the execution was Governor Alexander S. Brotherton, himself.

The second fax was the DNA report. Grayson immediately stuffed it into his brief case, and took off for ECU, one of the few universities offering a master's degree in maritime archaeology and, more importantly, actually had a resident professor who was a certified expert on Blackbeard.

Grayson arrived at ECU mid-afternoon and drove directly to the brand new Harris Building, a modern structure used by the maritime archaeology department. He located Dr. Charles Goforth's office, where he was greeted by the tall, lanky professor wearing an ill-fitted brown suit with a blue and yellow striped tie.

As he sat across from Goforth's desk, Grayson explained the case history of Dani Alverez and the kidnapping predicament of Mandy Vernon. After presenting his hypothesis about the familial relationship between Toby and Blackbeard, Grayson showed Dr. Goforth the report on the DNA findings.

Dr. Goforth listened patiently, then carefully studied the report. There was a pause, the professor grimacing, as if in deep thought until finally he spoke. "The hypothesis you are grasping for seems incredible. I'll need a little while to do some research on this."

"Time is a commodity we don't have! My client is going to die in two days!"

"Well, I've got another idea. Let's walk over to the criminal justice building and see my friend, Hardie Ferguson. Hardie is a professor and also a retired criminal defense lawyer. Just the other day, he was telling me a story about a case that might fit."

They walked next door to the building that housed the school of social work, including the department of criminal justice. After exiting the elevator on the third floor, they entered an office at the end of the hallway.

They waited about five minutes when a short, balding man in his early sixties, wearing a maroon blazer and khaki pants greeted them at his office doorway. He ushered them into his small office, where Dr. Goforth made introductions and explained the situation, then reminded Ferguson of a recent conversation between them at a social function at the Chancellor's house.

"You'll recall the genetic argument you told me about. You know, a person could inherit homicidal tendencies."

"Oh, yes," Ferguson said. "I read about it in a law journal; it was rather far out."

Without further coaxing, Ferguson told them about the law review article, which analyzed a case where a genetics expert was allowed to testify about four generations of men with verifiable violent tendencies."

Ferguson, with a flair for the dramatic, began waving his Bic pen in the air as he proceeded with his explanation. "First," he snapped, "the defendant was convicted of a violent murder. Second, the defendant's father, his grandfather and his great-grandfather's DNA all showed violent tendencies."

Ferguson smiled resolutely, then continued. "The geneticist had been able to obtain blood or bone samples from four generations and matched their DNA patterns. Remarkably, an identical pattern of DNA was found common to each man. It was theorized these common strands of DNA signified inherited violent traits."

"Did it help the defense's case?" Grayson asked curiously.

"Well, it sounded really good, but in the end, no cigar. The guy still got the death penalty, but the point is the genetic evidence was accepted by the court as scientifically valid and reliable."

"Could you get me a copy of that law review article, Mr. Ferguson?" Grayson asked.

"Of course, how soon do you need it?"

"Yesterday!"

"How about tomorrow?"

Driving back to Hampton, Grayson felt very much alone. He longed for Martina's voice. His insides ached at the thought of what she and her family must be experiencing. He dialed her phone number on his cellular phone.

The distant buzz stopped. "Hello," came her familiar voice.

"Martina, where are you?"

"Mama and I are on the way back to the motel. We just left Dani at the prison. Just two visits left."

"Listen, there's been a little progress," he said, then told her about his discussion with the ECU professors.

"Do you think these professors can help us?"

"I don't know, but I'll tell you — I'm actually a little awestruck by this new finding. Can, can you believe we are probably dealing with the great-great-great-grandson of Blackbeard?"

THE WHALER cruised past Thorofare Bay, heading south toward the village of Atlantic, a very old town originally known as Hunting Quarters. Although the docks were crowded with commercial fishing vessels, Gunny was able to squeeze the Whaler between two larger boats.

He walked around the waterfront area of the town and asked the standard questions to anyone and everyone who would listen to him, but still, no luck. Finally, on his way back to the boat, discouraged once more, he approached a dark-headed, full-figured woman, probably in her early forties. She was sweeping the steps of a general store near the docks.

"Excuse me, ma'am, could I ask you a question?"

The woman smiled cordially. "Sure, what can I do for you?"

Gunny told his story and showed her the photos of Mandy. Immediately, her eyes squinted and her pronunciations became more deliberate.

"I've not seen the child, but I know Toby Greene very well, in fact, too well," she declared ruefully.

"What do you mean?"

She clenched her fists as an expression of disdain formed on her face. "Well, by God, I use to live with the good-for-nothing son of a bitch!"

Gunny couldn't believe his ears.

"You lived with him?"

"Yes, about five years ago. He left me 'cause I couldn't have children. God, I'd hate to think what a child of his would've been like," she added scornfully.

"What do you mean?"

With bitterness in her eyes, the woman's voice grew louder. "He's the meanest, most self-centered man I've ever known! All he cares about is himself and a stupid notion he's related to Blackbeard."

"Is he actually related to Blackbeard?"

"I don't know. Who cares?" the woman snapped, still upset at the mention of Toby Greene's name.

"Have you seen him lately?"

"Thank the good Lord I haven't, but I did hear he came into the docks three or four weeks ago for supplies. Seems like he was injured and needed some bandages and stuff."

"Any idea where he's holing up?"

"He could be most anywhere. He knows these waters as good as any man alive."

Gunny thanked the woman and headed back to the boat. With daylight waning, he was all too aware that to try to navigate Core Sound in the dark would be foolhardy. Rather, it made more sense to spend the night in the village of Atlantic, then move out at first light.

As he lay in the cabin of the Whaler, his eyes closed, a feeling of anticipation began to build inside him. *The end is near, I just know it!* he thought, as sleep overtook him.

*

November 21st
39 Hours Until The Execution

Shattering the serenity of the reddish-gray dawn, the twin Evinrudes roared alive. Gunny steered the Whaler into

Core Sound, again heading south. In the first two hours, he had little to no luck. He hailed two fishing boats, the first a trawler, the second a sports fisherman, but the crew of neither boat could provide any helpful information. After four hours, Gunny began to doubt his strategy, wondering if Toby's trail in mid-Core Sound had grown cold.

Gravely aware this was Dani Alverez's last full day on earth, Gunny changed his search plan. He had to use the short time remaining as efficiently as possible. Instead of stopping at every little village and town along the shore, on a hunch, decided to turn eastward and cross back over to lower Core Banks.

The waves were capping, and the wind was becoming increasingly stronger and colder. The Whaler held steadily on its eastward heading, the bow now pointing toward the sparsely populated barrier island known as Core Banks. This elongated sandy strip extended down to its southernmost point at Cape Lookout marked by a statuesque black and white, diamond-covered lighthouse, the upper half Gunny could see in the distance.

Steering between two lines of slanted stakes that marked the channel, Gunny navigated slowly through the shallow water, finally shifting into neutral as the Whaler drifted near a rickety, wooden landing dock. He cleated the Whaler down, hopeful the craft would be secure in the uncertain seas that seemed to be forthcoming.

After wading ashore onto a narrow beach, then up a path, Gunny soon spied a shack where a young man dressed in blue jeans and a red Wolfpack sweatshirt sat on a porch swing. He was waving his hand cordially in greeting. "Can I help you?" he offered as Gunny walked closer.

Gunny asked if the young man had seen anyone matching Toby or Mandy's description, but his response was negative. Nevertheless, Gunny decided to check it out and was able to rent the young man's four wheeler.

"By the way," Gunny asked, now more concerned than ever about the weather conditions, "have you heard a weather report?"

"Sure have. Supposed to be a real nasty storm coming in. Small craft warnings, high winds, rain and all. If I were you, I wouldn't be on the water later on tonight. It could get real bad!"

The four-wheeler turned out to be an old rusted Toyota pickup truck with a five-speed manual transmission and big tires. As Gunny spun northward up the beach, he could see the reflection of the Cape Lookout lighthouse in the rear-view mirror. Speeding across the hard sand, the Toyota's tires just inches from the foamy surf, Gunny glanced left, the land still so low the waters of the sound were visible through the sea oats. To the east, the gray Atlantic Ocean hurled increasingly larger waves, crashing violently onto the beach, sending finger streams of foamy sea water flowing high onto his beach pathway.

As the Toyota splashed through the surf, Gunny spotted two fishermen ahead. He stopped to talk to them, making the usual inquiries and receiving the usual negative responses. Three more times he stopped to speak to other fishermen, his efforts still for naught.

Approaching Drum Inlet, located at the northern tip of Core Banks, Gunny saw even more fishermen, but he might as well have been talking to the sea gulls - nobody had seen anything. He turned the Toyota around and gunned it down the beach, convinced if Toby had been there, someone would have seen him.

BACK ON the Whaler, Gunny studied the chart, hoping for divine intervention. He decided to set a course to the western shore toward the town of Davis, said to be the most unspoiled village on Core Sound.

When the Whaler was just north of Davis, near Jarrett Bay, Gunny cut the engines to review his chart again. With daylight waning, he knew this would probably be his last chance to save Dani, and maybe Mandy. It was crucial his choice of search locations be on the mark!

As the boat drifted aimlessly with the current, Gunny tried to match the configurations of land shown on the chart with the waters and shorelines before him. Something just didn't match up. There was an island off to starboard that wasn't supposed to be there. In the exact spot where this island should've been on the chart, there was nothing shown but water — extremely shallow water.

Taking a magnified view of the uncharted island with binoculars, Gunny could barely make out a structure of some kind. Concluding it was probably just a duck blind and further investigation would be a waste of precious time, he steered the Whaler back into the channel. Once more, he pointed the bow south headed to *who the hell knows where.*

Then, on a whim, his attention returned to the little island. His angle of view of the strange structure he'd seen earlier was now unobscured. From this angle, he could clearly tell it definitely wasn't a duck blind, that is, unless they made duck blinds out of orange brick.

Cutting the engines, Gunny checked his guide book. One reference indicated some of the little islands in the area were old abandoned menhaden processing plants. Figuring this was an old fishing plant, Gunny's first inclination was - forget it, move on.

Just as the Whaler was about to pass the mouth of Jarrett Bay, Gunny heard himself say, *Wait a minute! The water is shallow, it's poorly marked and in the middle of nowhere. That island would be a perfect hideout for old Toby!* Gunny quickly swung the wheel to starboard, the Whaler heeling slightly, then turning to the right, its new heading Jarrett Bay and the uncharted island.

Gunny noticed the blue water getting lighter, fading to sky blue, then to a soft baby blue, and soon it was white, foamy and rippling, the bottom clearly visible.

Suddenly, it was too late. The inevitable grinding sound instantly put a crushing damper on Gunny's optimism. The craft dragged into the shallows, then lugged to a dead stop - grounded and stuck.

"Damn!" Gunny exclaimed as he tried to push the Whaler back toward deep water with the boat hook, but his efforts were for naught. The 5,000 pound craft might as well have been a mountain - it wouldn't budge. The boat was lodged firmly on the shoal, still a hundred yards from the mystery island, high and dry, planted in a foot of water.

Gunny was beside himself, but he forced himself to regain his composure and think.

After a moment, it occurred to him he might be able to get a little help from Mother Nature. Quickly locating his tide tables, he studied it carefully.

"Hoorah!" he finally exclaimed when he discerned the tide was rising. *Maybe there's still some hope!* he thought.

*

Pondering what he could say to the governor, given the opportunity, Grayson knew whatever it was, it would have to be concise, convincing and take place within the next twenty-seven hours. If and when the time came, it would absolutely be his last-ditch chance to convince Brotherton to stay the execution.

He decided he really needed something undeniable, something that drew media attention, something with pizazz — like maybe a solid, verifiable connection to the real Blackbeard.

With a stiff neck and a tension headache, Grayson sipped on his ninth cup of coffee of the day. On his second sip, the fax machine buzzed and a multi-page document from Professor Hardie Ferguson began scrolling out.

Grayson perused the ten-page law review synopsis, which discussed the use of human genome research as affecting criminal behavior. *Could this theory prove Toby had inherited his violent tendencies from Blackbeard?* Grayson had serious doubts.

The synopsis was quite complex, but as Grayson paged through it, he began to get the gist of it. It suggested that the revolution in genetics presented new reasons for criminal conduct. It quoted cases where murderous behavior had been provoked because of inherited genetic defects or mutations in the perpetrator. It discussed specific situations based on inherited traits such as depression, alcoholism and attempted suicide. But these types of cases, Grayson decided, just didn't seem to fit here.

Then Grayson came across the case of *State of Mississippi v. Garland E. Ziglar.* Ziglar was convicted of murder after he gunned down the manager of a convenience store. His antisocial behavior had been detected when he was an adolescent. *Just like Toby.*

As Ziglar grew older, he engaged in petty crimes and deviant sexual behavior. *Hmm, both thieves, both sickos,* Grayson reflected.

Ziglar had committed a number of assaults, which culminated a convenience store murder. In his capital murder trial, DNA from three generations of male ancestors, each with a common mutation for violence, was offered as a reason for his aberrant behavior. Therefore, his lawyer argued he should not be sentenced to death.

Toby's father had been a rough, tough brawler and had once beaten a man to death. His grandfather had been a violent, mean-spirited man. *Could the genetic link of violence extend all the way back to Blackbeard?*

"Nah, no way," Grayson finally decided, shaking his head at the realization that Ziglar's case only went back three of four generations. *No,* Grayson reasoned, *in order to go all the way back to Blackbeard, they would be looking at fifteen or maybe even twenty generations. Trying to knit together that many generations would be spreading the genetics too thin.*

But then, Grayson noticed an addendum to the faxed material. It was a photocopy of a newspaper clipping entitled, "DNA Trace On Ancient Bones Leads to Teacher." Reading the article, he learned that back in 1997, DNA from a nine thousand year old human skeleton known as the Cheddar Man was used to establish a blood tie with a modern-day school teacher who lived just a half mile from the cave where the bones were discovered.

"Wow!" Grayson exclaimed. *If DNA holds up nine thousand years, a mere 280 years from Blackbeard to Toby is nothing.*

CHAPTER

62

THERE WAS a chill in the autumn air as darkness closed in, the blue water appearing black as tar. With the tide rising, Gunny decided he might as well wade in and check out the little island while he was waiting.

Dropping anchor, he exchanged his jeans and sweatshirt for his brand new, midnight blue wet suit Grayson had bought him. Tugging and pulling, he wiggled into the four ply suit, hopeful it would keep him from freezing to death should he be confronted with prolonged exposure to the elements. For added protection, he strapped on his cartridge belt with his holstered Beretta and extra magazines.

As he waded through waist-deep water, he made his way into the shallows, trudging along until he reached a muddy bank, where he grabbed an overhanging root and pulled himself up the steep, slippery bank. At the top, standing in the midst of swamp grass, bayberry bushes and scrubby pines, he peered toward the interior of the densely wooded island which he judged to be only about three or four hundred yards in diameter.

Instinctively drawing on his recon experience, he decided first, he would walk the entire perimeter of the tiny island before plodding headlong into its dark center. Slowly, carefully creeping along the bank, he stepped through ruts and furrows cut by the tidal erosion.

Darkness now fully set in, the only light coming from a half moon that occasionally peeked through the clouds. When he reached the west side of this nearly-round island, he noticed just ahead was a deep cutaway in the bank. As he got closer, he could see a small inlet partially hidden by overhanging trees and bushes.

Gunny assumed the little inlet led into the interior of the island, but upon peering into the opening, all he could see was nebulous shadows against a backdrop of darkness. Deciding to ford the stream, he stepped into knee-deep water and waded across, then climbed up the opposite bank. Walking along the steep slope that ran above the stream, Gunny slipped deeper and deeper toward the dark center of the island.

The view ahead was black as coal. As he stepped through the darkness, a fleeting moon glimmer momentarily illuminated a striking silhouette. It was in the creek just ahead. Its shape bore the contour of a gigantic shark, and seemed to be staring ominously at Gunny, forbidding further entry.

Gunny, careful to stay in the shadows, inched toward the strange object floating in the water as if it were a boat. Sidestepping slowly along the bank, finally, he could see the entire silhouette.

By damn, I've found him! Gunny concluded, as he stopped not thirty yards from the vessel. The sleek-shaped craft was definitely a racing boat and had two bubble cockpits. *This has to be the refitted Fountain yacht described by the Jackson guy.*

Forcing himself to remain silent and motionless, Gunny watched and waited, searching for any sign of movement. Seeing none, he skulked closer, until finally recognizing something. It was a man, albeit a very large man. He was standing on the bank next to the boat.

Gunny, now less than ten yards away from the craft, tried to blend into the pine tree forest that ran along the creek bank. Crouching and keeping in the shadows, he could see the brick structure in the background, which appeared to be the remains of a factory, presumably a menhaden factory.

Floating in the creek directly behind the shark-shaped boat was the white fishing boat. *This is really it! I've found that son-of-a-bitch's hideout.*

An ear-piercing crack, a sound as intrusive as a rifle shot in the dark, rudely interrupted the quietude of the night. In his excitement, Gunny had become negligent. He'd stepped on a fallen tree branch, which snapped, startling the evening, blatantly announcing to all within ear shot an intruder had encroached.

Gunny froze in his tracks and held his breath. But, in a blink of time, a metallic click-clank sounded, the sound made when a rifle bolt is being pulled and released. With zero time for processing, automatic gunfire suddenly blasted, instantly followed by a string of repetitive thuds splattering into the nearby creek bank. Gunny hit the ground and crawled for cover behind a pine tree. Another volley of gunfire reverberated through the forest, this time ripping holes in the pine tree just inches above Gunny's head. Gunny, his pistol drawn, dared not shoot back for fear Mandy might be in his line of fire.

But then, as suddenly as it had started, the gunfire abruptly stopped. Other than the echo from the blasts that still rang in Gunny's ears, there was nothing but an eerie silence.

Daring a peek from behind the tree, Gunny could see the big man, presumably Toby, climb aboard the Fountain yacht, drop into the port cockpit, and close the bubble canopy behind him. The engines roared alive, coughing out enormous clouds of gray smoke, and the shark boat began to move, creeping very slowly at first as it headed out of the inlet toward open water.

Realizing the craft was going to pass directly in front of him, Gunny considered jumping down from the bank onto its deck, but before he could get into position, it was too late. The boat began to rapidly accelerate, and in another second, was shooting down stream toward the inlet like a hot rod on a drag strip.

As it whizzed by, it was just a blur. Nevertheless, wishfully, Gunny was convinced he'd glimpsed his daughter's blond hair in the starboard canopy. In seconds, the shark boat brushed through the overhanging tree branches at the entrance of the inlet and skimmed out through the shallows and into Jarrett Bay. Heeling sharply, the sleek craft made a U-turn, then roared toward Core Sound.

Gunny, still clamoring along the creek bank, tripped and rolled down the hill, then splashed into the creek. Springing to his feet, the water up to his hips, he high-stepped through the murk, gradually making it out of the creek, back to the shallows of the bay. Quickly retrieving the Whaler's anchor, he climbed back aboard his freshly re-floated boat, fired up the Evinrudes, and slammed the dual throttles forward. The chase was on!

Desperately, Gunny scoured the horizon. Only a minute had passed, but to his great dismay, the shark boat was gone, vanished, out of sight. As the Whaler surged full blast into Core Sound, a flicker of moonlight allowed a passing glimpse of the shark boat's shiny black hull. But only a heartbeat later, the mysterious craft was enveloped into the blackness of the night.

The Whaler was fast, but despite the urgency, Gunny dared not risk the narrow, uncertain channel at maximum speed. Hitting a shoal at high speed would be disastrous and would end his quest forever. He ran the boat as fast as he dared but with every passing minute, he was losing ground.

Grateful for his new radar, he flicked the on switch, and blindly started pushing buttons. The screen blinked on in shades of green, and the scanner began doing 360s on the dial. Suddenly, a shiny blip began flashing.

The whitecapping waves pounded the Whaler as the

wind velocity accelerated, buffeting the little boat hard to port with each gust. To make matters more miserable, a cold, steady rain was falling, which reduced visibility to a grayish haze.

Gunny, struggling to hold the boat in the channel, kept one eye glued on the suspect blip, his other eye attuned to the turbulent waters ahead. It only took a moment for him to figure out that the channel marker buoys showed up on the radar screen. *Thank God for that,* he murmured. Otherwise, he'd never be able to find the markers out in that murky soup.

Trying to hold the boat on the crest of the mounting waves was virtually impossible. All he could do was maintain headway and keep the bow steeped upward. Time and time again, the Whaler powered up the curl of an attacking wave, only to be slammed back down into the sea, as cascades of cold salt spray repetitively whipped back into his face. Wiping his brow with each frigid drenching, his eyes flicked warily back and forth between the radar blip and the hostile froth rising before him. It made him *daresome.*

It had been agonizingly slow, terribly uncomfortable and scarier than hell, but after three hours, the little boat was still boldly pounding through the sea, in pursuit of the elusive blip. Holding tightly to the helm, Gunny's arms ached and his feet throbbed from hours of standing and balancing himself as the boat ceaselessly rose onto the swells, dived down into the troughs, rocked with the wind and rolled with the waves. Even though he wore the four-ply wet suit, cold rain and blinding spray had seeped in, leaving him shivering and miserable.

Still, he kept the boat moving onward, trusting and praying that before this day ended, he would find his child.

IT WAS a few minutes after one o'clock in the morning, less than twenty hours before Dani was to die. For the past hour, Grayson had been sitting in his office, still trying to figure how the genetic information might save Dani. He was too wired to sleep, and with the events about to take place, sleep was a luxury he couldn't afford.

The sound of footsteps on the staircase distracted him from his deep concentration. He thought he was supposed to be the only person in the building.

The office door abruptly opened and in walked Charles Goforth, the lanky ECU professor, attired in a baggy brown checked sports coat and wrinkled, non-matching blue trousers.

"Mr. Forrest, I'm glad I caught you. This was so important, I decided to drive up right away rather than phone. I hope I'm not intruding."

Relieved, Grayson invited Dr. Goforth to have a seat.

Dr. Goforth set his brief case down and pulled out a note pad, then sat down in the chair across from Grayson.

"Okay," he said anxiously. "You already know about the history of Blackbeard's skull. You know, of course, Lieutenant Maynard ordered Blackbeard's head chopped off and his headless body thrown overboard into the waters near Ocracoke, probably in the area we now call Teach's Hole."

"Uh huh."

"And everybody knows the old legend that the headless body swam around the ship three times before sinking."

"Yeah, I know all about that, Professor," Grayson said, hoping Goforth hadn't driven all the way to Hampton just to discuss the renowned Blackbeard myth.

"But, I bet you don't know why Blackbeard swam around the ship without his head?" Goforth asked.

"No, can't say as I do. Do you?"

"Well, some say that Blackbeard was swimming around, looking for his head because he didn't want to meet the devil without it."

"So what?"

"Anyhow," Goforth continued, unperturbed by Grayson's lack of enthusiasm, "Upon Lieutenant Maynard's return to Hampton, the royal governor of Virginia, Alexander Spotswood, threw an enormous celebration. Dignitaries from miles around attended, and the center of attention was Blackbeard's decaying head."

Grayson forced himself to nod politely, but actually, he was thinking — *this news flash is ancient frigging history.*

"Long lines of 17th century curiosity seekers filed past the skull, all carefully studying the grotesque head." Goforth's eyes suddenly brightened as he looked up at Grayson.

"Guess who took all the credit?" he asked.

Grayson wasn't in the mood for a guessing game, rather, he just stared blankly at the professor.

"Spotswood, the governor! He took full credit for the slaying of Blackbeard, and even told his admiring guests he considered the execution of Blackbeard to be the most important accomplishment of his career. After this celebration, the pirate's head was staked up on the bank of the Hampton River near the entrance to Sunset Creek."

"Sunset Creek," Grayson said, interrupting. "I know the exact location. That's near where I keep my boat in dry storage."

"Well, things back then weren't quite so modern. The Hampton River was a very heavily traveled body of water, and Blackbeard's head was mounted near the river's entrance as a warning to all seafarers that piracy would not be tolerated. Finally, the skull was removed and taken to an inn in Williamsburg where it was placed on display. It remained there for a good many years, but then, it mysteriously disappeared."

"What happened to it?"

"No one knows for sure, "but eventually it wound up in the hands of a wealthy Boston collector. Now get this! Coincidentally, the skull went on tour just a few months ago, and was put on display in Norfolk."

Grayson suddenly perked up, sliding to the edge of his chair. "Go ahead, Professor."

Goforth's eyes widened dramatically. "Guess what happened?"

"What?"

"Somebody stole it!"

"Who?" Grayson could feel a tickle of excitement as the suspense mounted.

"They don't know, but the suspect was a big, bearded, Blackbeard look-alike!"

"No shit!" Grayson exclaimed. Pausing, he held his breath. "But, uh, how come it wasn't in the news?"

"Uh, I don't know. Somebody may have put a hush on it for some reason."

Grayson shook his head, a puzzled expression on his face.

"So, that's it in a nutshell," Goforth said as he sat beaming, apparently waiting for a puppy-dog pat on his head.

"Are you suggesting, Dr. Goforth, the skull stolen in Norfolk could have been swiped by our boy, Toby?"

"Exactly!"

"So, if this DNA matchup between Toby and Blackbeard

is accurate, what might Toby be planning to do next? Might we predict his actions based on those of his great, great, great-grandfather?"

Goforth leaned back in his chair as his fingers fiddled with his lip while he quietly pondered, searching for an informed response. Then, looking off into the distance as though he were traveling back through history in a time machine, he slowly began to vocalize his speculations.

"I think," he said, his words coming slowly and deliberately, "I think Toby is enraptured with the legend of Blackbeard and has a notion he can reenact it."

Abruptly, Professor Goforth stood up and began to pace back and forth while continuing to talk.

"Let's assume Toby was the thief in Norfolk. If so, his willingness to steal the skull right out from under the noses of armed guards demonstrates his fanaticism. Add his willingness to try to kill your friend Gunny."

"What does that tell you, Doc?"

"Well, Mr. Forrest, it surely shows how intensely desperate this man is to accomplish something for the sake of Blackbeard." Goforth paused, then posed his own query.

"What if Toby really believes Blackbeard's headless body swam around Maynard's boat looking for its head? What if he believed the old pirate was worried without his head, he wouldn't be presentable to met the devil?" Goforth looked up, his eyes wild and dancing in fantasy.

Grayson cut a sharp look back at the giddy professor and wondered if he wasn't a bit on the eccentric side.

"You've got to be kidding, Doc!"

"I know, I know," Goforth admitted, shaking his head, as if to concede his very own hypothesis was even too outlandish for him to swallow.

"And another thing that makes no sense at all," Grayson interjected. "Why would Toby have kidnapped a young girl— Gunny's daughter Mandy?"

Goforth raised his index finger as though anxious to

reply. "You know, the real Blackbeard had at least fifteen wives, maybe more. Most were just teenagers. Maybe Toby is just acting out that legacy."

AT FIRST it could not be heard over the whipping of the wind and the crashing of the waves, but finally the buzz of the cell phone caught his ear. "Hello," he yelled into the receiver.

"Gunny, where are you?" Grayson asked as he sat behind his desk in his warm, dry office.

"I'm in the middle of a frigging hurricane chasing Blackbeard. I'm near Ocracoke, I think. I can just barely hear you; we have a bad connection. Speak louder!"

"I've got to tell you the news!" Grayson tried to make his voice heard over the fuzzy static on the line.

"Talk louder!" Gunny screamed, still struggling with the helm, still trying to hold the boat on course, fighting to keep the infernal waves from pounding the small craft from abeam.

"Now, listen to this, Gunny! Certain characteristics of the DNA in the skull fragments matched the DNA in the blood. Do you know what that means?"

"Grayson, I can't hear you," Gunny shouted - then the connection went dead.

*

2:00 A.M.

The blip moved northwest, but all Gunny saw were mountains of raging waves, seething with foamy anger, all aimed right for the little Whaler.

As the Whaler was pushed high onto the crest of a large swell, Gunny glanced down at the radar screen. Unexpectedly, the blip he had been chasing was motionless. It had stopped! With his knuckles, he rapped on the plexiglass cover of the radar unit, but the blip still did not move - it really had stopped, and what's more, the Whaler was actually gaining on it.

And, if Gunny's dead reckoning was correct, he was headed back to Ocracoke.

VII

THE PIRATE

CHAPTER
65

THE SHARK boat, adrift in the churning waters of Teach's Hole, had ceased forward movement. When the bearded pirate exited the cabin hatchway, he was wearing a black, hooded wet suit. The wet suit, in conjunction with the hood and his facial whiskers caused him to bear a striking resemblance to a gorilla in tights.

Amidst a torrent of rainfall, the shark boat bounced up and down at the whim of the angry sea. Toby hopped around the deck on one foot, trying to pull his only swim fin over his right, size twenty foot. He cursed the loss of the other fin, but now it was too late to find a replacement. He figured he must have lost it on the beach when he dug that temporary grave.

Toby next strapped twin scuba tanks on his back, pulled down his facemask, and inserted the regulator mouthpiece. As he sucked compressed air into his lungs, he reached inside the cabin and grabbed a bulging waterproof bag, which he carefully hooked onto his buoyancy vest. As he held tightly to the cabin cleats, he made his way forward across the bouncing deck to the anchor bin. Lifting the Danforth out, he held it before him and gingerly stepped off the bow, unceremoniously splashing into the swirling sea, the anchor line uncoiling behind him.

He quickly descended twenty-six feet, set the anchor flukes deep into the sea bottom, then slowly ascended to the surface. Momentarily caught between the rolling swells, he exchanged his regulator mouthpiece for his snorkel and began to swim toward the nearby beach. Soon approaching the shallows, he stripped his single fin from his foot and waded through the surf, heading directly for a large white stone protruding conspicuously out of the sand.

Against a gale-force wind and rain pounding down, he stepped up on top of the stone and gazed east as though he were getting his bearings. That done, he stepped back down on the sand and began taking measured strides inland, counting aloud with each stride. Still counting, he forded a shallow salt marsh pond, crossed a patch of sea oats and high-stepped through a thicket of bayberry bushes.

Exactly on his 75th stride, he stopped directly under an ancient live oak tree, a tree so old that 280 years hence, it might well have shaded Blackbeard himself. Pulling his prybar knife from his leg sheath, he knelt under the tree and began scraping away at the sandy ground.

It had taken him five minutes to scratch and dig down two feet when he finally felt it. As he scooped away more sand, he could see a patch of black plastic. With cupped hands, he cautiously carved away the sand encased around it, until at last, a long, black bag was uncovered, a body bag.

Carefully lifting the bag from the hole, he held it closely against his chest, cradling it like a mother would her baby. With his eyes uplifted, he rose to his feet, the long, narrow bag still nestled in his arms. Walking guardedly, he retraced his steps back through the bayberry thicket, across the patch of sea oats, through the salt-water pond until he was back at his beginning point on the water's edge.

Momentarily placing the bag and its fragile contents on the white rock, he refitted his mask, put his fin back on and re-inserted his regulator mouthpiece. Grasping the bag in both hands, he waded back into the sea, quickly descending as a fizzle of bubbles followed him into the depths of the hole. He kicked vigorously, swimming westwardly along the hole's sandy sea floor, his initial objective on the verge of becoming reality.

After swimming west exactly 125 feet, Toby descended, diving to a precise, preplanned point on the sea bottom. There, he began to scratch away sand with his bare hands. Detecting a nearly invisible fracture, he inserted the blade of his prybar knife into the crack. He pressed down hard on the handle, applying steady pressure. Soon, a large trapezoidal sand-colored rock pried upward.

After repositioning his body above the rock, he grabbed it with both hands. With all his strength, he pulled upward, struggling, straining, eyes bulging, veins swelling, until finally, there was discernible movement. Zealously, he persisted. He pushed, tugged and manhandled the huge protective rock, slowly sliding it to the side. Strangely, now exposed was the rounded end of a concrete drain pipe a yard in diameter.

Toby, still breathing through his regulator mouthpiece, removed his scuba tanks and held them out in front of him. He inserted the base of the tanks down into the round opening of the concrete pipe, the width of the double tank scuba rig only an inch smaller than the width of the pipe. Still holding the tanks out front, the air hose leading back to his mouth, Toby dove head first down into the narrow pipe. With his tanks leading the way and with a frenzy of air bubbles fizzing back up into his face, he kicked his fin and descended into the dark, round hole as though he were headed into the center of the earth.

Toby squeezed his massive girth against the circumference of the drain pipe. Inching his way down, it got increasingly tighter and more snug. Then, near catastrophe - his entire body was down inside the pipe, but his downward movement had crawled, then dragged to a stop. He had lost his momentum. The pipe was too small and his body was too large. He was stuck, it seemed.

He was past the point of no return. He could not go

forward; he could not go backward. Fearlessly, he pulled and pushed, sucked in and wiggled. Soon, ever so slightly, he moved downward. He pushed, slithered and contorted his body. Finally, he made more progress and descended deeper and deeper, until at long last, a hollow metallic clunk signaled his scuba tanks had found bottom. Groping the curvature of the sidewall, his fingertips fell into the crevice of a vault door guarded by a wheel lock. He turned the wheel and pushed, forcing the vault door open, enabling the agile giant to squeeze his wide body, scuba tanks and all, into the black hole.

Toby's hand slid across the inside of the vault door, coming to rest on the interior wheel lock. He pushed the door shut and began turning the wheel, the watertight door locking, leaving him sealed away from the outside world.

Flicking on his underwater flashlight, he shined a beam through the black water, exposing an encasement the size of a mini van. He reached upward, his fingers touching a lever. When he pushed it, the outer cover of a switch box opened. He clicked the first two toggle switches, and the watery cavern instantly illuminated. With the flip of another switch, the hum of an electric motor filled the chamber, and soon, an air pocket began to form near the ceiling. Amidst the underwater echo of gurgling water being siphoned away, the water level started to fall, and in minutes, it was pumped out leaving the room dry.

Toby removed his regulator mouthpiece, now able to breathe the stale, compressed air that filled the cavern. He opened his waterproof bag, then reverently he removed the cranial remains of his beloved patriarch. The cherished skull bore remnants of silver streaking its crown. There were dips on its face, which had once been eye sockets. Along the base of the skull, a chip recently carved by Toby's own sword was plainly visible.

Toby removed a pint bottle of Jamaican rum from his vest pocket, twisted off the cap and poured several ounces into the upside down skull. For a moment, he held the skull out before him, his eyes glazing over, his face drawing into a tight grimace. His demented thoughts intensified, totally focused on just one thing—his great, great, great-grandfather's *Vow of Vengeance.*

With zealous fanaticism glowing in his black sinister eyes, Toby lifted his sacred grail to his lips, and like a priest polishing off the communion wine, he turned the skull upward. As he drank, an obscure etching of letters could be discerned in the interior cranium of the upturned skull, the letters spelling out Blackbeard's final command. The letters read:

D-E-T-H T-O S-P-O-T-S-W-O-O-D

Ironically, it had been exactly 284 years ago to the day when Blackbeard had uttered these words an instant before he was beheaded, right here in Teach's Hole.

Toby, overflowing with maniacal veneration, cautiously opened the black body bag as though it were hallowed, revealing an intact human skeleton. After gently propping the skeleton against the side of the underwater tomb, he used bailing wire to affix the chipped skull to the top vertebrae of the skeleton.

Leaning the bones back against the wall of this man-made Davey Jones purgatory, Toby extracted a black linen sheet from his vest and draped it over the skeleton, painstakingly tucking in the sides as though it might bring warmth to the old pirate while he waited in repose for his audience with the devil.

Toby peered solemnly into the eye sockets of his predecessor as though searching for a sign of approval from his revered patriarch. As he stared into the skull's empty occipital sockets, he cleared his throat. "Soon, my great, great, great-grandfather," he vowed, his bizarre words echoing off the walls of the submarinal tomb. "Soon, you will be presentable to your father who will offer you sanctuary. Soon, you will be reunited with Satan!"

CHAPTER
66

AS GUNNY entered Teach's Hole, the blip was still on the radar screen, but the shark boat was nowhere to be seen. High velocity winds battered the Whaler about, and the deluge of rain was blinding. Visibility was near zero.

Gunny let go the anchor and paid out all of his line, hoping the hook would hold. As the Whaler bounced and swayed with the churn of the sea, the anchor line quickly stretched taut.

Unbeknownst to the weather-blinded skippers, their boats were silently swinging them on a collision course with destiny.

Then, at last, Gunny's heartbeat surged—there it was! The elusive shark boat was dimly visible through the spray of downpouring rain. As it swung closer, Gunny was able to tell that both canopied cockpits were empty.

With the moment of truth upon him, Gunny was struck with the irony of this unbelievable moment. *Soon, right here in Teach's Hole, there will be a final showdown. This,* Gunny thought, *would be a repeat performance of the final show-down between Blackbeard and Maynard in 1718.*

Gunny slid off the stern of the Whaler into the sea and was immediately greeted by a cold, salty wave. He pushed off from the Whaler's hull and swam through the turbulence, stroking vigorously against the current, slowly making his way to the pirate boat.

Despite an aching backside, he managed to heist himself up and over the transom of the black yacht, then roll onto the rear deck. With his Beretta drawn and held out in front of him, he cautiously edged past the closed F-16 canopies headed forward toward the cabin hatchway.

He grasped the latch, turned it and pushed. The door cracked just wide enough for Gunny to see her. Like an answer to his prayer, Mandy was lying on a berth, her eyes closed. She looked like a sleeping angel.

He began to step down into the cabin. But suddenly, massive hands clawed into his shoulders. His equilibrium was thrown off-balance. He felt himself being pulled backward toward the stern, a sense of *deja' vu* whooshing through him. On instinct, his muscles flexed and he jerked forward, instantly breaking Toby's grip. He spun around, putting himself head-to-head and face-to-face with his attacker, the same overgrown brute, the same maniac as before, but now dressed in black from head to toe. The demented bastard held a pry bar knife threateningly out before him!

"I'm ready for you this time!" Gunny chided, as he leveled the Beretta and pulled the trigger, firing point blank at the head of this beast-like wild man.

But to Gunny's bewilderment, just as he squeezed the trigger, Toby's arm swung upward and struck the gun, throwing the bullet off-course. The Beretta slipped out of Gunny's grip and tumbled to the deck, while the misguided shot nicked Toby's shoulder.

Showing no concern for his flesh wound, Toby's first response was a taunting laugh, but in a flash, he slashed out with his prybar knife, his eyes glowing in delight at the upcoming slaughter he foresaw.

Then, there was blood. The blunt blade connected with Gunny's abdomen. A grin of sinister satisfaction on his face, Toby pushed down hard on the knife, as he dragged the blade deeper into the raw flesh of his prey.

As Gunny staggered backward, both hands clutching his midsection, Toby scooped up the Beretta, pointed it at Gunny's head and began to squeeze the trigger. Gunny's reaction was automatic. In a flash, he jumped into the air, spinning his body a quarter turn, his right leg thrusting out and slamming into Toby's gun-holding hand. Amidst the explosion of the gun blast, the Beretta was punted up and out of Toby's grasp as a wild bullet grazed the hairs of Gunny's thinning scalp.

The pirate howled like a rabid dog, then zealously, lowered his head and attacked in a battering-ram charge. Gunny, bleeding from his stomach and totally exhausted, had nothing left. If he tried to fight, he would die. If he stood there, he would die. In utter desperation, a split-second before impact, Gunny threw his near-limp body over the side and into the relative safety of Teach's Hole.

Toby, determined to exact his revenge, snatched the Beretta from the rolling deck. Holding the gun out before him with both hands, he aimed it, trying to get a bead on Gunny, who was floundering in the brine, his head intermittently submerged in the foamy, never-ending swells.

The noise of the crashing waves overshadowed the crack of semi-automatic gunfire, as multiple deadly bullet plinks peppered the water, each bullet trailed by a jet stream that criss-crossed its target.

Survival instincts took over. Gunny raised his arms over his head, his lean body quickly submerging, sinking like a rock. Bullets continued to stream through the water, chasing after him as he descended deeper into the hole. Finally, the sixteenth and last lead missile jetted down toward him. Had any of the bullets met their mark?

Toby didn't know, and Gunny wasn't sure.

Toby grabbed his sword and in one quick slice, chopped the anchor line in two. Then, clamoring back to the cockpit, he closed the canopy, cranked the engines, and slammed the throttles forward.

Resurfacing and gasping for air, the first sound Gunny heard was the roar of engines, but also, he heard another sound, a higher pitched sound, like a scream. When he saw her, he was astounded. There Mandy was, standing helplessly on the aft deck.

"Help me, Daddy!" she cried as she waved her arms in distress.

But Gunny was totally powerless to do anything except keep his head out of the water and listen to the fading roar of the engines.

CHAPTER
67

November 22nd
3:45 A.M.
17 1/4 Hours Until The Execution

GUNNY FLOATED in the tempestuous waters of the hole, his aching body cast about like a cork. His wet suit had a long rip extending from his chest down to his navel. When he felt inside the rip, he touched raw meat.

The bone-chilling bite from the cold November water had drastically lowered his body temperature. That, along with excruciating pain, incessant frustration and utter hopelessness was rapidly causing his iron will to crumble. He had fought the good fight, but it had been to no avail. He could do no more.

The thought of his own demise was not so dismal, rather, it was somewhat comforting. He could end his struggle and sleep forever. With his eyes closed, he allowed himself to be swallowed into the cold, black abyss.

His limp body sank deeper and deeper, his own thoughts of death now having vanished - but something gnawed at him, nagging, refusing to allow him to just quit. Unfinished business was a wedge, denying him his eternal rest. His mind would not shut down, but was affixed on the vision of Mandy's endearing face and the recurring echo of her desperate cry for help.

His inner being revived, opting to rejoin the living. Instinctively, he began to reach upward with cupped hands making dog paddle-like movements while frantically kicking his feet and struggling for dear life to reach the surface. At last, his arms aching and his lungs on the verge of exploding, his head burst out into the open. Gasping for air and treading water, he searched the western horizon for the black racing yacht, but it was not to be seen. It had already disappeared into the darkness of the vast Pamlico.

The Whaler, rising and falling with the never-ending swells, was still clinging to its anchor line some fifteen yards away. Painfully, Gunny slowly sidestroked in its direction, all the while wondering if a vital organ in his midsection had been ruptured.

With Mandy the nucleus of his thoughts, he edged closer to the Whaler, until at last, he was able to reach out and grab the stern swim ladder. As he held on to the bouncing ladder, the boat repetitively surged violently upward, then violently downward.

The boat was uplifted on a giant wave, then recoiling down, it plunged deep into the water. *It was now or never;* he had to take advantage of the boat's low position. Gunny threw himself up onto the swim platform, then hurled his mangled body over the transom, painfully banging his right shin on the top of the starboard engine as he flopped down onto the deck.

Shivering from exposure, he lay on the wet deck, his eyes closed. The hard fiberglass felt as comfortable as the feather bed he used to sleep on at his grandmother's house.

His respite was fleeting, however, as the horror of reality soon reappeared. Groggily, he crawled through the hatchway down into the cuddy cabin, where he cut away the blood-saturated fabric of his wet suit. In the dim cabin light, he could see just one laceration, which extended from his right nipple, angling across his chest, down to his lower abdomen. Although it was a nasty-looking wound, fortunately, it did not appear to be very deep, and the blood was already clotting. After applying a makeshift bandage of gauze and tape, he forced himself back out to the open cockpit.

The waves had become higher and more violent. Trying to balance himself in an upright position was like trying to ride a roller coaster standing up. The bouncing deck was boomeranging up and down so violently even crawling was difficult.

Careful to keep his body flat against the cabin top, he crawled spider-like, wiggling his way over the cabin and across the foredeck, where, hand over hand, he raised the anchor.

Back at the helm, he turned the ignition keys. The engine ground, whined, coughed and sputtered - and finally roared alive.

"Thank you, Lord!"

The blip on the radar screen indicated Toby was moving fast, already five miles away, headed northward on the Pamlico. The wind remained rampant, and the rains continued to beat down. Nevertheless, Gunny pushed the throttles all the way forward and charged onward, now more determined than ever.

Just after passing the Ocracoke lighthouse beacon, an unexpected, extremely intimidating gust of wind threw the Whaler into the base of a gigantic swell. Gunny clutched the helm tightly, trying with all his strength to force the boat back up onto the wave, but it was too late. Although he saw it coming, there was nothing he could do but duck behind the windshield. As the huge wave crashed down on the Whaler, the cockpit was instantly flooded.

As he struggled with the helm, trying to regain control, he heard the heartening sound of the bilge pump sucking out the overflow. Once more, he and his little boat had miraculously averted disaster. That was the good news, but the bad news was the Fountain yacht was outdistancing the Whaler three to one, and was almost off the radar screen.

Feeling slightly faint, Gunny popped the top of a canned Pepsi and took a gulp. Then, in an effort to snap out of his funk, he began crowing Marine chants. "You're a United States Marine; you're a lean, mean fighting machine." Then, in his flat, off key voice, he howled, "From the halls of Montezuma, to the shores of Tripoli, we are proud to claim the title of United States Marines..."

He sang the entire hymn as loud as he could. His personal pep rally seemed to be working. For the moment, he was born again. He pushed the throttles forward and held the compass on 000' degrees. He was headed due north: *Damn the torpedoes! Damn this gale! Damn that crazy pirate!*

An hour passed, then two, as Gunny struggled to hold the Whaler on course. The small craft would climb the unrelenting swells, then slide down into the troughs, again and again.

Still monitoring the radar blip, watching helplessly as it continued to elude him, ironically Gunny felt a certain admiration for Toby's exceptional skill. The pirate seemed to thrive on the tumultuousness of the stormy sea, apparently undaunted by the extreme conditions.

The Whaler was tough, but it couldn't keep up with the high tech, cutting-edge Fountain, particularly as Gunny fantasized it being piloted by an apparition with nearly three centuries of expertise. It was all Gunny could do to keep the pirate boat on his radar screen, although by now, it looked to be ten miles ahead and approaching a wide expanse of water, probably the Albemarle Sound.

CHAPTER
68

5:00 A.M.

HIS CELL phone buzzed. "Hello," Gunny shouted, trying to make himself heard over the blow of the wind and the crash of the sea.

Grayson, his voice vaguely audible, was eager to tell Gunny about the DNA findings. "There's a 99.8 percent chance they're related. Blackbeard really was Toby's great, great, great-grandfather!"

Gunny, caught between the devil and the deep blue sea, listened as best he could, all the while frantically trying to keep the Whaler angled into the waves. Finally, unable to decipher much of what Grayson had just told him, he began blurting out squibs and blotches about seeing Mandy and the brutal attack at Teach's Hole.

"I'm chasing him north; he's almost to the Albemarle," Gunny screamed, "but he's getting farther and farther away!"

"Listen, Gunny, you've got to catch him! It's our last chance; you know. Tonight's the night! Dani's execution is less than sixteen hours away.

"I'm doing the best I can! What the hell are you going to do?"

"Well, word is tonight just after the execution, our illustrious Governor Alexander Spotswood Brotherton plans to put himself in the national political spotlight. I'm going to attempt a last-ditch confrontation and try to convince him to grant a stay. But, don't hold your breath."

"Who?" Gunny asked, not sure what he had just heard.

"Brotherton."

"I heard you say Brotherton, but I also thought you called him Spotswood."

"I did. Spotswood is Brotherton's middle name." Grayson paused as he mentally connected with Gunny's telepathy. "My God! You don't think...I mean, it never dawned on me until I just said that...uh, no way, do you think, Gunny?"

There was no answer. Grayson was stammering into the silence of a dead connection.

*

Both boats, one nine miles ahead of the other, plowed through eight-foot swells as a hint of light began to form in the eastern sky. High winds persisted as dark, anvil-shaped clouds continued to dump down torrents of rain.

The respective captains of the two small vessels steered northward, each unswervingly focused on his own individual mission. The captain of the black shark boat fanatically focused on revenge, the captain of the Boston Whaler zealously affixed on a dual mission of justice and mercy.

Gunny tried to reconcile this dilemma. Surely if the governor knew Toby Greene was responsible for the murders he would have to stop the execution of Dani Alverez. *Surely the governor wouldn't be so power hungry he would intentionally let an innocent man die.* But, then Gunny conceded the unthinkable: *That bastard would sell his soul to the devil for power.*

Approaching collapse, Gunny felt like a waterlogged rat with a hangover. He hadn't slept in twenty-six hours. He was cold, hungry and bone tired. The stitches in his butt felt like they were broken, his chest hurt, and so did his

stomach. But he was resolutely determined to keep on going, whatever it took.

By 8:00 A.M. he had reached the southeastern tip of the
Albemarle Sound. But the elusive radar blip had crossed
the Sound and was headed toward the North River in the
direction of the Currituck Sound.

Unfolding his wind-mangled chart, Gunny studied it
carefully, trying to determine where Toby was heading. For
a moment, a grin of satisfaction formed on his face when it
dawned on him that if Toby were foolish enough to enter
Currituck Sound, he would be trapped. If he were trying to
get to Hampton that way, he would be in for a big surprise,
because it was a dead end. Currituck Sound was land locked
to the north, east and west and so shallow it was only navi-
gable in a flat bottomed boat.

"Come on, Toby! I dare you," Gunny chided to the
empty wind.

As both boats continued steadfastly north, the shark
boat's blip, twelve miles ahead, suddenly disappeared from
the Whaler's radar screen. Unbeknownst to Gunny, Toby
had steered his craft into a narrow, ditch-like cut-through
that passed through the town of Coinjock, only a few miles
south of the Currituck Sound.

The savage winds grew worse, blasting across the
Albemarle with such intensity Gunny had little to no control over his vessel. The Whaler was being blown about like
a feather in a whirlpool. Sensing the little boat could not
endure much more, Gunny buckled on his waterproof fanny
pack, which held his money and truck keys, strapped on his
orange life jacket and waited for the inevitable.

Mighty swells would lift the Whaler upward, sending
it soaring to a higher summit, then, like a kite suddenly
deprived of wind, the small craft would come crashing
downward, splashing violently into a cavern of water, over
and over.

Amazingly, the unsinkable Whaler would pop back to
the surface to await the next onslaught, which invariably

was quick in coming. The gigantic waves continued to slam into the small boat, tossing it up and down like a toy. All Gunny could do was hold on.

It finally happened! His worst fear realized when a monster wave rose from underneath, and in one swift surge, heaved the Whaler skyward and cast it forth like a javelin. The boat careened through the air, aloft for nearly as long as was the Wright Brothers' first flight. Then, the doomed craft splashed down with a morbid thud, crashing hard onto a shoal.

Gunny was catapulted up, then out into the torrential black water, which immediately dragged him under but quickly spit him back to the surface. Like a cat with one of its nine lives left, Gunny lifted his head, coughed up water, then pawed and kicked his way toward a soggy mud bank, where he grabbed a handful of weeds. Pulling with his hands and slithering with his body, inch by inch, he wiggled and pawed his way up the mud-slick slope.

At the top, he struggled to his feet, then stumbled toward a grove of scrubby trees, which offered minimal protection from the still-pouring rain. Collapsing onto the mushy ground, he lay motionless, his body soaked through and through and caked with mud from head to toe.

In his momentary repose, he looked out toward the water where he spotted the remains of the Whaler. Its stern was resting high and dry on a shoal, and its bow was still floating as though the tough little boat were trying to emulate its skipper's adamant refusal to surrender. Gunny nodded his head in admiration for the craft.

"What a shame. You've been one great boat, and I'm going to miss you."

Gunny, glad to be out of the rampaging water, forced himself to his feet and set a northerly course through a low-country forest. He trudged a swamp, crossed a thicket, then passed under the thick branches of a pine tree forest. At last a very welcome vestige of civilization came into view, a paved road. *Somebody has got to be nearby,* he thought hopefully as he turned to the right and began his arduous trek north up the road.

Clueless as to where he was, he continued to plod along, when up ahead he saw a road sign. Squinting his eyes, trying to focus, finally he could read it: *Shiloh-6 miles.*

As best he could recall, the village of Shiloh was not too far from Elizabeth City, where he had left his pickup truck. If he could just get to his truck, maybe, he could somehow head Toby off, but he would have to move quickly!

Every muscle and joint ached. His chest, stomach, butt and every other part of his body throbbed. But being the over-achiever he was, he tried to ignore his discomfort by forcing himself to pick up his pace. He broke into a run, hoping against hope to somehow get there in time to save the show. As he ran, he continuously fought the urge to stop and lie down. Even the watery ditch on the side of the road looked inviting.

Determined not to quit, Gunny plodded along, half running, half walking as his mind traveled back to Viet Nam. This reminded him of the time when his chopper went down over a Viet Cong regiment. He hid in a camouflage of mud for three days before the VC moved away. After that, he had waded for miles through rice paddies before reaching the safety of his unit. That was back when he was 20, and now he was 51. Reluctantly, he had to concede there was a difference.

CHAPTER
69

November 22nd
2 P.M.
7 Hours Until The Execution

UNDER OVERCAST skies, a limousine passed through the community of Phoebus, crossed a narrow causeway that traversed Mill Creek, then entered the United States Army Base of Fort Monroe. In the distance to the east, as far as the eye could see, lay the Chesapeake Bay. Off to the south, Hampton Roads Harbor dominated the expansive water view. As the limo pulled up to the gate at Fort Monroe, a sharply dressed United States Army corporal with military police insignias on his sleeves gave a snappy salute.

The limo with its lone passenger, front man Roger Keller, drove along the waterfront, finally stopping in front of the Chamberlin Hotel, where a number of news media vehicles were parked. News crews from the major networks were setting up equipment in anticipation of the spectacular events scheduled for that evening.

Keller stepped out of the limo and climbed the front steps to a tiled portico, which spanned the entire width of the hotel. He was greeted by a plain clothes security officer who checked his identification.

"This way, sir," the officer beckoned, as he directed Keller through the exquisitely carved mahogany doorway into the grand entrance of the newly renovated hotel.

Keller's attention was immediately drawn to the historical paintings, prized etchings and original photographs, all depicting the rich heritage of the Chamberlin that were displayed high on tapestry-draped walls of the lobby.

Keller, having grown up in nearby Newport News, knew the old hotel quite well. When he was eight years old, he learned to swim at the Chamberlin's pool. In high school, the Chamberlin had been the setting for his senior prom, and some years later, his own wedding reception had been held there.

A short, trim man in his mid-forties who spoke with a European accent held out his hand. "Mr. Keller," he announced, "I am Gustov Kipfer, the hotel manager. Welcome to the Chamberlin. We are honored the governor has chosen us for his great celebration."

After standard cordialities and hand shaking, Keller accepted the offer for a guided tour of the newly renovated hotel. Kipfer, leading the way out onto the portico, suddenly stopped as he gazed out toward the Chesapeake Bay.

"Let's start at the beginning. This site is quite extraordinary." Kipfer raised his arms, holding them up like a maestro. "We are located on Old Point Comfort, the western shore of the Chesapeake Bay. For an enemy ship to get to Washington, D.C. it would have to pass within a cannon's shot distance from this very point."

Keller followed his host back through the hotel entryway as Kipfer continued his canned speech, obviously designed specifically for VIP visitors.

"As you enter the Chamberlin, you are immediately struck by the historical paintings and artwork on the walls. To my left is an oil painting of the very first hotel located on this site. It was known as the Hygeia and it opened in 1820."

As they stared up at the magnificent oil paintings, Keller asked, "What are those smaller oil portraits to the left of the Hygeia?"

"Oh, I'm delighted to tell you, they depict some of the old hotel's more famous guests, including Chief Black Hawk, Edgar Alan Poe and Mark Twain."

"That's quite remarkable. After tonight, you may want to display an oil portrait of Governor Brotherton."

"We would be quite honored, sir."

Kipfer led the way as they walked leisurely across a massive, marble-floored lobby, a lobby the size of a small auditorium. A series of semi-enclosed anterooms, each custom decorated with antique parlor furniture, lined the wall to their left. As they walked, Kipfer pointed farther down the hallway. "To your far right, are other splendid paintings. Over there, you can see the painting of General George McClellan's Union Army marching past the Hygeia in September of 1862."

Keller, a barely detectible frown on his face, instinctively snapped his head toward Kipfer. He opened his mouth as though he wanted to lash out in response, but instead, elected to remain silent.

Still strolling down the mammoth hallway, suddenly, Keller stopped when he noticed a large portrait on the wall to the left. Pausing, he looked up devoutly. "Now, that's my favorite!" he declared as he stared up at a portrait of a young Robert E. Lee standing near the construction site of Fort Monroe.

"Ah yes, we are very proud of that painting," Kipfer replied.

Becoming impatient, Keller looked at his watch. "We'd better cut this tour short. I also need to inspect the roof garden preparation, if I may."

"Certainly, follow me, sir." They walked back down the hallway, passing an oil painting of Hampton Road's famous sea battle between the Monitor and the Merrimac, which hung from the opposite wall. Approaching the elevator, Keller glanced at another oil painting on the wall to his left, which prompted him to stop dead in his tracks. As he turned toward the painting, his face went flush.

"Is that what I think it is?" he asked.

"Yes sir," Kipfer replied, detecting Keller's further dissatisfaction. "It's a painting of Jefferson Davis, President of the Confederacy, after he was captured by the Union troops. It shows him as he waited in his cell at Fort Monroe."

"That will not do!" Keller huffed, his voice loud and authoritative. "You must remove it before tonight! It does not present the appropriate image of Virginia."

Kipfer, cognizant of the significance the governor's gala event would have on the future of the Chamberlin, could not afford to let an oil painting spoil the event.

"Yes, sir. It will be done."

They entered an elevator where an elderly gentleman attired in a black tuxedo asked what floor they wanted. "Roof Garden," Kipfer replied, as the elevator operator manually pulled the door shut. After rising eight stories to the top floor, they exited into a large elegantly decorated foyer dominated by massive antique gold-leaf mirrors and sparkling Waterford crystal chandeliers.

As they passed through one of the multiple archways that led into the grand ballroom, Keller, awe-struck at the architectural beauty, pivoted a full 360 degrees as he gazed at the inspiring decor.

"There have been major changes since I was here last!" he exclaimed enthusiastically.

Kipfer had a glint of pride in his eyes. "Oh, yes, we've enlarged and totally renovated the ballroom. This is probably the most luxurious ballroom in the entire South! Certainly, its location, as well as its view, is unparalleled."

The ballroom was rectangular, the size of two basketball courts. Covering three walls were pearl white French windows, which rose thirty feet from the polished oak floors to a ceiling fringed with gold leaf crown molding. The ceiling was adorned with scores of Waterford chandeliers, which had the capacity of creating a blinding dazzle when fully illuminated. To the east, French doors opened onto an elegant terrace, offering a panoramic view of the bay and harbor.

In the ballroom, television crews busied themselves, setting up equipment and connecting the twelve big screen television monitors, strategically placed throughout the room. Waiters were setting tables with white damask tablecloths, rose arrangements and silver candelabras.

A wooden podium, complete with a built-in microphone, had already been centered on the head table. Behind the podium, the floor-to-ceiling French windows provided another marvelous view of the Chesapeake Bay.

Kipfer ushered Keller across the ballroom floor and through the French doors onto the roof garden. As they walked along the cracked tile deckway, Kipfer explained that the terrace garden would not be open to the public until spring.

A dark, foreboding sky to the southeast signaled the approach of inclement weather. Despite the dark skies, the view of the convergence of the majestic Chesapeake Bay with the busy Hampton Roads harbor was breathtaking.

"From here," Kipfer said, turning to the northwest, "you can see nearly all of Fort Monroe, including the numerous gun emplacements that once protected the bay from foreign encroachment."

Keller nodded.

"Also, over to the south," Kipfer said, extending his arm and using his finger as a pointer, "is the Interstate 64 Bridge-Tunnel to Norfolk."

The two men leaned against the roof garden railing as they stared out into the bay. "Is that a destroyer headed this way?" Keller asked, directing Kipfer's attention to a large gray ship in the channel just past the hotel's pool and tennis court.

"Yes, I believe so. You know, sir, the main channel to Hampton Roads Harbor is less than a hundred yards from the Chamberlin's tennis courts."

With that, they walked back into the ballroom. Just inside the door, Keller, his face rigid and expressionless, stopped and turned toward Kipfer. "Mr. Kipfer," Keller said sharply. "Let me explain the agenda this evening."

As the hotel manager produced a small pad and a pen

from his coat pocket, Keller, in a no-nonsense tone, began to explain the timing of the upcoming events.

"First, there will be a non-alcoholic cocktail hour. I emphasize non-alcoholic. Is that clear?"

"Yes, sir, we have already been instructed alcohol might offend some of the guests."

"That's correct. We'll do our serious drinking when this is over."

Kipfer allowed a knowing smile to briefly slip on his face. "I understand, sir."

"Now, the dinner must be served promptly at 7 o'clock and dessert at exactly 7:45. All plates must be removed from the table by 8:15 in preparation for the governor's speech, beginning at 8:30. The execution will be at 9 o'clock sharp, followed by a political announcement." Keller's cold blue eyes stared daggers at Kipfer. "Do you understand, Mr. Kipfer?"

Kipfer was quick giving his unequivocal reply of assurance. "Yes sir! I will personally see that everything is absolutely perfect."

Keller, his head cocked to one side, glared directly into Kipfer's eyes. "It damn well better be!"

Momentarily taken back by Keller's directness, Kipfer paused, gulped, then stammered, "Oh, oh, yes sir, we have triple checked everything. I, uh, assure you, sir, everything will be fine."

CHAPTER
70

3 P.M.
6 Hours Until The Execution

IT HURT each time he put one foot in front of the other; nevertheless, he forged ahead, painfully plodding down the macadam road. As of yet, he had not seen a living, breathing creature, not even a bird, much less a person. No houses, no vehicles, nothing but low country thickets, scrubby trees and a road flooded with water. As the rain continued to beat down, Gunny slogged his way along, passing an open field to his left and a pine tree forest to his right.

After another half mile, he saw some buildings, barns of some type in the woods to his left, but still no vehicles or people. Finally, just ahead, a white framed house came into view. Picking up the pace, Gunny ran through the soggy front yard, longing for a friendly face, a hot meal and some dry clothes. He had to find a telephone.

It was a small bungalow, probably a vacation home. No lights were on; no vehicles were in the yard, and no signs of life. As he peeked into the window of the detached garage, he wasn't sure whether to laugh or cry.

What the hell! he finally decided as he pried up the window, crawled through the opening, and gawked at the only pathetic hope that seemed available to him. It was a glorified bicycle—a Moped. It was rusty, dirty and had seen better days. He inspected the two-cycle engine, which seemed intact. There was air in the tires, oil in the reservoir and, by damn, the gas tank was half full.

He rolled the mini-motorbike to the doorway, threw his leg over and straddled the seat. With high hopes, he jumped down hard on the starter—but nothing caught. A second time, he jumped down on the starter, this time harder, and again, nothing. On the next attempt, it caught, coughing and wincing at first, but soon it settled down and began to hum like Gunny's grandmother's Singer sewing machine.

With new resolve, Gunny rolled the Moped along the gravel driveway to the hard surfaced road. Maybe he should have left a note, but he didn't. He just climbed onto the bike, pushed off and began to pedal-putt away, heading up the peninsula toward Elizabeth City.

As the Moped purred north, there was no traffic and very few houses. After passing a plowed-over soybean field to his right, Gunny finally saw another sign of life, a double wide trailer with a light on inside. Rejecting the thought of stopping, he decided he could get back to his truck quicker by Moped than by stopping and having to explain his outlandish predicament.

As he buzzed along, his visibility partially obscured by the rainfall, he managed to decipher the writing on a sign up ahead: *Welcome to Old Trap Community.*

When his eyes returned to the road, a gloss on the hard surface ahead became dimly discernible, but before he could react, the motorized bicycle went out of control. The little cycle hydroplaned across a slick of water. Then, just as suddenly, the Moped kerplunked, sank and abruptly stopped, but unfortunately, Gunny did not. Instead, his bruised and battered body shot over the handlebars like a human cannon ball, and in a flash, he belly flopped down, splashing into the waist deep overwash.

He quickly revived himself and grimly trudged to his wounded mount, picked it up by the frame and dragged it to higher ground. *Now I know why they call this place Old Trap,* he muttered as he dried the spark plug, then jumped down hard on the kick starter.

The little engine spit, sputtered and once again, began to hum. Breathing a sigh of relief, Gunny climbed back on and was off and away, full speed ahead.

In the next few minutes, he passed several farmhouses, a number of outbuildings and a *Welcome to Shiloh* sign. Then, four miles further, the sign he'd been waiting for came into view. *Pelican Marina—3 miles.*

The arduous trip continued for twenty minutes more, until at long last, he could see his beautiful truck up ahead at the Pelican Marina. The Dodge Ram was so pretty he felt like kissing it right between the headlights.

The Moped slid to a halt beside the Ram. With no time to waste, Gunny quickly dismounted and heisted the little motorcycle into the bed of the pickup. Hopefully, he would be able to return it when this was all over.

Once in the truck, he switched on his cell phone and immediately punched in Grayson's number. Grayson answered on the first ring, his voice anxious and more desperate than ever.

"Damn, I'm sure glad to hear from you!" he declared, hoping for good news. "What's up?"

Gunny explained about the chase, the demolished Whaler, and about Toby heading up the North River toward Currituck Sound. "Now, fill me in on what's going on at your end?"

"It's probably too late," Grayson replied, his voice monotone. "The governor won't take my calls, and there's nobody else to appeal to."

"Surely someone has the power to stop the execution," Gunny implored.

"Only the governor can, and that son-of-a-bitch can't wait to see Dani die so he can announce his candidacy for President."

"Grayson, did you understand what I said earlier just before the line went dead? You know, about Spotswood!" Gunny asked.

"There was a lot of static on the line, but I got the gist of it. I checked with a maritime history professor, and he thinks Toby, in his own deranged way, has substituted governors. You know, in Toby's mind, he's blaming Brotherton for what Spotswood did to his great, great, great-grandpa nearly three hundred years ago!"

There was a moment of silence as Gunny pondered this new information. Finally, he responded, his words very deliberate. "Okay, it's beginning to fall into place. It's clear to me Toby has got to be headed to Hampton to knock off Brotherton. He's planning to carry out the last wish of his infamous ancestor, and he's got my daughter with him!"

Grayson exhaled. "All I know to do is try to get into the banquet room at the Chamberlin Hotel and make one last 'Hail Mary' effort to see the governor in person. Maybe I can beg or even embarrass him into delaying the execution."

Grayson was unconvinced at his own words, but, he was staunchly determined to try.

Gunny pointed his Dodge pickup toward Hampton and drove as fast as he dared, all the while pondering what Toby's next move might be - *How would he get to Hampton by water? The Currituck Sound was landlocked, the only inlet from the ocean is fifty miles south.* But somehow, Gunny just knew Toby was capable of performing whatever magic it took to get that black shark boat into Hampton Roads Harbor. After all, he was the 21st Century Blackbeard!

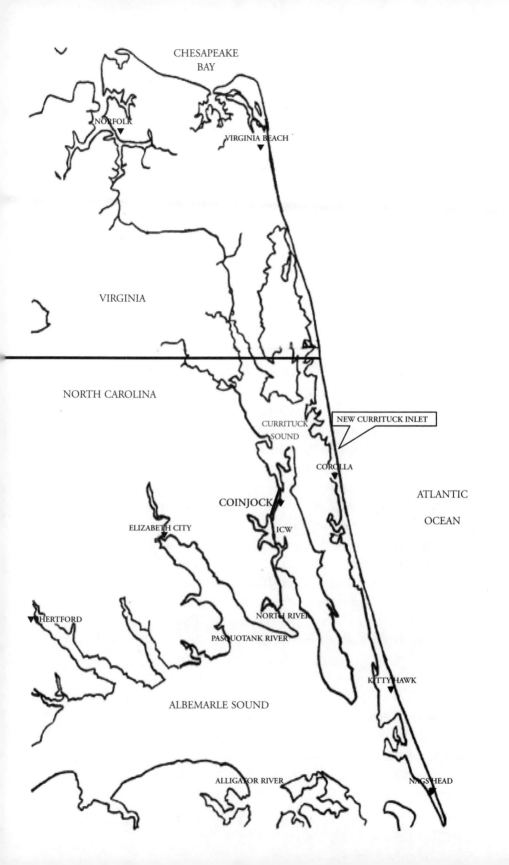

71

THE BLACK Fountain, still heading north, neared Coinjock, a small town situated along the Intracoastal Waterway cut-through. Here, in this waterway, scarcely wider than a ditch, there was no margin for error, particularly with the low visibility and heavy rainfall.

Nevertheless, the Fountain clipped smartly through the no-wake zone at a devil-may-care speed as boats docked on both sides of the waterway bounced violently up and down, back and forth, repeatedly wham-blamming against pilings. With wind gusts peaking at fifty miles an hour, the current was swift and the waves were rising high and breaking hard. This normally placid canal-like waterway was roaring like class three white water.

Toby, from within the safety of his bubble, reduced throttle and slowly turned to port, the bow of the Fountain falling off plane, veering to the left toward Chapel's Marina. With the boat coasting swiftly toward the fuel dock, Toby raised the canopy and stuck his head up into the wind-blown rain. Skillfully guiding the yacht, he reversed the engines' thrust, and the craft crabbed left and stopped parallel to the dock.

A young man in an orange foul weather suit braved the elements as he walked cautiously out on the fuel dock to greet the newly-arrived customer.

Toby stood beside the open bubble canopy, rain splattering off his black, tent-sized poncho. "Fill up both tanks!" he demanded gruffly.

Noticing the wild look in the strange man's eyes, the teenager immediately felt uncomfortable. Nevertheless, his father taught him to always deal respectfully with the clientele.

"Sir, this is a beautiful boat, and uh, and it holds a lot of fuel," the teenager said as he wiped the rain from his forehead. Then, after a moment's hesitation, he cautiously added, "Uh, sir, we have a policy we must first check your method of payment. Can you give me a credit card?"

"Turn on the pumps!" Toby ordered, his eyes as cold as a man- eating shark.

Hoping to sound tougher than he felt, the boy took a deep breath and looked up at Toby. "Uh, sir, I'm not supposed to fill anyone's tank without checking a credit card or getting a deposit."

Like a tiger on a chimp, Toby bounded down onto the dock, his enormous right hand shooting out and grabbing the helpless boy by the throat. "Tell the man inside to turn on the pump or I'll kill you right now!"

The teenager's face was turning tomato red, until at last, Toby's grip relaxed. The youngster coughed, then gasped for air, before finally screaming out in terror, the shrillness of his cry muting the roar of the gusting gale.

"Turn on the pump, Dad!" the boy yelled, Toby's massive hand still resting on his throat. "Please, Dad, turn on the pump, please, now!"

Panic stricken, Mr. Chapel, the boy's father, immediately flicked a switch behind the counter. When the gas pump started, Toby released the boy, then calmly inserted the nozzle into the thousand gallon port tank and began filling it, all the while continuing to glare menacingly at the terrified young man.

"Hello, this is Currituck County Sheriff's Office. How

may we assist you?"

His voice quivering, Herman Chapel reported the robbery in progress.

"Sir, please stay on the phone. We're dispatching two units to your location; they should be there momentarily. Please stand by."

Toby, his beard drenched from the still-pouring rain, had finished filling the second fuel tank. Shortly, the engines were again roaring and the black Fountain was speeding north on the ICW, its destination still in question but the Currituck Sound now seemed to be unavoidable.

"Listen here," Chapel said excitedly, holding the telephone to his ear, "the boat just took off heading north. Maybe you can head him off at the bridge on Highway 158."

"Ten-four on that! I'll divert one of our units to that location," the dispatcher responded.

In half a minute, the black craft, still speeding up the narrow channel, neared an overhead bridge. Up ahead, Toby could see the figure of a uniformed man standing on the bridge beside a patrol car, blue light flashing. The deputy was staring down, watching intensely as the black boat rapidly approached.

Toby shoved the dual throttle controls forward to full speed. Instantly, the Fountain leaped ahead, quickly accelerating from fifty to eighty in less than five seconds. The roar was deafening, so loud Deputy Frazier was forced to put his hands over his ears. His body cringed as the bridge vibrated and the incredible craft blasted by underneath him. Totally astounded, his mouth dropped open, but all he could do was look down in utter amazement as the pirate boat raced up the waterway.

CHAPTER
72

THE SHARK boat exited the narrow channel into a wide body of water. Although visibility through the near-blinding rain was minimal, the boat raced out into the shallow sound, traveling at well over fifty miles an hour and still accelerating. Entering Coinjock Bay at that speed in a high draft boat would normally be considered foolhardy, yet Toby steered his craft straight across the Currituck.

As the craft skimmed the shallow waters of the lagoon-like sound, Toby wasn't worried. He he'd fished the sound for many years and knew every inch of its thirty-mile length and four-mile width. He had traveled it on numerous occasions in a flat bottomed jon boat all the way from its northern-most point, where it connected to Back Bay near Virginia Beach, down to its southernmost point, where it adjoined the Albemarle Sound. Sure, it was shallow, but Toby knew all he had to do was keep the Fountain up on plane and she would draw no more than a foot of water. That way, she would glide right across the Currituck, almost like a hydroplane.

Having studied the history of the sound, he was about to use what he'd learned over the years to perform a feat others would later deem impossible. He knew back in the 18th century, the water in the Currituck Sound had been

salty or brackish. Back then there had been many inlets to
the ocean along these banks, and the last of these, the New
Currituck Inlet, had closed in 1828.

Normally, the only direct water route from the Currituck
to Hampton Roads harbor would be through the ICW,
known as the Albemarle and Chesapeake Canal, which ran
roughly parallel to the Dismal Swamp Canal. But Toby had
no intention of exposing himself to that risk because there
he could easily be trapped in a lock or at a drawbridge with
no place to run.

The only other water passage to Hampton Roads harbor was via the Atlantic Ocean to the Chesapeake Bay. But,
there was one major problem with that route: From the
confines of Currituck Sound, the nearest inlet to the ocean
was all the way down the North Carolina coastline some
fifty miles south to Oregon Inlet, located below Nags Head.

Actually, however, as the crow flies, the ocean was near
the Currituck Sound—a mere two hundred feet in places—
but yet, it was so far away—a solid strip of sand blocked all
passageway to the open sea.

Ignoring this geo-physical barrier, Toby steered due east.
The Fountain yacht was on a collision course with a solid
bank of sand. Nevertheless, Toby focused intently on his
GPS readout, careful to keep the boat on a precise,
preplanned heading.

As the Fountain's speed increased, the depth finder
showed less than a foot of water under the keel. The craft
was on plane, only a few inches of hull in the water. The
boat was almost flying—it had to be—otherwise, it would run
aground and be stuck high and dry in a foot of water.

The Fountain's radar image showed Currituck Banks as
a narrow strip of land less than a half mile distance dead
ahead and approaching very fast. Mandy, dazed and hor-
ror-stricken, sat strapped in her seat under the starboard
F-16 canopy. Looking to her left, the instrument lights tinted
the deranged giant a burnt orange color, exposing a maniacal grin on his hairy face. Displaying no fear, he slammed

both throttles all the way forward, the craft now pushing close to top speed.

As Mandy watched the speedometer needle climb past eighty-five miles an hour, she couldn't help but think of the hundreds of gallons of gasoline just pumped into the boat's fuel tanks. She shuddered as she envisioned the boat crashing into Currituck Banks, then in a flash, exploding into a ball of hell-fire. She began to tremble uncontrollably, imagining her frail body being blown to bits.

The black shark boat, barreling at break-neck speed, was so close to the banks Mandy could see the sea oats blowing on the dune. A high speed crash was imminent! Mandy was mortified, certain in a matter of seconds, she would be dead. Silent tears slid down her face as she realized her fifteen short years of life were over.

In this fleeting moment, her panic-stricken mind focused on her greatest regret. She would never be able to tell her daddy how sorry she was about the heartache she'd caused him. He'd been such a wonderful father. She would give anything if she could just tell him how much she loved him - but now time had run out.

Speeding at nearly one hundred miles an hour, the hull of the black Fountain jarred violently as it skimmed onto a sandy barrier beach, which sloped upward thirty degrees. In the next instant, the bow pointed up, and the craft shot skyward like a tomahawk missile en route to impending doom. Momentarily aloft, there was just enough momentum to send the boat soaring over the flooded banks, but gravity quickly overtook the short-lived flight. The bow angled downward and the craft dropped like lead and smashed violently into the crashing curl of a massive Atlantic breaker, then nose-dived through the froth into the ocean shallows.

Mandy's shoulder harness held her fragile body tightly in her seat. Looking out of her bubble, she could see nothing but water, which now totally engulfed the Fountain. Surrendering to her fate, her panic soon subsided as she closed her eyes and waited. The Fountain's descent was rapid, soon stopping abruptly with a dull grinding thud as it struck the shallow sea bottom. Now, it was only a matter of time.

But moments later, there was the sensation of buoyancy, and the boat began to float. Mandy's racing heart felt like it was about to beat a hole in her chest. Finally, mercifully, the craft popped cork-like back up into the raging surf.

Incredibly, this magnificent vessel had survived and was now ready to confront the savageness of this Atlantic gale.

PEERING OUT at the hostile sea, Mandy contemplated whether she should feel happy to be alive or sad to be compelled to continue in this hell that had befallen her. Suddenly, however, her dismal train of thought was disrupted by bizarre words, words like none she had ever heard.

"Oiy'm the greatest pyreat alive," Toby proclaimed, speaking in a freshly acquired Elizabethan tongue. "Never fear, mi Mary. Oi've guided this craft across the Currituck and into the open sea." Toby was boasting gleefully, seemingly inebriated as he took a sip from his bottle of Jamaican rum, then wiped his mouth with his sleeve.

Despite his bravado, Toby was no fool when it came to piloting a boat and knew full well the significance of positioning his craft in the high seas. A boat getting ahead of the crest could fall bow first down into the wave, then pitchpole over. And a boat going too slow could slide into a trough and risk swamping, or worse, being driven under the wave.

Mandy, looking through her bubble, stared at the treacherous waves, which skyscraped above the craft, then turned her head to look over at Toby. It was painfully clear with this demented social reject controlling her destiny, she had not escaped death—it had only been briefly postponed.

Even a Navy frigate would've had difficulty maintaining

headway in these heavy seas. The Fountain yacht was being tossed about like a twig, but somehow Toby was managing to keep his craft afloat and pointed north. Now, however, this crazed mariner was faced with the immense task of navigating through the graveyard of the Atlantic, north, all the way to the Chesapeake Bay, a distance of thirty-eight perilous miles, in the midst of a full scale Atlantic gale.

Mandy, still strapped in her seat, had been staring out at the sea, but she was beginning to feel a bit queasy.

"Excuse me," she said cautiously, her voice activating the intercom. "Do you have anything for sea sickness?"

Toby looked at her through the plexiglass. "Aye, you're feeling a bit quormishie, huh?" he said, whiskers twitching, revealing a cocky grin. "Look in the compartment in front of you. There's some pills. Take three of them."

Mandy located the bottle and took two dramamine tablets and washed them down with a Sprite.

"I know you don't give a damn about me," she said ruefully.

"You just don't want me to puke all over your precious boat."

Toby grinned. "Hush, mi Mary, you know I adore you."

"Oh pla-eee-ase!" Mandy blurted in disgust.

Repeatedly, the sea raised the small craft high on its crest. To Mandy, it was like the boat was headed into the stars. At the peak, the boat would be momentarily suspended until a powerful wave would send it careening downward into a trough.

Mandy, feeling she had nothing to lose by asking, summoned her courage.

"Excuse me, but can I ask you a question?"

"What, my deary?" Toby replied, a sugary tone to his voice.

"Why are you doing this? I don't understand."

Toby straightened his massive body and turned toward her. As he looked through the plexiglass, staring squarely into her eyes, his expression displayed a faraway look, a look so foreboding Mandy wished she'd never broached the subject.

"Just as moiy' great, great, great, great-grandfather left his legacy to me," Toby extolled, his voice stinging with satanic resolve. "This, is my legacy to him and to the future!"

"But why?"

"Blackbeard can rest in peace after tonight."

"What's going to happen tonight?"

"Tonight, vengeance is mine! After tonight, Blackbeard can meet the devil without shame."

A puzzled look came across Mandy's face as she innocently exclaimed, "You're not serious? You're putting me on, aren't you?"

But then, darts of venomous hatred shot from his dark piercing eyes. "Oi'm as serious as death can be, my little Mary!"

Mandy instantly shrank from her captor's stare as her mind retreated to the fond image of her daddy. She couldn't help but recall an expression Gunny would probably have used in describing this wannabe pirate.

He would've said, *This guy is nuttier than a fruitcake.*

CHAPTER
74

4 1/4 Hours Until The Execution

SEATED AT his desk, trying to come up with a game plan, Grayson was interrupted by a phone call. He answered to hear Martina's somber voice.

"Hello, Grayson. What's the word?"

"Not good. How's Dani doing?"

"They let us spend three hours with him this afternoon. Then, we'll be allowed another hour from 6:30 until 7:30 this evening. That'll be it," she said with a sigh.

"Martina, tell Dani I'm sorry I let him down. Ask him to please forgive me."

With that, Grayson could speak no further. He paused to wipe tears from his eyes as his helpless frustration clashed with pent-up rage.

"You've not let him down, Gray. It's the system that's failed him, not you."

Grayson couldn't restrain himself. He had to vent.

"Damn it, Marty! This system is so intent on vengeance it has ignored due process! And as much as I hate to admit it, I'm part of the system. It was my job to force the system to recognize the basic Constitutional principle of fairness!"

Grayson paused, took a deep breath, then shot a final blast of rage. "That's what a criminal defense lawyer does!"

"Gray, it's not you. Please don't blame yourself. Dani

doesn't blame you and neither does my mother. And, you know, I love you!"

Instantly, with those three *magic words*, the phone line went quiet, until finally, Grayson took a deep breath and replied, in his softest voice. "Uh, I love you too, Marty. I wish I could be with you right now!"

With that, neither could speak.

After a tender goodbye, Grayson hung up and looked at his watch. He realized he had to get going. It was already five o'clock, only four hours were left. *But what am I going to do when I get there?*

A cold drizzle fell as Grayson drove across the Mill Creek causeway. He passed the stern-faced MP at the main gate who saluted him into Fort Monroe. Parking his Cherokee near the base marina, a block away from the Chamberlin, he opened his umbrella and headed toward the hotel where guests were already arriving. Men in tuxedos were holding umbrellas over women in evening gowns exiting chauffeur-driven limos. As he neared the main entrance of the hotel, he could see the guests presenting their invitations to plain-clothes guards at the top of the hotel steps.

Wearing his blue blazer and khaki pants and holding his purple and gold ECU golf umbrella over his head, Grayson didn't exactly blend. As he approached the steps, he paused, knowing he didn't have a snowball's chance in hell of getting past the guards. But he had to try.

"Here goes nothing," he mumbled as he closed his umbrella and walked nonchalantly up the steps, looking neither left nor right.

"Excuse me, sir. May I see your invitation?" asked the security guard standing on the portico at the top of the long staircase.

"I'm Grayson W. Forrest, Attorney. I, uh, don't have my invitation with me because, uh, an emergency kept me from getting home to pick it up or, uh, even having time to change into my tux, as you can see! But, the governor is expecting me!"

The six-foot, four-inch guard stared down at Grayson. He showed no emotion as he patiently permitted Grayson to throw his best pitch.

"I need to speak with the governor as soon as he arrives," Grayson said, feeling somewhat proud of his impromptu performance.

"We know who you are, Mr. Forrest, and the governor is expecting you. That's precisely why we've been given specific instructions not to allow you to enter or be anywhere near this hotel under any circumstances. That's the governor's direct order. Sorry, sir."

"You don't understand! The governor's life is in jeopardy! I've got to see him."

A local reporter standing at the bottom of the steps noticed the commotion and instantly shot an inquisitive stare up toward Grayson. Sensing the likelihood of bad press, the guard put his hand on Grayson's shoulder.

"Come inside, Mr. Forrest, and let me hold on to that umbrella."

Grayson handed his umbrella to the guard and stepped into the lobby where two other plainclothes guards stood at the ready. The younger guard was big enough to have been a linebacker for the Washington Redskins and the older guard was shorter and thinner and carried himself like a drill sergeant. With the linebacker on one side and the drill sergeant on the other, Grayson was escorted into a nearby anteroom.

The no-nonsense drill sergeant did the talking.

"Mr. Forrest, if you cause any trouble, we're instructed to arrest you and have the MPs lock you away in the stockade until this evening is over."

Grayson sensed these guys weren't kidding and wouldn't hesitate to carry out their orders if he continued to protest.

"Okay, I'll leave if you will give the governor a note from me."

"Fair enough," agreed the drill sergeant as he glared unflinching at Grayson.

Pulling a note pad from the breast pocket of his blazer, Grayson began writing:

> *Governor, your life is in great danger. Toby Greene, a descendant of Blackbeard, is en route to assassinate you. It was Toby Greene who killed your nephew and niece, not Dani Alverez. Please delay the execution until you can verify this.*

Grayson folded the note and handed it to the security guard. The other guard, the linebacker, his oversized right hand holding tightly to Grayson's forearm, opened the main door and ushered Grayson down the steps. As Grayson led the way, with the guard close behind prodding him along, they walked through the misty rain back down the street to Grayson's Cherokee.

"Now, get the hell out of here! If we see you again, we'll arrest you on sight. You understand?"

Knowing he had just come very close to being locked up and should feel quite fortunate to be driving away, Grayson replied with a token nod. Immediately, he started the engine, made a U-turn and drove away, heading back past the MP checkpoint and across the causeway.

Now what? he thought.

EXITING THE causeway at the first ramp, Grayson drove into the community of Phoebus. Parking the Cherokee on a side street, he scurried the half block back to the waterfront. As he walked along the bank of Mill Creek, brainstorming for an idea, he spotted a small jon boat tied to a private pier. It had no motor, but there were some oars lying on its rusty deck.

Grayson inserted the oars in the locks, cast off the line and gave the little boat a shove seaward. Climbing over the transom, he took his seat amidship, his back toward his destination. He began to row as the mist-sprinkled water rippled from the wake and the little boat glided quietly across Mill Creek, carrying Grayson back to the forbidden shores of Fort Monroe.

Under bleak, rainy skies, the short voyage went undetected, the jon boat quickly and quietly crossing the creek and sliding onto a marshy shoal. Grayson, in his Bass Weejun tassel loafers, stepped down into ankle deep, slime-coated water, now ready to begin his risky hike back to the hotel. He knew stealth would be crucial to his success, but each time he took a step, the quietness of the night was interrupted by the disturbing sound of water squishing from his tasseled loafers.

As he crept along a sidewalk, he passed through a neighborhood of large, historic homes, obviously the residences of high-ranking officers. He walked near the tree line, hoping to blend; he hopscotched from the cover of one parked vehicle to another; and on one occasion, he found it necessary to detour through someone's back yard.

As he sneaked through the darkness, he passed the thick concrete walls of the original fort, which had been surrounded by a moat. Continuing on, he twice saw headlights approaching, prompting him to jump behind the cover of bushes. Finally, as he turned a corner, the lights of the Chamberlin Hotel came into view.

I know which way not to go; I don't think I'll try the front door again, Grayson murmured to himself. Instead, he approached the back entrance near the loading dock where two delivery trucks were parked. Removing his drenched, blue blazer, which he knew would stick out like a flashing neon light, he hid it under a clump of ivy. Then, rolling up his sleeves, he headed for the dock, still cautious to stay in the shadows.

He slipped through the darkness and took a position behind the dumpster. When the coast was clear, he stepped into the light and rushed toward the kitchen door. Grabbing the door knob, he twisted it and pushed, but it did not budge. "Damn, it's locked!" he muttered as he made a rapid retreat to the darkness behind the dumpster.

Seconds later, before he had time to consider other options, the door flew open, and two men carrying garbage cans came out walking toward the dumpster. The man in the rear shut the door gently behind him, leaving it slightly ajar so it wouldn't lock them out.

Grayson rushed to the door, opening it just wide enough to duck inside. He immediately found himself in a busy hallway near the kitchen. Quickly slipping into the first room on his right, he was surrounded by rows of double decker washers and dryers. On a long table in the center of the room, were stacks of neatly folded linens, towels and *freshly washed and ironed white uniforms.*

*

"Ah, yes!" Toby exclaimed, gratified to spot the channel marker dead ahead. Rewarding himself, he tipped his bottle up for another slurp of rum.

The rain had almost subsided, and the wind gusts were now more moderate. The shark boat, riding high on the crest of the sea, only occasionally slipped down into a trough. Toby, proud of his piloting achievement, steered his craft toward the entrance to the Chesapeake Bay.

Although the evening was misty and dark, Toby could see the lights of Virginia Beach off to port. It was near this location, he recalled, his tremendous tragedy had occurred when he lost thirty-two kilos of cocaine, which seriously dented his reserves and cost him nearly a million dollars, not to mention the loss of his favorite M-60 machine gun.

In a few minutes more, he saw the lights of the Chesapeake Bay-Bridge Tunnel ahead. The long span of illumination extended as far as the eye could see in both directions, stretching from Virginia Beach across the bay entry way to the Eastern Shore of Virginia. It had been off the shore of Assateague, farther north on the Eastern Shore, where Toby had dumped the corpses of those greed-driven divers who helped him construct Blackbeard's subterranean tomb.

*

6:15 P.M.

The Chamberlin Hotel's roof top ballroom was filled with Governor Brotherton's eager supporters. It was quite an eclectic group. There were wealthy tobacco men from Richmond, opulent livestock producers from eastern Virginia, self-proclaimed leaders of the religious right, retired Army officers from Fort Monroe, affluent members of the judiciary, a number of prosecutors, including Arnold Bledsoe, and a variety of other disconcerted citizens from all over the country. They all stood together in their formal evening attire sipping piously on non-alcoholic beverages and making polite social chatter.

Governor Brotherton sat at the desk in his hotel suite reviewing his speech, probably the most important speech he would ever make. Priscilla, his frail wife, walked in from the bedroom dressed in a designer gown. Although she normally avoided formal gatherings, on this particular evening, she had made a special effort to extend herself socially, realizing how important it was to her husband's political career.

"What do you think, Alex?" Priscilla asked, hopeful for her husband's approval. With a twinkle in her eye, she twirled like a fashion model as she proudly showed off her strapless, powder blue evening gown adorned with hand-appliqued beaded pearls.

Brotherton barely looked up. "You know, timing is everything, and my timing on this announcement is perfect."

He raised his right index finger, trying to accentuate the positive points of his plan. "First, the execution will be on live television seen by more than two hundred million people. Then, as soon as Alverez is pronounced dead, I'll announce to the entire nation my candidacy for President of the United States of America!"

Looking over at Priscilla who was still waiting for a compliment, the governor smiled. "It's a win - win situation!" Priscilla nodded, her smile now a bit contrived.

"What do you think?" she repeated, this time with a hint of anger in her voice.

"Oh, you look wonderful," Brotherton finally said, as he ambled over and gave her a perfunctory hug.

"You will make a wonderful first lady, my dear."

A knock came and the door immediately opened. Roger Keller, a wide grin on his face, stuck his head in the doorway.

"It's about that time, sir," he announced, then with a knowing wink, he added, "Everything is ready."

Keller, a stickler for details, had covertly arranged for one of their own people to control the sound system in the death chamber. It was important to eliminate the possibility of negative publicity, like embarrassing slip-ups in the execution process or annoying, self-serving, final statements by the condemned prisoner.

Brotherton was glaring narcissistically at his reflection in the hall mirror.

"Not bad for sixty something, huh?" he said.

Keller looked at his watch.

"Sir, if we're going to stay on schedule, we'd better get going."

Slipping his notes into his breast pocket, the governor, exuding pomposity, beckoned to his wife. "Let's go, my dear."

His hand on Priscilla's shoulder, he nodded at Keller as he ushered his wife out the door and down the hallway. Just before the distinguished couple reached the elevator, Brotherton, a sly grin on his face, turned and looked back at his closest henchman.

Keller, eagerly awaiting the look back, was bursting with enthusiasm.

"Break a leg, Governor!"

CHAPTER
76

6:55 P.M.
2 Hours, 5 Minutes Until The Execution

GOVERNOR AND Mrs. Alexander Spotswood Brotherton made their grand entrance into the hotel ballroom, where they were greeted with wide smiles and spontaneous applause. The governor, now in his element, hobnobbed with his supporters, most of whom had paid ten thousand dollars each just to be there.

Reverend Rufus K. Jones stepped up to shake the governor's hand.

"Governor, on behalf of the thousands of members of my television congregation who love the Lord Jesus Christ, I want to thank you for what you're doing to save this great country of ours."

Reverend Jones, now gushing with enthusiasm, grinned nauseatingly, then added, "I feel assured you will have a rocking chair in heaven."

"Governor!" came a call from the doorway.

Brotherton excused himself and stepped to the side of the ballroom, where a guard, somber-eyed, whispered, "Sir, you did know Grayson Forrest tried to get in a little while ago and we shooed him away?"

"Yes, I had heard. Good work, Joe," Brotherton replied as he scoped the room, anticipating the next contributor he might engage in social chat.

"Sir, were you told what Forrest said?"

"No, but knowing that eccentric upstart, he was probably still babbling about that Blackbeard nonsense."

"Well, sir, as a matter of fact, he was, but this time he claimed the pirate was headed here to assassinate you."

"Poppycock! That boy would say anything to get me to stay the Alverez execution."

"Sir," interrupted Roger Keller, who had just tapped Brotherton on the shoulder. "It's time for you to go to the head table for the invocation."

The illustrious group headed toward their respective seats as waiters soon began serving. Governor Brotherton and Priscilla sat near the center of the head table just to the left of the podium. To their immediate left was the newly re-elected, ultra- conservative United States Senator from Virginia, Roscoe W. Barefoot and his wife. To the governor's immediate right sat his nephew, Dr. Jim Johnston, making his first public appearance since testifying at the Alverez trial some four months earlier.

Senator Barefoot stepped briskly to the podium. As the crowd applauded briefly, he adjusted the microphone, then waited for the applause to subside.

"Ladies and gentlemen," he announced, his voice deep and forceful, "Please let us welcome the man who will save our great nation and lead us forward just as he has done for the Commonwealth of Virginia. I am proud to introduce the Honorable Alexander Spotswood Brotherton!"

Five hundred plus people rose, clapping thunderously. Governor Brotherton, a trusting, grandfather-like smile, shook hands with the senator, then stepped behind the podium.

When the applause finally faded, Brotherton began. "I welcome you to this great historical occasion. There is much to accomplish tonight, but I believe the first thing we should do is have a wonderful dinner." After a few approving chuckles, Brotherton introduced the Reverend Rufus K. Jones for the invocation.

Reverend Jones, decked out in his blue silk suit and alligator shoes, stepped forward smiling. In his resonant voice, he orated a five minute prayer, heedful to give thanks both to the Lord Jesus Christ as well as the esteemed governor and what both had done to accomplish what was about to happen tonight.

Dinner was served as the exclusive invitees bubbled with excitement at the very thought they were about to witness the most extraordinary event of their lives.

They could not imagine just how extraordinary it would be.

*

Attired in a freshly washed and starched white uniform, Grayson entered the ballroom from the kitchen door. Observing a tray of water pitchers on a nearby table, he calmly picked up two of the pitchers and walked from table to table, deftly pouring water into glasses.

The prime-rib dinners had been served, and the governor's guests were busily eating and chatting away, no one noticing the busboy working his way toward their table.

Grayson attempted to keep his back to the governor, hoping to remain undetected. When he had emptied his last water pitcher, he decided to slip back into the kitchen for refills. Just as he pushed the swinging door to exit the dining room, he heard a buzz.

As he looked around, he saw his fellow busboys staring back at him. *Oh, God, my cell phone!* he finally realized. Quickly, he rushed through the kitchen, turned down a hallway and ducked into an employee rest room. After locking the door behind him, he pulled his cell phone from his pocket.

"Hello," he whispered.

"Grayson, this is Martina. What's going on there?"

"I'm in the ballroom posing as a busboy at the governor's banquet. I'm probably going to have only one chance to talk to the governor because when he spots me, he'll certainly have me arrested, but I'm going to try anyway. What's going on there?"

"Dani has only ten more minutes with me," Martina said, her voice quivering. "Mama is under sedation at the motel. Thank God she isn't here to see this. Anyway, at 7:30, they'll take him away to prepare him for the execution. He wants to talk to you, okay?"

Martina sat in a small conference room near the execution chamber with Dani sitting across the table from her. His hands were uncuffed, but his legs remained shackled. She handed him the phone.

"Mr. Forrest," Dani said softly, "How are you?"

"Oh, Dani, are you all right?"

"I'm fine, but I'm worried about you and my family."

"Dani, I want you to know it's not over yet. I'm in the same room with the governor, and I'm going to try to get him to delay the execution. Gunny is somewhere out on the highway headed this way. We believe the pirate is planning to assassinate the governor, probably tonight."

Dani paused and took a deep breath. Then, finally, he said, "Sir, I pray you will be successful, but if you're not, I want you to know you are the kindest man I've ever known. I appreciate what you've done for me."

Dani's voice was sincere and amazingly self-assured.

Grayson's eyes became instantly moist, and he began to stutter. "Uh, uh, Dani, I'm...I'm so sorry it seems to be turning out this way. I'm sorry our great system of justice has let you down. I'm sorry I've let you down."

"But, sir, you've not let me down. I'm grateful for the love and respect you have shown me and my family. Uh, I'm sorry, but it's time for me to go. I, uh, must say goodbye."

"Your time is up! Come with me, sir!" ordered a guard as he unplugged the phone from the wall. Those dreaded words— *Your time is up! Come with me, sir!* —seemed so final as they continued to reverberate in Martina's ear.

Dani hugged Martina one last time. "I love you!" he said, as he was being led away.

77

THE DRIVE from Elizabeth City took Gunny through Norfolk and onto I-64. Except for having to slow down for an approaching ambulance, he'd been making excellent time, speeding along at well over sixty miles an hour. In short order, he passed Willoughby, Norfolk's beach community, and was nearing the Hampton Roads Bridge-Tunnel. In the distance, on the other side of the James River, he could see the lights of Fort Monroe's Chamberlin Hotel standing tall, stalwartly guarding the harbor entrance.

Much to Gunny's dread, however, traffic began to slow down, and soon started to back up as he neared the tunnel. Then, it came to a dead stop.

"Oh, crap!" Gunny exclaimed, slamming on his brakes as his truck came within inches of bashing into the rear bumper of a Lincoln Town Car.

*

With the lights of urban Norfolk visible to port, the sleek black yacht, now proudly flying Blackbeard's personal ensign from its stern antenna, was speeding west across the bay. Soon, within sight was a long chain of stationary headlights which seemed to span the entire width of the approaching harbor entrance. The Hampton Roads Bridge-Tunnel resembled a giant Christmas decoration, making it an ideal beacon to guide Toby toward his destination.

*

The line of traffic hadn't budged as Gunny's frustration mounted, prompting him to suddenly realize he had not smoked a cigarette since sometime the day before. Instantly, he was in deep need of nicotine to allay his rising sense of desperation. Fumbling in the console, he located a crumpled pack of Camels with two cigarettes in it. He stuck one in his mouth, lit it and took a deep drag. Between puffs, he looked at his watch, nervously noting valuable time was passing.

Gunny's pent up stress was beginning to take its toll. His stomach was drawing into a tight knot, and he felt like he was going to explode if this damn traffic didn't hurry up and start moving. *Damn, I wish I had a drink!* he thought.

Deciding some fresh air might help, he stepped out of his truck, walked to the bridge wall and stared out toward the bay. Taking deep breaths, he looked at the empty water. Suddenly, from out there somewhere, he heard it! It was the identical sound he'd heard before - first at Jarrett Bay, then later at Teach's Hole. It was the groan of the same twin thousand-horsepower engines.

Looking east, he glimpsed a shiny black speck getting larger by the second. It had to be Toby, after all who else would be out in this muck? As the speck grew bigger, there was no doubt. The same shark-shaped craft was now so close the colorful bridge lights were reflecting from the craft's aluminum hull.

"What audacity!" Gunny exclaimed when he spotted the pirate flag flying from the radio antenna. *Blackbeard is back for his revenge! This is incredible.*

As the pirate boat neared the tunnel, Gunny found himself in the same, all-too-familiar position of futility - so near, yet so far away, and still unable to save Mandy. All he could do was lean over the wall, wave his arms back and forth, and yell at the top of his lungs.

*

As the Fountain approached the bridge-tunnel, Toby pulled out his rum flask and slurped another gulp. With rum dripping from his beard, he crooked his mouth into a sinister smirk. He looked over toward Mandy, his dark eyes staring through the plexiglass. "Deth to Spotswood!" he mumbled, his words slurred.

Mandy dared not return his look, rather she looked straight ahead as she wondered where this jaded madman was taking her.

As the boat sped along the channel, it passed over the underwater tunnel with neither Toby nor Mandy noticing the tall black man on the adjoining bridge leaning out over the rail.

*

8:15 P.M.
45 Minutes Until The Execution

As he entered the harbor, still boldly flying Blackbeard's own Jolly Roger, Toby kept his boat well offshore near the middle of the harbor and away from other traffic. The night was dark and the wind was kicking up white caps as the pirate steered an invisible course toward a secret destination on the river bank, a destination known only to him.

Soon, just as Toby pulled back on the throttles, the sound of crushing sand emitted from under the hull. The sharkboat had run aground. Unfettered, Toby looked at Mandy, a sly grin on his face.

"Ah, right on schedule," he said, his voice monotone. There, on a submerged sandbar on the Hampton River, the jet black pirate boat had come to a stop only three football fields' distance from downtown Hampton.

Through the drizzle, Mandy could barely make out the obscure point of land nearby. Her mind began to race with morbid thoughts of what might be getting ready to happen. Whatever it was, she knew it would be something awful.

Toby, mindful of the rising tide, lugged his spare anchor out and set the flukes down into the sand. Quickly back aboard, he raised Mandy's canopy. "Have some fresh air, mi Mary," he said benevolently, then disappeared in the direction of the stern. Mandy, twisting around in her seat, was able to observe him open a compartment on the deck behind her. He was bending down and lifting something out. Whatever it was, it had a propeller at one end.

Perplexed, she studied the strange-looking apparatus and noticed a curious feature. A long antenna-like pole was tied to the side of the thing. It only took her a moment to identify the pole thing, itself. *What would Toby be doing with a fishing rod?* she wondered. Somehow, she really didn't believe he was going fishing.

She continued to watch him as he reached into the compartment once again, this time to retrieve a large bag. Immediately, a glimmer of hope triggered in her mind. Toby, it seemed, was getting ready to leave the boat. *Maybe, just maybe, this would give her a chance to escape.*

Soon, however, her hope was snuffed out. With a roll of duct tape in one hand and liquor bottle in the other, Toby gruffly ordered her to put her hands behind her. With sad resignation, she complied as he taped her wrists together, then her ankles.

"Open your mouth, deary!" he demanded as he twisted the cap off the liquor bottle.

"Please don't kill me!"

"Open your mouth or I'll cut your throat!"

Petrified, Mandy complied. She opened her mouth, and he dropped three pills on her tongue. Forcefully holding the bottle to her lips, he poured rum in her mouth until it overflowed onto her chin and neck. "Swallow!"

Mandy coughed, spit up and finally swallowed. The pirate tore another strip of duct tape and stuck it over her mouth. She shook her head and gagged, but shortly her world became hazy. This was the end; she was certain of it. Then, oblivion overtook her.

Toby slithered into a black wet suit, strapped on scuba tanks, and dropped the forty pound submersible into the water. In a moment, he was over the side and wading toward deeper water, pushing the submersible in front and towing a black sea bag behind. When the water reached chest high, he grasped the rear control bar of the submersible and silently buzzed away, soon disappearing into the depths of Hampton Roads.

C H A P T E R
78

8:30 P.M.
30 Minutes Until The Execution

ONE MORE time, Gunny looked at his watch, regrettably noting it would all be over in just thirty minutes. He couldn't fathom being helplessly stuck in traffic while Dani Alverez was executed.

As he pounded on the steering wheel in frustration, waiters at the Chamberlin Hotel were clearing the dessert dishes and pouring coffee. Still performing his busboy duties, Grayson gradually worked his way toward the head table.

The lights in the ballroom had been dimmed, Grayson now feeling less anxious he was going to be recognized before he got his final chance at the governor. Dipping his hand into his pants pocket, he felt the folded DNA papers, as well as the report on genetic similarities provided him by Professor Ferguson. He wasn't quite sure how he could use them, but maybe he could show them to the governor to somehow verify the pirate really did exist.

As he stood against the west wall, Grayson contemplated his options. He considered, perhaps, just walking up to the podium, grabbing the microphone and telling the entire audience the Blackbeard story. Thinking about it for a moment though he quickly rejected that plan, concluding he would probably just get himself arrested without an opportunity to get his point across.

Grayson, feeling he just had to do something, considered another, more direct plan. It seemed more logical to just calmly walk up to the governor, sit down next to him, and tell him about Toby's scheme. Then, he would show him the DNA papers for verification. Surely he would at least listen, rather than cause a scene.

But, before he could make his move, the governor rose from his seat and stepped to the podium, then tapped on his water glass with his spoon. "May I have your attention, please?"

Scratch that idea. Now what?

Quickly, the ballroom became silent as waiters and busboys scurried out of the way. All eyes were on the commanding figure standing before them.

"I want to thank the management and employees of the Chamberlin Hotel for the splendid dinner. This grand hotel is truly a magnificent historical restoration and a most fitting site for this momentous occasion."

The governor paused for a round of applause, then continued. "Here we are at Fort Monroe, the defender of the Chesapeake for nearly two hundred years. It is here tonight, ladies and gentlemen, the great Commonwealth of Virginia, along with majestic Fort Monroe, once again will make history..."

Brotherton's words were once again met with a huge round of applause.

*

As though homing in on a beacon, the battery-powered submersible reached its clandestine destination at the underwater base of a piling. The channel marker extended up from the depths and towered twenty feet above the water's surface, a red flashing navigational light located at its tip. The water was seventy feet deep, making the piling a perfect submarinal dock from which to launch the attack.

With his visibility limited in the dark, murky water, Toby

blindly tied a bowline attachment to the piling a few inches above the sandy bottom. Next, still breathing through the regulator, he unstrapped his scuba tanks and hooked them to the tethered submersible. Then, uncoiling some quarter inch line, he tied one end to his waterproof bag, the other end to his belt. Finally, he unfastened the fishing rod and grasped it tightly in his left hand.

After taking one last deep breath, he looked up, dropped his air hose and pulled the release strap of his weight belt. With a kick from his single fin, he began his ascent, exhaling as he rose.

Preceding him, a stream of air bubbles gurgled to the surface. The pirate had arrived.

*

Gunny sucked the last bit of smoke from his last nonfiltered Camel and flicked the butt over the bridge rail. Trying to stay calm, waiting for the traffic to move, he stared out through the drizzle at the lights of the Chamberlin Hotel on the far side of the river.

He felt so helpless, utterly unable to do anything except bow his head and close his eyes. Reverently, he prayed to a God he wasn't even sure existed that he wouldn't lose the only person in his life who he truly loved. Finally, when he raised his head and took a deep breath of fresh air, he sensed the crud in his mind had cleared and now a new determination had enveloped him.

With new resolve, he made himself a solemn vow.

I promise, if I can have just one more chance at Toby, I won't blow it!

79

8:35 P.M.
25 Minutes Until The Execution

THE FLASHING red navigational light reflected a crimson tint across the channel. Using a snorkel to breathe and the single fin to kick, Toby swam against a swift current toward the nearby seawall. Once there, he pulled himself up onto the ledge, where he sat as he removed his fin and mask. Next, he reached for the line tied to his belt and slowly, very deliberately, pulled the line toward him, dragging the seabag through the water and up from the depths.

*

"Crack cocaine is in our cities, our schools, and on our streets, and alas," the governor preached, "even on our beaches!" Histrionics his forte, Brotherton shook his head as he play- acted his feigned disgust.

"We, now acting together, have this great opportunity to use the lessons we have learned in our great Commonwealth to teach the entire United States how to control crime!"

It was Brotherton's finest hour; his delivery was eloquent.

"Tonight, in less than twenty minutes, you will witness our new Fast Track Death Penalty Law take effect. It will be the culmination of legislation I, along with many of you, have devoted our lives."

As the governor continued his self-serving speech, he received standing ovations with each salvo of bravado. Grayson, standing unobtrusively along the darkened sidewall twenty feet to the governor's left, watched and listened. With butterflies fluttering in his nervous stomach, he looked at his watch. It was 8:38.

*

From a compartment in his black wetsuit, the marauder extracted a .22 caliber Colt Woodsman handgun and screwed a silencer on the muzzle. He heaved the black bag to the top of the wall, then pulled his massive body up behind it. After crouching momentarily near the unlighted tennis courts, he crept through the shadows toward a double row of hedges that ran adjacent to the swimming pool. As he sneaked along, in his right hand he held the handgun at the ready, and with his left hand, he tightly gripped the bag and fishing rod.

At the edge of the hedgerow, he shot like a rocket across a partially illuminated exposure, zipping unseen past a security guard who was standing on the nearby steps staring obliviously toward the bridge-tunnel. Sliding under a clump of bushes, Toby found transient safety behind a large air-conditioning unit.

Shortly, there was a muffled spinning sound. A thin, nearly invisible fishing line with a pyramid-shaped weight attached suddenly soared skyward, wrapped around the roof guardrailing, and dropped silently back to the ground.

"A perfect cast!" Toby whispered jubilantly as he pulled a coil of rope from the sea bag and attached an end to the dangling fish line. Quickly, he pulled the rope up and over the railing, which left a double line hanging down from the first-floor roof some three stories up.

*

Like an obedient servant, Grayson continued to stand un-obtrusively against the wall, his true identity still undetec-ted. Peeking at his watch, panic began to overcome him when he saw it was already 8:40. *I've got to make my move,* he told himself. *I just can't stand here like a potted plant.*

*

8:40 P.M.
20 Minutes Until The Execution

The 280 pound giant reached up, grabbed the rope and with his raw brute strength, began pulling his body upward, gradually hoisting his mass up the rope. A thin, nearly invisible line tied to his ankle trailed down to his seabag below. His beard-shrouded face looked like it was going to pop as he strained, pulling with every ounce of energy he could muster. Finally, sixty seconds later, he made it to the top and rolled himself over the eave onto the gravel roof. Without missing a beat, he quietly pulled his seabag up behind him.

From his vantage point on the lower roof, Toby gazed up toward his destination, the roof garden, which was at the very top of the eight story hotel. He had six more levels to climb, but not even Blackbeard himself could have cast a line to that height.

Toby, peering through the exterior window of room 242, saw no discernible movement. The room appeared vacant. He inserted the blade of his prybar knife under the window sill, and with a swift downward push, the window broke free. Cautiously, he forced it up.

The pirate, eyes dark and deeply set, squeezed his enormous body through the window, then immediately searched the room, closet and adjoining bathroom. Satis-fied he was alone, he opened his seabag and poured its contents onto the bed. It was time for his transfiguration as he began to dress in preparation for his long-awaited debut at Governor Spotswood's gala affair.

*

Gertrude "Trudy" Bullins looked at her watch noting there was only fifteen minutes left until the execution. After placing her linen napkin on the table, she leaned over to her troll-like husband and whispered into his ear. "Dumpling, I'm going to the ladies room. I'll be back shortly."

"Hurry back, sweet pumpkin," he whispered, revealing one of his rare smiles. "You don't want to miss the action, do you?"

Trudy, sixtyish, stylishly dressed in her new rose-colored evening gown adorned with family heirloom diamonds, walked briskly across the ballroom toward the lobby elevator. *Being around these tea tot'lers is hell,* she muttered under her breath as she headed to her room. *I'll just have a quick triple vodka and be back in time for the grand finale.*

*

Gunny, still stuck on the bridge, continued to ponder. *If I were Toby, where would I park my boat? Maybe near the hotel, itself,* - - momentarily, however, Gunny quickly negated that possibility because it would be too near a busy shipping channel. Next, he considered the base marina, but quickly nixed that idea also, since the base marina is controlled by the military police.

Then, Gunny recalled the final episode in the legend of the real Blackbeard when Governor Spotswood ordered Blackbeard's detached head be hung from a stake for public viewing. The location of the morbid display, called Blackbeard Point, was near the mouth of a creek in Hampton, not far away.

"Hmm," Gunny mused.

8:50 P.M.
10 Minutes Until The Execution

TOBY ONLY needed one more minute to be fully dressed and impeccably adorned as the spitting image of Blackbeard, but abruptly an interruption came. The metallic click of the door unlocking, then opening, was followed by the flick of a switch. The room was suddenly illuminated.

Trudy Bullins was stupefied at the incredulous sight before her. The gargantuan buccaneer was garbed in a jet black coat with a matching black, three point hat. His long black beard was combed, cleaned and freshly braided, and a huge sword hung menacingly from his hip.

She opened her mouth to scream, but before she could summon a sound, a .22 caliber projectile silently entered her forehead and ripped through her brain. Still wide-eyed with a frozen expression of astonishment permanently affixed to her face, Trudy's body, clad in her new rose-colored gown, crumpled forward and collapsed onto the plush, thick, royal blue carpeting.

*

As his speech drew to a close, Alexander Spotswood Brotherton was extremely pleased with himself. He felt his performance had been particularly spectacular.

"My good friends," he piously proclaimed, "what you are about to see is a live event that will change our criminal justice system forever. From this day forward, murderers will know they will have to pay for their evil deeds with their life !"

The volume of Brotherton's voice grew louder. "From here on, they will think twice before taking the life of a fellow human being!"

The audience listened solemnly, each guest earnestly believing he or she was hearing first-hand an oration that would rival some of the greatest speeches ever made in America.

"At this time, ladies and gentlemen, we are going to dim the lights and turn on the monitors. Remember, what you are about to see is live, and may well be the most memorable and historic event any of us will ever witness in our entire life."

The lights dimmed as twelve wide screen television monitors came on simultaneously. For the first two minutes, the picture focused on an antique wooden arm chair, which except for the scorch marks on the arms, was really quite attractive and might have complemented the decor of a fashionable home. This chair, however, was somewhat unique in that it featured arm and leg straps as well as intimidating electrical wiring.

Moments later, the television audience could see two uniformed guards, one on each side, leading a frail figure into the viewing area. The young prisoner wore leg shackles and walked slowly, taking baby steps imposed by the short length of chain between his ankles. As the young black man got closer to the camera, his freshly shaven head became visible.

Following directly behind the shackled man was a priest, Father O'Reilly, an open Bible before him. A faint murmur could be heard as he read passages from the Gospel of Luke. As the group got closer to the camera, Dani Alverez's expressionless face became more distinguishable. The young man showed signs of neither resistance nor fear as he was slowly ushered toward the wooden chair.

The governor glanced in the direction of his nephew, Jim Johnston, who was staring intently at a monitor. Brotherton couldn't help but inwardly gloat at this, his finest hour, certain he was about to pull off one of the greatest media events in the history of television. Not only would he get his own personal revenge for the terrible murders of his family, but more importantly, this single event could easily vault him into the position of becoming the most powerful man in the world.

*

Grayson, still unnoticed, slipped closer to the head table, now less than ten feet away. Standing at parade rest, his back to the wall, and his hands clasped behind him, he knew it was now or never. He took a deep breath as he readied himself for his move.

The room was morbidly quiet, the enthralled audience staring intensely at the telecast of the condemned man who was about to take his seat in the electric chair. Then, Grayson's moment came! Waving the DNA papers in the air and screaming like a wild banshee, he sprang toward the podium. "Governor, I have new evidence that proves Alverez is innocent! For the sake of justice, please delay this murderous execution until you can review it!"

The governor's coveted timing was spoiled. Grayson's bizarre interruption had driven a wedge into the moment. The hushed audience, their attention momentarily drawn away from the TV monitors, shifted their focus toward this seemingly berserk busboy.

Before Grayson could protest further, however, two plain clothes, gorilla-sized goons grabbed him by the arms and dragged him across the ballroom floor and through an archway toward the nearest exit. Grayson resisted, pulling back, trying to snatch free, but the goons held on tightly.

"Governor! Governor!" Grayson screamed at the top of his lungs. "I've got to talk to you. You're making a terrible mistake. It's a matter of life or death!"

Grayson thrashed and jerked, but the goons maintained their tight grip as they swiftly manhandled him down the hallway and out of sight.

Empathizing with their beloved governor, the audience looked on at what they perceived as a cheap political shenanigan. "My friends," Governor Brotherton said in his most composed manner, "Please excuse the distraction. As I am sure you understand, there are always agitators trying to thwart our efforts to make America a safer place to live. Now, please turn your attention back to the monitors," he requested, his voice totally unruffled.

Meanwhile, the goons were dragging Grayson down the back hallway. Viciously, they began to beat him with their fist, pounding him hard in the face and stomach. They kept punching him over and over until he dropped to his knees. Then, the most devastating blow yet, a kick to the side of his head with a steel-toed boot sent him collapsing face-down to the floor.

After dragging him into a closet, and just before closing the door, the smaller goon said goodbye with a final kick to Grayson's side. Blackness overcame him as he slipped into unconsciousness, terminating his quest to save his client from the electric chair.

CHAPTER

81

DANI SAT in the wooden arm chair as one of the guards looked down at him compassionately. "Mr. Alverez, I know this is tough. Please, sir, just cooperate. Let's get it over with."

The middle-aged officer pulled Dani's arms up and gently placed them on the chair's arm rest, which bore the scorch marks where more than eighty other arms had briefly laid before a surge of electricity had left them lifeless. The other officer stared down stone-faced at Dani. He showed no emotion and said nothing as he strapped Dani's arms down tightly against the cold hard wood.

Dani's trouser legs had been rolled up, exposing a portion of his freshly shaven left leg. A wet substance was wiped onto the hairless area and electrodes were fitted. Similarly, cold liquid was wiped onto Dani's freshly shaven head, then more electrodes were pasted on his bare scalp.

*

There was no one in the second floor hallway to see the pirate peeking out of room 242. Suddenly, Toby darted across the hallway, pushed the "up" button, then immediately darted back to the safety of room 242 to await the elevator's arrival. Shortly, when the elevator door opened,

Toby, dressed to the nines, his seabag on his shoulder, rushed out of the door and into the elevator. But, as the elevator door closed, he sensed he was not alone. Through the corner of his eye, he saw a short, elderly man in a tuxedo and top hat who was eyeing him very curiously. For a long moment, Toby and the gentleman exchanged wary looks, then Toby winked.

"This is just part of the show," Toby said, his lips curving into the semblance of a quickly contrived grin.

The man smiled, exposing his toothless gums. "Okay, Mr. Blackbeard, roof garden, I presume?"

"No, seventh floor.

The elevator stopped on the seventh floor, one floor below the roof garden. Before departing the elevator, Toby looked furtively both left and right, then bid the elevator operator goodbye. Rushing down the hallway, his seabag in tow, he stopped at the door of room 721 and knocked. Receiving no response, he pulled his sword from its scabbard and thrust the blade through the wooden door panel. With three sharp, twisting jabs, the broad blade had bored a hole large enough for Toby's arm. He reached in and turned the door lock, then pushed the door open.

Upon entering the vacant room, Toby went directly to the window. As he looked out, his eyes momentarily glazed over in dreamy wonderment at the sight of his ultimate destination, the roof garden, which was only one story above and just ten feet to his left.

*

8:55 P.M.

Warden Pugh, dressed out in his best suit, entered the small execution chamber. "Dani Alverez," he said grimly, "as you know, I am the warden, and in that capacity, I am hereby ordered by the Circuit Court of Virginia Beach, Commonwealth of Virginia, to read the following warrant to you."

Looking straight in Pugh's eye, Dani calmly replied, "Sir, I am innocent of the charges."

"Sir, the law requires me to read this warrant to you."

Dani calmly nodded.

"By the authority of the Circuit Court for the City of Virginia Beach, Commonwealth of Virginia, it is decreed that Dani Alverez be incarcerated in the Virginia Department of Corrections and on the 22nd day of November of the year 2002, that a sufficient amount of electricity be passed through his body until he is pronounced dead."

When Warden Pugh completed his obligatory reading, Dani looked up at him. "Sir, I forgive you and everyone who is part of this."

"Okay, we're ready!" Pugh coldly announced as he looked toward the executioner, a tall, ruddy-faced man standing near the doorway of the execution chamber.

Father O'Reilly leaned down and laid his hands on Dani's shoulder. "Peace be with you, my son."

"And also with you, Father," Dani replied, seemingly at peace with himself.

Tears in his eyes, Father O'Reilly squeezed Dani's right hand. "Goodbye my son."

When the priest exited the death chamber, the executioner checked the electrode connections on Dani's head and leg, then he also exited to his station just outside the door where the electrical circuit levers were located. The rules required him to stand on a rubber mat because of his close proximity to the electric chair. Shortly, the chamber door clanged shut, leaving Dani alone in the death chamber to await the shock of 20,000 volts.

"Our father, who art in heaven, hallowed be thy name," Dani prayed loudly, his voice quivering as tears began to slide down his cheeks.

*

8:57 P.M.

The window of room 721 opened, and the pirate, bedecked in full battle regalia, stepped out onto the eight-inch ledge.

Cautiously, seven stories up, he sidestepped along the ledge, inching his way across until he was directly below the roof garden.

No guests had ventured outside the comfort of the ballroom, but rather, all eyes remained riveted on the television monitors, the condemned man still sitting in the antique electric chair awaiting death.

Only one guard was stationed out on the roof garden, a veteran Virginia State Policeman, Edgar Syriani.

The glow of the lighted cigar at the far end of the roof garden alerted Toby as he peeked over the top of the wall. Syriani was gazing out toward the Chesapeake Bay, studying the variety of lights that could be seen through the haze of the night. The lights of a commercial ship heading toward the channel were visible to the east. Directly in front of him, out on the bridge-tunnel, he could see the headlights of the hundreds of vehicles stuck in a traffic jam, which had just now begun to move.

The only reason Syriani volunteered to man this damp, chilly station outside on the roof was because it allowed him to puff on his stogie. This was one of the few pleasures he enjoyed these days after losing his beloved wife of thirty-five years to cancer the previous year and then, six months later, tragically losing his only daughter in an automobile accident. In just one more year, he could retire, but now, he was at loose ends as to what he would do with his time.

Syriani glanced back toward the ballroom window where he could see the reflection of the high-paying hypocrites who sat inside, anxiously gawking at the monitors. He had no desire to see the execution and actually felt anybody who did was downright sick. He wished it would hurry up and get over with.

And at that instant, it was over. What to do with his leisure time when he retired would never again be an issue. A .22 caliber bullet silently entered Edgar Syriani's medulla. With hardly a sound, he fell backward, collapsing face up onto the cold, wet deck of the roof garden. His glowing stogie still in his mouth.

*

Dani trembled as he gazed out through the viewing window toward the witnesses staring back at him from the other side. He had been relieved to learn his mother was not going to witness the execution. Martina, thankfully, had been able to convince her it would be better if she remained under sedation back at the motel until this was over. Dani focused on his beautiful sister's kind face as she mouthed out to him, "I love you!"

"I love you, too," he mouthed in reply, just before looking up toward the ceiling to await the jolt that would end his final moment of torture. Oddly, it reminded him of sitting in a dentist chair, trying to distract himself with pleasant thoughts. Try as he might, however, there were no thoughts, pleasant or otherwise, sufficient to dispel the rising terror of the moment.

Then, he remembered the beautiful stained glass window in his small church back home in the Caymans.

"Thy kingdom come, thy will be done, on earth as it is in heaven," Dani prayed, imagining himself kneeling at the altar in that small church so many thousand miles away.

Martina, tears streaming down her face, watched her little brother intensely in these last seconds. She felt a sense of pride at Dani's display of courage as he sat facing his imminent demise.

While beads of sweat dripped from the nose of the heavyset warden, the cold-eyed executioner focused on the warden's face, awaiting his nod. Warden Pugh watched the clock on the outside wall, preparing to exercise the near

God-like power he had long enjoyed.

Dani, still looking upward, continued to pray. "Give us this day our daily bread and forgive us our trespasses as we forgive those who trespass against us." As Dani prayed, he took deep breaths, not knowing which would be his last.

The last seconds ticked away. "And lead us not into temptation but deliver us from evil."

CHAPTER
82

IN THE roof garden ballroom, all eyes had returned to the monitors where they remained as Brotherton continued his fervent speech.

"This will be a heralded moment in our history, ladies and gentlemen. You should not feel sympathy for this murderer, but rather, you should feel joy for America and be grateful for the victims who will never be. This new law will save lives! Thousands upon thousands will live because of the Fast Track Death Penalty Law."

The monitors showed Dani seated in the electric chair, his mouth was moving, but no sound was audible. The handsome governor was gloating vainly, now on the verge of his moment of glory. Although his expression exuded great pride, a detectible gleam in his eyes betrayed his hidden obsession for power, power he would certainly soon realize.

Theatrically, Governor Brotherton looked at his diamond studded Rolex. "Ladies and gentlemen, my watch is synchronized with the clock in the death chamber. Precisely at nine P.M. Warden Pugh has been directed to throw the switch to the electric chair." With a few scattered claps that threatened to escalate into yet another accolade of applause, Brotherton raised his hands, quelling the overture and sending a controlled hush through the ballroom.

"The same electricity that will terminate the life of this convicted murderer will also be the electricity that will light up the future for justice in America."

Brotherton drew his lips into a tight smile and raised his hands, holding them palm out toward the audience. "My friends and supporters, please join me in a ten second count down to justice!"

Then, as he looked down at his watch once more, Governor Alexander Spotswood Brotherton began his final countdown. "Now, watch my fingers! All right, here we go: *TEN*," he roared, as the audience followed suit, echoing him. Dropping a finger, *"NINE!"* Dropping another finger, *"EIGHT!"* Everyone bursting with anticipatory adrenalin, *"SEVEN!"* they screamed so loudly the room vibrated.

The guests were on the edge of their seats, and except for the absence of party hats and noisemakers, they could have been waiting for the ball to drop at Time Square. Too excited to breathe, much less blink, *"SIX"* they shrieked out wildly.

Now, having lowered his left hand, the governor was showing five fingers of his right hand. His grin widened as the word, *"F-I—V-E,"* began to sound from his mouth. Much to his chagrin, however, a deafening explosion blasted through the rear of the ballroom, shattering the glass in the French doors leading onto the roof garden. Instinctively, every eye snapped toward the diversionary smoke that suddenly began to billow from the shattered windows.

Before the audience could process the significance of the explosion, another, this time louder, earsplitting reverberation erupted from the glass windows behind the head table.

Like a bad dream, Toby Greene, dressed in all black, resembling a Hollywood swashbuckler, leaped through the imploded opening. His black, braided pigtails streamed out from under his three-point hat. Smoke, rising from his charcoal beard, cast his face in an eerie, demonic haze. His eyes, wild and deranged, shot forth a piercing glare, a glare of hate, unswervingly affixed on the governor.

Toby was a one-man arsenal. His double-shoulder harness holstered twin .45 caliber Glocks; his right hand wielded a gigantic broad sword; and in his left, he held an M-4A carbine. The M-4A, an ultra light assault rifle, only fourteen inches long, contained two 30-round magazines banana clipped together. The high tech weapon employed an infrared aiming laser designed to fire three round bursts at the squeeze of the trigger.

The governor, his five fingers still suspended in the air, whirled around to see the monstrous pirate. All he could do was stare in disbelief. The hellish demon was raising his sword with his left hand, while pointing the M-4A out toward the terrified dinner guests with his right.

A security guard, Albert McBride, reacted quickly, immediately drawing his Sig Sauer nine millimeter and leveling it at the pirate.

Holding the mammoth sword high and taking slow, deliberate, robot-like steps, Toby closed on the governor. "Deth to Spotswood!" he yelled in a blood-curdling howl, the governor unmistakenly the focal point of his threat. Then, a second time, this time like it was a satanic curse, he wailed, "Deth to Spotswood!" his subhuman cry so terrifying the audience froze as the words of vengeance echoed off the walls.

The pirate was only one body length away when his immense sword began its downward swoop. Instinctively, Brotherton raised both hands in a fruitless effort to protect himself from the impending slice.

Special Agent McBride pulled the trigger once, firing one round, then paused. Seeing no reaction, he fired three more times in rapid succession, striking his target with all three shots directly dead-center chest. But Toby was unfazed, the impact of the bullets only a minor irritation. The triple jolt did, however, throw the slash of the sword off course, causing it to miss its mark and slice clean through the solid wood podium like it was a chunk of cheddar cheese.

The pirate, stepping forward to regain his balance, raised the M-4A, an infrared dot suddenly appearing on McBride's forehead. Then, a short burst of automatic gunfire and McBride was dead.

The governor's reprieve would be only temporary. Again, the sword was raised high, its target still the head of the now utterly petrified governor who was staring up in horror as the glistening blade of death came down. He opened his mouth to scream, but there was no time.

Governor Alexander Spotswood Brotherton was decapitated, his headless trunk crumbling to the floor while his handsome head was launched airborne. With every white hair still sprayed perfectly in place, Brotherton's head skimmed a dinner table, bounced onto the oak hardwood, then rolled like a lopsided bowling ball across the dance floor, colliding with the ornate shoe molding on the west side of the ballroom.

From its resting place, the eyes seemed to stare back up at Toby, the mouth of the late governor still open as if he were still trying to scream.

Ironically, the executioner had become the executed.

Toby, the M-4A pointed upward, let go with a barrage of automatic gunfire into the ceiling. The bullets shattered the glass chandeliers and blasted away much of the overhead plaster. Like falling sleet, countless slivers of Waterford crystal fell upon the mortified guests. Amidst a chorus of screams, the governor's high-society friends began to stampede like cattle, stumbling, tripping and crawling for sanctuary from this hell on earth in which they had suddenly found themselves.

Reverend Rufus K. Jones, the unfaltering self-proclaimed shepherd of the multitudes, panicked like a lost sheep. He tried to escape by running across the ballroom, directly into Toby's line of fire, but a short blast from the M-4A quickly ended Jones' ministry. With blood oozing from his mouth, the minister fell lifelessly to the floor.

Then, another man fell dead, a man who had been personally invited to the momentous occasion by the governor, a man for whom the governor had paid the $10,000 per-plate fee. One of the bullets that had passed through Reverend Rufus K. Jones' heart ricocheted back into jury foreman Braxton Hornsby, striking him just above his nose, directly between his eyes. Hornsby died never having to answer for his evil crime against the American jury system.

With the agility of an Olympic track star, the pirate hurdled his massive body gracefully over the head table in pursuit of the governor's severed head, then chased it across the dance floor. Quickly upon it, he wedged it between his boot and the shoe molding and stabbed it onto his sword, skewering it like a shishkabob. Holding his trophy high, Toby's face was emblazoned in an expression of maniacal glee as he resounded his most cherished taunt, a taunt which broadcast to all the world the fulfillment of his most coveted achievement: "Deth to Spotswood!" he screamed in a supernatural wail of eternal damnation.

Rookie security guard Burt Finley advanced with his 357 Colt Python revolver drawn. "Drop that gun, now!" he boldly ordered.

Blackbeard grinned then, as nonchalantly as if he were about to squash an ant, he casually fired a blast into Finley's gun-holding hand, sending the revolver clanking to the floor. For a long, painful second, there was a period of morbid silence, the suddenly meek security guard vexed with horrific dread of what he knew was about to come. "No, please! No!" he screamed, his trembling voice crying out for mercy, but there would be none.

"He who challenges Blackbeard dies!" the pirate roared out defiantly, as he callously sent a three round burst of fire into Finley's stomach.

With the skewered head held high, the pirate knocked

over a table, stepped on Finley's corpse and bolted directly through the midst of the cowering audience. Barging through the double French doors, he scampered across the roof garden stopping only when he reached the edge of the roof.

Pausing, he hooked his skewered sword to his belt, grabbed the rope he had secured earlier, and rolled over the parapet. Repelling down, he bounced off the hotel wall once, twice, three times before his feet finally crunched down onto the gravel of the lower roof.

He scurried along the roof until he located the entwinement of double-line rope he had used on his earlier ascension. After dropping the bitter end off the roof, he threw himself over the wall and slid down the line, landing in the bush beside the air-conditioning unit.

CHAOS REIGNED inside the ballroom. The elevator door opened and a four man team of wide-eyed MPs exited, their handguns drawn. But as they passed under the archway into the ballroom, they came to an abrupt halt at the sight of the carnage that lay on the blood-saturated floor before them. Five bodies, one headless, lay prostrate amidst a carpet of broken glass. Scattered throughout this once glamorous, now bullet-riddled ballroom were scores of people, many seriously injured, most of whom were groveling behind overturned tables. Some were in shock, some were delirious, some were nauseous—all were terrified.

"Who did this? What happened?" demanded an excited young soldier, directing his question to Priscilla Brotherton. Blood spatter covering her new dress, the governor's widow lay semi-conscious on the ballroom floor, unable to respond. To her right, leaning against a post, sat Dr. Jim Johnston, his head shaking, his eyes red and tearful. The sad-faced doctor, totally bewildered he could have been so wrong, stared catatonically down at the floor. He was totally dumbfounded.

Roger Keller crawled out from under a table. His hands were trembling and his face was wet with nervous sweat. "He, he...killed the governor!" Keller stammered.

"Who did this?" demanded the corporal, himself astounded by the human carnage that surrounded him.

"A pirate! Blackbeard!" Keller whimpered hysterically as he pointed out toward the roof garden. "He jumped over the wall."

The MPs rushed out onto the roof garden just in time to see a large shadow moving rapidly across the lighted lawn, then disappearing into the darkness of a double row of boxwoods.

*

Skewered sword in hand, Toby crept to the seawall and quietly lowered his large frame down to the concrete ledge below. Lapping water slapped at his feet as he dumped his firearms, ammo and bullet proof vest into the water. He reached down into a crevice and retrieved his single fin and placed it on his right foot. Then, locating his dive mask, he stretched the rubber strap over his head.

Two military police officers had been patrolling the hotel grounds when they overheard the emergency radio call. Seconds later, they had glimpsed a shadow near the seawall. They raced in that direction.

Toby, his face mask in place, had just grabbed his skewer when the faces of the two MPs appeared at the top of the seawall. "Stop where you are! You're under arrest," the corporal yelled as both soldiers aimed their handguns at the pirate.

Toby stared up into the barrels of the Army-issue Berettas, both of which were in point-blank range of him. Now, unarmed and without his protective vest, it seemed that surrender was his only option. Reluctantly, he dropped his sword and raised his hands over his head.

"Don't move or I'll blow you away!" the corporal yelled, his gun pointing directly at the pirate's chest.

The MPs, after radioing for backup, slid over the wall, both soldiers carefully eyeballing the suspect, both ready for any furtive movement.

The pirate, arms stretched high above his head, suddenly dropped his right hand down toward the back of his neck. In a flash, a green oval object shot out of his hand and landed between the MPs.

"Grenade!" the corporal screamed.

Before either MP could react, the pirate, scooped up his sword and leaped off the ledge splashing into the water. The hysterical MPs followed suit, also jumping for their life into the black brine, hoping they would be spared from the impending shrapnel blast.

Three seconds... Four seconds... Five seconds... Silence... Six seconds... Seven seconds... Eight seconds... Nine seconds... Ten seconds.

*

The goggly-eyed MPs soon surfaced, both huffing and puffing, both spitting and snorting as they dog paddled back toward the ledge. "Damn! Must'a been a dud," the corporal said with a gasp.

A half minute later, a host of military police arrived just as the two spooked soldiers were climbing back up onto the seawall. When the sergeant of the guards saw them, he stopped dead in his tracks. "Where the hell is he?" he demanded as he looked around in disbelief.

"Out there somewhere," was the meek reply of the corporal as he nodded vaguely in the direction of the channel.

"I'll be damned. You let him get away!" After another few moments of head shaking and cursing, finally the sergeant regrouped and started barking out commands.

"Lock and load! Get some search lights out there! Call for a boat!"

Minutes later, multiple rays of light began to criss-cross the harbor entrance. The beams glistened across the black water, but the only identifiable movement was the motion of the rippling waves, occasionally kicking up a white, foamy slosh against the seawall.

Soon, a legion of law officers, including military police, Hampton cops and Virginia State Police arrived, most of whom congregated along the Chamberlin's waterfront. Every eye peered into the glare of the shiny black water as they searched for the pirate. An Army Patrol boat arrived shortly and began a search pattern, zigzagging back and forth across the seascape.

Then, only minutes later, a sighting was made.

"Out there!" came a tenacious yell from a sharp-eyed soldier, as he pointed excitedly out into the channel toward a marker post a hundred yards away.

Spotlights were brought to bear, their beams shining on the marker post which was usually capped with a red light near its top, but now the marker had a new embellishment - Toby, now attired in his black wet suit, was balancing himself at the top of the post, defiantly waving his mighty sword on which was still speared the now yellowing head of Alexander Spotswood Brotherton.

"Deth to Spotswood!" he again bellowed then, belly laughing, he made an obscene gesture with his middle finger.

A sniper-trained MP leveled his scoped M-14 at the pirate, but before he could align the cross hairs, Toby plunged back into the water, once again disappearing into the blackness of the harbor.

The sergeant, exasperated, looked back toward the hotel, hoping his superiors had not witnessed this debacle. But then, insult was added to injury. What he saw would certainly be his Waterloo, if not worse. In place of the stars and stripes, which had always flown so proudly from the hotel flagstaff, he saw a black flag bearing the figure of a skeleton, stabbing a heart with a sword. Blackbeard's personal ensign now waved triumphantly over Fort Monroe's Chamberlin Hotel.

*

Lying on a cold damp floor, flat on his back, Grayson opened his eyes and saw only the black of darkness. He moved his arms as he felt around, blindly trying to determine where he was, but each movement sent pain radiating throughout his body. When he raised up on his elbows, his rib cage hurt so badly he wished he had remained unconscious. Groping blindly with his hands, he reached out, first touching the soggy strings of a wet mop, then inches away, he felt the corner of a door. He struggled to his feet and found the doorknob, but it wouldn't turn. It was locked. He was stuck in a frigging broom closet.

He yelled, he shouted, he threw his entire weight against the wooden door, all to no avail. The door would not budge. Finally, he found a light switch and flicked it on, making visible assorted cleaning materials, a vacuum cleaner, mops, brooms and a tool box.

"A tool box," Grayson muttered optimistically, as he opened the lid and rummaged through the jumble of hardware inside. He soon saw what he needed - a crow bar. Holding the steel bar with both hands, he wedged it into the door jam and pried as hard as he could until at last, the lock popped.

Out in the congested hallway, Grayson recognized some of the same dinner guests. Now, their faces were sad-eyed, confused and panic stricken. Some were lying on the hallway floor disheveled, trembling and crying, while others were wandering about aimlessly, their eyes glazed, everyone was in shock.

Grayson walked down the hallway and passed under an archway that led into the ballroom, but what he saw stopped him in his tracks. His heart cried out in utter revulsion at the blitzkrieg of death that lay before him. Bloody bodies blocked streams of red, causing a pond of blood to pool in the center of the ballroom floor.

"What happened?" he asked a familiar-looking older man who was standing aimlessly in the center of the ballroom.

Judge Bullins looked more like a lost puppy than a bull. He stood zombie-eyed, weaving back and forth, spastically jerking his head around.

"Trudy, where are you? Trudy! Trudy!" he cried out.

"What happened?"

Disorientation was written all over the judge's pained face. "A pirate exploded a bomb, shot a bunch of people, and cut off the governor's head." Bullins continued to pan his head jerkedly around the room as he resumed his hopeless search. "Trudy! Trudy! Where are you, Trudy?"

It was hard to recognize this pitiful old man as the tyrannical judge who had sentenced Dani to death. In fact, the old man was so pathetic that Grayson *almost* felt sorry for him.

Grayson looked at his watch—it was 9:13. *Dani is dead!* he silently admitted to himself. Pausing to wipe the tears from his eyes, he couldn't believe after all these months it was over, just like that. With all his heart he had tried, yet no one would listen. His greatest dread now realized, he fought back tears of despair as a rumbling from inside overcame him. A torrent of pent- up rage was boiling like a volcano ready to erupt.

CHAPTER
84

THERE HE was in his white, blood spattered busboy suit, beaten all to hell, his face hurt, his head ached and he thought he had a broken rib. What's worse, his spirit was crushed—his innocent client had just been put to death.

A number of burning questions gnawed at him. He couldn't fathom why the governor, the prosecutor, the police, the judge, the jury and practically everyone else didn't give a tinker's damn about the immorality of an innocent man being executed.

Is our system of justice being manipulated by a few self-centered demagogues who would trade away the freedom guaranteed by our Constitution to satisfy their own lust for power?

Grayson felt as if he were trapped inside of a pressure cooker. As he smoldered, he surveyed the survivors scattered about the ballroom. They were a sad lot. But then, he spotted the worst of them. There he was, king of the assholes, decked out in his slightly ruffled tuxedo, standing over near an exit door. Just the sight of Arnold Bledsoe left Grayson irate! *What a miserable excuse for a chief law enforcement officer!* Grayson muttered as his rage bubbled into his red zone, a rage that would be contained no longer.

Grayson went ballistic. Homing in on his target, he rocketed across the ballroom like a missile approaching ground zero. In a flash, he was two inches from Bledsoe's nose, glaring unmercifully straight into his eyes.

"You stupid son-of-a-bitch!" Grayson yelled accusingly, as darts of fire shot from his eyes. "You just wouldn't listen, would you?"

"Get out of my face you twerp," Bledsoe retorted sharply, his eyes squinting as he glared back at Grayson.

"If you'd done your job, if you'd sought the truth, which was your sworn duty to do, you stupid prick, this would not have happened!" Pausing to catch his breath, Grayson grew more infuriated with each word. "You pompous asshole, it's your fault Dani Alverez and the governor are dead, not to mention all these other people!"

"Get out of my sight!" Bledsoe ordered, his face now as red as Porky Pugh's neck.

Grayson inhaled deeply, trying to regain his composure as he pondered his next move. But it was no use - the die was cast. He had already taken the plunge, and his next move was irrevocable. "I owe it to Dani, and by God, I owe it to myself! He clenched his right fist into a tight ball and swung it toward Bledsoe's face with all the force his pent-up frustration could carry. And in a blink, there was sweet pain when his knuckles impacted squarely into Bledsoe's cavalier nose, which was immediately squashed flat and spurting out a geyser of blood.

Bledsoe folded like a cheap lawn chair, his hands covering his face in a hopeless attempt to curtail the blood flow. A second later, he fainted, belly flopping, nose first, down on the sticky floor.

In the very next moment, a husky MP, a no nonsense expression on his face, raced toward Grayson and grabbed him firmly by the arm. "Sir, are you Grayson Forrest?"

Well, here goes my first arrest and probably my law license. They probably disbar you for assaulting the Chief Commonwealth Attorney.

"Yes, I am," Grayson calmly responded, feeling some

satisfaction at seeing the bloody-faced prosecutor lying motionless on the floor in front of him.

Just as he was prepared to hold out his wrists, ready for the cuffs, he noticed that the MP showed no concern for Bledsoe, rather, in a very formal tone, he said, "Sir, we have an urgent phone call for you. Please come with me."

As Grayson was being ushered to the elevator, his right hand still clenched in a fist, his mind dwelt in delight on his perfect Muhammad Ali knock-out punch. Holding his arms close to his sore rib cage and rubbing his trophy fist, he followed the MP to the elevator, which took them down to the main floor lobby. There, at the registration counter, the MP put a phone receiver to his ear.

"Are you still there, ma'am?" he said. After a pause the soldier then handed the phone to Grayson.

"Hello," Grayson said, unable to imagine who would be calling him.

It was the unfamiliar voice of a lady who identified herself as Mary Payne. "Mr. Forrest, I'm the secretary for Homer Thomas, Virginia's Attorney General."

Just as he had suspected, Grayson was now quite certain the coverup was about to begin. "Yeah, so?"

"The Attorney General has asked that you immediately report to the penitentiary in Mecklenburg County. Mr. Forrest, this is urgent and must be kept absolutely confidential and completely under wraps. I repeat, you are directed to make no statement to the media and tell no one where you're going."

"Lady," Grayson replied as he lashed out sharply, totally unwilling to play ball with these pricks any longer, "It's pretty damn amazing! An hour ago nobody from your office would even talk to me. Now that you've killed an innocent man, I get a personal invitation from you. What kind of a fool does Thomas think I am?"

"Please, Mr. Forrest..."

"You people are trying to shut me up, aren't you? You're afraid for the public to find out you've killed an innocent man!"

"Sir, uh, all I'm at liberty to tell you is...uh...uh, it's about Dani Alverez. The situation is grave, and you must get here quickly. I'm sorry, but I am not authorized to answer any other questions."

Grayson felt like his brain was going to explode. He screamed into the phone, "Look, dammit, lady! You tell that son-of-a-bitch you work for that he's just as responsible as the governor was! And you can tell him that I'll tell any damn body I want to about this catastrophic travesty of justice!"

"Please, Mr. Forrest, please wait and hear Mr. Thomas out first."

"Well, what the hell does he want?" Grayson demanded.

"I'm sorry, sir, but I have my orders. Now, will you please leave immediately for the penitentiary?"

CHAPTER

85

AS GUNNY sped down the streets of Hampton, he spotted the entranceway to the Fisherman's Wharf Restaurant, which he believed to be located near Blackbeard Point. Swerving to avoid an exiting car, his pickup zoomed across the near-vacant parking lot and screeched to a halt in a space adjacent to the Hampton River. Quickly out of the truck, he darted across a grassy strip that bordered the river, his hopes sky high.

Looking to the right, he scanned the west side of the curving shoreline in search of the shark boat. He strained his eyes until they ached, but all he could distinguish through the mist was the fuzzy contour of an endless riverbank disappearing into the darkness of Hampton Roads harbor.

To get a better vantage point, Gunny ran up the restaurant steps. He peered back to the right, but still all he saw was the same empty blackness. Looking left, out into the distance toward Fort Monroe, he could see flashing blue lights, but the Chamberlin Hotel itself was hidden from view, blocked by the bridge-tunnel.

Gunny strongly suspected all the blue light commotion had something to do with Toby Greene, which would confirm his assassination theory. Nevertheless, because he'd received no response from any of his last five attempts to phone Grayson, he couldn't be sure what was going on.

He looked back to the right, this time forcing his eyes to focus on a point of land outlined by tall pines and lying less than a quarter mile away. *Blackbeard Point has got to be nearby*, he surmised. It just didn't seem likely for Toby to pass up an anchorage bearing the namesake of his beloved ancestor. But still, the shark boat was nowhere to be seen, its location a mystery cloaked in darkness, lying somewhere beyond the limits of his vision.

Bounding down the steps, then re-crossing the grassy riverbank, Gunny leaped down onto a narrow beach that ran along the river's edge. Jogging cautiously over the rut-strewn sand, a wooden privacy fence extending out into the water was blocking the beachway. Not to be deterred, however, Gunny waded out into hip-deep water, rounded the fence, and quickly sloshed back up onto the beach on the other side of the fence, now in the backyard of somebody's waterfront mansion.

A flashing navigational light several hundred yards up river was casting an eerie crimson glow that tinted red both the color of the water and the hue of the hazy night air. Sensing the pirate boat had to be nearby, Gunny's rising adrenaline overcame his good judgment. Through the blackness of the night, he broke into a run along this shadowy beach, his long legs stretching out into a sprint, hopefully carrying him nearer to his daughter. But, just ahead in the darkness, another obstacle waited. This obstacle was silent, deadly and had no conscience.

Running at full throttle, Gunny's 51 year old heart was beating like dueling bongos as his nicotine-ridden lungs gasped for air. Then, suddenly, like being raked with a hockey stick, his chest collided violently with something, forcing a guttural, "Ugh!" to belch out of his mouth. His legs swooped straight out from under him, plopping him down hard, flat on his back in the gritty sand.

He lay stunned, trying to shake off a feeling of oncoming shock. "What in the hell was that?" he muttered.

Finally, apprehensively, he raised himself up on his elbows and looked up at his unlikely assailant. An immense fallen pin oak had washed up on the beach and now blocked his way. *Damn, I've been clothes lined by a frigging tree!"*

Shaking his head in disgust, he struggled to his feet and took a closer look at the sharp ends of the pin oak's broken limbs, grateful he had not been punctured by one of its spear-shaped points. Then, almost magnetically, his eyes were drawn seaward. Through a haze tinted red by the intermittent strobe from the nearby buoy, Gunny thought he glimpsed the shark boat. But when he blinked, the vision vanished.

Puzzled, he rubbed his eyes as he tried to figure out whether the imagined sighting was real or just some kind of mental mirage prompted by wishful thinking. But the haze flashed red again, then back to black, over and over, back and forth. Amazingly, when the light glowed red, he could see the silhouette of the shark boat, but when the red flashed off, the silhouette would disappear.

Studying the shape of this now you see it, now you don't image, Gunny sensed an exuberant fizz from within. It appeared that his long vigil might be coming to a head.

CHAPTER
86

CAUTIOUSLY, LOOKING and listening for any sign of life, Gunny waded out toward the yacht. He pulled himself up and over the gunwale and peered warily through the plexiglass of the port-side bubble, but no one was home. The starboard bubble was so steamy he couldn't see through it. Placing his forehead against the glass, he vaguely saw what appeared to be hair, blond hair. In fact, it was Mandy's blond hair!

"Thank God!" Gunny cried out excitedly. Clawing at the hatch cover with his fingernails, it wouldn't open. It was locked. "Mandy!" he screamed as he pounded on the hatch cover, but she didn't move.

He looked around the deck for a tool. Maybe he could pry the canopy open. Nothing caught his eye, but he did notice an anchor line leading off the stern. Hand over hand, he pulled the anchor in, grabbed it with both hands and directed the pointed fluke into the seam at the edge of the canopy. Gouging down hard, he pried the rim upward. As more pressure was applied, the canopy began to bend, then finally the lock snapped.

When Gunny raised the bubble, he found his daughter slumped over in the seat, her wrists, ankles and mouth duct taped. She was cocked over, drooping forward, motionless and unresponsive. He carefully stripped the tape from her mouth and gently shook her. "Mandy! Mandy, honey! It's all right now! Wake up, okay?" She didn't move.

Hoping beyond hope she was still alive, he untaped her wrists and ankles and held her tightly in his arms.

"Oh Mandy, please be all right! Open your eyes and talk to me, please!"

A slight twitch in her eye gave him optimism.

"That's it, baby, wake up! It's okay now. I love you, Mandy."

With that, her eyes popped open, and she looked up, dreamily gazing into the desperate eyes of her father. After blinking herself back into reality, she tried to speak.

"I...I, uh, love you too, Daddy! But, where have you been?" she asked, her brow furrowing as a puzzled expression formed on her face. "I...I was afraid that you were so mad at me for running away that you gave up on me."

Teary-eyed and totally overwhelmed with delight, Gunny stammered, "I...I would never give up on you, honey. I love you. Are...are you okay, baby?"

The tender moment was fleeting, quickly spoiled by the foreboding sound of someone sloshing through the water, the sloshes growing louder and closer with each successive step.

Gunny tried to get Mandy up, frantically pulling and tugging on her, but it was too late. In one giant stride, Toby leaped up onto the deck and was upon them. Gunny shoved Mandy back down into the seat, then turned to take on the most deadly confrontation of his life.

Toby stood on the stern, his vengeful eyes focused on his adversary, a ferocious snarl visible through his drenched beard. "My revenge will be done when I kill you, Maynard!" he roared out threateningly.

Weaponless and desperate, Gunny reached down and grabbed the Danforth anchor, lifting it chest-high.

Undaunted, Toby was fixated — he had to destroy his archenemy, Lieutenant Robert Maynard, who he perceived to be in the skin of this black man standing there before him.

Pointing the skewered sword at Gunny, Toby growled like a rabid dog, then broke into a savage charge. Gunny heaved the anchor, fluke first, directly into the pathway of the attacking madman, but the thirty pounds of steel merely bounced harmlessly off his chest and fell to the deck.

Zealously, Toby, his sword high, continued his advance. "Deth to Maynard!" he yelled wildly, his scream loud and haunting.

Gunny began to sidestep along the starboard sideboard as he rapidly retreated toward the bow. But Toby gave chase, quickly closing the distance, his menacing blade swinging back and forth like a pendulum, slicing through the air to within an oily frog hair of Gunny's back side. In seconds, Gunny had backed up all the way to the tip of the bow. There was no place else to run.

Toby, still on the attack, was quickly within range. Hate pouring from his cold eyes, he slashed violently down toward Gunny's skull. Gunny tried to lunge out of the way, but he wasn't fast enough. A soggy whack sopped down hard against his shoulder, but there was no pain; it was more like a smack from a rotten cabbage.

It was only then, just as the red flashing beacon cast its eerie intermittent glow, that Gunny discerned what had actually struck him. Repulsively refreshing, the putrid head of Alexander Spotswood Brotherton had been his life savior. Even in this moment of impending doom, a momentary grin slid across Gunny's face as he thought: *It's about time that good-for-nothing son-of-a-bitch made a positive impact.*

Gunny quickly recovered and stepped across to the port foredeck, painfully aware that if he lost his footing and fell, it would all be over.

With every passing second, Toby's sword cut closer and his words got louder. "Deth to Maynard!" he screamed over and over.

After dodging another sword slash, Gunny leaped aft, springing himself up and over the twin bubble cockpit and back toward the stern. To his great horror, however, he landed on the side of his foot, lopsided and off balance. The momentum from the jump was too much - he could not compensate. He tumbled, cartwheeled, then crashed onto the aft deck, the back of his head ramming violently against the hard, unforgiving aluminum transom.

Eager for the kill, Toby vaulted the cockpit in hot pursuit, now certain victory was within his grasp. Gunny, lying helplessly on his back and wedged tightly against the transom, was dead meat for sure.

The used-up old Marine frantically groped for anything with which to grip onto in order to pull himself upright. When his right hand touched the base of the VFR radio antenna, he clasped his fingers around it and pulled for all he was worth.

The glistening blade of Toby's sword was just before entering its downward arc, and directly on course for Gunny's cranium. Using the antenna as leverage, Gunny tried desperately to pull himself up onto his feet, but to his dismay, the antenna snapped off in his hand, and he collapsed back down onto the deck. He was doomed!

Miraculously, the trajectory of the blade was off course, missing its mark, only creasing Gunny's left arm. Toby jerked the sword back and wound up for another whack. This time he could not miss.

Still lying on the deck, both hands clutching the broken antenna, Gunny focused on Toby's attacking sword. Just before the sword began a crash dive down toward him, Gunny lashed the antenna like a whip, the point cutting deeply and the shaft flailing across Toby's unsuspecting face. The pirate stepped back and took pause.

It was a moment of unanticipated opportunity. Gunny, suddenly the aggressor, sprang to his feet. Twice more, Gunny whipped the antenna across the pirate's hairy jowl until the blasphemous devil stepped back in retreat.

Like the calm before the storm, the moment was dominated with a foreboding silence, a silence soon interrupted by an uncanny howl, an eerie sound emitting from somewhere deep within the gut of this gargantuan man. The attack was to be demonic. The monster pirate was seeing red and blazing with the wrath of Satan. Certain this was the end, and by now being too exhausted to resist, Gunny could only stand and aim the pointed antenna out in front of him.

Maniacally, Toby stormed forward, determined to exact his retribution, but his own zeal was his Achilles' heel. The sharp point of the antenna jabbed smack dab into Toby's right eye. Blood spurted and the pirate squealed like a stuck pig.

Toby's fanaticism would not be deterred. The blood-blinded pirate brushed a matting of ooze from his eyes, then holding his sword in a tight death grip, he raised the skewered blade above his head. Snorting like a wild boar, he began to swing the sword in a full circle, hell bent that his final act of revenge would be the decapitation by proxy of Maynard's 21st century surrogate.

Gunny was determined to use the moment to his advantage. He lunged forward, jumping high into the air and snapping his right leg up into a flying jump kick, his target, Toby's head. With the force of a sledge hammer, Gunny's right heel slammed hard into Toby's temple. Like a wounded elephant, the dazed pirate crashed down, collapsing and slamming onto the aluminum deck with a resounding thud.

Gunny would take no chances. He had to make absolutely certain Toby was out for good. Methodically, he sent a powerful karate chop to the pirate's neck, followed by a violent punch to his solar plexus. Then, finally, with his right foot, he kicked down hard into Toby's groin.

Toby, lying face up on the deck, was barely semi-conscious. Writhing in pain, he was blinded by blood coagulating in his punctured eye. His dream was lost. All that was left for the pirate, it appeared, was death.

But then, like a devil that wouldn't die, Toby lifted his bloodied head. True to his promise, Gunny grabbed the skewered sword and raised it high as he glowered down hatefully at the murdering demon who lay there before him. "It's time for you to go back to hell!" Gunny shouted, unconsciously reenacting the role of Lieutenant Maynard at Ocracoke on an earlier November 22nd.

Gunny guided the sword to its apex, ready to swing down into the pirate's throat. Just as the sword began to fall, a shrill scream suddenly interrupted Gunny's long awaited moment of vindication.

"No! No! No! Daddy, Don't!" Mandy shrieked frantically.

Dropping the sword back down to the ready, he stared incredulously at his daughter, his eyes demanding answers.

"Daddy! I'm pregnant! He's the father."

With a befuddled expression on his face, Gunny glared at his daughter, his face furrowed in a gaze of disbelief.

"He raped me!" Mandy cried out, as more tears began to flow down her pale cheeks. "Just don't kill him, Daddy. It just wouldn't be right."

Looking down at the huge body sprawled out on the deck before him, Gunny paused and shook his head. Finally, he regretfully conceded, "I guess you're right. If I kill the son-of-a-bitch, I'd be lowering myself to his level."

With that, he threw his arms around Mandy and pulled her toward him.

"I love you, baby. You're going to be all right." As they embraced, he gazed tearfully into his daughter's eyes. At long last, he felt a sense of relief that now she was safe. They were finally together again as a family.

"Oh, Daddy, I've missed you so much!" Mandy exclaimed as she glanced over Gunny's shoulder, looking back toward the stern of the boat. Then, she saw him.

"Oh, my God! Watch out, Daddy!"

But it was too late!

LIKE A flash of lightning, the blade of death found its target, the razor edge slicing into the raw flesh of Gunny's side. Amidst a starburst of blood spatter, the momentum sent Gunny careening over the side and splashing head-first into the shallow water.

Surrounded by water, tinting redder by the second, Gunny struggled to his feet. In shock, his eyes half closed, he stood like the living dead, unable to discern the dire moment that was upon him.

With the skewered sword in hand, Toby leaped off the stern, his eyes red and wild and still affixed on his single-minded goal of completing his final act of revenge. "Deth to Maynard!" spewed out from his saliva-spitting mouth. Through the dark water, semi-blindly, he high-stepped toward his wounded prey.

Mandy, daring a peek from her refuge in the cockpit, saw her daddy holding his bleeding side and stumbling in the water. Toby was right behind him, closing in for the kill. She had to do something!

Mandy had never driven a boat in her entire life. Nevertheless, she had to try! She turned the keys to the right, and like magic, both engines fired, both growling out like a pair of junk yard dogs.

Gunny, still stumbling through the water, had just cleared the width of the stern with Toby in close pursuit. And in a blink, Toby's sword blade was within range. A lateral cross slash was all it would take to behead Gunny.

He surrendered to the inevitable.

Then, the course of destiny drastically changed. Mandy pulled back hard on the double-levered throttle, the drive train clunking into reverse. Suddenly, 2,000 horsepower blared with the sound of endlessly repeating mega-blasts of exploding dynamite. The momentum from the reverse torque whiplashed Mandy forward, slamming her forehead into the instrument panel as the shark boat barreled backwards, speeding stern first like a bat out of hell, straight for the narrow beach.

Toby, wide eyed, like a deer caught in a spotlight, was bedazzled when he saw the stern of his own boat bearing down upon him. He whirled around and squared off with it, his skewered sword raised high as though he, the invincible, could somehow thwart the law of physics.

Toby was cursing God in his loudest, most angry voice when the stern of the Fountain crashed into him. Still gripping his sword, his elbows now hooked over the transom, he was carried on his final voyage, racing him toward his last destination.

Further time for the pirate on earth was abruptly canceled. Stern first, the shark boat plowed aground onto the beach directly into the fallen pin oak tree. Toby, seething with three hundred years of hate, his sword still held high, was violently jammed into a spear-like point of a broken pin oak branch.

At the very instant of his impalement, as though guided by the hand of fate, the momentum from the reverse thrust threw Toby's sword upward, flinging it high into the air. It tumbled end over end as Governor Alexander Spotswood Brotherton's head somersaulted from right side up to upside down. The sword landed point first, drilling deep into the sandy bank above the pin oak tree, the blade oscillating and undulating like a tuning fork.

As the shishkabobed head continued to vibrate, the late governor seemed to gaze out unconcerned that his lust for power had been so appallingly destructive to the American system of justice. His callous expression was as dispassionate as his attitude had been toward the execution of Dani Alverez.

Ironically, the governor's head came to rest at the very location where Blackbeard's head had once been displayed nearly 300 years earlier, giving new meaning to the name, "Blackbeard's Point."

Mandy, rubbing her banged forehead, saw Gunny had collapsed. He was face down in the water, drowning.

Unconcerned for her own safety, she bolted over the gunwale and waded over to his waterlogged body, his head still submerged. Struggling to keep him from sinking, she rolled his limp body onto its back and lifted his head out of the water. "Hold on, Daddy! Please hold on! I can't lose you now!"

Almost immediately, Mandy's attention was diverted upward to the ratcheting, reciprocating roar of fanning rotor blades, followed by a beam of light that shone down. As if in answer to her plea, a Coast Guard helicopter had appeared from out of nowhere and was hovering over them like a mother hen. Momentarily, a rescue swimmer came sliding down a line.

EN ROUTE to the penitentiary, Grayson, still steaming with anger, was doggedly resolved he would not allow the government to dupe him into helping them cover up this horrendous fiasco of injustice. Just having to deal with the government, particularly now with his entire body in pain, was intolerable. What he really wanted to do was just hold Martina and cry.

It was 1:00 A.M. when he approached the penitentiary. As he neared the main gate, he drove past a sizable crowd of death penalty protesters who were holding an all-night vigil. The group numbered over a hundred people of all ages, many of whom were holding candles. One man carried a banner that read, DEATH PENALTY INHUMAN.

As Grayson's vehicle got within earshot, the quietness of the dismal night was interrupted when a college student with a microphone blared out, "Why do we kill people to show people that killing is wrong?"

Giving them a thumbs up as he passed, Grayson drove through the gate and into the parking area, impertinently parking his Cherokee in a space reserved for the assistant warden. After taking a deep breath, he marched into the reception center where he was greeted by a female reception officer.

"You must be Mr. Forrest," she said brightly, as she looked up from her desk. "They're expecting you, sir. Please come with me." She unlocked a door and escorted him down a hallway to a conference room beside the warden's office.

Upon entering the room, Grayson was immediately startled at the unusual scene. There, sitting at a round mahogany table were Martina, Warden Pugh and a tall, trim, silver-haired man in a blue, pin-striped suit. Behind the man's horn-rimmed glasses, his drab green eyes showed signs of great stress and strain. There were two vacant chairs at the table.

"Mr. Forrest, I presume," the man said politely, as he swiveled a quarter turn in his chair to face Grayson.

"That's right."

Grayson looked at Martina, but before he could decipher the strange expression on her face, the man spoke once again. "Thank you for getting here so quickly, Mr. Forrest. I am Homer Thomas, the Attorney General of this Commonwealth. Please, sit down."

Well, hooray for you, Grayson muttered under his breath as he sat down in the chair beside Martina. Under the table, Martina's left hand slid across his leg and came to rest against his sweaty right palm. As Grayson gently squeezed her hand, he tried to read her expression through the corner of his eye but soon abandoned his efforts when the Attorney General resumed his speech.

"The events of this evening have been mind-boggling," Attorney General Thomas stated, then he paused to shake his head as a sad grimace cut deeply into his face. "It has been an horrendous testimonial to the state of affairs of this Commonwealth. I so very much regret that I supported this legislation, and I hope that history will forgive me."

For the moment, Grayson elected to keep his mouth shut until he could confirm his strong suspicion about the purpose of this bizarre meeting. There was really no question about what the Attorney General was trying to do. Obviously, he wanted to put a hush to this bureaucratic debacle. As Thomas rambled on, a voice inside of Grayson's head kept screaming, *You old political hack! What the hell are you trying to say? Just get to the point!*

The mental torture of listening to this oratory of quizzical platitudes was surpassing Grayson's ability to cope. The inner voice kept up its rebuff. *You bastards have killed an innocent man, and now you're worried about the political ramifications.* Grayson decided he couldn't stand to listen to much more of this bullshit. With his patience wearing thin, he was on the verge of screaming.

Looking at his watch, he made his decision. *I'll give this asshole just one more minute, and then I'm going to tell him to kiss off! After that, I'm out of here.* Glancing at the second hand on his watch, he feigned attention to what he perceived to be meaningless, political babble.

"Why this happened," Thomas drolled, "I really don't know. But I, as the Commonwealth's highest law enforcement officer, have a duty to the people of Virginia to assure that justice is done."

Yeah, yeah, yeah, Grayson mumbled, almost loud enough to be heard, as he stared impatiently at his watch, the seconds ticking away. Fifty seconds had passed with just ten to go before he would walk out. His plan was to take Martina by the hand, stand up and say, "Stick it, jerk! We're out of here," and then, he and Martina would leave.

Grayson's legs flexed as the second hand signaled a full minute had passed. As he grasped Martina's hand and leaned forward, preparing to make a move, a knock came at the conference room door.

"Come in," General Thomas responded.

The door opened to disclose a hefty prison guard standing in the doorway. "We're here, sir."

"Come in. Have him sit down."

Grayson's mouth fell open in astonishment, his adrenalin coursing. "Oh my God! Dani, you're alive! Thank God!" Grayson screamed as he looked up unbelievingly at Dani standing there cuffed, shackled and grinning like a possum. Ignoring the stoic prison guards, Grayson sprang to his feet and pounced on Dani, embracing him with both arms. The guards were visibly tense at this overt violation of their near-sacred no contact rule, but they took no action to quell the enthusiasm of the moment. As Grayson hugged Dani so tightly that it hurt, he searched futilely for words that might adequately express his feelings. Stammering excitedly, however, the only words that would come out of his mouth were, "Dani, thank God!" which he repeated over and over.

When Grayson finally looked down at Martina, he could now plainly see her previously indecipherable eyes. Although wet with tears, they were dancing with delight. He winked. She winked back.

Marveling at this magnificent moment, Grayson still didn't comprehend what was going on. What he did know, however, was that he was deliriously, ecstatically happy that Dani was still alive. Whatever happened, it must have been a miracle!

"Now, ladies and gentlemen," Mr. Thomas began once again, "would everyone please have a seat?"

Dani took a seat in the empty chair beside Grayson, the two guards standing so close behind them that their breathing sent air ripples frizzing across Grayson's scalp. Shaking his head in disbelief but glowing with jubilation, Grayson could barely contain himself. "Marty, what happened?" he whispered, his voice low and muffled.

Before Martina could reply, the Attorney General interrupted, his tired eyes peering over the top rim of his reading glasses.

"Please, I know this is a joyous moment for you, but for our Commonwealth, it is an extremely sad time in our history. Please, listen to me. It's very important."

Perhaps Mr. Thomas isn't such a jerk after all, Grayson decided. Gathering his composure and trying to restrain himself from screaming out in euphoric elation, Grayson looked up attentively, his attitude much more respectful.

After a moment of silence, Mr. Thomas began to speak once more. "I realize that it is quite unusual for us all to be sitting here together like this, but I really don't know what to make of all this tonight. Excuse me," he said, pausing as he removed his glasses and rubbed his weary eyes.

Finally, his glasses back in place, he continued. "In order to preserve justice and prevent an irreparable mistake, I usurped the authority and ordered the execution stayed. As you know, only four hours ago Governor Brotherton was assassinated by some self-proclaiming Blackbeard the Pirate. Furthermore," Thomas said as he gave a knowing nod in Grayson's direction, "I was quite aware that Mr. Alverez's defense revolved around the existence of a modern-day Blackbeard. For that reason, I felt it incumbent upon me as the chief of our justice department to take the unprecedented action of staying the execution until this matter can be investigated.

Meanwhile, Mr. Alverez will remain in secure custody. Are there any questions or comments?"

"I should say there are!" Grayson asked excitedly. "How did you do it? I mean, stop the execution? I didn't think you had the authority." Then, taking a momentary reflection on his last comment, Grayson smiled, and quickly added, "Now don't get me wrong, I'm overjoyed that you did, but just how did you pull it off, sir?"

"Mr. Forrest, I'm not at liberty to comment on that at this time, but I can assure you that it will become known in due course." Without further ado, the grim-faced attorney general stood up, thanked everyone for their patience and unceremoniously left the room.

With the stone-faced guards still standing behind them staring blankly, ready to pounce, Grayson turned and placed his arm around Dani.

"Dani," he said, his voice tender and soft, "I'm so sorry you've had to go through all this. Please keep being strong. I have faith that it's all going to work out."

"Don't worry, Mr. Forrest, I'll be all right."

Teary eyed, Grayson watched the guards lead Dani back to his cell. When the conference room door closed, Grayson turned and embraced Martina, squeezing her tightly as she pulled close to him.

"I'm so happy and grateful for this moment," he whispered.

As their lips touched, Grayson knew he was hopelessly in love.

They walked down the hallway hand in hand. A buzzer sounded, the reception room opened, and they rushed through, exiting into the crisp night air. Grayson looked at his watch, surprised it was almost 2:00 A.M. and he wasn't the least bit sleepy. He was so wired he couldn't sleep if he tried.

"Where are you spending the night?" Martina asked.

"With you, I hope," Grayson replied, a sheepish grin on his face.

Martina's face broke into a broad smile, followed by a giggle.

"That sounds wonderful, that is, as long as my mother's snoring doesn't keep you awake."

Grayson looked at Martina with a contrived frown, then they burst into laughter.

With the enormous tension of the previous 24 hours, the image of Grayson, Martina and Mama sharing a bedroom struck them as hysterically funny.

*

At the motel, Grayson obtained his own room from where he tried to phone Gunny but got no response. After a hot shower, he poured himself a scotch on the rocks, his mind drifting off, as he reflected on this, the most astounding day of his life.

After a few minutes, his trance-like thoughts were interrupted by a tap on the door. He invited his early-morning visitor in. They sat down together on the edge of the bed, each exploring the other's eyes, each searching for the right words for this moment. Finally, Grayson managed to speak.

"Tell me what happened in the death chamber," he said softly.

Martina sighed, her expression immediately somber.

"You just wouldn't believe it. It was the most phenomenal thing I've ever seen. Dani was strapped into the chair and those electrode things were hooked to his head and leg." Martina paused, took a deep breath, then continued. "He was looking out through the viewing window and could see me in the witness area. He mouthed to me, 'I love you,' then, with just seconds to go, he began to say the Lord's Prayer."

Grayson listened intensely, hypnotized by Martina's big brown eyes. "What happened next?"

"There was a clock in the witness viewing area that displayed the official time. At exactly 8:59, I thought I was going to have a heart attack as the seconds ticked away. I was also looking at my own digital watch, which had already turned to nine o'clock."

Grayson, all ears, listened impatiently. "Okay, go ahead."

Taking another deep breath, Martina continued. "Amazingly, Dani was still alive, still praying. Out of the corner of my eye, I looked at the wall clock, knowing that at any time it would display nine o'clock, and the electricity would be turned on and my brother would die."

Martina struggled to continue as Grayson waited in high suspense for her next words. "I kept looking at the clock, but it remained 8:59. I looked down at my watch, which showed 9:01, I looked back at the clock which continued to say 8:59. I looked back at my watch again, which by then said 9:03. I thought I had actually gone insane or was having a nervous breakdown."

"So, why didn't the clock ever get to nine o'clock?"

"I don't know."

EPILOGUE

EARLIER, ON that fateful night, Gunny had been heliovaced to Riverside Regional Hospital, where he underwent surgery. It had been nip and tuck, he almost didn't make it. But, he pulled through and recovered quickly. Six days later, he was released from the hospital to the care of his daughter.

Mandy had weathered the ordeal well. She had grown from a self-centered teenage brat into a kind and caring young lady who was adoringly appreciative of her loving father. She was in good health except she was pregnant. Abortion was out of the question because she was already five months pregnant. Also, Gunny didn't think abortion was moral. On March 15th, Gunny became a doting grandfather to a strapping, black-haired, eleven-pound, eight-ounce boy.

*

Three days after the stay of execution, Grayson filed a Petition for Writ of Habeas Corpus in the Virginia Beach Circuit Court, alleging that new evidence had been found. Because Judge Buford Bullins had been institutionalized, grief-stricken by the loss of his wife, a substitute judge signed a temporary stay of execution and set the petition for a hearing. On December 1st, the court found that the new evidence entitled Dani Alverez to a new trial.

Begrudgingly, Commonwealth's Attorney Arnold Bledsoe, yielded to public pressure and dismissed the charges against Dani Alverez. On March 15th, Dani was released from custody a free man.

A federal investigation into the Fast Track Death Penalty Law was launched by the United States Department of Justice in conjunction with the Virginia Attorney General's office. Shortly, all prosecutions under the new law were ordered stayed until the matter could be reconsidered. Eventually, the legislature repealed the fast track law, deciding it was unconstitutional and denied due process.

Attorney General Thomas used his influence to coerce the Justice Department and the Federal Bureau of Investigation to begin an extensive investigation into child kidnapping rings such as the one that had taken Mandy. That, in conjunction with his efforts to rectify the injustice of the Alverez case, would make Thomas a popular political figure with a future in government.

The portly warden, Alton "Porky" Pugh, received a special humanitarian award for pulling the plug on the clock at two seconds until nine o'clock. This unlikely humanitarian claimed he had received a divine message, which proclaimed execution immoral. He maintained he was called by God to take matters into his own hands. It was noted, however, Pugh was wearing an earphone connected to a radio receiver, allowing him to monitor the governor's roof garden speech. Whether his actions were actually based on a message from on high, or more realistically, as a result of his fast thinking upon learning the governor had been attacked by Blackbeard, we will never know.

Shortly after that eventful November 22nd date, Pugh retired and collected a lump sum, sizable pension. A rumor developed that he made an offer to purchase the assets of the crumbling Grace of God Ministries, which filed for bankruptcy protection shortly after the untimely demise of its leader, the Reverend Jones.

Dani Alverez was quoted as saying that God saved him through an unlikely array of angels, which included Warden Alton "Porky" Pugh, Mr. Homer K. Thomas, Gunny Lincoln Vernon, and of course, Grayson Quentin Forrest.

Grayson's mother, Louise, had a difficult time with the thought of her wonderful white son being in love with Martina, who Louise openly conceded was beautiful, intelligent, considerate and otherwise perfect, except she was, in fact, black. Nevertheless, the courtship continued.Rosa Alverez withstood the trauma of her only son's near execution. Later, after weeks passed, she did feel some distress at the thought of her only daughter being smitten over a white man; however, she was compelled to recall how good he had been to her Dani. For that reason, she was determined to overlook Grayson's whiteness since he had, after all, been declared an *"angel"*.